DEPRAVED

DIFFERENCE

A Detective Shakespeare Mystery

By
J. Robert Kennedy

Detective Shakespeare Mysteries
Depraved Difference

Tick Tock

The Redeemer

James Acton Thrillers
The Protocol

Brass Monkey

Broken Dove

The Templar's Relic

Zander Varga, Vampire Detective
The Turned

DEPRAVED DIFFERENCE

A Detective Shakespeare Mystery

J. ROBERT KENNEDY

ISBN: 1461075858
ISBN-13: 978-1461075851

10 9 8 7 6 5 4

For my wife, my daughter, my parents, my friends.
All of you made this possible.

DEPRAVED DIFFERENCE

A Detective Shakespeare Mystery

ONE

Tammera flipped closed her laptop, the satisfying snap signaling the end of another long day, and shoved it into its well-travelled case. She lifted her dark brown suede jacket off the chrome coat-rack monstrosity she hid behind her office door, stuffed her arms in the sleeves and shrugged it up her shoulders. With her knock-off Prada purse over one shoulder, the case over the other, she pulled her long brown hair from under both, and marched to the elevators, tossing a wave and a half-hearted smile at the bored security guard perched behind the reception desk.

He glanced up from the sports section. "Goodnight, Miss Coverdale."

"Goodnight, Joseph." She pressed the down button. "Hold down the fort 'til I get back."

"Leaving us?"

She jabbed at the button again. "Heading to Boston for a few days."

The elevator chimed. "Have a good trip!" said Joseph, his head already buried in his paper.

"Thanks!" *Not bloody likely.* Tammera stepped onto the elevator and hit P3 as the doors closed. She leaned against the rear wall of the elevator, resting her head against the glass. She looked up at her reflection in the mirrored ceiling and sighed. The investment bank she worked for needed an extra body in Boston and she was it. A flurry of emails to cancel weekend travel plans had followed the bad news. Her fiancé was *not* happy and a rip-roaring fight ensued. *As if he has a monopoly on being pissed.* He demanded she quit. She called him an idiot. *Quit in this economy? In my industry?* She growled and took a deep breath to calm herself as she fumbled through her purse for her keys.

When the doors opened, she stepped from the elevator into the nearly deserted parking garage, the few remaining cars belonging to the skeleton nightshift, or other poor SOBs like her—no longer a junior, but not senior enough to slack off. A shoe scraped on the pavement behind her. Her heart raced as she spun around to see a man's gloved hand swing toward her head. She screamed but it was too late. Excruciating pain raced through her entire face from the jarring impact, her eyes filled with tears as she fell backward, her flailing arms, desperate to find something to hold on to, sent her keys flying over the railing to the next level. Her head bounced off the cold concrete floor and her world blurred, her keys hitting the ground in the distance, the last sound she heard before blacking out.

She awoke, her mind a fog of pain and confusion. She slowly opened her eyes to find her head resting on her chest, her blouse torn and her nylons ripped at the knees spread immodestly before her in what appeared to be a straight back chair. She tried to close her legs, but felt something pulling against her ankles, preventing them from moving. Still groggy from the blow, it didn't occur to her to be afraid. She tried to lean forward to see what the problem might be and winced, the movement sending her head throbbing with levels of pain she had never experienced before. *Where am I?* She steeled herself and tried to lean forward again, but found she couldn't. *How did I get here?* She tried to remember, the fog in her head slowly clearing. Suddenly her memory returned with all the force of a sledgehammer, jolting her back to reality. *Somebody punched me!* Her mouth still stung where she had been hit and she tasted the salty blood from her swollen lip. A run of her tongue over her teeth revealed two loose. She tried to reach up to touch them, as if shoving them back into place would help, but discovered her hands clasped behind the back of the chair, something holding them tightly together. Her heart started to pound and she felt the room spin as her situation became clear. *I've been kidnapped!* She took a deep breath to steady herself. The roar in her ears slowly settled as she regained control. She looked at her surroundings. It was dark, but not completely, some light from what most likely were street lamps, shone through dirty, cracked windows far overhead, years of pigeon feces blocking much of it. She was in what she guessed to be an abandoned warehouse, a musty smell and stray

2

pallets strewn about the only contents. She opened her mouth to call out for help when footsteps behind her echoed off the walls and ceiling, their slow, methodical approach shoved her heart against her ribcage, faster and faster, as they neared. Too afraid to turn around, it was everything she could do to not shut her eyes and pray for deliverance from this nightmare.

The footsteps stopped behind her, so close she heard the rustling of nylon scraping nylon, as who she was now certain was her captor reached into a pocket. *It must be a gun. I'm going to die! Oh, God, please help me!* She yelped as a gloved fist thrust in front of her face. She jerked her head away to avoid the expected blow and squeezed her eyes shut. Then she heard something strange. Voices. But far away, almost recorded. Yet familiar somehow. Opening one eye a crack, she was shocked to see a cell phone held in front of her, a video playing on it. Her captor clutched her by the hair and yanked her head to face the phone. Her eyes teared from the pain as he twisted the ball of hair he held tighter. She opened both eyes to watch.

"Holy shit, man!" said a voice on the recording. "Look at what they're doin'!"

"Are you getting this?" asked another excited voice.

"Yeah, dude, we're gonna be famous!" The view flashed to the person's face recording it, rampaging acne betraying his age, then to his equally challenged friend, who hammed it up for the camera with a small dance and a Gene Simmons salute. The phone was turned back and held high to record over the people in front. On the screen Tammera watched two young men kick and punch a woman, her unconscious body offering no resistance. One man lifted his steel-toed boot and brought it down hard on her head, eliciting a collective gasp and another "Holy shit!" from the kid taping it, as the subway car screeched to a halt. The two men bolted out the door and the passengers rushed in front of the camera as the kid moved closer to the woman's motionless body.

"Dude, we gotta get outta here!" yelled his companion. The camera jerked as its operator was dragged out. The angle spun around and froze on the image of a woman as she shoved her way off the train.

It was her.

She sobbed as the memories of that night flooded back, the horror of seeing that poor woman murdered before her eyes, the feeling of helplessness at being able to do nothing. And the shame. The shame of slinking away, rather than being human enough to at least give a statement, something she did rectify the next day, but only after much soul searching. The man flipped the phone closed, the snap of the case yanking her back to reality as he stepped around to face her. A Yankees baseball cap, drawn down low, and large, reflective sunglasses allowed her to see herself, but not him. A dark blue windbreaker, zipped tight to cover as much as possible, kept most of his emotionless face hidden from view.

He stared at her.

"Wh-what do you want from me?"

Again he just stared.

But she knew what he wanted. He wanted justice, he wanted someone to pay. Yes, she had done nothing, but what was she supposed to have done? She was one woman! They were two men!

"I wasn't the only one that did nothing!" she cried. It sounded feeble. She looked at herself in his glasses. Blood trickled down her chin, her eyes red and swollen from her tears reminded her of the woman. Pathetic. Helpless. "Did-did you know her?"

Again, no response.

"I-I know I should have done something! I know that, but nobody did anything." She leaned forward as far as her bindings would permit as she attempted to make a connection, her pleading eyes tried to bore through the glasses, to see if a conscience she might reason with lay behind them. "I was scared. We were all scared!"

He held the phone up between his thumb and forefinger, slowly rocking it back and forth as if wagging a finger at a child.

She knew what he meant. *Not everybody was scared.*

He pressed a few keys and activated the video camera. With his left hand he held it out to record her. With his right he pulled a gun from his belt and pointed it at her head.

Her eyes focused on the end of the barrel as it became her entire world. She saw the gloved finger on the trigger begin to squeeze.

"Oh, God, please no!"

She squeezed her eyes shut and screamed as he squeezed the trigger.

Merissa winced as she slowly rotated her wrist, trying to loosen the still tender scabs built up over the past week. She pushed the cause, a pair of handcuffs, up her arm in search of some relief. They slipped back down. She growled in frustration and was about to try pulling her hand through the cuffs again, when she thought better of it, and grabbed the chain they were attached to with both hands and yanked it instead. In the darkness above she heard the other end scrape against what she had determined must be a metal pole spanning the ceiling of her dungeon, as it slid toward her, providing a little more slack. *I feel like a dog on a run.* And that was exactly how she was being treated since her abduction several weeks before. Each day a platform lowered from the ceiling above with a bottle of water and a tray of food. She had been too scared to approach the first couple of days, and after what seemed an eternity, but was more likely only minutes, the rattling of chains sent her into a panic, each pull by her captor causing the platform to rise a few more inches, and with each pull, she pushed with her bare feet against the floor, trying to force the wall at her back farther from the horror in front of her. When the platform finally reached the ceiling, it filled the hole in the floor above seamlessly, leaving total darkness. The unknown sounds of her captor set her imagination ablaze with visions of some hellish reality just overhead, the mysterious clanging of metal, creaking of footsteps on wood, the sounds of things impossibly large scraping across the ceiling of her dungeon, followed by a silence even more terrifying.

On the third day her tremendous thirst and hunger won out, hours of sobbing and the occasional screaming fit having exhausted her. This time she welcomed the sounds above indicating the impending arrival of her daily meal. She inched toward the lowered platform and stole a glance up at the bright hole in the ten-foot high ceiling which revealed nothing except the silhouette of her captor, the lack of details far more horrifying to her, leaving her fertile imagination to fill in the blanks of what terror now possessed her. She snatched the food, and as soon as she removed it and the bottle, the platform rose, signaling an end to the feeding.

She cowered against the wall, staring at the ever shrinking hole above as the platform completed its return trip, sealing her in once again. In complete darkness, she placed the sandwich on her lap, and twisted the top off the bottle, downing at least half of it before she stopped. She breathed a sigh of relief, her thirst temporarily quenched. She felt for the sandwich with her spare hand, seized it and took a tentative bite. As she slowly chewed, the flavors almost overwhelmed her. Either desperate hunger made everything taste better, or her captor was a wizard with food. After swallowing the first delicious bite, she devoured the rest of the sandwich and finished off her water. She was about to toss the bottle when she thought better of it, the pressure on her bladder nearing the breaking point after holding it for so long. She felt the ground for the top she had discarded, and soon found it a few feet away. She screwed it back on the now empty bottle, and placed it against the wall for later.

Later proved to only be a few minutes. She grabbed the bottle, removed the top, then stood up and dropped her pants and panties to her ankles. Carefully positioning the bottle, she let as controlled a stream as she could manage go, the satisfying sound of the urine actually going into the bottle a welcome relief, this being something she had never tried before. *If only I were a guy.* She harrumphed to herself. *If I were a guy, then I wouldn't even be here.* The pitch of the stream quickly got higher as the bottle filled, finally rushing over the top, the warm fluid spilling on her hands. She clenched, cutting off the stream, and cursed. *Lovely.* She shook her hand then screwed the cap back on. She put the bottle on the floor then hiked her panties and pants back up, not completely relieved, but no longer in danger of having to squat in what was her new home.

Her strength restored, she turned to thoroughly exploring her surroundings by touch, confident her captor wouldn't return until the next day. She began first by facing the wall she had been sitting against since she arrived, save the brief moments she had spent retrieving the food and relieving herself. With both hands pressed flat against the wall in front of her, she slowly made her way to her right. She ran her hands over every square inch of the wall she could reach. Immediately in front of her, the wall felt damp and soft. She scratched at it with her fingernails, and she felt some of it peeling away, the sound reminding her of digging a latrine when camping as a child. She scraped some into her other hand and sniffed it, then rubbed it between her fingers, the gritty feeling unmistakable. *This is a dirt wall!* She shook the dirt from her hands, and reached upward. At about shoulder height the texture suddenly changed, from the cool, damp, softness of the earthen wall, to the colder, dry, hardness of another material entirely. She ran her fingers across the rough, pitted surface. It seemed to be consistent, no indentations or breaks in the feel, except for the distinct, even line, separating it from the dirt portion of the wall. *This is concrete!* Excited by this find, her mind raced as she continued along the wall. Could she dig her way out? If this was an outer wall, it might not be that far to dig? She shook her head. She'd never be able to dig enough in one day. *And what would he do to you if he thought you were trying to escape?* She shuddered at the thought, and continued her exploration.

Her shoulder bumped into something.

She yelped, jumping back, listening for what she did not know. Silence. She tentatively reached out, her hand coming into contact with the same cold, dampness she had felt all along. She turned, running both hands along their respective surfaces, until they met. *It's only a corner! Settle down!* She breathed a sigh of relief, and continued along this new wall. It didn't take long for her to confirm there were three more corners. *And no door.* She got down on her hands and knees, and began to explore the floor, reaching out in wide circles, running her hands along every square inch, then crawling forward another few feet. The entire floor seemed to be of the same consistency as the walls. She reached the end of her second pass, and turned to make her third, feeling almost like a lawnmower, trying not to miss any of the surface. She moved several feet from the wall, running her hands about, finding nothing she hadn't already found. She reached far ahead to plant her hands then drag herself toward her next search area, when her left hand found empty space. Falling forward, she felt her hand hit something cold. She continued to collapse, the chain overhead screeching in protest, then breaking her fall as all the slack she was granted was used up. Now on her side, she pulled her hand up out of the cold void, the distinct feeling and sound of ice cold water finally registering. *What the hell is that?* She changed position so she could explore with her free hand, and felt around. She found a small area of concrete, perhaps four feet square, with a smaller square cut cleanly in the middle, that went down about six inches, at which point there was water.

She had no idea what this was, or why it would be there. *Could it be part of the plumbing?* "Eww!" she exclaimed, rubbing both hands on the dirt floor in an effort to remove any unseen sewage. She smelt her hands and didn't notice anything. She stuck her tongue out to touch it to her hand then stopped. *How desperately do you need to know?* She made a mental note of the location of the hole in the map she was now creating in her head, and continued her exploration, finding nothing else of interest. She crawled to the nearest corner, and thought about what she had learned. She had dirt walls that turned into concrete higher up. The floor was dirt, with some sort of concrete hole leading to water. She knew there was a ceiling above her, with a wood floor on top of her, suggesting a house or cabin of some sort. *I'm in a basement.* She nodded to herself. She was definitely in a basement, dug out to be deeper than any basement she had ever been in before.

She had repeated her explorations several times, but found nothing she had missed. The occasional sound of rushing water from the hole she had discovered suggested it might indeed be linked to the plumbing of wherever she was. Rather than use the floor and live with the smell, she had taken to using this hole as a latrine. Her routine had continued, unchanged, for what she now thought to be weeks, but with no sense of time, she was only guessing.

But today was different.

Today she felt different. After eating, she had fallen asleep, which wasn't unusual, but when she woke up, she felt different. She felt clean. Her mouth, which had become disgusting to her, tasted fresh. She ran her tongue over her teeth, and they felt smooth, clean for the first time since she had been taken. She tasted the distinct grit of toothpaste, as if she had not had any water to rinse. And her hair! Her head no longer itched. She reached up with her free hand and ran it through the smooth, clean hair, not a single knot, no hint of the matted greasy mess that had been there before. She ran her fingernails against her scalp, and realized they had been clipped. She reached down and felt her toenails finding they too had been trimmed. As she ran her hands up her legs, she immediately realized something else was different. *What the hell?* She felt her pants, then her shirt. They were different. *I'm wearing different clothes!* As she explored her body using only touch and smell, she realized she had been cleaned and groomed.

Everywhere. From her hair and ears, to her toes, to her—. She shuddered to think of it. But there was no doubt. He had definitely cleaned her. *Thoroughly.* She drew her knees up and she hugged them to her chest, burying her head and closing her eyes. *What else did he do to me?*

As she sat there, moaning, trying to come to grips as she rocked herself like a small child, she heard something overhead, then an odd zapping sound, followed by a flash of blinding light. She squeezed her eyes shut and jumped to her feet, her hands flat against the wall behind her as she felt her way into a corner. Finding the corner, she froze and held her breath, listening for the telltale signs her captor might be about to join her. There was nothing. She tentatively opened her eyes, holding her free hand up to shield them from the light. She rapidly blinked and tried to focus, her eyes no longer used to the brightness. It took a few minutes for her eyes to adjust, but when they did, she found a lone light bulb hanging from the ceiling. She stepped under it, closing her eyes and enjoying the warmth as the bulb bathed her in light for the first time since she had been taken captive. It felt wonderful. *Almost like sunlight.* She stood, lost in this nearly forgotten sensation, for several minutes, then opened her eyes again, and looked around her, seeing her prison for the first time. It was definitely a basement, made of concrete walls that turned to dirt about five feet from the floor. The floor was dirt, the only exception the small square where the water hole was. Above were wooden rafters that appeared very old, the distinct lines of the platform cut into the floor the only break. And there was the pole, running the entire length, a pair of handcuffs clasped to it, then to a chain that led down to her own pair.

She slowly spun around, taking in every detail, not sure how long the light would last. As she did, she noticed something on the walls. She stepped closer and gasped. Long gouges were scratched into the dirt by fingernails, as if someone had tried to climb out, the bloody streaks left on the concrete, three feet from the ceiling, indicated the extent of their success.

She wasn't this dungeon's first captive.

For the first time in weeks, she screamed.

Aynslee Kai leaned back in her chair and tried to stretch all the kinks of a hard day's work from her body. It was useless. When she got home she would pour a glass of cabernet sauvignon, grab a Tess Gerritsen novel, and run herself a hot bath. Though the evening newscast had ended long ago, her work as the entertainment reporter was never over. She loved her career choice but hated her job, covering celebrities not exactly hardcore news. Her dream? CNN anchor. *Yeah, me and every other person in this business.* She hoped her talent would be spotted eventually so she might escape the cubicle assigned three years earlier, its plain, light blue walls pale reminders of the sky of which she had no view, the single plastic "window" merely providing a better view of the enclosed offices lining the outer walls, devouring the sunlight, leaving nothing for the minions like herself, relegated to serving within the bowels. Art prints clashed with a collection of cartoon clippings, their humor long lost, plastered about in a futile attempt to brighten her cell but instead serving to remind her of her miserable existence and lack of success. It was taking longer for her talent to be recognized than she had planned. At first she thought she had hit the jackpot to get assigned the entertainment beat. It meant regular face time almost every night, but she soon realized she would never be taken seriously as long as she did it. Usually reporters rotated out or quit, but she hadn't moved on yet. Friends told her it was because she was too pretty. She thought that was BS, half the female talent on the air these days had implants and West Coast noses.

About to call it a day, she heard the familiar double-tone of an email arrive. She glanced at her watch. Almost midnight. *Forget it, I'll look at it tomorrow.* She shutdown the notebook, disconnected it from the docking station and slipped it into its carrying case. Checking her BlackBerry to make sure it was on, she headed out the door. As she waited for the elevator a young intern joined her. He seemed to always be there whenever she was leaving, almost as if he lurked around the corner in wait for her. It creeped her out. She nodded at him and pulled out her iPod to try and head off a conversation.

"That's a nice iPod, Miss Kai."

Too late!

"How many gigabytes does it have?"

She shrugged her shoulders. "No clue."

"You probably just got it 'cuz you liked the color!" He laughed. The awkward guffaw made her cringe. Thankfully the elevator chimed a soon definite end to their conversation as the doors opened. She stepped aboard and to her dismay, he did as well. "Me, I got an eighty-gigabyte model. As soon as I got it, I ripped my entire CD collection. It took me weeks, I've got hundreds of CDs you know. I have over six thousand songs on it. If you'd like I could put together some playlists for you."

Having tuned him out, it took her a minute to notice he was waiting for a response. "Sorry, I didn't catch that, I'm a little distracted, working on a story, you know."

"I was wondering if you'd like me to put together some playlists for you?"

How do I get rid of this guy? In as disinterested a tone as she could muster, she said, "Sure, leave them on my desk." His face brightened. *That probably backfired.* The elevator opened on the ground floor and she burst from it like a bull at the rodeo. A quick glance over her shoulder confirmed she had left her stalker behind as she raced to the subway. She scrambled down the station steps, swiped her transit pass, pushed through the turnstile and headed to her platform. It didn't take long for her train to arrive. She sat at the front of the car, her body pressed against the side, her purse on her lap, her notebook case strategically occupying the seat beside her, the strap wrapped several times around her arm. She turned up her iPod and retrieved her BlackBerry to check her email, curiosity winning out.

The email contained no text, only a video attachment. She activated it. As the clip played her jaw dropped and her eyes opened wide. She looked around to make sure no one had seen it then ran to the door as the subway slowed at the next station. She dialed the news director as she rushed to the other side of the platform.

Logan kicked a discarded Pepsi can and watched as it clanged away from him, coming to rest near Joe, the resident drunk who slept in front of their building, or in the lobby on cold days. He looked at the shithole he lived in and sighed. It wasn't supposed to be like this. He had never really expected to be rich or famous, but a dishwasher at a pizzeria without a penny to his name, and a family that refused to speak to him, was not where he thought he would be at eighteen. He had been stoned, after all, when he and Aaron had videotaped the woman being beaten on the subway a year ago. When they returned to his parents' house they posted it on YouTube and every other site they could think of, but not before recording an outro featuring the two of them horsing around for the camera. *That part was really stupid.* He kicked a beer bottle, the hollow echo of the glass rolling on the concrete sliced through the uncharacteristic silence. Joe stirred. Within hours their handiwork had been downloaded thousands of times. It even made the local news and over the next few months the coverage of the incident and the debate over the morality of leaving the recording of a woman's murder on the Internet drove over one hundred million curious and depraved to view it. When his father found out he kicked him from the house, saying anybody who stood by and watched a woman get beaten to death was no son of his.

Fuck 'em. Who was he anyway? He had never been proud of him, never patted him on the back for a job well done. *Did you ever do anything to make him proud?* Logan sighed as he looked up at the building he and Aaron, tossed as well by his mom, had rented a small bachelor pad in a year ago. He hadn't even known neighborhoods this seedy existed in New York until they moved in, but it was all they could afford with the odd jobs they were able to find. It had turned into a yearlong bender of booze and drugs. A bender he was tired of. But Aaron seemed perfectly content to keep going this way. *I'm just so tired.*

"You okay, kid?"

Joe's gravelly voice startled him. He looked at Joe, lying on his side, hugging a brown bag Logan was sure didn't hold leftovers from lunch.

Logan shook his head. "No."

He stepped into the lobby, checked the mail, tossed the bills in the garbage and dragged his weary body to his apartment. After he shouldered the warped door closed behind him, he heard voices on the other side of an old acoustic divider pillaged a few months ago to try and give each other some privacy for when they were getting busy with the honeys. There had yet to be any honeys.

"Hey, Logan, that you?"

"Yeah." Logan stepped around the divider and saw Aaron and a man he had never seen before laughing on the couch as they watched TV, the hijacked cable feed their biggest accomplishment in three months. How long their rooftop handiwork would last, they didn't know.

"Dude, this is Wolf, he's new in the building." Wolf stood and shook Logan's hand. He looked old, maybe thirty, blonde hair, kind of nerdy looking.

Wolf pointed to a case of beer sitting on the table. "Beer?"

Logan already liked him. He grabbed a bottle and twisted off the cap, flicking it toward Aaron who ducked and laughed. After a long swig Logan sat down in a nearby beanbag chair, its innards long-since replaced with newspaper and other semi-soft scraps, and ran his fingers through his shoulder-length, scraggly hair, trying to rid himself of the knots caused by the hairnet his boss forced him to wear all day.

"Tough day at work?"

"I hate that fucking place." Logan proceeded to scratch his goatee. "It's hot, it's noisy and the boss is a prick. And look!" He held up his hands for them to see. "I've got dishpan hands for fuck's sake!"

Aaron laughed. "Life sucks, dude!"

Wolf nodded and reached into his pocket. "Maybe this will help take your mind off it." He pulled out a small Ziploc bag and fished out three blue pills.

"That better not be Viagra, you fag!" yelled Aaron, causing Logan to spray his beer toward the kitchen.

Wolf smiled. "Nope, better." He popped one and handed the other two to the roommates. They both swallowed the pills and washed them down without question. Within minutes Logan began to relax, the tension in his neck and shoulders eased as his troubles of the past year slowly melted away. His entire body felt light, almost as if he could float from the chair if he chose to. He looked at Aaron and giggled, his eyelids starting to feel heavy. Aaron slumped forward and hit his head on the drywall board perched atop four cinder blocks serving as their coffee table. The beer bottles rattled from the impact, caps and beer can ashtrays jolted into new resting places. Logan giggled uncontrollably at the sight. He pointed at Aaron and looked at Wolf who spit out his pill as he watched Logan. This made Logan laugh even harder as the room spun around him. He reached out to steady himself on the floor, but grasped empty air instead, the floor not where he expected. He spilled his beer as he fell forward and passed out.

Aynslee stood her ground. "This is my story and there's no way in hell I'm giving it up!"

Jeffrey Merle, the news director, sat perched on the edge of his desk, his arms folded over his chest, propped up by a small potbelly. "Aynslee, this is too big for an entertainment reporter. Shaw is our crime reporter, I want him to run with this."

"No friggin' way, Jeff," she said as she crossed her arms and avoided eye contact with Jonathan Shaw who lounged in a nearby chair, a look of self-importance on his face she would love to smack off. "This was sent to me specifically, it's my story or I walk to another station with it." *Might have crossed the line there.* She knew Jeff didn't like to be threatened. But she had his balls in a vise. The killer had sent the email to her, not the station. If she walked they'd lose the exclusive. And she knew he knew it.

Jeff stood and walked around his desk. He sank into his high-backed leather chair and clasped his hands behind his head, revealing a hint of perspiration under each armpit. He looked between her and Shaw intently for a minute as he pondered the situation. Aynslee waited. To say patiently wouldn't be accurate. Her heart pounded and her face was flush. She clenched her fists tight, her fingernails digging into the skin so hard she was sure they were drawing blood. She knew this was her big chance to break out from her three year rut. She also knew this might mean the beginning of a new career. *He's going to fire me.*

Jeff broke the silence with a sigh. "Fine, it's yours. Now get out, we lead with it on the six a.m. broadcast." He picked up the phone, ending the meeting. Aynslee missed the expression of shock on Shaw's face as she marched from the office, her head held high. She passed her cubicle and headed straight to the bathroom, closed the stall door and vomited.

Logan's chin rested on his chest and his head throbbed as if he had just woken from a weekend bender. He felt someone struggling behind him and when he opened his eyes and turned his head, he saw it was Aaron. They were sitting on the floor, backs pressed together. Logan tried to stand, but couldn't, something tight against his chest preventing him. He looked down, and saw some type of cord wrapped several times around his chest, holding him to Aaron, and his arms straight to his sides. He looked around the room and saw Wolf near the window, looking out on the street below. He yelled into the gag stuffed in his mouth, the muffled sound snapping Wolf from his reverie. He slowly shifted his gaze to Logan. Logan went silent, the expression, or lack thereof, on Wolf's face sent his heart racing in fear. Wolf strode over to the coffee table where a notebook computer was set up. He stroked his finger over the touch pad and the screen saver disappeared, replaced by a media player. He clicked the button to play the selected video full-screen so both Logan and Aaron could see it.

Logan's heart leapt into his throat when he saw the video they had posted almost a year ago. *Oh my God! This dude must have known her!* Logan couldn't bring himself to look away from the video; he still found it morbidly fascinating. Fear, and a modicum of shame, helped him keep a straight face at the scene they had added, however Aaron, either not as strong willed, or still ignorant to the danger they were in, let out a single laugh. Logan thought he caught a near imperceptible change in Wolf's expression, but it lasted a mere moment.

Wolf pulled a cell phone from his pocket and started recording, holding the phone out in front as he reached behind him. Logan knew what was coming, but knowing and seeing were two entirely different things. When the gun appeared he screamed into his gag. Aaron sobbed but his muffled pleas had no effect on the impassive Wolf who continued to hold the phone, capturing both in the frame as he raised the weapon. He squeezed the trigger as Logan closed his eyes and turned his head away. The blast caused him to jump as a warmth spread over his legs. He was surprised to feel no pain with so much blood pouring out until he realized it wasn't blood. He had pissed his pants. He twisted his head to see Aaron but couldn't. He spun the other way and saw his friend's head lying on its side, a huge hole oozing blood and brain matter onto his shoulder. The world turned black.

Merissa sat cowered in the corner and rocked back and forth, hugging her knees, as she had for hours, the realization she wasn't the first person to be kept there sinking in. If she wasn't the first, then she most likely wouldn't be the last. And she doubted he had just *moved* his previous captive. *Or captives.* She knew they were dead. They had to be. She wracked her brain, trying to remember any news stories that might have mentioned someone being kidnapped and released. Or found dead. She kicked herself for not paying attention to the news. *If I get out of this, I'm going to start reading the paper.* But she knew she was never getting out of here. *No! Don't give up!* There was always hope. As long as she was alive, there was hope. But if she was going to die, there was no way in hell she was going to give that bastard the satisfaction of dying by his hand. She would fight the son of a bitch with everything she had. If she were going to die, it would be because of something *she* initiated. She wasn't going to just sit by passively and let some deranged psychopath have his way with her, then just kill her when he was finished getting off. *That's better!* She felt a renewed sense of determination, the depression of the past several hours turning into anger. It was time to take control.

Footsteps passed overhead, toward the center of the room, causing her heart to race, and her newfound determination to immediately waver.

Feeding time.

The light switched off, plunging her jail into total darkness before the platform began its slow descent. *I guess he doesn't want me knowing what he looks like.* It reached the floor with a thud, the light from above setting it apart from the rest of the darkened room as if its offering the feature attraction at a museum. She knew he would wait until she retrieved the food. Not wanting him staring at her, she quickly got up, grabbed the food and water, and scurried back to the wall. The chains rattled as her captor yanked on them, beginning the platform's ascent, the light from above slowly, relentlessly, shrinking, eventually into nothingness. Her tomb once again sealed in darkness, the light flickered, then blazed, a beacon to her despair.

She took a deep breath, trying to settle her nerves once again. She eyed the food, wondering if it would be drugged this time. *But do you really want to be awake?* She thought about it. At least if she were drugged, she didn't have to know what he was doing with her. But if she were awake, could she maintain control? What would happen if he discovered she were awake? Surely he would kill her? Maybe that's what happened to the others? Maybe they figured it out too, and that's what got them killed? She reached for the water, then stopped. *No! You need to take control!* Her hand hesitated, as if in its own battle of wills, inching toward the bottle, then darting back. *Don't do it! Don't do what? Don't drink it because you'll pass out? Or don't not drink it because you'll be awake?* She was pretty sure it was the water that was drugged. After all, it would be the easiest. Just add some drug, shake the bottle, and voila, knock-out juice. She took a deep breath and grabbed the bottle. Twisting the cap off, she raised it to her mouth.

No!

She tipped the bottle, the water rushing out toward her mouth. It hit her closed lips, and ran down her chin then neck. She stopped, the horror of her decision and its possible ramifications pumped adrenaline through her body. She quickly poured the water on her hands, washing them as best she could, then gave herself a quick camper's bath. She ate half the sandwich before she could change her mind, and waited to see if it had any effect on her. After a few minutes her eyes drooped and her limbs tingled then went numb. *Dammit!* As she lost consciousness she took satisfaction in now knowing he was drugging the food. *Next time....*

She awoke to sensations of a warm, comfortable bed, soft sheets atop a deep, cushioned mattress caressed her body as classical music played nearby, the smell of burning incense filled her nostrils, the pleasant vanilla scent causing her to breathe even deeper. For a moment she thought someone had rescued her, but when she felt the weight of a warm body on top of her, gently kissing her neck, she realized it was all a terrible nightmare. She was at home in bed with her husband. She breathed a sigh of relief and inhaled his cologne as she reached to embrace him. She stopped, not recognizing the scent. She opened her eyes and saw a man with a physique too well sculpted to be her husband's on top of her naked body, his eyes squeezed shut as he thrust himself at her, a look of frustration on his face. She was about to scream out for help when she noticed her rapist wasn't hard. *Let the bastard suffer!* A smile spread across her face as she watched him, sweat building on his forehead, his face turned red in anger, the veins on his neck and face popping out as he continued in futility. He stopped and opened his eyes. She closed hers and wiped the smile off her face.

"No!" he screamed. She only felt the first blow, the pain excruciating as the fist connected with her nose, the shock radiating outward, overwhelming her. She could imagine nothing worse until the next blow landed, hitting the side of her cheek. She felt her captor quickly move. She opened her eyes, thinking it might be over, but as she focused through the blur, she realized he was merely repositioning himself to straddle her chest. She screamed as he raised his fist and dropped it like a sledgehammer. She squeezed her eyes shut as a second blow rapidly followed, this one on the other side of her face. He continued to punch her, left then right, left then right, like an unstoppable juggernaut. She quickly numbed to the pain, it already overwhelming her senses.

Please, God! Please end it!

The blows didn't stop, but the pain did, as she finally, mercifully, blacked out.

Logan awoke with a start, puzzled to still be breathing. *I'm not dead!* He didn't feel like he'd been shot. He debated on whether or not he should open his eyes. *Maybe he's gone?* He opened one eye a sliver and immediately squeezed it back shut, the image of Wolf squatting in front of him, still holding the phone, burned into the back of his eyelids. Logan cursed himself. If he had kept his eyes shut he might have lived a little longer. And now he was going to die. *Why is he waiting?* Logan sat there and again curiosity won out. He opened one eye to see what was going on. The muzzle flashed six inches from his head. His brain never had a chance to register the sound.

In the editing room, Aynslee, still shocked Jeff had let her keep the story, debated how much of the killing to show. He had always been sweet on her, something she used to her advantage from time-to-time, the tight fitting top she still wore a shameless reminder of today's success. But the more she reviewed the footage, the more she wondered what she had gotten herself into. *Why was it sent to me? Who sent it? How do they know me?*

The excitement over a career-making story drowned out the warning bells in the back of her mind. The logical part of her brain screamed to leave this story to someone else, to run in the other direction, but the ambitious part spoke in a whisper, a whisper so alluring she couldn't resist it, the siren call of the promised fulfillment of all her hopes and dreams, of everything she had ever wanted, too strong to not overcome any fears she may have.

She stretched in the chair and spun it around, lifting her feet as she smiled at the fantasy. Something caught her eye and she dropped her foot, stopping the spin of her chair. She spied the intern as he stood behind a nearby divider, staring at her through its plastic window. He smiled and waved. *How long has he been standing there?* She quickly turned and tossed a casual wave over her shoulder in the hope it would be enough to ward him off, and returned to the debate of how much to show. *It's just so graphic!* She leaned forward toward the console and undid the last cut showing the shooting. *But, violence sells.*

A knock at the door caused her to jump. She laughed to herself at the sudden realization of how on edge she was from the video, and turned to see who had interrupted her. The intern's grin stretched from ear to ear, his face pressed against the glass fogged a small section. *Please don't draw a heart!* He waved at her, the exaggerated motions indicated he wanted to come in. Before she could shake her head he opened the door.

"Hi, *Ayn*slee." The way he stretched out the first syllable of her name made her cringe. *And what happened to "Miss Kia"?* His nasal voice caused a momentary feeling of pity. *What a geek!*

"Hello…" She didn't even remember his name.

"Reggie."

" … Reggie. What can I do for you?"

Reggie looked at the floor, his hands grasped at each other, the rapidly forming sweat glistened as he spread it around. Aynslee sat on her hands. "Well, *Ayn*slee, I've been thinking a lot about our conversation last night."

What conversation? "Yes?"

"Well, I've been trying to figure out what kind of music you'd like in your playlists."

What the hell is he talking about? She flashed back to last night. *Definitely backfired.* "Oh, you don't have to worry about that, Reggie. I've got plenty of music on my iPod already, actually I'm not sure if I have enough room."

"Not enough room?" This clearly excited him. "Do you have iTunes on your computer here? Never mind, I'll get you set up and create some playlists for you so that you can just update your iPod when you leave for the day, depending on the mood you're in." Before she could stop him he headed out the door then spun around. "I'll set up some themes for you, maybe dance, classical," and then he paused and raised his eyebrows up and down suggestively, "or love songs." Another toothy grin followed by a guffaw and the door shut leaving Aynslee wondering what the hell had just happened.

Her BlackBerry demanded her attention as it vibrated across the desk. She snatched it and read the subject line. Adrenaline rushed through her body as she saw it was blank, the incident with Reggie forgotten. She opened the message and saw it contained a lone video attachment. She activated the file and smiled as she saw what it contained. *CNN, here I come!* Then the wave of shame hit.

TWO

The rain fell in icy cold sheets, so hard Leroy's exposed skin stung with each tiny impact. He pulled the threadbare remains of his trench coat as high as he could in a futile attempt to escape the downpour. Soaked to the bone, his skin numb from the cold, his hands shivered. He plodded forward, unsure if he could still feel his feet. *But at least I still have you.* He caressed the bottle of Jack Daniels hidden in his pocket, the brown paper bag shredding at the touch of his fingers, it too failing to escape the onslaught. He carefully pulled the bottle containing its precious elixir from his pocket, his shaking hands threatened to drop his hard earned reward. He rushed the bottle to his lips, as if once pressed against them, the bottle would never drop. He took a long swig to dull his misery a little more. His hands stopped shaking for a moment then swiftly resumed their previous rattle as he returned the bottle to the one pocket with no holes. "I need to get out of this rain."

"What about the warehouse?"

Leroy nodded. "Good idea." He stumbled forward, willing his legs, numbed from the cold and alcohol, to carry him the few minutes' walk to the shelter. He pushed forward, through the driving wind and rain, the occasional swig fortifying his resolve. He rounded a corner and smiled. "There it is!"

"Quit gawking and get a move on!"

Leroy's nostrils flared in annoyance and shuffled the last few feet, all the while warily examining his surroundings, on the lookout for anyone who might seek to steal his own private refuge.

"Get in there you fool, there's nobody around!"

Leroy grunted and pushed open the door with his shoulder. It scraped on the concrete floor, the top hinge having let go long before. He cringed at the screech of metal, looked about one last time to see if anyone had heard, then entered as rapidly as his tired body could muster, shoving the door closed behind him. The storm howled outside, the wind rattled the peeling walls and painted over windows of the abandoned warehouse, its hollow shell, emptied of anything of value by the owners, the remainder by looters, acted like an echo chamber, the din from the storm a dull roar Leroy found peaceful, much like the roar he heard in his ears on occasion. On cold rainy days like today, or long winter nights, the respite it provided was welcome, much more than a packed shelter with rules to be followed. Here, Leroy was answerable to himself, free to enjoy the peace and quiet this refuge provided from the city noise. Even on a stormy day like today, it was still quiet compared to the din that was New York, the noise from millions of inhabitants so close by, silenced. And that was why Leroy loved his little piece of paradise, a place where he didn't need to worry about thrill seeking kids beating him, or worse, hauled away by cops looking for an easy bust. This was his place and his alone. He took a belt from his bottle, placed it on the concrete floor and peeled off his clothes until he wore nothing but his stained underwear. Taking another swig, he looked around for the mattress he had rescued from a garbage bin a month ago and stashed here. It was gone.

"It's over there in the corner."

Leroy looked and smiled. He stumbled toward it but stopped short when he saw a chair with someone sitting in it, their back toward him.

"Who the hell is that?"

"I don't know," replied Leroy. He tiptoed his way around the chair. "It's a chick!"

"Are you sure?"

Leroy double-checked. Skirt and tits. "Yup."

"Get rid of her."

Leroy eyed the woman, her head slumped forward on her chest. He glanced back at his clothes, decided against dressing before confronting the unwelcome guest, and stepped in front of her.

"Hey, lady, this is my place," he slurred. "You go find your own place!"

"You tell her, Leroy!"

Leroy took another swig. Emboldened, he continued, "Hey, Bitch! Get out of here!" He stumbled forward and tripped headlong into the woman, knocking her from the chair. He crashed to the floor and found himself lying beside her, face-to-face. He stared at her through his drunken stupor. Confused, he rubbed his eyes, trying to focus. His vision cleared for a moment, revealing a hole in her forehead, a small trail of dried blood running the length of her face. "Holy shit!" he yelled as he struggled to his feet and ran toward the entrance, his uncoordinated legs causing him to fall more than once.

"Where're you goin'?"

Leroy stopped.

"She ain't gonna hurt nobody now."

Leroy nodded. He approached the body again, picked up his dropped bottle, thankful it hadn't shattered, and took a long drink. As quickly as his shaking hands would allow, he set about taking her watch, ring, bracelet and necklace. He saw a purse on the floor nearby and opened it. He removed the wallet, relieved it of cash and credit cards, then started back toward his clothes.

"We hit the mother lode today!"

He nodded as he thought of how much he'd be able to buy when he pawned his newly acquired goods. He leaned down to check on his clothes when the door blew open and banged against the wall, the sound echoing through the empty warehouse. "Shhh!" he hissed, stumbling toward the entrance. He lifted the door, its single good hinge itself on its last legs, and shoved it back into place. It took several tries to get it to stay closed, but once successful, he returned to his clothes. *Still wet.* He looked at the bed, took another shot of courage and headed back. He lay down, facing away from the woman, and passed out.

Officer Steve Scaramell watched the road as his Training Officer, Officer Brent Richards, poured coffee from a thermos into an insulated cup, tore open two sugar packets with his teeth and dumped them into the dark brew, then retrieved a swizzle stick from the dash and stirred the liquid. Finished, he tossed the stick back on the dash and looked at the road. His partner's eyes where they should be, Scaramell returned to surveying the surroundings.

The downpour had convinced them to do a quick warehouse district tour to kill some time and avoid having to get out from the shelter of their radio car. Scaramell, on the force less than a year, was relegated to the passenger seat, which was fine by him since he hadn't learned to drive until the Academy and was still a little nervous behind the wheel. His partner, however, seemed able to drink coffee and gnaw at beef jerky while engaging in a high-speed pursuit. His laissez-faire approach to paperwork, protocol and driver safety, had at first shocked Scaramell, but in time he learned to ignore it. He was the "rook", here to learn, and if lucky, correctly distinguish the good habits from the bad.

He spotted an open door on an abandoned warehouse and pointed. "Looks like the winos are busy again." Richards nodded, pulling the patrol car up to the warehouse. They climbed out and trotted over to the entrance, weapons drawn. The sheets of rain prompted Scaramell to shoulder the door open and rush in quicker than his training dictated, leaving him to be first to spot a pile of clothing laying nearby on the floor. "Oh great, a fuckin' *naked* wino." He hated dealing with drunks; they usually wanted to be your friend then puked on your shoes.

"Look." Richards pointed to the other end of the warehouse where someone lay on a mattress and another on the floor, near a toppled over chair. He holstered his weapon and Scaramell followed suit. "Looks like a 10-64," said Richards as he walked toward the pair. Scaramell quickly flipped through his mental file of codes. *Quality of Life*. A little disappointed the call had become completely routine, he followed his TO.

"Okay, wakey, wakey!" called Richards as he approached the man snoring on the mattress. No response. Scaramell gave a gentle kick to the ass of the one lying near the chair, a woman, probably so strung out on crack she had no idea she had just partied with a bum who hadn't seen a shower since the administration changed. Still no response. Richards booted the mattress, unwilling to touch the near naked man.

"Wake up!" The man stirred, looked up and rubbed the sleep from his eyes.

"Whaddya want?" he demanded before realizing it was a cop. He struggled to his feet, nearly losing his balance as he rocked on the soft mattress. The man's tired bones cracked, making Richards cringe, the foul stench of body jam occupying every orifice so overpowering, it caused him to gag. "Oh, sorry, officer. H-how may I be of s-shervice to you?" He cocked his head to the right. "Shuddup, I'll handle this." He hiccupped then farted.

Scaramell watched the walking petri dish for a moment, then turned his attention to the hooker. His jaw dropped as he saw the bullet hole in her forehead. "Holy shit!" He yelled as he drew his weapon and spun toward the wino. Richards snapped his head around, looking at him then the girl. "She's dead!"

"What?" Richards drew his weapon and spun full circle, his trained eye searching the warehouse's every corner. Scaramell continued to cover the wino while his TO scanned the warehouse. Richards turned his weapon on the wino. "Call it in!"

Scaramell grabbed his mike and radioed for backup, his heart thumping against his chest at the excitement of his first homicide.

"I told you we shouldn't have stayed here!" said the wino. He shook his head. "No, you shut-up!"

"Who the hell are you talking to?" Richards approached the man cautiously, his weapon aimed at the man's chest.

"N-nobody," replied the man who lowered his chin and whispered, "Get out of here while you still can, they can't see you!"

"The guy's nuts. Better search him."

"Fuck that, rookie, I ain't touchin' him," replied Richards. "You have at it."

Scaramell holstered his weapon and looked the man over. He wore only underwear, but unless he had a package that would make a porn star proud, he definitely carried something in his shorts. Scaramell pointed. "Empty it out."

"Empty what out?"

Scaramell pulled out his Tazer. "Do you really want me to use this?"

The wino raised his hands. "J-just a second." He inched his hands lower, his eyes never leaving the Tazer. With his left hand he pulled his underwear out by the elastic, stretching the threadbare material, exposing a tear in the front from which a watch clasp dangled out. His right hand shook as he pulled at the gold clasp, freeing the watch and a testicle. Scaramell groaned and almost squeezed the trigger. The man looked at the officers, sheepishly tucked his shame back in and turned slightly to the right, hiding the hole from view. He emptied out the remaining contents of his underwear onto the mattress. Scaramell motioned for him to back up as he snapped on a pair of latex gloves and examined the stash. Credit cards, cash, jewelry, and a driver's license. He retrieved the license and read the name to his partner.

"Tammera Coverdale."

Merissa came to in a blinding orange haze and excruciating pain, lying in a heap on the hard, dirt floor she had grown accustomed to over the past several weeks. Her entire head roared as if on fire, the pain so intense she didn't know where it hurt most. She gingerly touched her face and winced as she explored the split lower lip. A trickle of blood ran down her finger, skirted her palm then continued down her raised arm. She gently pushed on the lip to try and stop the bleeding and was rewarded with a gush of blood. It was split in two, her finger merely occupying the empty area where her lip should be. She moved her hand up to her nose and pinched it slightly. She gasped at the sharp pain then again at the pain in her chest. She remembered some of the blows missing her face and landing on her chest and collarbone. She took another breath and shooting pains coursed through her entire upper body. *Something's broken.* She tried to steady her breaths, making them as shallow and regular as she could. The pain subsided somewhat after she regained control and she returned to her self-assessment. She touched her eyes, the lids and surrounding area protruding at least an inch, and determined the orange haze was the light shining through the lids of her swollen shut eyes.

Overhead she heard the familiar sound of footsteps then the chain rattling as the platform lowered. She didn't feel much like eating, she was in so much pain, she didn't know if she even could, however rather than risk another beating, she decided she better get whatever today's offering might be. The platform hit the floor and she crawled toward the sound, her head throbbing now that she was leaning forward on hands and knees, each movement of her body sending shooting pains from her broken clavicle. She found the platform and reached further in. Her hand grasped a piece of wet cloth which after a moment turned ice cold. She jerked back then tentatively reached forward again, gently felt the cool, wet cloth and concluded it was an ice pack. She picked it up and before she could explore the remainder of the platform, she heard the chain rattle as her captor grabbed it to haul the platform back up. *I guess that's it.*

She crawled back to the wall, made more difficult this time by her free hand now holding the ice pack. The effort left her breathless, her gasps triggered spasms of pain. She sat against the wall and took as long, shallow breaths as she could, until she finally had regained control. After a few minutes the pain in her chest subsided, and she turned her attention to the icepack. She placed it on her eyes and after several minutes of gently applying the cool ice to each, the swelling eased enough for her to see again. Nothing had changed in her surroundings. The lone light illuminated what she now knew was definitely a basement in a home, having just experienced the upstairs. Her split lip throbbed for attention. She pressed the ice pack against it and winced, her eyes tearing. She pulled the cloth away, the slowly melting ice mixing with the blood and flowing down her hand and arm.

I can't let this go on.

She held the icepack to her left eye and rested her head against the dirt wall. *It has to stop.* She knew it had to stop. She wasn't willing to be the victim any longer. How many more beatings would she have to endure? How many more attempted rapes? How many more days of being treated like an animal? Staying alive was one thing, but this wasn't life. This was existence. This had to stop. *This will stop.* Decision made. But as she thought about it, she realized as soon as it stopped for her, it would most likely start for someone else. She had to somehow help them with what she had learned. But how? What had she learned that may help someone else? She knew he drugged the food. She knew he was trying to rape her when she was drugged and it was happening upstairs. How could she let someone know this so they might use it to their advantage? She knew she wouldn't be able to trick him again. This knowledge would be of no use to her, but to someone else it might just let them escape.

But how can I get a message to them without him knowing?

She examined her surroundings. She couldn't carve it into the floor or walls, he would see any message immediately, and she couldn't reach the ceiling, it was too high. She growled in frustration then took a breath, reviewing each item available to her. She eyed the water hole and smiled as the solution dawned on her. It might take a few days, but it would work.

It has to work.

"Miss Kai?"

Aynslee raised her head off her desk with a start, not certain what had woken her. She rubbed her hand across her chin, wiping off a spot of drool. She reached for a Kleenex to wipe up the more embarrassing puddle on her mouse pad when she heard someone clear their throat. Her hand flew to her chest as she jumped in her chair, shocked to see someone standing at the entrance to her cubicle. A quick glance at the clock on her desk confirmed she had slept for several hours after pulling an all-nighter editing a report for the 6 am broadcast. The voice that had woken her belonged to a tall, lean man in his mid-thirties. He wore a tailored suit cut to hide what was clearly a very athletic frame, his square jaw, pronounced cheekbones and slightly protruding Adam's apple revealed no hint of excess body fat. His short, dirty-blonde hair had a functional style, clearly a barbershop cut rather than a salon, and his clean shaven face revealed no scars or blemishes. She found herself assessing him in Hollywood terms, her old beat taking over. *A young Tom Selleck without the porn star mustache.* Tall, dark and handsome. *Who are you and where have you been all my life?*

"Sorry to startle you," he said, his voice, not too deep but not too high either, drew her in. Its sincere quality made her feel like he *was* truly sorry. She wasn't sure what swooning was, but was certain she was doing it right now.

"That's okay," she replied as she yanked herself from her fantasy. "How may I help you?"

He reached into his suit pocket and pulled out a wallet, flipping it open to reveal a gold shield. "I'm Detective Hayden Eldridge, I'm investigating the murders of Tammera Coverdale and two John Does. Do you have time for some questions?"

"Yes, yes I do." She stood, straightened out her skirt and blouse, ran her fingers through her hair, giving it a toss, then motioned down the hall, hoping her makeup wasn't smeared down one side of her face. "Perhaps we should do this in the conference room?"

"That would be fine."

She snatched her purse and led the detective down the hall as she surreptitiously fished a small makeup mirror from her purse, quickly making sure she didn't have a Tammy Faye outbreak, or worse, the imprint of the mouse pad running down her cheek. In the clear, she returned the mirror to her purse and when they reached the conference room, held the door open for her guest. She closed it behind them and motioned to a seat across the table from where she then sat down. The detective removed his jacket and draped it across the back of his chair before sitting.

"Now, how can I help you Detective, Eldridge, was it?"

He nodded as he pulled out his note pad and pen, swirling it to get the ink flowing. "When did you receive the first video depicting the murder of Tammera Coverdale?"

"A couple of nights ago, Wednesday I guess, while I was heading home on the subway. Actually, that's not right. I guess I received it just before I left. The email arrived before I left but I didn't bother checking it." She leaned forward on the conference table. "You see, it had been a late night and normally I work the entertainment beat so I figured any email at that time of night could wait."

"Yes, I've seen your reports on the news."

Aynslee smiled, about to twirl her long brown hair, when she caught herself. *What am I, fourteen?* "Oh, you have?" She wasn't sure she sounded disinterested enough.

"So the email arrived Wednesday evening," prompted Eldridge, evidently choosing to ignore the flirtatious note in her voice.

"Just before midnight."

Eldridge jotted this down. "And you actually read it when?"

"Maybe fifteen minutes later. I read it on my BlackBerry and immediately came back to the office."

"And that's when you notified the police?"

"Well, no, I called my news director."

Eldridge looked up. "And then *he* called the police?"

"Well, no, *he* called a production meeting, and our lawyers, who then made contact with your department the next morning, after we aired the story."

"And it never occurred to you to contact us immediately?"

Aynslee blushed. "Well, of course it *occurred* to me, however Legal said we were within our rights to hold off until it aired."

Eldridge grunted and returned his attention to his pad. "And you received the second email when exactly?"

"Early yesterday evening, maybe eight o'clock. I was editing my piece for the eleven o'clock news when it arrived."

"And you notified us …"

She looked down at her hands sheepishly. "After the broadcast."

"Uh huh. And you have no idea who is sending you these emails?"

"No, none, and our geeks can't trace the emails either."

"Yeah, we have our own techs looking into that as well. It seems they are recorded on a cell phone and then the suspect uploads them using a hijacked residential wireless connection."

"What do you mean?"

"Well, I'm not a techie, but our resident geeks explained it to me. Apparently if you don't secure your wireless network at home, anyone can piggyback on it and surf the Internet, send email, pretty much anything they want."

"And that's how he did this?"

"Yes, we've traced the two emails to completely different parts of the city."

"Really." Her voice trailed off, her mind spinning, already wondering how to work this into her next broadcast.

"Did you recognize any of the victims?"

It took a moment for her to notice he had spoken. "No, no I didn't," she said, shaking her head.

Eldridge folded his notebook and returned it and the pen to his shirt pocket. "Okay, I guess that about does it for now." He stood and put his jacket back on, extending his hand to Aynslee who joined him at the door.

"Thank you for your time and I'll contact you if I have any more questions."

"You're quite welcome." She shook his hand, his grip firm and, most important, dry, immediately telling her she was dealing with confidence. She stole a quick glance at the other hand. *No ring!* "Do you have a card in case I need to reach you?" *Clever girl!*

"Of course." He handed her a business card from the inside pocket of his sport coat then headed toward the elevator. He paused and turned back to face her. "And Miss Kai?"

Her heart skipped a beat. "Yes?"

"Next time you get an email from a killer, call the police immediately."

She blushed. "Yes, Detective." *What, you thought he was going to ask you out?*

Shaw glared as what was obviously a detective left that little bitch's office. *Steal a story from me?* He was pissed. *He* was the lead crime reporter. If there was a crime, *he* got first dibs, no one else. If *he* wasn't interested then it was up to *him* to kick it to one of the more junior reporters. And never in a million years would he pass something on to a walking set of tits far younger than he was when he got his first break. The pencil in his hand snapped, startling him from his mental tirade. He looked around to make sure nobody had noticed and turned to his computer, wondering how to get her emails forwarded to him without her knowing. Looking up from the computer in frustration, he saw the geek lurking about and waved him over.

"Yes, Mr. Shaw?"

Man, I used to pummel kids like this in high school. "Reggie, my boy, have a seat!" He motioned toward an uncomfortable chair facing his desk and leaned forward, lowering his voice. "Reggie, is there any way to get somebody's email forwarded to another person without them knowing?" He knew from the rapid flushing of Reggie's cheeks he was taken aback by the question, almost as if caught with his hand in the cookie jar. *The little shit's probably reading everybody's email.*

"Wh-why? Do you think someone is looking at your emails?" Reggie squirmed in the chair, gripping the arms, the cheap plastic shining with the sweat pouring from his palms.

Yahtzee! Shaw shook his head and leaned in closer still. "No. I want you to forward someone's emails to me without their knowing."

Reggie's jaw dropped. "I-I can't do that!" The glare from Shaw caused him to lower his voice. "I would need management's permission."

"Listen, kid, I can make your life here a living hell, or I can make it very pleasant." Shaw leaned back in his chair and drummed his fingers on his desktop. "Which is it going to be?"

Reggie gulped.

"Tick-tock, kid."

Reggie looked at the floor. "Wh-who's email do you want forwarded?"

Shaw grinned. On the inside. *Fucking wimp!* "Aynslee Kai."

Merissa sat huddled in the corner as she came to terms with the decision she had made. She saw no other alternative; she was going to die, she could do nothing about that now. The question was what to do about it. It had taken hours to decide, but she knew she had only one choice. She pushed herself forward on her knees, clasped her hands and looked toward heaven. She wasn't a religious person, she hadn't attended church since she was a child, she wasn't even sure how to do it. She had prayed while trapped here, more to comfort herself than anything else, but this time, based upon what she had decided to do, she figured it was best to pray formally. *Dear God, I know suicide is supposed to be a sin, but I have no choice. I know he is going to kill me, but if I die on my own terms, maybe I can save the next person he takes. Please forgive me.* She made the sign of the cross and collapsed forward, her shoulders shaking as the torrent of emotions spilled out. Her chest filled with despair, her mind with the questions she had asked for weeks. *Why me? What did I do to deserve this?* Her inner strength broken, she questioned her decision. Perhaps she could escape?

"No!"

She startled herself, not having heard her own voice spoken beyond a whisper in weeks. It was enough to shock her from her bout of self-pity. She wiped the tears off her face and rose to her feet. Removing her shirt, she wrapped it around the chain that still bound her to the ceiling, then, using her handcuffed hand, she looped the cloth covered chain around her neck, momentarily appreciating the irony that what had kept her prisoner would soon set her free. She knew it would be painful, but nothing compared to the pain she had already experienced. With the chain secure around her neck, she relaxed her knees and dropped toward the floor, gravity slowly tightening its grip. The pain wasn't as bad as she had feared, the cloth from the shirt softening the chain's pinch at first. It tightened with every inch she lowered herself, the pain taking hold soon replaced by a far worse sensation. Suffocation. She gasped for breath, the reflex actions of her body not succeeding, the chain now too tight to let any air pass. She fought the urge to get up, knowing if she did she would have to go through this all again. Her gasps became shorter and shorter, her clouded mind no longer able to resist her survival instinct. Her suffocating body demanded she stand. With her one hand chained close to her neck, she was forced to reach with the other to try and pull herself up using the now tight chain. Grasping at it above her head she tried to lift her body to relieve the pressure. For a moment she tasted the sweet relief of a tiny amount of air making its way into her lungs. She pulled harder. Her oxygen deprived body unable to coordinate the attempt at self-preservation, her bare feet slipped on the dirt floor and she flipped over, her feet now extended out in front of her, her body facing upward, her full weight pulling on the chain as her arms and legs flailed, all coordination now lost. It took less than a minute for her to blackout from the lack of oxygen, the Technicolor display provided by her brain not the least bit interesting to her in her final moments.

Aynslee's eyes drooped as she dialed what must be the fortieth number in the past two hours. As soon as the detective had left, she had written down the name he had mentioned, Tammera Coverdale, then confirmed with Legal the police hadn't released the identity yet and got the green-light to run with it. At the moment all she could do was report on the video clips themselves, but now she had a name. And she also knew the police didn't have names for the second set of victims, meaning they probably hadn't even found them yet, a story in itself. She had searched the Internet for hours, calling every listing for Coverdale she found. Three dozen phone calls to New York based Coverdale's had proven a bust. She had moved on to Jersey, the fourth listing for Coverdale, Hugh and Elise. *Work with me,*

Jersey! The phone rang in the earpiece of her headset, pulled low on her ear to lower the volume. It rang several times, Aynslee's finger hovering over the button to end the call. Her heart leapt and she yanked her finger away as the clicking sound of a handset being lifted off its base crackled through the earpiece. She shoved it into position and took a breath.

Silence.

She waited a few more seconds, unsure of what to do, then decided to speak first. "Hello, my name is Aynslee Kai, I work for WACX News, I—."

"Leave us alone!" a woman's voice cried, then the line was cut.

Bingo! Aynslee snatched her purse and jacket off her coat rack, ran down the hall and grabbed a camera crew.

Lance, not his real name, twirled the straw in his definitely not virgin Shirley Temple and stared at the vision in front of him. He was all man, he could tell. Tight jeans showed off his firm ass (he had checked!), a white denim shirt, untucked with the first three buttons open, displayed his tight, sweaty chest to the world. Lance was swooning. *He's sooo cute!* A little young maybe, but that just meant he would get a chance to teach him a few new tricks that would change the boy's life forever. They had talked for about fifteen minutes, every moment of it perfection! *I have to have this dreamboat!*

He was dancing with a long time on-and-off partner, when he spotted this vision eyeing him from the bar. A quick smile fired in his direction was enough for Lance to abandon his partner on the dance floor and sachet over to the bar. Introductions (his name was Charles!), a round of drinks, and a little bit of leg and arm rubbing, and he was ready to do anything this boy wanted. *Anything!*

"It's kind of loud in here, you wanna go somewhere quieter, where we can..." Charles paused and looked at Lance slyly as he ran his finger from under Lance's ear, down his neck then as far down his bare chest as he could, yanking at the top button of his shirt. He leaned in and bit Lance's earlobe, then whispered, "Talk?"

Lance didn't know if his loins leapt more from the throaty whisper or the red-hot touch, but it didn't matter. *You dirty dog! Talk indeed!* He threw his boa around his neck, took Charles by the hand and dragged him from the club. They hadn't even made it a block when Lance couldn't help himself. He dragged Charles into an alleyway, shoved him against the wall, and ground his hips into him. Reaching down between his legs to check out his package, he cooed, "Oooh, is that for me?"

Charles smiled and reached into his pocket, pulling out a couple of tablets. "E?" Lance nodded and stuck out his tongue, closing his eyes. Feeling Charles place the tablet on the end of his tongue, he flipped it back into his mouth and swallowed. He opened his eyes and turned his head to the side, kissing his young delight on the side of the neck, then flicking his tongue over his Adam's apple. He looked up and a mischievous feeling spread over him. Slowly he dropped to his knees and unbuckled Charles' belt. As he undid the fly he felt the Earth start to spin but kept going, determined to reach his prize. He fumbled with the button, his fingers suddenly uncoordinated, then collapsed.

Aynslee burst from the station van, her camera man and sound engineer scrambling to keep up. She rushed up the steps to the Coverdale's small Cape Cod style home and, when everyone was in position, rang the doorbell. Her heart pounded as she waited, thinking of the scoop that had fallen into her lap. This was huge. Not only would she be revealing exclusively to the world who the victim was, but also get an interview with the family to boot. *I wonder have they been notified?* She had a moment of doubt about what she was doing, then shoved it aside. *If they know the name, then of course they've notified the family.* As they continued to wait, her excitement started to wane. *Are they not home?* After a minute with no answer, she rang again and knocked several times, but still no one came. She tried to peer through the glass block window to the side and in desperation placed her ear to the door. She listened for a moment and thought she heard sobbing. She decided to take a chance and motioned to the cameraman to start rolling. The red light on, she leaned closer to the door. "Mrs. Coverdale, this is Aynslee Kai, WACX News, I'd like to talk to you about your daughter, Tammera." She listened and this time heard a definite cry from the other side of the door, near the floor. "She's in there," she whispered to her crew, pointing toward the door and down. Lowering her voice, she tried to soothe the door open. "Ma'am, I'm the reporter who was sent the footage of your daughter's murder. I'm just as confused as you are about all of this, and I'd like to talk to you about it, to find out what kind of a person your daughter was so the world can know she was an innocent victim, not somebody caught up in some sordid affair." The sound guy, Steve, gave a thumbs up as they heard someone unbolt the door.

Aynslee doubted the friends of the poor, disheveled woman who opened the door would recognize her, her eyes bloodshot, her nose bright red and swollen from crying, her hair in knots, having not seen a brush in days. She was gaunt, her face pale, her cheeks sunken, dark circles under her eyes adding years to her face. She was a woman who had lost the will to live. When she saw the camera pointed at her she yelped and slammed the door shut.

"No cameras!"

Aynslee waved off her cameraman, Mike, who nodded and turned off the light but left it recording, aimed at the ground. "I've turned off the camera, Mrs. Coverdale. Can I speak to you now?" The door slowly opened again and they saw the middle-aged woman step back and head deeper into the house without saying a word. Aynslee looked at Mike and Steve, shrugged her shoulders and stepped inside, following the woman. They found her sitting in a chair in her living room, hugging a throw pillow.

Aynslee sat across from her and pulled out a notepad. "Ma'am, first let me start off by saying how truly sorry I am about your loss." She looked at a picture sitting on the end table next to her of a young woman. It was hard to be certain, but she bore a definite resemblance to the victim. "Is this her?" The woman nodded. "What can you tell me about her?" Aynslee jotted down the name emblazoned on the school sweater worn in the photo.

The woman took a deep breath, as if steeling herself for what she was about to say. "She was a wonderful child, our only child. She had a terrific job that was taking her places and she had a fiancé who loved her very much. They were getting married this fall."

Aynslee scribbled in her pad. "And what was the fiancé's name?"

"Jeremy Rush. They were so much in love. They planned on having children right away." Her voice cracked. "Grandbabies," she whispered as she bent over and burst into tears, her hand reaching blindly for a tissue from the box sitting next to her.

Aynslee opened her mouth to ask another question, but found her voice cracking as the enormity of what she was doing hit. *Someone died! This is real, this isn't an out on the town segment!* She closed her mouth and waved her hand back and forth in front of her neck. This time Mike turned the camera off for real. Aynslee knew she wasn't going to get anything else from the distraught woman, and didn't want to regardless. She had enough to throw together a small segment for the next newscast; it would have to be enough. Rising, she walked over and placed a hand on the woman's shoulder and said softly, "I'm truly sorry." She motioned to her crew and they walked out the door, a sobbing victim left behind, Aynslee fighting back her own tears, her crew uncharacteristically quiet.

Elise heard the door click shut, the reporters gone. She curled her legs up under her and leaned over, resting her head on the arm of the La-Z-Boy recliner, still hugging the pillow. Her body racked in sobs, every muscle ached from crying for days. *My baby is gone!* She couldn't understand why. Why would God do this to her? Why would God take her child from her? No parent should have to outlive their child. *This isn't right!* She looked up at the ceiling and through it, as if directly into God's eyes. *Damn you!* She wailed. She was losing her faith. That, combined with her grief, was leading to a spiral of depression she didn't care if she ever came out of. She didn't want to. She pictured her precious, beautiful, baby daughter. First steps, first words, first day at school. Last supper, last hug goodbye, last wave from the curb, last phone call, last sound of her voice.

And where the hell was her husband? Why wasn't he there to support her? She knew he was hurting as much as she was, but he was too much the traditional male. He needed to be on his own to grieve; no one could see him cry. But she needed him. Here. Now. *I can't be alone.* And at that moment she knew exactly what she needed to do. She needed to be with Tammera. Standing, she strode with purpose to the bathroom, opened the medicine cabinet and pulled out the bottle of sleeping pills prescribed to her husband months before. Opening the bottle, she poured them into her mouth as she heard the front door open.

Merissa awoke to pain, excruciating pain around her neck from where the chain had bitten into and torn her flesh, the shirt she had wrapped around it only delaying the inevitable. But it was nothing compared to the searing, jolting shock she experienced when she took that first breath. It felt as if someone had punched her full force in the throat, her collapsed esophagus trying to pop back into shape as her body forced air through it. She focused on her breathing as she tried to control the pain, keeping her breaths slow and steady. The pain gradually subsided as her airway returned to normal. Her instincts forced a wave of relief to flow through her as she realized she was alive, but as more oxygen made it into her system she became aware of her surroundings. She lay on the basement floor, the light gently swung above her, the platform still in place, the chain removed, not only from around her neck, but her wrist as well. She wore a fresh blouse, her old one nowhere to be found. *I've failed!* Her relief turned back to despair as she grasped that she was still alive, the exact opposite of what she had hoped to achieve. She had failed, and now with the chain removed, might never get another chance.

A creak overhead snapped her back to reality, signaling the return of her captor and the lowering of the platform, but instead of food, she saw a pair of legs standing on it. Her pulse raced as he pulled on the chain, the thumping in her chest gained strength as his ankles, knees and then waist were revealed,. The platform was half way down when she saw he had his back to her, an opportunity she dared not pass up. She rose, careful to remain out of sight, and on adrenaline alone, her body still weak from her ordeal, she charged the platform, throwing herself at it as hard as she could. The platform swung away from her, the chains groaning in protest, her captor letting out a surprised yelp as he fell backward and toppled off the platform. His head hit the ground hard, knocking him senseless.

Merissa struggled onto the platform, grasped the chain, and pulled on it. Her first few tugs did little, but she kept going, fighting the instinct to try and climb the chain like a rope in gym class, knowing she wouldn't have the strength to make it. As the platform inched toward the hole, and freedom above, she never took her eyes off her captor. She heard him groan and roll over onto his back, his hand reaching up to touch the back of his head. "Come on!" she cried, furiously pulling on the chain, tears flowing freely, her heart pumping so hard she heard the blood pulsing in her ears like a drummer nearing the end of a tribal dance. She watched as he shook his head and when their eyes made contact, he realized what was happening. He struggled to his feet, jumped up and grasped the platform edge. "No!" she screamed as it rocked under his weight. She reached up and gripped the floor above. Pulling herself up, she swung her right leg over as he did the same on the platform below. She almost had her second leg up when she felt an iron grip on her foot pull her down. She grasped at the floor with her hands, desperate to find something to grab on to.

"Help!" she screamed, her partially crushed windpipe limiting the volume. As he pulled her further down, she flipped over onto her back, dropped her free foot below the floor and kicked with all her might. It connected and the grip loosened as she heard a groan of pain. Tearing her foot free, she rolled back onto the floor, jumped to her feet and ran into the darkened room. She bumped into a table and grasped around for something, anything she might use as a weapon, but found nothing. A grunt behind her caused her to spin around and watch as he struggled up off the platform, the light from her prison silhouetting his upper body, all semblance of humanity lost, replaced by the image of a beast crawling from a primeval pit in pursuit of its prey. Charging forward she ran headlong into a wall, then feeling along it she found a doorway and stumbled through. She raced down a hallway, screaming for help the entire time. *There has to be a door at the end of this!* She heard his shoes squeak on the floor as she hit the door at the end of the hall hard. She recovered and groped for the doorknob and after several precious seconds found it. It turned in her hand and the door loosened ever so slightly as she pulled on the knob, but it wouldn't give. He was in the hallway now. "Help!" she yelled again as she pulled on the knob with her entire body weight. She reached up and found a deadbolt. Turning it she tugged again at the door. It opened several inches before he hit her full force from behind, slamming her body against the door, forever closing it, the bolt's click, like the trigger cocking on a gun, signaled the end of all hope. He threw her to the floor and dragged her by the hair back to the platform. She grasped at his hand, trying to loosen the viselike grip. He tossed her like a sack of potatoes back into her dungeon. She plunged through empty space then the bottom half of her body hit the platform, now six feet off the floor, spinning her around so she fell headfirst. She hit the floor hard, her head bending back, snapping her neck, releasing her from the prison that had become her own personal hell.

THREE

Detective Hayden C. Eldridge stared at the crime scene photos the lab had sent. A seven year veteran of the NYPD, he had made detective three years ago and loved not wearing the uniform anymore. *Uniforms don't get to look at crime scene photos. Or see it through to the end.* He flipped to the next photo, wondering if he was missing something his more experienced partner might have caught. His excitement at the news his partner would be Detective Justin Shakespeare, a veteran of homicide, lasted for exactly two hours after they met. Eldridge looked at the empty chair at the desk across from his, a chair that was empty far more often than it should be, and shook his head. Following the standard introductions by the lieutenant, Shakespeare had shown him around for a few minutes, then took him to his favorite lunch place. He would learn over the years Shakespeare had a lot of favorite lunch places. This one was a hot dog vendor in Central Park.

"Listen, kid," he had begun, half a hotdog and accompanying bun, sauerkraut and relish filling his mouth, "I've got less than five years left until I can retire. I'm not puttin' my neck out for no one or no thing. I'll tell you what I know from the comfort of my desk, but I ain't gettin' involved in no big cases." Eldridge had felt disgust not only over his new partner's eating habits, but his lack of ethics as well. Since then he worked mostly on his own. When assigned a case, Eldridge was left to investigate while his partner chatted up his girlfriend at a small fifties diner in Queens, poking his head in from time to time. Eldridge taught himself the ropes and became quite a good detective if he did say so himself. And little of it thanks to Detective Shakespeare.

But today he wished his partner was here, just to be a second pair of eyes. He had gone through the photos dozens of times, and his lieutenant was close to calling in the FBI on this one. He had convinced him to hold off; he didn't feel it was a serial killer, just some crazed wacko. But if he didn't make some progress soon, he'd lose the case to the Feds, which would piss him off as it would any detective. The first victim, discovered by a wino in an abandoned warehouse, was identified as Tammera Coverdale, 34 years of age, engaged to be married with no prior record, minimal debts, a good job and two parents, still married. Nothing in her background so far had suggested any motive for her murder. The other two victims from the second video however looked like they were in their late teens. Enhancement showed tattoos, facial piercings, unkempt hair and it looked like it had taken place in a rundown apartment. They appeared to be the complete opposite profile of the first victim, yet he had no doubt they were linked. *But how?*

He leafed through the photos, the grainy shots obscuring much of the detail. He'd sent the kids' photos to missing persons but he doubted anybody had reported them yet. It may be weeks before they found the bodies if these guys lived in the type of shit hole he thought they did. *One tip I'll give you, kid, is ignore what's in front of your face. Look at the background, that's where your clues'll be.* Shakespeare he wasn't, but he had kept his promise of *telling* him everything he knew, he just never *showed* him anything. Eldridge looked at the remaining photos, one at a time, ignoring the victims. On the third photo he found what he was looking for. A pizza box, the red logo of a smiling, mustached Italian staring up at him with the company's name emblazoned across the top, the first half covered by one of the victim's arms. He snatched the Yellow Pages and flipped to Pizza. Scanning the listings, he soon found a small advertisement with the same smiling face, kissing his fingers as if he had just tasted the best pizza pie this side of Palermo. He knew if Shakespeare saw the ad he'd be calling ahead to have a pie waiting for when they arrived. He jotted down the address and phone number and trotted from the squad room.

It took Lance a few minutes to pierce through the fog that possessed his brain, a splitting headache, far worse than most of his recent hangovers, pounded like a high school drummer. The throbbing in his head was a distant second to the excruciating pain in his arms. He looked up and saw his familiar leather handcuffs wrapped around his wrists and over the hook in his bedroom ceiling, a hook he had installed months before for this very purpose. He had obviously taken part in last night's festivities; either that or his lover knew all his secrets. The thought of having a stalker tantalized him, but the pain in his arms from dangling for an unknown number of hours must mean his lover passed out before taking him down; he would have used his safe word before letting himself be abandoned like a piece of meat in a butcher's shop. He tried to call out when he felt the ache in his jaw from the ball gag filling his mouth. He chuckled as he tried to remember last night. He had woken in this situation a few times before, but only if he'd had too much to drink. He struggled to focus his pounding head. What had he done last night? He didn't remember drinking that much, he usually didn't drink very much at all, he found it affected his performance too much—brewer's droop was not to be tolerated.

He swung himself so he could see the rest of the room and was startled to see someone sitting on his settee, their eyes closed. *Charles! Now I remember!* But he didn't. He remembered the alley, taking some E, then just when the good times were about to begin, he remembered feeling drowsy and then nothing. *And now here I am, bound, gagged, and I don't remember any of the fun!*

It never occurred to him to be scared as he grunted to get his lover's attention. Charles opened his eyes, picked up a laptop computer sitting beside him, and brought it over so Lance could see the screen. He pressed a key and a jerky video played, showing the awful beating he had witnessed last year, the comments of those nasty boys who had taken it still sickened him. He started to look away when the video stopped, frozen on the face of a passenger as they turned to shield their eyes from the gruesome beating. It was him.

Charles placed the laptop on the bed and pulled out a cell phone, activating its video camera. Lance was confused, not sure if this was all part of the role playing he was used to, and how the video of what happened a year before had anything to do with it. When Charles pulled a gun out, his eyes bulged as the gag muffled his screams from the neighbors.

As his GPS announced he had arrived, Eldridge pulled into the first spot he saw and eyed his surroundings. *Man, I hate this part of town.* Most buildings were in a desperate need of repair, a coat of paint the least of their worries. Litter drifted down the streets and sidewalks like tumbleweed, an abandoned lot nearby the home to the shells of several cars, one of which appeared to be the new home to a failed Wall Street broker, or a bum with a sense of humor, the "My Other Home Is On Park Ave" sign replacing the rear window eliciting a chuckle from Eldridge. He grabbed the photos and climbed from his car. He looked around and spotted his destination, a small white with red trim restaurant, the freshly painted-over brick causing it to stand out from its neighbors. A large sign stretching the building's entire width announced Giovani's Pizzeria had the best pizza in town. *I wonder if Shakespeare knows about this place?* If it weren't for the bars on the windows, it would look almost inviting.

He gripped the door handle and took one last look around, spotting a kid eyeing his car. Eldridge made eye contact with the kid and held open his jacket, revealing his shoulder holster. The kid ran. Eldridge opened the door and stepped inside. It took a moment for his eyes to adjust but not for his nose. A smile spread across his face as he took in the delicious aroma of fresh baked pizza dough and melted mozzarella cheese.

"A little bit of normalcy in an island of insanity, eh?"

He looked to where the voice came from, expecting an obese, hairy Italian with stained wife-beater t-shirt. Instead, he found a man, clearly willing to risk his own cuisine, but who appeared to successfully resist overindulging too often. With the exception of a very neat mustache, the man was clean shaven, a smidge of flour on one cheek highlighting their ruddy color, a near perfect match for the restaurants red and white décor. He wiped his hands on his flour covered white apron and pushed a tress of hair back under the crisp chef's hat barely containing his dark, wiry mane. The clean, simple restaurant was a welcome respite from the depression lying on the other side of the door.

Eldridge nodded. "Not at all what I was expecting." He walked over to the counter and sat down on one of the several stools.

The man laughed. "Welcome to Giovanni's, I'm Giovanni Deangelo, what can I get you?"

"What am I smelling?"

"That, my friend, is the world famous polo pizza, a hand tossed crust brushed with a delicious garlic pesto sauce, topped with mozzarella, onions, hot peppers, black olives and spicy roasted chicken, all baked to perfection in a wood burning pizza oven, by yours truly."

"Sounds great!" Eldridge's stomach demanded attention. "I'll take a slice."

"It'll be ready in five minutes, my friend."

Business first I guess. Eldridge pulled out his badge. "I'm Detective Eldridge, Homicide, I need to ask you a few questions."

"Sure, how can I help the NYPD today?"

Eldridge pulled out a photo of each of the three victims and lined them up on the counter. "Do you recognize any of these people?"

Giovanni took one look at the photos and grunted. "Yeah, I know two of 'em." He pointed to the first photo. "That no good bum is Logan, he worked here until three nights ago. This other one is his equally no good friend, but I don't know what his name is."

"What happened three nights ago?"

"Nothin' three nights ago, but he didn't show for his shift last night so if you see him, tell him he's fired."

"Do you know where I can find this Logan?"

"Yeah, he lives on the second floor of that cesspool across the street." He turned around, grabbed a wood pizza paddle, opened the oven and expertly extracted two pizzas. He sliced them with a large pizza knife then slid an oversized piece on a cardboard tray. Placing it on the counter in front of Eldridge, he smiled. "On the house, Detective!"

"Thanks, but I'll pay, don't want anyone accusing you of trying to offer a police officer a bribe!" Giovanni laughed and watched as Eldridge picked up the slice and took a tentative bite of one of his few vices. *Oh my God!* Eldridge savored every chew, each one releasing a new sensation, the rich taste of the garlic pesto sauce, the crunch of the sautéed onions and tang of the hot peppers as they clashed with the sweetness of the olives, all combined to produce an experience he never expected could come from a pizza. Thirty years of pepperoni, green peppers and mushrooms or the occasional Hawaiian were blown away, his appreciation for the tired staple of American cuisine turned into a fine dining experience. It pained him to end the experience, but he had to. He swallowed then leaned back from the counter, pointing at the pizza. "That is the best damned pizza I have *ever* had."

The restaurant's namesake smiled and took a slight bow, clearly pleased with the response. "Nothin' but satisfied customers for Giovanni's."

Eldridge scarfed down the rest of the slice and wiped his mouth with the napkin. "The boys at the precinct will definitely be hearing about this." Eldridge paid his host and headed to the door. He pointed at a decrepit building across the street. "Is that the cesspool?"

Giovanni walked around the counter and nodded. "Yup, feel free to make a few calls and have it knocked down."

Eldridge smiled and pushed open the door. "I'll see what I can do."

He walked across the street to the building Giovanni had pointed out. Most of the surrounding buildings qualified as dives, but his destination truly was a cesspool. He strode up to the door-bum sitting outside, his hat on the ground in front of him filled with the day's take of twenty-seven cents, and held out the photo of Logan. "Seen this guy?" The man leaned forward, snatched his hat and shook it without saying a word. Eldridge sighed and reached in his pocket. Pulling out two quarters, he tossed them in the hat.

"Second floor, first door on the right."

"Thanks." Eldridge pulled open the door, noting the brick propping it open was tagged with a local gang symbol, marking the territory of whoever dealt from this building. He kicked it aside and entered the lobby, the immediate smell of urine and feces assaulted his senses. He gagged as he fished a handkerchief from his pocket and held it over his mouth and nose. The dim lighting was intermittent, the lone remaining fluorescent bulb on its last legs. He looked for a means of escape. An elevator to his left looked like it had been pried open one too many times to be considered reliable. He opted for the stairs to his right. He climbed to the second floor and knocked on the door the vagrant had indicated. As he expected, nothing. He knocked again. "NYPD, open up, I need to ask you some questions!" Again no answer. *Whenever you need to enter a place without a warrant, listen very carefully for the person crying for help.* Eldridge had used his partner's logic a few times in the past and it hadn't bit him on the ass yet. He turned the knob and pushed. The door swung open.

The smell of stale beer, cigarettes and marijuana were overpowered by the unmistakable stench of death, the source not immediately evident, a torn, stained acoustic divider hiding much of the bachelor apartment from view. Pizza boxes, beer cans and unopened mail covered every exposed surface, an overflowing outdoor metal garbage can, no longer able to keep up with the volume, the need to empty it on a regular basis apparently lost on the occupants, filled the entrance closet. The sink, piled high with dishes and the occasional pizza box, swarmed with cockroaches. Eldridge gagged and wondered how many he couldn't see. He shivered, disgusted by the sty that lay before him, the filth at a level only teenaged boys could stand for any length of time. He stepped around the divider to see the rest of the apartment and found his two victims, tied back-to-back, their heads slumped over, blood and brain matter sprayed across the floor and wall behind them. Nearby lay the pizza box he had seen in the blow up.

Aynslee sank in her chair and let her shoulders sag as she closed her eyes for a moments rest. She slowly exhaled, and even debated mimicking the meditation postures she had seen on TV. She kicked off her shoes and drew one leg up under the other. As she drew up the second leg she realized this position wasn't meant to be performed in a chair with arms. She dropped the leg, let out a deep sigh, and spun the chair to face her computer. Opening her eyes, she saw a Post-it note stuck to her monitor. "iTunes installed and synched with your iPod! Reggie!" She prayed the strange design drawn under his name wasn't a heart with a Cupid's arrow through it. Logging into her machine, she saw the iTunes icon on her desktop and wondered how he had managed to get on there without her password. *I've got to figure out how to get rid of him.*

Her BlackBerry vibrated with a new message. She launched her email program on her computer and saw amongst the dozens of emails, a newly arrived one with no subject line. *Oh no!* She opened the attachment. If it weren't for the first two emails, she would have deleted this third one after a few seconds of watching, the video of a man, an apparent sexual sadist, ball gag stuffed in his mouth, screaming out in terror or pleasure, similar to some smut-films sent her by friends as a joke. But the fear in his eyes when the gun appeared eliminated any doubt as to it being the genuine article. She closed her eyes as she saw the trigger squeezed. *Not again!* As with the others, the video ended with a shot of the body, then nothing. The email contained no text and the "from address" had her own email address in it. It contained nothing to indicate who it was from and why they were doing this. Or why they were sending it to her.

She leaned back in her chair, eyes closed, and took a deep breath. *How many will there be?* She opened her eyes, the images she had just watched merely playing themselves out on her eyelids. She picked up her Blackberry to find Detective Eldridge's number and hesitated. *CNN!* Her thumb hovered over the scroll button as a battle of wills raged in her head. *You promised!* She pressed the button. *But what about you? You need this! And he's already dead.* She quickly cancelled the call.

She stood up and yelled, "I got another one!"

You're so weak.

Reggie heard her beautiful voice ring out across the office. Standing, he watched as she waved toward Mr. Merle's office, a huge smile on her face. *And what a smile.* His heart raced as he pictured her smiling at him as he gently lay her across his desk, leaning in for a kiss, one so passionate he would be the envy of all of his friends. If he had any. The beginnings of an erection shocked him into sitting down. He snatched his keyboard and covered the obvious bulge in his pants as he looked around to make sure no one had noticed.

"What the hell happened?" The seething voice of Shaw sent his manhood racing for cover as his mouth went dry. Shaw stormed into his office and leant over his desk, his face inches from Reggie's. "I thought we had a deal?"

It took a moment for Reggie to regain his voice. "I-I'm sorry, sir, but I c-couldn't do it."

Shaw leaned in closer. "Why the hell not?"

Because I love her. "It wouldn't be ethical," he squeaked. *Where did that come from?* Shaw turned beet red and Reggie felt himself get lightheaded as Shaw's hot breath blew on his face like the snorts of an angry bull in

Pamplona. He bit his cheek. Hard. Shaw glared at him for another moment then stormed from the office. Lifting the keyboard, Reggie looked at the rapidly expanding urine stain in his pants. *Shit!* He jammed the keyboard back over his crotch and whimpered, wondering if hiding under his desk until everyone had left for the day was at all possible.

It wouldn't be ethical? Shaw couldn't believe what he had heard. *That little shit has the nerve to talk to me about ethics?* He stormed into the men's room and slammed the door to one of the stalls shut. He leaned forward against the cold, metal wall, his clenched fists supporting his weight. He banged his head on the wall, his rage consuming him. Desperate for a release, he punched the metal, hard. The pleasure from the resulting dent was fleeting, the searing pain shooting through his hand caused him to gasp. He clamped his mouth shut, trying not to cry out. Closing his eyes, he took several deep breaths and flexed his fingers, checking to see if he had broken anything. He started at the sound of the bathroom door opening. Through the crack in the stall he saw the little shit, Reggie, standing at the mirror doing something. He threw open the door and stormed from the stall, ready to tear another strip off the kid, but before he could, Reggie spun around, yelped, slapped a keyboard over his crotch and ran into the now vacant stall, slamming the door behind him. Not knowing what to do, Shaw headed to the gym to work off some steam.

Eldridge eyed two soiled mattresses, laying in opposite corners, probably rescued from some nearby dumpster, the ratty beach towels substituting for sheets failing to cover the urine stains from what he hoped were the previous owners. *Then again…* He picked them up by the finger tips, not confident the latex gloves he now wore would be enough to protect him from the filth. Each corner had a few personal items belonging to the boys, mostly porn magazines with some of the more choice pages pinned to the walls, a poor attempt to turn this disgrace into a home. One corner contained a backpack with "Logan" written in pen across the top. Unzipping it, he rooted around for any identification but turned up nothing except a folded piece of paper stuffed in the bottom. He retrieved it and carefully unfolded the torn foolscap, revealing the beginnings of a letter that read, "Dear Mom & Dad, I want to come home." *I guess life here wasn't so good after all.*

Turning his attention to the bodies, he raised his hands to make the frame of a camera and positioned himself to approximate where the killer must have stood. He crouched a bit to get the angle, making him think he was taller than the killer by about half a foot. He heard voices on the other side of the divider as the officer controlling access to the scene acknowledged someone's arrival.

"Hey, Detective, where's your partner?" asked a sarcastic voice from behind the divider.

"Ha ha," said Eldridge to the grinning face of Vincent "Vinny" Fantino, a criminalist with the Crime Scene Unit, as it came into view. Eldridge and Vinny had become quite close over his years as a detective. Vinny had been on the force for over fifteen years, and knew his stuff. Eldridge considered him his "go to" guy if he wanted a quick, accurate answer. He also considered him a friend.

"If I know that waste of space, he's probably stuffing a Philly sandwich in his mouth or his tongue down the throat of that girlfriend of his." Vinny shook his head as he surveyed the scene. "Why any woman would want to kiss that fat bastard, I'll never know." Vinny's eyes settled on the victims and became all business. "So, what have we got here?" he asked as he looked for a clean spot to place his kit. Giving up, he settled on a less dirty spot instead.

"Not much I'm afraid. According to the pizza guy across the street, this one is named Logan and worked for him until a few nights ago." He pointed to Logan's presumed roommate. "No idea who the other is. How long would you say they've been dead?"

Vinny snapped on some latex gloves and examined the gunshot wounds, gently moving aside some hair matted down with dried blood. "Based upon the insect activity, I'd say two, maybe three days."

Eldridge nodded. "That fits the timeline. The Logan guy showed up for his shift at work three nights ago but never showed last night. The video was emailed two days ago."

"I'll get a more definite answer when I get him back to the morgue." Vinny rose and moved to the other victim as one of his techs entered the room with the photographic equipment.

Eldridge headed to the door, pulling off his gloves. "Make sure you guys take measurements of everything. We should be able to tell how tall this guy was from the angle of the gun in the video and the surroundings."

Vinny didn't look up. "Will do, I'll let you know if we find anything helpful."

Chelsie waited by the rear employee exit, eyeing the poorly lit parking lot through a tiny window in the door with trepidation. Earlier in her shift a customer had sat alone for hours sipping a bottle of Chalk Hill Chardonnay, all the time never taking his eyes off of her. It had creeped her out, and his hundred dollar tip hadn't helped. Guys sitting alone in bars, even high-priced wine bars, who gave big tips to young waitresses, usually wanted something. And sometimes, especially after an entire bottle of wine with no food, they waited outside in their cars to get it.

Which was why she now waited at the exit for Denis, the bouncer. Denis rarely had to lay a hand on anyone, the sheer enormity of him scaring most people straight, but whenever there was an altercation, it never lasted long, and he never lost. Her boss, Yannick, was a great guy and always insisted on Denis walking the waitresses either to their cars, or in her case, the nearby subway station, just in the event a patron was thinking with the wrong head. Most nights she was of the opinion Yannick was a bit too paranoid, and she sometimes missed her train by having to wait, and Denis, who would insist on waiting until she stepped onboard, was not much of a conversationalist. But tonight was different. She looked at her watch and as if on cue, Denis lumbered around the corner. "Sorry, Chelsie, Mr. Leroux had me moving some cases of wine."

"No problem, Denis, there's plenty of time." There wasn't, but Denis, more brawn than brains, took any hint of criticism to heart, so she decided a little white lie couldn't hurt. He opened the door for her and followed her outside, all the while making sure no one was around. Their footsteps echoed on the pavement of the nearly empty parking lot, only a few staff cars and vehicles abandoned by intoxicated patrons remaining. The rattle of a car starting at the far end sent her heart pounding a little harder. She quickened her pace as she dialed her parents' number, knowing her mother would never get to sleep if she didn't. It rang twice before her mother picked up. "Hi, mom, just a quick call, I'm heading to the subway now. I'm really tired so I'm not going to call tonight, okay?" As they crossed the street she listened while her mother prattled on about getting her rest. "Gotta go, Mom, love you!" she said, cutting off the now repetitive conversation. She loved her parents but sometimes they worried too much. As she was about to enter the subway station she looked back toward the parking lot and saw the car pull out and head away from them. Breathing a sigh of relief, she gave Denis a quick hug, her arms barely reaching his shoulders, and raced down the platform and onto the just arriving train.

Taking her seat on the subway, thankful to find one empty for a change, Chelsie turned up her iPod and closed her eyes, imagining herself at a Duran Duran concert, even though she wasn't alive when they were last popular. Retro Eighties nights at the bars were always her favorite, the music so much more upbeat and fun than the depressing music that came out of the nineties or the rap crap posing for music today. She could dance for hours with her girlfriends, belting out the lyrics at the top of their lungs until they were hoarse the next day. She smiled at the thought and made a mental note to text her friends when she got home to set up an outing for tomorrow night. As she eased in for the long ride home she felt the day's tension slowly melting away. She hated her waitressing job, but the tips were good and the courses she was taking would eventually get her a better gig, but for now she had no choice but to stick it out. Leaning her head against the glass, she felt the subway vibrate as it sped to the next terminal, the periodic clicking of the tracks gently pulsing against her scalp and through her body, acting as a poor man's massage chair. She quickly eyed a new arrival as he sat beside her and settled in. *Not bad, too old though.* But then anything over thirty was too old to her. He smiled at her as he opened a copy of the New York Times. Returning the smile, she resumed her position at the window, singing Hungry Like The Wolf on stage with Simon Le Bon.

Chelsie opened her eyes slightly, as she often did, just to make sure nothing she should be concerned about was happening, and could have sworn the man beside her was slightly closer than she remembered. She looked at him and cringed. His eyes were closed, head tilted back slightly, nostrils flared. *Is he sniffing me? Ew!* She shuddered. *Good luck, creep!* She laughed inwardly. *Okay, that was mean.* He opened his eyes and pulled a handkerchief out of his pocket and straightened himself, giving his nose a quick wipe. She immediately closed her eyes, feeling kind of silly, and guilty at thinking the worst of some innocent guy who just had a runny nose. She stole a quick glance to see if he had caught her staring. He shuffled his paper and flipped to the next page. *Okay, he's not that old, but still old enough to be boring.* He looked at her and smiled. Embarrassed at being caught, she blushed, and quickly averted her eyes. She looked at her watch. *Treats?* She nodded to herself, pulled the headphones off and stood. The man looked up at her and smiled again, swinging his legs into the aisle so she could exit. She scooted past him, and this time there was no doubt. She could hear him draw in a deep breath, through perfectly clear nostrils, as she squeezed by.

Double ew!

She hurried to the exit as the subway came to a halt. The doors opened and she stepped through, tossing a quick look over her shoulder at her former seatmate. He was staring directly at her, but didn't move. She rushed onto the platform and up the stairs, all the while stealing glances behind her. As she emerged on the street, she breathed a sigh of relief as she hurried toward the small corner store, her strange encounter now over.

This wasn't her usual stop, but she wanted a treat since she wasn't feeling tired, and there was an all-night corner store here, only a few blocks from her apartment. And tonight it had the added bonus of getting her away from some bum sniffing freakazoid. Her mother would probably flip if she knew this was a frequent routine of hers, but she found walking at night, alone, exhilarating. She was never scared in her own neighborhood. It was only ten minutes at a brisk pace to her apartment, and the few people out at this time of night had yet to give her any problems.

She grabbed a few toiletries and a tub of Cherry Garcia, paid the bored clerk, then strolled toward her apartment, her purchases swinging at her side, her mind on her music, turned low so she might hear any goings on around her, as the events on the subway and at work slowly drifted into the past, memories to be forgotten over the coming days. She crossed a small side street and looked up at the night sky, seeing if she might catch an errant star in the light polluted sky of New York.

She started at the sound of a van's sliding door. She spun toward the sound and gasped as two hands reached out from the dark interior and yanked her inside. She opened her mouth to scream when something jabbed her in the leg, the unexpected pain from the needle piercing her skin silencing her. Looking down in shock she saw a needle sticking out, her captor's gloved thumb pushing the plunger down, injecting its contents into her. Her mind still wasn't processing what was happening, the situation so unexpected, the events happening so quickly, she didn't know what to think. *What the hell?* Almost immediately a warm, relaxing sensation rushed through her veins as if she had just downed a large shot of JD. Within moments, as every muscle in her body loosened, she felt the van slowly spin, then the world go dark, the clunk of the van door slamming shut a distant echo sealing her fate.

FOUR

"Tonight on Larry King Live, Aynslee Kai. Entertainment reporter last week. Hottest crime reporter in the country this week. Why is a serial killer sending her videos? We'll ask her later in the show, but first—"

Eldridge shook his head. *She's milking this for all it's worth.*

He flipped the channel to the local newscast and there she was again, wearing the same form hugging top and skirt as the day he had met her. It was as becoming then as it was now. The way she carried herself said *I'm good looking, I know it, and I'm going to use it to get me where I want to go.* He didn't get the impression she would cross any lines, the lack of sway in her hips when they had met giving that away, but he figured she would use her sexuality to bend people to her will. And he had no problem with that. He had even had to pour on the charm himself a few times to get a female witness, and even a couple of male witnesses, to tell him what he wanted to know. But this one could be a challenge. He needed her to cooperate, but he had a feeling her career came first and everything else, including civic duty, a distant second.

"—fourth murder victim. I must warn you, what you are about to see is very disturbing."

Eldridge leaned forward on his couch. *Don't tell me.* A video played, showing a man tied up and gagged, pleading for his life. A gun slowly came into view, the finger on the trigger relentlessly closing. The image froze then the broadcast cut back to Aynslee. "We just can't show you any more than that. The identity—". Eldridge shut the TV off in disgust, threw the remote on the table and grabbed his phone to find out where Aynslee was. *I guess our little talk fell on deaf ears.*

Chelsie woke with a start. Looking around, she saw nothing, only an inky black like she had never experienced before. Not even a hint of a reflection from some stray, indirect light source spoiled the perfect darkness. *Where am I?* She racked her brain, trying to remember what had happened. *The van!* Her memories surged forth, a tsunami of remembrance that sent her heart racing with adrenaline, as the events of earlier came back. *Somebody grabbed me! And drugged me!* She rubbed her leg where the needle had pierced through her nylons. It felt slightly hard, almost like after a vaccination. *Is this the van?* If it was, they definitely weren't moving. She listened for a motor. Nothing. She listened harder. *Are we parked?* This excited her. If they were parked, she might have a chance. She listened for the sounds of pedestrians. All she needed was to be able to get someone's attention. They could call the police. They could get help, or even help her themselves. She strained to hear something. Anything. But all she could hear was the sound of her own breathing. *Maybe I'm not in the van?* This admission made her notice her bum was quite cold. And damp. She reached with her right hand and was shocked to feel something completely unexpected under her. *Is that dirt?* She felt the floor some more, and was soon certain of it. This was dirt. This was definitely not a van. *A cave?* She had visions of werewolves and vampires flash through her head. *You watch Twilight entirely too much.*

She decided to take a chance. Maybe she wasn't alone. Maybe there was someone else there, and they could work together, help each other. "Hello?" Her voice barely made a sound, her throat so dry. She swallowed and tried again. "Hello?" This time it was louder, the distance of the echo surprised her, revealing an area larger than she expected. She called out again. Nothing. She waved her hands in front of her face, and something heavy dragged down her left arm. She probed the smooth, hard object encircling her wrist with her fingers and found a part jutting out, leading to long, cold rings of metal linked together for as far as her arm could stretch. *A chain!* Pulling on it, she heard it rattle against something metallic far above her head. She rose and grasped for something, anything. She soon found a strange feeling wall, almost cave-like. As she followed it, dragging her chain with her, she heard metal scraping on metal overhead. The further she moved down the wall, the more the chain stretched, then every few feet a surge of scraping sounds accompanied by more slack. She rushed around the walls, her hands spread out in front of her, feeling the surface, desperate to find a door or window, any means of escape. She bumped into another wall and yelped, tears filling her eyes. She quickly felt around the corner, and stumbled headlong down this new wall, her heart pounding faster and faster, tears streaming down her face, her hands shaking more and more as she found each corner, and no way out. Her teeth chattered, her jaw vibrating with fear, tiny moans escaping her chest as she rushed again around the room, hoping she had missed something, anything.

But she had missed nothing.

She finally collapsed in a corner, exhausted, and hugged her knees, pressing her chattering jaw into them, trying to settle it, her mind a swirl of panic, as it raced to process the situation. She was trapped. She was a prisoner. She was going to die. To be raped. To be eaten. Hannibal Lector was nearby, watching her, laughing to himself as his next meal exhausted itself. Some creature, some beast, was waiting to tear her apart, some dirty, perverted, fat old man was going to make her his sex slave, and rape her, forcing her to have his babies for years to come, and they too would be trapped here with her.

She heard footsteps above her and let out a blood-curdling scream.

"Just up here on the right please."

Ibrahim nodded to the portly woman in the rearview mirror and pulled his cab up to the corner of 42nd and 5th. He stopped the meter and turned to face her. "That'll be seven-fifty, madam."

The woman already had a ten-dollar bill in her hand and passed it through the partition to him. "Keep the change," she grunted as she opened the door and swung her legs out, relying heavily on the frame to pull her bulk out and onto the sidewalk.

"Thank you, madam!" He had started driving the cab three weeks ago and still got excited when someone handed him cash. He found he would sometimes just rub his thumb over the stack of bills, the paper's wrinkled, almost fabric-like texture, thrilled him. But it was the smell he couldn't get enough of. The smell of a thousand hands that had handled the worn bills before him, buying a thousand things he had never heard of before coming here. In a single day he now handled more money than he had seen in his previous life. Having fled the violence in Sudan two years ago with his wife and daughter, he had struggled ever since. His cousin had managed to get him a job as a cabby but took a large cut of his take under the table. *There is no thief worse than one who is family.* He could have lied about how much he made each night, but then he would be no better than his cousin and as anyone who knew him would tell you, he was honest, almost to a fault. He placed the new bill in his pocket, adding it to the wad he had already accumulated today, checked his driver side mirror and was about to pull out when he saw something move behind him. Startled, he whipped around to look. A man knocked on the trunk and pointed, holding up a carryon luggage case.

Ibrahim climbed from the cab, his heart still beating fast, and popped the trunk, placing the man's bag inside. Slamming the trunk closed he asked, "Where can I take you, sir?"

"La Guardia, please."

They both climbed in and Ibrahim pulled out into traffic. "No problem. Things are pretty backed up so it will take a little longer than usual." The man said nothing as he sat in the back seat behind Ibrahim. The large, dark sunglasses he wore revealed nothing about his eyes, the rest of his features hidden behind the shadow of a Yankees cap pulled low. Ibrahim shuddered at the complete lack of emotion displayed on his passenger's face as he stared straight ahead. *There is something definitely wrong with this man.* He pressed a little harder on the accelerator, eager for this fare to end.

They drove in silence for almost ten minutes. While passing on a side street the man leaned forward. "I need to get something out of my bag. Can you pull over, please?" Ibrahim nodded and pulled into the parking lot of a gas station. He popped the trunk and reached to take off his seatbelt when his passenger shook his head. "I'll get it." The man climbed out and walked to the back of the cab. The car rocked slightly as the man did something in the trunk. Ibrahim watched in his side mirror for him to come back but he didn't. *What's taking him so long?* He rolled down his window.

"Can I help you, sir?"

Silence.

Both fear and curiosity gripped him. *Should I go look?* He knew he shouldn't. He had heard too many stories, and the memories of the

Janjaweed's brutal attack on his family were still fresh in his mind. He looked around the gas station parking lot. At the other end a family redistributed their luggage for a vacation, but other than them, he was alone. How long was he supposed to wait? He decided to risk it.

He stepped from the cab, and, cautiously leaning out, eyed the back of the vehicle. His passenger was nowhere to be seen. *Did he skip out on me?* "Sir?" He crept to the back, his heart pounding like a drum, his mouth dry with fear. As he neared the rear he heard a shoe scrape on the pavement behind him.

"Miss Kai, I thought we had an agreement."

Aynslee looked up from her laptop and saw Detective Eldridge frowning at her from the entrance of her new office. *Four real walls!* "Detective Eldridge," she smiled, knowing full well why he was there, the elation of the Larry King interview suddenly pushed to the background, a knot in the pit of her stomach replacing it. "Please, have a seat." She motioned him toward one of two office chairs in front of her desk.

Eldridge sat, looked around for a moment then fixed his gaze on her.

Are you interested in career women? "As you can see I'm moving up in the world," she laughed, the half-heartedness of it betraying her nervousness. "No window yet, but better than my old cubicle any day." *Unbelievably better!* When she had arrived this morning to a standing ovation from the staff, she saw Jeff at the end of the hall with a big smile on his face, leading the cheering. She knew she wasn't the first reporter from the office to get on Larry King, but she was the latest, and she might as well enjoy the attention while it lasted. Next week it might be someone else, that damned intern for all she knew. Jeffrey shook her hand then motioned her into the new office. She pretended it wasn't a big deal, but as soon as she closed the door, she did a happy-dance no one saw. *Because I have four walls and a door!* Immediately she took a few photos and emailed them to her mom and dad.

But one glance at Eldridge and she knew he could care less, his stare unwavering.

No small talk. "Yeah, well, I guess you're here to talk about the video. I'm sorry about that, but ..." She trailed off, hoping he would say it was okay. *Please say it was okay!*

He didn't.

"Well, you know how it is, everything is about getting the story out first, early bird gets the worm, that type of thing."

Eldridge said nothing.

Aynslee smiled, his lack of response making her uncomfortable. *Say something!* "Look, if I tell the police then that means it goes public and I lose my exclusive. I can't afford that!" It sounded feeble even to her.

Again, Eldridge said nothing.

Those eyes! It's like he's looking straight into my head, like he knows what I'm thinking. "Okay, you're right, I should have called you first, and I'm sorry I didn't, but I'm not going to apologize for thinking of my career first." *But I just did!* "The guy was already dead, what harm is there in a few hours delay?" She cringed. *No, I'm not heartless!*

Eldridge blinked. Aynslee was sure it was the first time since she had started talking. And he still said nothing.

"Okay, you win!" said Aynslee, exasperated. "I promise, the next time I get a video, I will call you first. But you have to promise me that it won't get leaked to the press until I get my exclusive!"

Eldridge rose from his chair. "I'm glad we have an agreement," he said and he stretched out his hand. Aynslee reached to shake it when she noticed it was palm up. Sheepishly, she pulled a memory stick from her laptop and handed it to him.

"See, I was already making you a copy."

Eldridge walked from the office without saying another word. Aynslee slumped back in her chair and smacked her forehead. *I wish he was fat.*

Ibrahim awoke to find himself in near total darkness, the only light from the odd stray shaft making it through the walls of whatever prison he was in. He struggled to rise but found his hands and feet bound and tape over his mouth. It took him a moment to realize he was in the trunk of a car, most likely his own cab. The steady sound from the engine told him they were idling, the telltale sounds of other cars around him suggesting they were in heavy traffic. The car surged forward, slamming him into the front of the trunk, the loose tire jack digging into his side. He closed his eyes and tried to calm down but it was no use, memories of when the Janjaweed had come to his home in Silaya and tied him up, much like he was now, played on the back of his eyelids like a movie, perfect replays of a nightmare he would never forget. But then it wasn't dark. It was all too bright. He had been able to watch every single thing done to his family. When he had tried to close his eyes, one of the vermin reached around and pried his eyes open, forcing him to watch as the soldiers raped his wife and his daughter, a mere six at the time, laughing and pointing at him as they did it, man after man, hour after hour. Squeezing his eyes shut, he tried to rid himself of the memory, but it was no use, the sound of their screams, the desperation in their voices as the marauders savaged their innocent bodies, too fresh. He opened his eyes, the images of that day replaced by his new nightmare.

The car lurched to a stop, sending him rolling backward in the trunk so he now lay on his other side, facing where the trunk would eventually open, signaling the end of his life. At the front of the trunk he spotted a green light with what looked like writing. *What is that?* He struggled forward, trying to see what was written on it. *Push to Open!* Shoving with his feet, he forced his head toward the button and stretched out his neck, inching his nose ever closer. The car made a hard left turn and he tumbled back again, away from the button and away from possible freedom. Gasping for breath against the tape, he positioned himself for another attempt. Pushing with all his might, he lunged his head toward the glowing beacon and winced as his nose made contact. The button pushed in slightly as the car hit a bump. Losing his balance, his head rapped itself against the trunk lid, sending shooting pain through his scalp. Ibrahim moaned but focused again on his target. Positioning his nose, he pushed forward one more time and made contact. The button moved forward but didn't click. Fearful the next turn might send him sprawling again, he gave one final push, stretching his neck out as far as he could. This time the button clicked.

The trunk swung open with a rush of wind, the stifling heat replaced by sweet, fresh air. The car was travelling at least thirty miles per hour but he had to chance it, he knew the driver would notice almost right away the trunk was open. Using his head, he shoved the lid up and struggled to his knees. The flood of light momentarily blinded him as he leaned forward over the lip of the trunk. He made eye contact with the startled driver behind them, then poured himself onto the rushing pavement below.

Ibrahim heard muffled sounds as he gradually regained consciousness, a steady beeping to his left and several voices he could not place competed with the roar of pain filling his ears as his body screamed in agony, the overwhelming sensation drowning out almost everything else. Every nerve ending was on fire, the unbearable pain sent stabbing sensations from his chest as he breathed, each bone in his body carrying the pain to every extremity, no part of him was free from the torture, yet through it all there was something else. He sensed something other than the pain, something calming, something gentle. He focused on it, trying desperately to feel through the pain, and, finally breaking through the fog of agony, he found it—the tender, gentle squeeze of somebody holding his hand. He struggled to open his eyes. As the lids slowly parted, a blinding light caused his eyes to burn and tear up. He squeezed them shut.

"Doctor!" Someone in the distance was yelling. Or was it in the distance? He fought to hear, to cut through the roar, as the person continued to call for a doctor. The voice neared as he broke through the din raging in his ears. The grip on his hand tightened. It hurt but he didn't care. He focused on it and again tried to open his eyes. "Doctor, he's awake!" *Fatima, my beloved!* He forced himself to keep his eyes open. Blinking rapidly, the blur of images slowly focused. Directly in front of his eyes a dark mass moved and something wet splashed on his cheek. The mass coalesced into the worried, tear drenched face of his wife. To his dismay she pulled away and a man in a white coat replaced her, shining a light in his eyes, making him squint and tear up again.

"Well, Mr. Jamar," he said, "you're very lucky to be alive."

Lucky to be alive? What happened? The events of earlier flooded back like a tidal wave of emotions. He shook in fear as tears welled in his eyes, blurring the image in front of him again. His chest heaved and he gasped as spasms of pain wracked his body. The sounds around him faded as he passed out.

Chelsie sat collapsed in the corner of her prison, her arms, exhausted from tightly squeezing her still raised knees for hours, now dangled at her sides, her hands palm up on the dirt floor. Her head rested where it had fallen, on her shoulder and the dirt walls behind her, as she drifted in and out of a restless sleep that brought no relief. It had been days since she had been taken. At least she assumed days. There was no light where she was, no way to tell the passing of time. All she had seen of her captor was his silhouette as he lowered a platform from the ceiling. The light pouring in from above blinded her every time, but when they adjusted she was able to see food and water sitting on a tray in the middle of the platform. Too terrified to approach it, she would remain in her corner, watching it sit there for what she figured to be ten minutes, before the platform would rise back into the ceiling, leaving her in the dark again.

But now she was thirsty. So thirsty fear ruled her no longer and she prayed for the tray to return. *Please, let me have water!* She screamed silently in her mind, her mouth and throat too dry to make a sound, as she waited for what seemed like an eternity. She drifted back to sleep, her mind filled with visions of fountains, water rushing from their spouts, her dancing amongst the sprays, head tilted back, as streams of water landed on her face and in her mouth, the taste so sweet she swore it was the greatest she had ever had.

She stirred, creaking sounds overhead, footsteps on an old wooden floor, waking her. She clawed her way toward the center of the room where the platform would soon appear, so weak she couldn't manage to crawl. She looked up, at what she did not know, but nothing came. Nothing. Too weak from the effort, she collapsed into the dirt floor of her new home.

Like a choir of angels in heaven, the sweet chorus of a rattling chain sounded above her. She rolled over on her back and looked at the shaft of light growing steadily larger. Framed in the middle, the silhouette of her savior, her captor who she hoped was about to relieve her suffering. The platform reached the ground and she saw the life-giving bottle of water and a sandwich sitting on a plate, just out of reach. She crawled on her elbows, so weak she managed only a few inches at a time. She reached the platform's edge, the water a few inches from her now. She reached out to take it as the platform shifted. Above, her captor pulled the chain to raise the platform. *No!* she silently screamed. Lunging forward with her last ounce of strength she grasped for the bottle, her hands so weak, all she managed was to knock it over. It fell off the tray and she watched as the bottle slowly rolled in an arc away from her as the platform rose toward the ceiling, the sound of the plastic against the wood teasing her, reminding her of how close she had come to the prize she could no longer see.

If she had tears, her eyes would have filled with them, but all she could do was sob in silence as the tray made its inevitable climb to the ceiling, taking with it the water she so desperately needed. She watched the shaft of light get smaller above her and her mind closed in on itself, despair taking over. Then she saw it. The end of the bottle, hanging ever so slightly over the platform's edge. *Please, God, please!* The platform jerked up another few inches. The bottle rocked back away from the edge. Her heart sank, but the bottle rolled back toward the edge again, this time more of the end revealing itself to her, tantalizing her. The platform moved again, and again the bottle rolled back but this time on its return it teetered on the edge. Chelsie willed it on, begging for it to fall off the platform. She rose to her knees, her arms at her sides, too weak to raise them. She stared straight up and watched as the bottle slowly tipped over the edge. It fell toward her, almost as if in slow motion. She watched as it seemed to land gently at her knees, bottom first. Smiling upward to heaven, her dried lips cracking with the effort, she collapsed in a heap on the floor, the bottle a mere foot from her nose. She eyed the precious liquid it contained and reached out with both shaking hands, and, grasping it, twisted off the cap. Raising it to her mouth, she drank, the water rushing over her lips like desert rain over a landscape long parched by the sun.

The all-consuming pain from earlier was distant, dulled somehow into the background. Ibrahim felt groggy, a feeling of floating in a pool filled his senses now, the pain pushed to the bottom of a deep cushion of water, away from his tired and broken body. He smiled. Opening his eyes, the room was a blur. The same beeping sounds from earlier persisted, strange whirring sounds of machines pumping as they rhythmically sustained their charges' stranglehold on this world, and through it all, the sounds of misery. Coughing, moaning, crying. Memories from the United Nations hospital rushed back and anxiety gripped his chest, the beeping nearest him increasing its rate. His vision cleared and he saw he was in a hospital ward, curtains separating him from patients on either side. He noticed an IV connected to his right arm, a wire clipped to a finger on his left hand, and at the foot of his bed, his daughter, looking at something intently, while his wife dozed in a chair against the wall.

"Amina," he called, his voice weak and hoarse. His daughter looked up at him, her eyes wide with delight, a toothy smile spread across her face as she forgot completely about what had been occupying her attention.

"Daddy!" She jumped on the bed and crawled toward him to give him a hug. She squeezed him tight, burying her head against his shoulder. The pain forced its way toward the surface, but it was worth it to feel her once again. He tried to hug her back but he was too weak to raise his arms off the bed. The weight on his chest lifted as his wife picked their daughter up and placed her back on the floor. She smiled down at him, trying to fight back the tears of joy filling her eyes.

"Just lie still, my love, the doctor said you are going to be okay." She took his hand and squeezed it gently. "You were in a coma and just came out of it last night. They were able to give you some medicine for the pain after that."

Ibrahim nodded. He looked down at the foot of the bed, his daughter again enthralled with something. His wife followed his gaze. "Amina? What is that?"

"It's a DVD player!" An extremely excited Amina spun it around to show them.

"Where did you get it?" Fatima reached down and lifted the player so she and her husband could see it. "This looks very expensive!"

"A nice man gave it to me while you were sleeping. He told me to make sure Daddy saw it when he woke up."

Puzzled, Ibrahim and Fatima looked at each other. "Watch, I can make it play!" Amina proudly pressed the *Play* button. The blank screen was replaced by a jerky video.

"What is this?" asked Fatima. But Ibrahim knew within seconds what it was. He hadn't told his wife about the subway, too ashamed at what she would think of him. When they were raped, at least he was tied up with no way to help. He had no such excuse this time. He knew he should have helped that poor girl, but he hadn't. Paralyzed with fear, flashbacks of that day in his village filling his mind, he had sat there, gripping the seat in front of him, staring in horror. And that is exactly where the video stopped. As the camera spun around he saw himself sitting there, doing nothing. Fatima gasped and looked at her husband.

Nausea gripped his stomach and bile filled his mouth, an overwhelming sense of shame swept over him. He watched his wife's reaction to the video turn from horror, then, as the implications of what she had just witnessed sank in, disappointment. He turned his head away, unable to face her.

FIVE

Eldridge strode through the doors of St. Luke's Hospital and stopped in his tracks, the chaos before him overwhelming. Row upon row of chairs overflowed with coughing, crying, and bleeding patients, their loved ones demanding attention from the nurses scrambling to triage them in what appeared to Eldridge to be an almost futile effort to restore some order. The din of misery and anger was almost excruciating. He had the impression those waiting were in a competition with each other to be the loudest, in the hopes this may motivate the nurses to take them first. If someone didn't get control of this room soon, there might be new injuries demanding attention.

Eldridge loathed hospitals.

When he received the call that an attempted murder looked like it may be related to his case, and that the victim was in intensive care, he had tried to think of some excuse to not go, but it was no use. When he was thirteen he had minor surgery and contracted an infection, resulting in further, more serious surgery. Weeks of recovery, his mother and father at his bedside every moment they were permitted, had instilled a deep, illogical hatred of the buildings. Not the doctors or nurses performing their duties, but simply the buildings. His negative memories were rarely of those who attended to him, they were usually quite pleasant, but of the lonely despair he suffered at being there. The featureless, small rooms with their stark white curtains, intended to provide privacy, but merely making a mystery of the sounds from the sick and dying feet away on the other side of the thin sheet of plastic. His mind ran wild as he imagined them dying from the same thing he was afflicted with. Night after night he suffered in silence, sobbing into his coarse, sterile pillow, pleading for his mother to rescue him from his misery, or for God to simply let him die so he could escape his surroundings. After he recovered from the infection, it was months before he was able to sleep through the night, and for years he was tormented with nightmares, constantly reliving the sounds beyond the curtains.

Since then he had set foot in a hospital only once outside the line of duty, and even then it had been a debate. His mother had died in a car accident when he was sixteen, and the year from hell had begun. His father turned inward, mourning his loss and completely ignoring that his son had lost a mother as well. He eventually blamed his son for her death, his grieving mind concluding it was his son's fault since she was picking him up. He finally lost the will to live and when he had been diagnosed with lymphoma he refused treatment, instead seeing it as a way to reunite with his beloved wife. When his father lay dying in the very same hospital he had been treated in years before, they had barely spoken in a year. A nurse at the hospital had called to let him know his father had days left and that he should pay his respects soon. His debate on whether or not to go had dragged on too long and by the time he reached the hospital his father had already passed, a letter, still not opened to this day, clutched in his hand. He didn't need to open it to know it would be more about how it was his fault his mother had died. They were once a happy family but that last year was misery. Afterward, the solitude of the family home had turned out to be a mixed blessing, the intense hatred from his father replaced by the curse of quiet emptiness.

He sighed and steeled himself for the experience ahead. He tried to make himself as small as possible, drawing in his shoulders and maneuvering himself toward the reception desk, in an unsuccessful attempt to avoid contact with the unwashed masses, his efforts pointless as he finally had to push his way through the crowd. When he reached the reception area, he found dozens of people screaming at the nurses behind the desk, most demanding to know why the wait was taking so long. One guy from NerdTech pleaded with a nurse to give him a pass so he could get to the roof to install some cables, a uniform chatted up a nurse who appeared oblivious to the mayhem, a taxi driver tried to find out about a friend, and finally there was him, the one person not shouting, who didn't want to be there in the first place.

"Quiet!" The roar brought the entire area to a standstill as everyone stopped to find the source of the bellow. Eldridge smiled as he saw who had brought order to chaos with simply her voice. She was huge, at least three hundred pounds, black with short hair, her nurse's uniform fitting where it touched. She looked like someone who didn't take shit from anyone. The wedding band, long overdue for resizing, made Eldridge feel a twinge of pity for her husband if he ever dared cross her. "One at a time, people!"

Eldridge took the opportunity to raise his badge over the crowd. "Detective Eldridge, ma'am. I'm here to see one of your patients, an Ibrahim Jamar."

The officer chatting up the nurse rose from the counter he was leaning on. "Detective Eldridge?"

Eldridge looked at him. "Yes?"

"Officer Foster. Follow me, sir. I'll take you to the room," he said, then, turning to the nurse, added, "and I'll see *you* later." She smiled, about to giggle, when she saw the large nurse glaring at her.

Eldridge followed the uniform to the elevators. They didn't have to wait long for the oversized car to arrive. As they entered, Foster pressed the button for the ninth floor as almost a dozen people crowded in. Eldridge pressed himself into a corner and covered his mouth with a handkerchief as the person beside him sneezed and coughed without covering their mouth. He debated whether or not the punishment would be worth it if he shot the inconsiderate bastard. The ninth floor arrived before he had the chance. They exited along with most of the other passengers and headed down the hall toward the ICU.

Eldridge entered, thankful this area was much quieter. He pushed to the back of his mind that these were probably some of the sickest patients in the building. A row of beds stretched the length of the room, each separated by a sterile, white curtain. He shivered. Several beds down a fellow detective interviewed a black woman, a small child gripping her leg, clearly confused at what was happening. They stood at the foot of the bed of a man who had clearly seen better days, most of his body plastered or bandaged, the few exposed areas of skin remaining covered in small scratches or swollen with bruises. *How could this possibly relate to my case?* He strode toward them, unnoticed.

"Hey, Amber, what've we got?"

Detective Amber Trace looked up from her pad and nodded, a tiny scowl on her face. Eldridge knew full well he hated to hand over a case to someone else, but sometimes it couldn't be helped. "Ma'am, this is Detective Eldridge. He'll be taking over the investigation." Trace walked over to Eldridge and lowered her voice. "Mr. Ibrahim Jamar, cab driver, was assaulted and placed in the trunk of his vehicle three days ago. He managed to get the trunk open, and get this, jumped out while the cab was doing over forty. Talk about balls of steel!"

Eldridge let out a low whistle. "Desperation does wonders for even the Cowardly Lion." Trace stared at him, the literary reference lost on her. He decided to continue. "Why am I here?"

"Because of this." She strode over to a table and pointed at a portable DVD player covered in powder, the lab tech responsible packing his fingerprint kit. "Finished?"

He nodded. "Yup, probably just the family's, but I'll confirm that when I run them."

Trace nodded. "Okay, get back to Eldridge when you know." She flipped open the DVD player. "This DVD player was given to the daughter by an unknown male while her parents slept. Watch." She pressed *Play* and stepped back. Eldridge watched the video play out then pause on the image of a black man sitting, his vacant eyes staring at his hands gripping the back of the seat in front of him. Eldridge glanced over at the bed nearby, the man's face too bandaged to ID him. Trace nodded. "The wife has confirmed that this is her husband."

"This looks familiar to me. What am I looking at?"

"This is that subway murder those two punks taped last year. Remember? A whole crowd watched as two perps beat some girl to death because she refused to give them her purse or something like that?"

Eldridge knew exactly what she was talking about. Everyone knew about the now infamous murder. "It looks different somehow." He couldn't put his finger on it, but there was definitely something different about the video. He had of course seen the original a year ago, but since it wasn't his case, had made a point of not watching it again, the senseless brutality it portrayed holding no appeal.

Trace shrugged her shoulders. "Looks the same to me."

"But what's this got to do with my case?"

"Look." She played it again then paused it on a frame showing a woman, her eyes bulging in fear, her mouth open in mid-scream, running from the train. "Isn't that your first DB?"

Eldridge bent over and peered at the screen. "Tammera Coverdale!" Standing back up he looked over at this new victim then at the screen. "Two people that were on that subway attacked in a week? This can't be a coincidence."

"That's what I thought." Trace flipped her notebook closed and tucked it into her jacket pocket. "The case is all yours. I've got a DB with my name on it, some S&M gone bad." She slapped him on the back and headed toward the exit.

Eldridge watched the video once again, then approached the Jamar family, the wife now standing at the head of the bed holding her husband's hand, the daughter perched on the edge, dividing her attention between Eldridge and her father.

"Hello, sir, ma'am, my name is Detective Eldridge and as Detective Trace said, I'll be taking over the investigation into who did this to you." He flashed a smile at the little girl who turned away, her mother patting her on the head. "Sir, are you able to answer a few questions?"

The man opened his eyes a sliver and grunted an acknowledgement.

Eldridge retrieved his notepad and flipped it open to a new page. "What can you tell me about the person who did this to you?"

Ibrahim's head barely moved, the effort to shake it exhausting him. "Nothing," he whispered.

Eldridge prompted him, knowing full-well the victim always remembered something that might prove useful. "Was it a man?" Ibrahim nodded. "White or black?"

"White."

"What color were his eyes?"

"He had large sunglasses on and was sitting directly behind me, I never really saw his face." His voice faded and he slumped into his pillow as the last of his energy drained away, the effort finally proving too much.

Interview over. Eldridge turned his attention to the wife.

"I'm sorry, detective, but my husband is too weak." She gently stroked his hand, then turned to face Eldridge, the concern in her eyes betraying her deep love for her husband.

"That's okay, ma'am. I can interview him another time." Eldridge stepped toward the table containing the DVD player. "And your name is, ma'am?"

"Fatima Jamar."

Eldridge motioned to the DVD. "Where did the DVD player come from?"

Fatima frowned. "When I was asleep some man gave it to my daughter."

Eldridge smiled warmly at the little girl and knelt down so he was eye level with her. "What's your name?"

"Amina." Her tiny, high pitched voice was barely audible, half her face buried in her mother's leg.

"Well, that's a very pretty name, Amina. My name is Hayden and I'm a police officer."

She buried her head a little deeper.

"And how old are you, Amina?"

"I'm eight and a *half* years old."

Eldridge smiled at her emphasis on the half. "And can you tell me what the man looked like who gave you the DVD player?"

"He looked like you."

Eldridge chuckled. "So he was white like me?" She nodded. Eldridge stood. "Was he tall like me, or was he short like this?" Eldridge knelt down about six inches and did a silly smile. The little girl giggled and nodded. "So he was short like this?" She nodded. "Do you remember what he was wearing?"

Amina nodded, turning to face him as she overcame her fear. "A baseball cap."

"Anything else?"

"Sunglasses!"

"That's good! Was there anything written on the baseball cap?" She shrugged her shoulders. "Okay, you did very good, honey." Eldridge rose and addressed the mother. "I'll have an officer posted here until we get this resolved. If you need anything, or remember anything, just see him and he will contact me."

Fatima picked up Amina and hugged her. "Thank you, detective."

Foster watched the proceedings from the doorway, trying to catch every bit of the conversation as it drifted his way. New on the force with only a couple of years under his belt, he knew he wanted to be a detective. And the best way to learn was to observe. He straightened himself as the detective ended the interview and walked his way.

Eldridge leaned in close and lowered his voice. "Stay here and keep an eye on him. I don't want anybody near him except medical staff. And I want their ID checked."

Foster nodded. "Will do."

"I mean it, don't take your eyes off him, even if that piece of ass from downstairs comes up here, you got it?"

Foster's cheeks flushed. "Yes, detective."

Eldridge smiled and slapped him on the shoulder. "Good. Now, do you know where security is?"

"Not sure, first floor I think."

"No worries, I'll ask at the front desk."

As Eldridge walked away, Foster hoped the fine piece of ass *would* find him up here. He was about to get married and wasn't looking for anything except affirmation he could still catch the eye of a beautiful young woman. The thought of his fiancée however caused a twinge of guilt. *Maybe it's best she doesn't find me.*

The chaos had returned to the reception area, the nurse who had brought order earlier nowhere to be seen. Eldridge raised his badge over the crowd and yelled to a harried looking nurse. "Where's the security office?" A phone lodged between her ear and shoulder, she jabbed toward a hall to his right, not missing a beat in her conversation explaining to someone why they couldn't skip the line by phoning the front desk. Eldridge waved his thanks and navigated his way through the crowd in the direction indicated. Around a corner, a janitor prepared to mop what at first Eldridge thought were the spilled contents of a dinner tray. He looked closer and gagged. *Puke!* Eldridge stifled another gag as the odor reached his nostrils. Bile filled his mouth as he watched the dark, grey, damp threads of the mop slap a load of filthy water atop the vile mass of poorly chewed food. Eldridge covered his mouth and nose with a handkerchief. "Security?"

The man tossed his head over his shoulder, indicating a nearby door then swished his mop, spreading the mess in a large, wet, circle.

"Thanks." Eldridge sidestepped the vomit while trying not to look, and approached the plain, windowless door marked "Security". He knocked. The door whipped open, a portly, grey haired man, who Eldridge figured cared more about securing his next meal than protecting the hospital employing him, glared at him.

"What?"

Eldridge frowned. "I'm Detective Eldridge, Homicide," he said, flashing his badge. "I need to review the tapes for the ninth floor from a few hours ago."

"You gotta warrant?" asked the man as he poured himself into a seat in front of a bank of monitors.

Eldridge's blood boiled. He hated arrogance. *Bad cop it is.* "How long have you been on duty?"

"Six hours. What's it to you?"

"Then it happened on your shift."

This caught the man's attention. "What?" he asked, his voice a little quieter.

"A murder suspect approached the eight year-old child of his intended victim, right under your watchful eye!" yelled Eldridge. "You know what? Forget it! Where's your supervisor?"

The man panicked. "He's on his break!" He started furiously smacking keys. "No need to get him involved. You said ninth floor right? How long do you want to go back?"

Eldridge smiled to himself. "Let's go back six hours and start from there."

His muscles screamed from fatigue, the pain having turned into a fire that threatened to win out over his determination to eliminate the next target. The complete lack of control at the front desk had meant it took less than three minutes to convince an overworked nurse to provide him a pass. With swipe access to any maintenance area, he had pulled his cap down low and avoided the numerous security cameras. It was almost too easy, the camera layouts easily hacked from the city computers. After arriving on the ninth floor, he entered a maintenance room near the elevators and jammed a chair against the door so he wouldn't be disturbed. He climbed a set of shelves kitty cornering the back of the small room and pushed aside the grate to the heating ducts overhead. The tight fit wasn't a problem, but the stamped sheet metal had a tendency to bend then snap back into place with a loud pop. Pushing his limbs to the edges, he was able to avoid placing most of his weight in the center, preventing any noise after the first few feet. His spread-eagle technique was quiet, but slow. It took almost fifteen minutes to arrive at his destination, his strained muscles now paying the price.

And unfortunately, by the time he arrived, he had found a cop already there, talking to his target. He had tried to relax his muscles, but thought better of it. He couldn't risk being discovered—it would end his mission, and that was not an option. He peered through the grate again and his pain was forgotten. The cop was gone. Below him, the bastard from the subway lay surrounded by his family. And no one else.

Time's up!

Ibrahim lay in his bed and stared at the ceiling, the drugs doing their job of dulling the pain and his senses. The world moved in slow motion around him, the dots in the ceiling tiles a swirling blur of incomprehensible patterns he found coalesced into a vortex of shooting, black stars, when he spun his eyes. He smiled then something caught his attention from the corner of his eye. Looking at the far wall, he saw something moving. Or did he? *Is it the drugs?* He squinted. *No, it's definitely moving.* He saw a vent tile in the ceiling rise from one end. He peered closely, and squinted, trying to focus the blurred image in front of him, still not sure if he was hallucinating. *What is that?* He stared hard and his eyes sprung into focus for a moment as a hand propped up the tile with something dark and rectangular. *Is that a cell phone?* He tried to prop himself up to get a closer look, but the effort sent the room spinning out of control. He closed his eyes for a moment, then opened them again, determined to bore through the haze. His determination paid off as he was able to focus clearly on what he now knew was a grate in the ceiling, indeed held up by what looked like a cell phone. But it wasn't the phone that made his heart almost stop.

He raised his arm to point when the first shot rang out. He didn't actually hear it until after the burst of exploding pillow foam, inches from his head, registered. It all seemed surreal, the room coming in and out of focus, streaks of movement, echoes of screams, and through it all, the dull pain pushed to the background suddenly jumped to the forefront, his shoulder searing in pain as he heard a second shot. The drugs were good, but not good enough. The pain burned through the Demerol fog and he cried out, the entire room screaming into focus, his wife grabbing their daughter, shielding their precious offspring with her body as she looked in horror at his wound, the police officer supposed to be protecting him storming through the door, and the flash from the muzzle as the trigger squeezed for a third time.

Foster stood near the ward door, eyeballing everyone who walked past, but mostly keeping a wary eye out for the nurse, already having rehearsed in his head what he would say to her if she were to come see him. He had decided to play dumb. *What? You thought I was interested? But I'm engaged!* He shook his head as he thought about it. *You're an asshole!* He nodded. *And a coward.* He harrumphed, catching the attention of an approaching intern.

"Excuse me?"

Foster shook his head. "Nothing, just thinking out loud apparently."

"I get that way at the end of a twenty-four hour shift, too!" The intern flashed his ID and Foster waved him through. From in the room there was an unmistakable loud cracking sound. *Gunfire!* Panicked screaming was followed by a second and third shot. He pulled his weapon and raced into the room, shoved the intern to the ground and pointed his weapon at his head while he scanned the room, not certain who the shooter was. He spotted the wife and daughter cowering against the wall.

"Is he the shooter?" he yelled.

The woman, too terrified to speak, looked up at the ceiling. Two more shots came from above him. He saw the cab driver's body jerk from the impacts as both bullets found their marks, square in the middle of his chest. Letting the intern go, he swung his weapon toward the ceiling and spotted a tile closing over his head. He fired two rapid shots at where he guessed the shooter might be. The second shot ricocheted off a water pipe and reentered the ward, slamming into an oxygen tank at the far end of the ward, the resulting explosion ripping through the room, ejecting the nearby bed, along with its occupant, through the now shattered window.

Foster gaped in horror as a steady progression of explosions moved toward them as oxygen lines and tanks ignited. Grabbing the wife and child, he threw them toward the doorway and dove on top to protect them from the blasts. With flames licking at his back, he closed his eyes and prayed as the woman and little girl underneath him screamed. Within seconds the sprinkler system kicked in and began dousing the flames. He scrambled to his feet and grabbed the kid and her mother then ran toward the doorway with them, nearly tripping over the intern's body, a bed rail embedded in his skull, forever freezing a look of shock on his face. Once safe in the hallway, he turned back to see the sprinklers making swift work of the flames, the oxygen tanks having quickly burned out. It took a few moments for him to realize the bed their witness was in was now a smoldering shell, its occupant unrecognizable. As he turned to check on the wife and child a searing pain in his back jolted him to his knees. "Oh my God!" yelled the mother as he collapsed to the floor, the pain from a piece of pipe protruding from his back at last registering, the adrenaline keeping him going now wearing off.

"That's him!" Eldridge pointed at the screen showing a man in a baseball cap and sunglasses handing Amina the DVD player. "I want to know where he came from and where he—" He abruptly stopped talking as he noticed the coffee in the guard's cup ripple. The shaking became more extreme, the ceramic cup starting to dance toward the edge of the desk as the vibrations raced up his legs and through his spine. They both watched in shocked silence as the coffee mug crashed to the floor, its contents splashing across the tile, some of it onto Eldridge's shoes. "What the hell was that?" The fire control panel lit up like a Christmas tree, followed by the rapid beeping of the fire alarm system.

"I don't know! There's fire alarms going off all over the ninth floor!" He attacked the keyboard as he tried to bring up the security camera footage to see what was happening, but every feed showed static. "It's as if the entire ninth floor has been cut off!"

"Ninth floor," muttered Eldridge. "Shit!" He wrenched open the door and shoved through the confused masses as he fought his way to the elevators. He squeezed his way through the crowd and managed to find an empty elevator. He hit the button for the ninth floor. Nothing happened. He pressed again, and then the button to close the doors. Nothing. He stepped out of the elevator and found all of the cars had returned to the main floor. Realizing they were now disabled, awaiting the fireman's key to unlock them, he looked about for a stairwell. He noticed a throng of people streaming out a nearby door and pushed his way through the mass of sheep waiting to be told where to go. "Police officer, make a hole!" he yelled. Nobody moved out of his way, but at least they stopped moving as they stared at him. He maneuvered his way through the door and continued the battle on the stairs. He rounded the bend to the fourth floor and narrowly missed butting heads with the NerdTech contractor he had seen earlier. Pushing him aside, he hugged the wall, climbing one step at a time, eventually making it to the sixth floor where the crowds thinned out enough for him to take the steps two at a time. He raced the final three floors and threw open the door to the ninth.

He stepped into an assault on his senses. A steady stream of water from the overhead sprinklers had not yet cleaned the stench of acrid smoke hanging heavy in the air around him. He sucked in a full breath of lung searing soot, and, still slightly winded from running nine flights of stairs, coughed as his throat and eyes burned. He opened his mouth to let some water from the sprinklers in then spat it out on the soaked floor. Fishing a handkerchief from his pocket, he held it over his mouth and nose as he ran toward the ward where he feared his witness was no more.

The repetitive drone of the fire alarm was slightly hushed by the white noise from the sprinklers, but through it all, the screams of the victims pierced like a dagger through time, the intense desperation from the unseen sources vividly bringing back the memories of his youth, the frantic screams of a teenage boy, crying in pain as four nurses held him down while two others tore away at the packing in his open wound, the dried blood acting as an adhesive between the raw flesh and the cloth bandages. He had screamed for them to stop the entire time they clawed at him, but they wouldn't. They kept going, those holding his arms and chest trying to calm him, their platitudes unheard over his cries, the others holding his legs in viselike grips, spread eagled as the other two matter-of-factly pulled at the bandages, commenting about the dried blood, and telling the others to hold him tighter. It seemed like an eternity, but finally one of those torturing him stopped the procedure, realizing the pain was too much for a teenage boy to take, and gave him an injection to dull the pain.

He found himself standing at the ward door, now off its hinges, the tears streaming down his face unnoticed by those around him as they mixed with the steady shower from the sprinklers. He shook his head and looked around as the reality of the situation took hold again. Mrs. Jamar and her child were tending to Foster only feet away. He stepped toward them and knelt down. "Are you two okay?" he asked as he did a quick check of Foster to see if he was still alive. He detected a faint, but steady pulse.

Mrs. Jamar nodded. "My husband?"

"I'll check." He pointed at Foster. "If you see any medical staff, get them to take care of him." She nodded and looked for help as Eldridge stepped around the shattered door now lying in the hallway, and entered the room. The mayhem in the hall hadn't prepared him for the horror he now faced. Everything was burnt. Everything. The linoleum flooring was sticky, the slightly melted plastic adhering to his shoes, each step requiring a little extra tug on his part to move forward. The ceiling tiles had been blasted from their now dangling frames, exposing the plumbing and electrical conduits, still live wires sparked from shorts as they reacted to the sprinklers. The fires out, the water now only served to cool the room and wash the walls and contents free from the soot, creating puddles of dirty water at his feet as the floor drains failed to keep up with the steady downpour.

The worst of it was the beds. The still occupied beds. Eldridge looked down the length of the ward, the curtains once separating the patients all burnt away, the rods and hangers the only evidence remaining they had ever been there. He gaped in horror as several bodies moved, moaning in pain, the one nearest him reached out, writhing in agony, his charred body, unrecognizable as once being human, resembling more pork, long forgotten on the barbeque. Eldridge reached out to touch the man but then drew back as he looked at the outstretched hand, the now charcoal black skin hanging loose, almost as if ready to fall off the bone. "I'm sorry," he murmured as he approached the bed Ibrahim had occupied minutes before. One look and he knew there was no hope. The body lay motionless, completely consumed by the flames, only an unrecognizable lump remained.

Eldridge stood at the foot of the bed as a fire crew rushed into the room, one of them grabbing him by the arm and shaking him. "Sir! Sir! Are you okay?" Eldridge stared at the carcass that had been Ibrahim, not registering the arrival. The firefighter jerked him around to face him. "Sir!"

Eldridge looked at the man and remembered where he was. He centered himself as best he could as he tried to push the nightmare around him out of focus. "Yes, yes, I'm okay." He flashed his badge as his training kicked back in. "I'm Detective Eldridge, Homicide, and this is a crime scene."

"Not 'til we say it's safe. Wait out in the hall, one of your guys is out there." The fireman pushed him toward the door. Eldridge nodded, took one last look at Ibrahim and stepped back into the hall to find Foster on a stretcher, the piece of pipe jutting from his back preventing him from lying flat.

"Detective," said Mrs. Jamar, her voice trembling as if she already knew the answer. "My husband?"

Eldridge shook his head. "I'm so sorry." She burst into tears and collapsed against the wall, screaming in a language he didn't recognize. Her daughter, not understanding what had happened but seeing her mother crying, wailed as well. Eldridge stood in the hall, slowly turning as he took in the scene around him. Two medical staff pushed Foster toward a now waiting elevator at the end of the hall. Medical and police staff swarmed around him, waiting for someone to coordinate their efforts, no one seeming to be in charge, only the firemen apparently not needing to be told what to do.

What the hell happened here?

He realized that would have to wait. "Listen up!" he yelled. Everybody in the hall stopped what they were doing and stared at the one person willing to take control. "Medical staff, this room seems to have taken the brunt of it." He motioned toward Ibrahim's ward. "Coordinate with fire rescue and evacuate any survivors. Police and hospital security, I want this hospital locked down, nobody leaves. Begin a room by room search of this floor for any other survivors that may need help. Anybody on this floor who isn't supposed to be here, I want immediately detained for questioning. Extend the search up and down, just in case the explosion injured people on other floors. I don't want anybody missed." Nobody moved. Eldridge smacked his hands together hard. "Now, people!" Everybody scrambled, this time with purpose.

He sat in his van, taking deep, slow breaths as he tried to calm his still racing heart. It had been close. Closer than he had ever expected. *Who the hell expects the damned place to blowup?* His final shots had hit the bastard square in the chest. As soon as he saw the shots connect, he scrambled backward in the air duct, narrowly avoiding the returned fire from the cop. The blasts from the explosions had knocked him around a bit, and the confines of the duct had left his ears ringing, but other than a brief flash of heat taking his breath away, he was none the worse for wear. He checked his eyebrows in the rearview mirror. *Still there.* He took another deep breath. His heart still thumped as if it wanted to escape his chest and flee in another direction, but not from the blast, this panic entirely the result of his second close call.

Way too close!

After exiting the ducts in the utility room, he had fixed his disguise, removed the chair blocking the door, and cautiously exited the room unseen in the confusion. With the alarms and sprinklers in full effect, he joined a throng of people as they made their way into the stairwell. It was on his way down he had his brush with fate. As he rounded a landing, he bumped face to face with the detective he had seen questioning his target, the eternity the encounter dragged on for most likely lasting only seconds. Certain he had been made, his mission over, he prepared for one final fight, but the unceremonious shove he was dealt sent the hunter on his way, leaving the prey to return to its own hunt. He watched the detective continue on out of sight before he rushed out from the building and across the street

A loud squawk on the passenger seat nearly sent him leaping out the open window.

"Yo, Greedo, you there?" came the voice over his cell phone's two-way radio.

His pulse raced again. He took a deep breath and gripped the phone. *What a stupid fuckin' nickname.* "Yeah, I'm here."

"Where the hell have you been? I've been trying to reach you for hours!"

"I turned off the phone by accident, sorry."

"Yeah, whatever, you're probably sleeping on the job again!"

He decided to ignore that one.

"Listen, I've got a call for you, I texted the details to your phone."

He checked his messages and found the call. "Okay, I'll be there in thirty minutes. Out." He switched off the phone before he had to hear any more from that idiot. Starting the van, he reached up and flicked the switch for the NerdTech mascot on the roof, the darkened logo blinking several times before turning a bright mix of red and white as the bespectacled, ball cap sporting, grinning idiot came to life.

He nearly matched the grin on the roof as he made his escape.

Another one down!

Eldridge stood in a corner of a hospital waiting room packed with uniforms milling about, some whispering amongst each other, some standing alone like himself. None of Foster's family had arrived yet, his parents apparently on a retirement cruise somewhere in the Mediterranean, his lone sibling a brother serving in Afghanistan. One of the female officers said he had recently been engaged, resulting in a flurry of activity as his fellow officers called everyone they knew to find out who she might be. It took hours, but she was finally located and would be arriving any minute. Eldridge rocked back and forth on his heels, arms crossed, chin held in one hand, as he tried to piece together what had happened. He looked up as the doors to the operating theatres swung open and the surgeon working on Foster entered. All eyes were on the man as he looked around the room for someone in charge. With the brass having stepped out for coffee only minutes before, Eldridge decided that was him, and stepped toward the doctor. "What's the word?"

"He's going to make it," said the surgeon, a smile on his face. Sighs of relief rippled throughout the room, some officers hugging and thumping each other on the backs, others crying, finally letting go the emotions bottled up during their vigil.

Eldridge let out an audible sigh and looked up to say a silent prayer of thanks. "Can I talk to him?"

The surgeon shook his head. "He'll be out of it for a few hours at least. Maybe tomorrow."

"Listen, Doc," said Eldridge as he leaned in and lowered his voice. "I *need* to talk to him. I have to find out what the hell happened in that room."

The surgeon lowered his voice so only Eldridge could hear. "I realize that, Detective, but I am not going to jeopardize my patient for the sake of your investigation. Come back tomorrow morning."

Eldridge knew from the tone of finality in the surgeon's voice there was no point in pursuing it. Instead, he placed his hand on the surgeon's shoulder and raised his voice. "Thanks, Doc, we really appreciate everything you've done here tonight in saving our boy."

Several shouts of "hear, hear" filled the room and the surgeon nodded his acknowledgement to the crowd before returning to the operating theater. Eldridge headed out of the room, uniforms slapping him on the back as he went by, deciding if he couldn't talk to his witness, the security tapes would have to do the talking instead.

Arriving at security, he rapped on the door and this time was greeted by a very different man. "Yes?" The man's voice rumbled through the air, so deep Eldridge felt it vibrate through his chest. Eldridge imagined him shaming Barry White with little effort. A tall, barrel-chested man in his early fifties, Eldridge immediately thought either ex-cop or ex-military, or something out of The Green Mile.

Eldridge flashed his badge. "Detective Eldridge, Homicide. I was here earlier reviewing tapes before the explosion."

"Ah yes, Detective," said the man. "I'm Stephen Prentice, Head of Security." He extended a hand that dwarfed Eldridge's. "I assumed you'd be back." He waved Eldridge in and closed the door behind him, the already small room ever more so with the large addition. "I've had the tapes from the ninth floor already queued up for you, I think you'll find this interesting." He pointed to a monitor as the guard from earlier hit a key to start the sequence. On it the main hall on the ninth floor could be seen. They watched people run past the camera in a panic as the sprinklers sprayed water in every direction, some of it splashing on the camera dome. Prentice pointed. "Watch this." Eldridge leaned in as a door inched open, slightly down the hallway. A man wearing a ball cap exited, looked around and strode purposefully toward the stairwell, passing directly under the camera, all the while looking down at the floor. "We think this might be your man." Prentice pointed at the door. "That was a service closet he came out of, so he must have been the one who set off the bomb."

"Bomb?" Eldridge looked at Prentice. "Do we have any evidence of a bomb yet?"

"Well, I just assumed a bomb, but you're right, we shouldn't jump to any conclusions yet. Regardless, this man should not have been where he was."

Eldridge moved closer to the monitor. "Run it again." The sequence restarted and as the man was about to pass under the camera, Eldridge said, "Freeze it there!" The image froze, showing the top of the ball cap. "Back it up a few frames and zoom in on the hat. There's something written on it." The guard hit a few keys and the image skipped back. Dragging a mouse he zoomed in on the hat and it filled the screen, the image blurred due to the low resolution.

Prentice squinted at the screen. "I can't make it out, what does it say?"

"I'm not sure," said Eldridge, frustrated. "Maybe the lab techs downtown can clean it up a bit. Can you follow him to see where he goes?"

"Already did. We don't have cameras in the stairwells but he can be seen exiting on the main floor then leaving the building. After that, we just have him crossing the street and then he's out of camera range."

"Okay, give me a copy of that footage as well as the footage from earlier and I'll see what we can do with it."

Prentice picked up a CD from the desk and handed it to Eldridge. "Way ahead of you."

Impressed, Eldridge took the CD. "You were on the force?"

"Twenty three years before I got shot and had to take early retirement."

"Sorry to hear that."

"Well, twenty three years was about twenty years longer than everybody said I'd last. My mother always said I was too damned big a target." He laughed, the small room acting as an echo chamber for his cavernous tone.

Eldridge chuckled and glanced at the coffee mug to see if the liquid rippled. He waved his arm at their surroundings. "Some retirement."

"Ha! You'd be surprised at some of the shit that goes down around here. It keeps things interesting." He opened the door for Eldridge and extended his hand. "If I can be of any more help, you just let me know."

"Thanks, I will." Eldridge left the room and headed back to the ninth floor.

Vinny stood up and stretched his aching back with a loud groan. He and his team had been sifting for hours through what was left of the crime scene after the sprinklers were through. There wasn't much recognizable left. The bodies had all been bagged, tagged and sent to autopsy. Unfortunately, or fortunately, depending how you looked at it, nobody had survived. The few who had survived the initial blast had all succumbed to their wounds within minutes.

He glanced over his shoulder at the sound of footsteps, immediately regretting the twisting motion.

"Detective Eldridge! Trouble seems to follow you."

"Yeah, it's been one hell of a day," agreed his friend. "What can you tell me?"

"Nothin' much at this point. I've pretty much ruled out a bomb, though." He walked over to a twisted piece of metal at the far end of the room, partially embedded in the floor, and pointed. "I think this is the origin of the blast. It's in the proper position for an oxygen tank, and this looks like the bottom. If this exploded, it probably drove the base into the floor, the rest outward. The other tanks that exploded probably were blown onto their sides and then lit through their lines. This is the only one showing a downward trajectory for the base. I'll know more when I get back to the lab."

Eldridge nodded. "Not a bomb? That's good. If this guy graduated from guns to bombs we'd be in big trouble."

"So this is related to the two DBs from the other day?"

"Looks that way, at least some video we've got suggests it." Eldridge knelt down to look at the remnants of the oxygen tank. "Oh, and speaking of tape, the security cameras caught somebody unauthorized in the maintenance room down the hall. I need your guys to sweep it, see if you pick up anything."

"Got it." Vinny motioned for one of his team to take care of it. "So, what did you make of our two heroes from the other day?"

"What do you mean?" asked Eldridge as he rose.

"You didn't get my message?"

Eldridge shook his head. "What message?"

"Shit, I knew this was gonna happen," said Vinny, looking up at the ceiling in frustration. "I called your desk and Shakespeare answered, said he'd give you the message."

Eldridge frowned. "Well he didn't."

Vinny felt his blood pressure rising. "That fat bastard, he's good for nothing. Why doesn't he just retire or die like the dead wood he is? You know, if I was his Lieutenant I'd had shoved my size ten shoe so far up his—"

Eldridge cut him off. "What was the message?"

"We ID'd the two vics, they both had records. I sent the file over, should be on your desk unless that son of a bitch used it as a napkin. You know, if there was a pile of shit and him sitting on a bench, the flies—"

Eldridge smiled. "I have to interview the victim's wife then I'll be at the precinct."

Vinny nodded. "I'll finish up here and then I've got to pop home to feed the new dog, she can get cranky if she doesn't get fed on time. Won't take long."

"New dog? What happened to your old one?"

"Had to put her down."

"Sorry to hear that."

Vinny shrugged his shoulders. "It's always tough, but sometimes it's for the best."

"Sometimes."

Eldridge leaned into the private hospital room on the fifth floor of St. Luke's housing Ibrahim Jamar's wife and daughter, both suffering from shock. He was surprised to see they weren't alone, a familiar looking black man stood at the wife's bedside, the daughter curled up asleep at her side. It took a moment, but he remembered the man from the reception desk when he had first arrived, the taxi driver asking about a friend. He knocked gently on the doorframe. The man jumped, startling Mrs. Jamar.

"Detective," she said, her smile weak, but genuine. She motioned at the man. "This is my cousin, Rafi, he helped get my husband the job at the cab company."

Eldridge nodded to the man, who nodded in return, avoiding eye contact. *Shy? Or just shy around cops?* "Ma'am, I need to ask you a few questions, if you're up to it."

"Very well." She lifted herself up in the bed and Rafi adjusted some pillows behind her back to make her more comfortable. She closed her eyes for a few seconds, took a deep breath and opened them, looking at Eldridge. "Okay, go ahead."

"Can you tell me what happened after I left the room?"

"Nothing at first," she began. "I was sitting down against the wall with Amina, resting, when suddenly I heard a gunshot."

"A gunshot?" Eldridge wasn't sure why he was surprised. He knew this was no accident. An accident didn't explain the man in the service closet. But the timing didn't make sense. "Are you sure?"

"Oh yes, I'm certain," she replied, nodding her head vigorously. "I've heard a lot of guns in my life, Detective. There were at least three shots and at least two of them hit my Ibrahim."

But how did they get past Foster? Twice? "Did you see who fired the shots?"

"No, I didn't see anyone."

"You didn't see anyone?" *How the hell do you not see a man shooting at your husband three times?*

"No, but I think it was coming from over my head."

"What makes you think that?"

"That brave officer, he came into the room and started shooting at the ceiling. That is when the explosion happened."

Ricochet? "He shot at the ceiling?"

"Yes."

Air ducts? That would explain the service closet. Was he already waiting when I was in the room? "Did he say anything?"

"No, not that I remember. It all happened so quickly! All I remember is that there were shots, then the policeman entered and fired at the ceiling, then almost immediately there was an explosion and he saved our lives." She looked down at her daughter and gently squeezed her. "Is he going to be okay?"

Eldridge nodded. "Yes, he's out of surgery and should be fine."

She let out a sigh of relief. "Please, when you see him, thank him for us, will you?"

"Of course," said Eldridge. "I should be seeing him tomorrow morning, I'm sure he'll appreciate that." Fatima smiled. "Is there anything else you can remember that might be helpful?"

She thought for a moment then shook her head. "I'm sorry, Detective, that's all I can remember."

Eldridge reached in his pocket and pulled out a business card. He wrote his cell number on the back and handed it to her. "If you remember anything else, or need anything, don't hesitate to call."

She reached for the card and cupped his hand with both of hers, smiling. "Thank you, Detective."

Eldridge placed his other hand on top of hers and squeezed gently, returning the smile. "Take care of yourself and your little one."

He nodded at her cousin, then headed for the precinct. He passed the CD with the footage from the hospital over to the computer geeks then dropped himself into his uncomfortable desk chair. Sitting in the middle of his desk lay a file from the lab with a note stuck on it from Shakespeare. *The Italian prick had this sent up for you. Left a message on your cell and desk line. Enjoy!* Eldridge glanced at his desk phone, the red pulsing light indicating a message, then snapped open his cell and discovered it turned off. *Shit!* He pressed the power button and a moment later it vibrated, indicating a message. He shook his head and said a silent apology to his partner, remembering he had turned it off during the vigil for Foster and forgot.

He flipped open the file and smiled. *Logan Rochester and Aaron Davidson.* He scanned their rap sheets and yawned. Public drunkenness. Marijuana possession. Nothing of interest. Stretching, he looked at his watch. *This can wait until the morning.*

He headed to the stairs and bumped into Trace as she rushed from an arriving elevator. "Hayden! Glad I caught you before you went home. Got something for you." She shoved a file into his hands.

Eldridge opened the folder and glanced at the case report. "What's this?"

"Remember that DB I mentioned earlier, the S&M gone bad? Well, looks like he's yours." She snagged the elevator door as it started to close and wedged her foot inside.

Eldridge looked up from the file. "What do you mean?"

"Description fits your latest video and I'm willing to bet the ballistics will come back a match to the other three murders."

"Family been notified?"

"Yeah, his younger sister found the body."

Eldridge grimaced. "Shit. She okay?"

"Pretty fucked up when I got there. She apparently idolized him, couldn't think of any reason why anyone would want to hurt him." The buzzer sounded as the doors slowly forced themselves closed. "All the info is there in the file. Call me if you have any questions." She jumped on the elevator, and added, "Tomorrow!", as the doors closed shut.

Aynslee sat at her desk, finishing some paperwork after the evening newscast. This part she didn't enjoy. Paperwork with the entertainment beat had been easy. Actually, mostly nonexistent. But the crime beat? Everything had to be double and triple checked, everything said on-air backed with paperwork. Especially with murders. Legal double-checked her scripts, giving an opinion on almost every word. She had said "alleged" more in the past week than she probably had in her entire life.

And she loved it!

Sure she hated the paperwork, but she felt like she was finally doing something useful, something with purpose. The entertainment beat had been one of the most popular news segments, certainly the most downloaded on the website, but that was more a commentary on how pathetic society had become, than with the quality or importance of the journalism. What she was doing now *meant* something. It affected people's lives. And if she could figure out what was going on, it might make a difference. It might *save* lives. She sighed, a smile on her face as she emailed the script for the morning broadcast to half a dozen different people, finally finished for the evening.

The gentle ringing of the phone demanded her attention. She picked up the receiver and before she could say her name, she heard sobbing at the other end. "Hello? Is anyone there?" The sobbing continued. If she wasn't in the news business, she might have hung up, but she knew this was someone who wanted to tell her something, no matter the state they were in. "Why don't you tell me your name? My name is Aynslee Kai."

"S-Sarah Hanson." The voice sounded young, maybe in her mid-teens.

"Hello, Sarah, how can I help you?"

There was some more sniffing, then the rustling sounds of a sleeve being wiped over a nose. "Are you the reporter that has been getting the movies?"

Aynslee tried to hide the excitement in her voice. "Yes. Did you recognize someone?"

"He was my brother."

Score! But which one? She couldn't risk pressing too hard, she knew that would scare off her lead. She had to approach this one with kid's gloves. "And what was your brother's name?"

"William Hanson."

"And was he your older brother?"

"Yes."

"And how old are you, honey?"

"Thirteen."

Aynslee felt a lump in her throat, not sure if she should be talking to a child. Part of her thought she should end the conversation now, but another part knew the poor kid needed to talk to someone, and at this moment, it was her. "What would you like to tell me about your brother?"

"That he was a good person. Don't believe all the bad things that people are saying about him, that he was a pervert."

The tabloids had gone nuts since she had done her original broadcast. As of a few moments ago, nobody in the press knew the identity of this man, killed while wearing leather pants and a feather boa, a ball-gag stuffed in his mouth. The press painted him as a homosexual deviant, killed either by an ex-lover or in a sex game gone terribly wrong. She hadn't bought into that however. She sensed more going on here; all of the victims were somehow connected, there could be no way Tammera Coverdale, William Hanson and two unidentified teenaged boys travelled in the same sexual crowd.

"I never did believe what was being said, Sarah. Why don't you tell me about him?"

The conversation lasted almost half an hour. There was a lot of repetition, the heartbreaking innocence almost overwhelming her several times. The poor girl was lost, but by the end of the conversation, she seemed to be doing a little better. Aynslee encouraged her to talk to her parents about what she was feeling, and to call again if she ever needed someone to listen. The distraught girl refused to hang up however until Aynslee promised to tell the truth about her brother.

"You have to promise me!"

Aynslee sighed. "Don't worry, Sarah, I *promise* you that I will tell everyone the truth about your brother. You have my word."

The poor girl thanked her profusely before finally hanging up. Aynslee knew however the truth would be something in between an innocent girl's impression of her big brother, and the harsh reality of adult life. With pages of notes to fill at least a couple of segments, she reopened the script she had just sent, to begin completely rewriting it. But first she needed to confirm William Hanson was indeed the victim.

Eldridge stared at the road ahead of him, barely aware of the traffic around him, more on autopilot than an active participant in the driving process. His car stereo, forgotten on some talk radio station, cut out, replaced by the ringing of his hands-free kit. He grabbed the phone off the passenger seat and glanced at the call display. *WACX? Not another video!*

He hit the talk button. "Eldridge."

"Detective, this is Aynslee Kai, I hope I didn't wake you."

"You didn't, Miss Kai, how can I help you?"

"I just wanted to confirm with you the identity of the victim on the third video. I have it from a reliable source that his name was William Hanson. Can you confirm this?"

Eldridge pulled into a parking spot and opened the folder given to him minutes before by Trace. *William Hanson. Shit she's good.* "Yes, I can confirm that one William Hanson has been identified as the victim on the third video."

"Care to make a comment for the record?"

"Sorry, Miss Kai, but I can't comment on an active investigation. Good night." He hung up and pulled back into traffic, wondering how a reporter figured out the victim's identity at the same time as they had.

Chelsie sat in the corner, blindly cleaning the dirt from under her fingernails. She had no idea how long she had been there, imprisoned like a caged animal. There was no way to tell the passing of the days, except she was pretty sure she was being fed on a daily basis, and judging by the stomach cramps signaling the start of her period, it had been almost a week. In the entire time she had heard nothing from her captor. He had never said anything to her and didn't appear to have laid a hand on her since her initial abduction, for which she thanked God every time she thought about it. But this fact made her fearful of what he might ultimately want. *If it isn't sex, then what is it?* She shuddered at the thought of what his motivation might be.

But the worst part was the boredom. The fear had been pushed to the background, now that she knew the pattern. Every day she was fed. The interaction lasted several minutes, several terrifying minutes, then she was left alone. Now eating and drinking everything offered her, she had regained most of her strength, and had used that energy to explore her surroundings in the dark, groping inch by inch, using all of her other senses to get a clue as to where she might be, and if there was any hope of escape.

The painstaking work was assisted occasionally with the lowering of the platform. She had found that if she stood directly under the platform, she had almost a full minute where she could examine her surroundings, before she would have to move. And he was always in the same position, so by moving directly under him, he didn't appear to notice what she was doing. This tiny act of rebellion now fueled her determination, and had provided valuable information. It was clear she was in a basement or crawlspace dug deeper at some time, and the chain she was handcuffed to was attached to a pole near the ceiling that ran the length of her prison. The only item of interest was a hole with water in it, she had discovered while exploring the hard-packed dirt floor. She used it as a toilet when needed and, when desperate enough, as a secondary source of water, something she wished she had known about days earlier.

Sounds from overhead brought her back to reality. *Here we go again.* The now far too familiar scraping of something being dragged, followed by the rattle of chains, signaled another feeding. And it was a feeding. Like a caged animal at the zoo, this was her daily visit from the zookeeper. Her initial fear had been replaced by a humiliating desperation, which had now given way to a determination to survive. And for that, she needed her strength. The moment the platform reached the floor, she yanked the water and sandwich from the tray and scurried into a corner opposite the water hole. The length between feedings left her starving, but she knew not to rush things. She used the light to seat herself comfortably, and position her water and sandwich before being left completely in the dark. Then she waited. It only took a few minutes of waiting before she was returned to darkness, and the sounds overhead ceased. She breathed another sigh of relief, her worst fear being the ritual would change somehow, that he may actually come down on that platform one day, and finally do to her whatever it was he had planned.

She took a few moments to collect herself, steadying her rapidly beating heart. She closed her eyes and leaned her head back against the dirt wall. She unscrewed the cap on her water bottle, and took a sip of the cool liquid, swishing it around her mouth, then spitting it out, in a poor attempt to clean her teeth. She turned her attention to the sandwich, and took a tentative bite. As usual, it was incredible. Each day it was something different. And each day is was equally delicious. She savored every bite of today's smoked meat sandwich, slightly ashamed of herself for how much she was enjoying it, the added touch of the toasted sourdough bread and Dijon mustard setting it apart from the white bread, packaged sliced meat and mayo she normally made herself.

No matter how long she tried to make it last, it never lasted long enough. Finished, she took a large swig of water and within a few minutes her eyes drooped as all feeling slowly left her body. *That's odd.* She struggled to keep her eyes open, but her eyelids felt like they had lead weights attached to them. She gave up, and slid across the wall she was perched against, coming to rest in the corner, her head on her shoulder and the cold, dirt wall, fast asleep.

SIX

Eldridge sat at his desk, reading the files on Logan Rochester and Aaron Davidson. It was early morning, his favorite time to work in the squad room. With much of the night shift still out on calls and the day shift not yet in, it was mostly quiet, allowing him to get some actual work done. He preferred being out in the field, chasing down leads, putting the murderers in jail, but unfortunately a big chunk of police work was mundane, involving paper and computers, and requiring a desk. Apparently with an uncomfortable chair. He eyed the orthopedic, donut stained chair across from him, his partner having put in for one with a doctor's note claiming sciatica. *How the hell can you be on duty with sciatica?* He squirmed in his wooden chair, the resulting creak loud enough to reach back in time to the Barney Miller set it was probably featured on.

Comfort proving futile, he leaned forward and pulled up the video the two boys had made. The attack was brutal, young Patricia Arnette not standing a chance. The fact almost a dozen able-bodied onlookers watched while it happened was sickening. The attack had lasted for several minutes, two and a half of those caught on Logan Rochester's camera phone. And when the final deathblow was delivered, his laughter and that of his friend capped off a true low point in human indifference. Thirty-two year old Patricia was dead. Her parents without their daughter, her brothers without their sister, her husband without a wife and most tragic, her thirteen month old baby without a mother.

The crime's most horrid aspect though wasn't the beating itself, nor was it the fact the onlookers had just watched and let her be murdered. It was the aftermath. Within hours Logan and Aaron had uploaded the video, with a commentary added that would go down in the history of depravity, describing in detail how excited they had felt to see someone murdered in front of their eyes and laughing at the sound the poor girl's head had made when the skull was crushed under the boot of one of her assailants. By that evening over seventy five thousand downloads had occurred. The next day it had made the local morning news and the national evening news, resulting in tens of millions of downloads over the coming weeks.

But it didn't stop there, the sad state of today's society further brought to the forefront by people creating spoofs of the video. People recorded their own intros, outros and soundtracks. They set it to music and laugh tracks, these deplorable clips downloaded millions more times. The lone good to come out of the publicity was the prompt capture of the two killers now awaiting trial at Rikers Island. The family of Patricia had pressed the District Attorney to identify the passengers on the train and charge them, but he refused, saying a jury would never convict, considering they would have most likely stood by themselves.

Society was scared.

Or did they just not care?

Well, somebody cares. Somebody cares enough to kill those who let Patricia be killed.

Eldridge closed his laptop and headed to the stairwell, the sound of Patricia's skull cracking playing over and over in his mind, like a skipping record. With each step he took, the crack got louder in his mind, the snap of his shoes on the tile echoing through the stairwell, the laughter, the screams, the inaction overwhelming him. He stopped. What was it about this case that was affecting him so much? Was it that he might do the same? What would he do if he thought justice wasn't being served? Would he take it into his own hands like someone else obviously had? The opening of a door on the landing below ended his thoughts and he continued his descent. It didn't matter what he might do, he knew what he had to do. Murder was illegal. And he was a cop.

End of discussion.

"How's that hospital surveillance video coming?"

Frank Brata, one of NYPD's young but brilliant techs, looked up from his workstation and smiled when he saw who it was. "Good morning, Detective Eldridge!" Eldridge was one of Frank's favorites to deal with. He didn't understand computers very well, but he was younger than most others he dealt with on a regular basis, and at least he felt he could relate to him at some level. Not that they'd be hanging out, zooming chicks any time soon. *Okay, maybe he's a little bit older than me.* He pointed at one of his machines in the corner. "It'll take some time. I'm using some software developed for NASA to piece the common pixels from multiple frames together—"

Eldridge raised his hand to stop him. "Sorry, Frank, I don't speak geek. When will it be done?"

Frank laughed. Coming from Eldridge, he wasn't offended for some reason. "It'll have to go overnight, and there's no guarantee it'll come up with anything recognizable."

"Okay then, while you're waiting for your computer to do its magic, I've got something else I need you to do for me."

"Sure, what is it?" *Hopefully something cool!*

"Remember that subway video from last year where the girl was beaten to death?"

Frank nodded, the images from that video fresh in his mind. "Shit, how could anyone forget that? It was on pretty much every news cast and talk show for a month!"

"Do you know if we have the original video of that?"

"Yup, actually have the cell phone it was recorded on."

"Excellent. I want blowups of every person's face that was on that subway that got caught on tape."

"Way ahead of you, Detective." He hit a few keys and an image of William "Lance" Hanson, shielding his face, appeared. "The DA has me working on that already what with the case coming up and everything. I've got a bunch running through the software now, they should all be done over the next few days. This is the first one that's finished."

"Okay, send that to me and then the rest as you pull them, I'll have my cell with me."

"Where else would it be?" Frank spun back in his chair and began attacking his keyboard as Eldridge left the lab. He sent the image to Eldridge's phone then leaned back in his chair and closed his eyes, a daydream of him and Eldridge in a gun fight morphed into him being

Eldridge. Frank sighed. *Maybe then I could get a date.* He fired up World of Warcraft, then thought better of it.

Eldridge found the same familiar chaos in the hospital reception area, as if the explosion the night before had never taken place, the final body count of six, including Ibrahim Jamar, already a thing of the past. Arriving on the fifth floor, he was pleased to see the previous night's vigil had cleared out, a good indicator Foster was no longer in danger. He asked the duty-nurse in ICU to page the doctor then took a seat, leafing through an impossibly old Reader's Digest. After a few minutes the surgeon from the night before arrived, looking exhausted, the dark circles under his eyes adding ten years to his face. Eldridge rose from his chair and approached him.

"Hi, Doc, how's he doing?"

The surgeon looked at him blankly for a moment before remembering who he was. "Officer Foster? Quite well." He yawned. "I'm sorry, Detective, I caught your friend's case at the end of my shift, didn't want to leave until I was sure he was going to be okay."

"And, is he?"

The surgeon nodded. "We'll need to keep him here for a few more days and he'll have months of rehab, but he should make a full recovery. He's very lucky."

Eldridge smiled. "That's great to hear. Can I speak to him?"

"Just for a few minutes and only if he's awake," he cautioned, stifling another yawn. "He needs his rest. And so do I." He pointed down the hall. "Room Five-Forty-Two. Now I'm going to go catch some shut-eye." He shuffled toward a different hallway as Eldridge chuckled.

"Thanks again, Doc." He found Foster's room and, looking in, saw he wasn't alone, a small Asian woman held his hand, a concerned look on her face. Foster, almost as white as the bandages wrapped around most of his upper torso, was hooked to several machines tracking his vitals, as well as an IV drip. He took a sip from a plastic cup the woman held to his mouth. Eldridge glanced at her left hand and noticed an engagement ring. *Fiancée? Then what was that business with the nurse?*

Foster's eyes opened slightly wider when he saw Eldridge at the door. "Detective, come in." The voice was weak, but Eldridge detected a hint of its former strength, the slight curl to the sides of his lips suggesting a sense of excitement at his arrival.

"Good morning, Foster." Eldridge smiled and entered the room, nodding to the young woman. "I just wanted to see how you were, and if you're feeling up to it, ask you a few questions."

His fiancée stood and faced Eldridge, creating a barrier between herself and her husband-to-be. "Can't this wait until he's stronger?" she asked, her thick accent not diminishing the determination in her voice.

Wouldn't want to get in a fight with her. "I'll be brief, ma'am," reassured Eldridge. "I promise." He put on his best smile in an attempt to disarm her. It didn't work.

Foster patted her hand. "It's okay, Mahal, it's all part of the job." She frowned but sat back down, holding his hand even tighter than before. "Forgive my fiancée, Detective. She's just concerned, that's all."

"Of course." Eldridge extended his hand to her. "I'm Hayden Eldridge, ma'am. I wish we had met under better circumstances."

She eyed his hand for a moment then shook it. "Esperanza."

Eldridge approached the bed so Foster wouldn't have to raise his voice. "Tell me what happened."

Foster took a deep breath. "Well, I was in the hallway, watching the door like you told me to when I heard a shot from inside the room where the witness was." He paused for a moment, his breathing labored.

"Take your time," said Eldridge, realizing the kid hadn't had a chance to tell his side yet and as any good cop with important information to share, wanted to get it into the right hands as quickly as possible.

Foster nodded then continued, this time slightly more relaxed. "Well, almost immediately there were two more shots so I drew my weapon, entered the room and tried to identify the shooter. I heard another two shots that sounded like they were coming from above. I saw a ceiling tile move so I fired two shots into the ceiling ducts and I think I heard a ricochet just before the explosion. I grabbed Mrs. Jamar and her daughter, got them out of there, and that's when I noticed I'd been hit."

Eldridge nodded, noticing Foster appeared to be a couple of shades paler than when he walked into the room. *Better wrap this up quick.* "Did you see anyone suspicious in the hallway before?"

"No, not that I recall."

"Someone was seen leaving the service closet down the hall after the explosion. Did you see him?"

Foster thought for a moment. "No, certainly not after the explosion, I was pretty out of it once I realized I had a hunk of piping in my back." His fiancée winced and squeezed his hand.

Eldridge chuckled. "Well, Foster, you did a hell of a job last night. I spoke with Mrs. Jamar and she wanted me to personally thank you for saving her life and that of her daughter."

Foster smiled, modesty injecting a hint of red into his ghostly pale cheeks. "Nothing doing. If you see her, tell her I'm glad the two of them are okay and I'm sorry about her husband." Foster gasped and turned pale.

Eldridge stepped forward. "Are you okay? You want me to get the doctor?"

Foster grimaced and shook his head. "No, it's fine," he said, sounding much weaker than a moment ago. "I get these spasms of pain, it'll go away."

"He must rest now," said his fiancée, her tone leaving no debate the interview was over. Eldridge thanked them both and left Foster to the ministrations of his partner.

Aynslee lay on the couch of her small, Lower East Side apartment, sporting sweatpants and a Lululemon tee, happy she didn't have to impress anybody for the rest of the night. She stared at an episode of 24 she recorded on her TiVo the night before, but her mind wasn't on the show. Instead, it jumped all over the place, inevitably returning to the same thing that had consumed her for days. *Hayden Eldridge!* She found herself daydreaming about him at work, in the shower, in bed and at this very moment, on the couch while watching TV. *It's nothing more than a schoolgirl crush!* But what was wrong with that? She hadn't been "with" anyone in over a year and hadn't seriously dated anyone in over three years. She was chronically single. Her career came first, often at the expense of her love life. She had a slew of first dates, very few second dates, and almost no third dates. Her BlackBerry ran her life.

And the problem *was* her BlackBerry. As she thought about it she realized once the station had issued these to everybody, she was beholden to it. It accompanied her everywhere, a constant companion, truer than any dog could hope to be. It sat on the counter in the bathroom when she showered, it sat on her nightstand when she slept. If it went off, she would wake and answer it or read whatever message had come in. If she tried to turn it off she couldn't stop thinking about it. She could hardly go to a movie anymore. By the time the movie was over she would be racing from the theatre to check her messages. Once she had forgotten it at her apartment and hadn't noticed until she arrived at work. She lasted thirty minutes before she had to return home to get it.

It was crack.

She couldn't live without the damned thing. Looking at it, she growled in frustration. Her thumb hovered over the red power button. *Do it!* She did. Holding in the button, the screen flashed and the phone turned off. A sense of satisfaction filled her. *She* was in control, not the almighty BlackBerry. She threw it on the carpet and turned her attention back to Kiefer, her eyelids heavy. As she drifted off, Kiefer turned into Hayden, leaving a smile on her face as sleep took over. As she dreamt of Hayden saving her from a marauding terrorist, her BlackBerry kept vibrating, threatening to give away their position. As the terrorists closed positioning on them, the BlackBerry rang and she woke with a start. Looking down at the floor she saw it was still off. *It's no use!* She reached down and turned it back on. A few seconds later it vibrated, telling her a message had arrived. She opened it and saw the attachment.

Not again!

As Eldridge returned to the precinct his phone buzzed in his pocket with a message from Frank at the lab. *The hat has a NerdTech logo on it. See attached.* Stopped at a light, he opened the attachment and the enhanced photo clearly showed a stylized NerdTech logo, its annoying, grinning face unmistakable, everybody in the city probably seeing it at least once. And he knew exactly where he had seen it last. *That guy was at reception when I first got there!* Eldridge closed his eyes, trying to picture the man's face. A horn honked at him from behind and he opened his eyes to see the light green.

He waved at the driver who flipped him the bird. *White, maybe five-eight.* He slammed his fist into the steering wheel as he realized he had also come face-to-face with the man in the stairwell during the evacuation. He pulled a U-turn, eliciting several horn blasts and unflattering hand gestures, and headed back to the hospital. Weaving through traffic, he phoned Prentice who immediately answered. "I need you to check your footage for a NerdTech vehicle leaving your parking lots shortly after the suspect leaves the building. I'll be there in a few minutes."

Prentice's "10-4" rumbled through the phone. Eldridge tossed the phone on the passenger seat and fought his way to the hospital he had only just left. Arriving more than a few minutes later, he bypassed the reception area chaos and headed directly to the security booth. Prentice greeted him and pointed toward a monitor. "Nothing yet," he said. "We're looking at the footage of the parking garage exit." They both leaned in, Prentice resting a massive hand splayed on the desk, the knuckles white with the strain of supporting his huge frame, as they watched vehicle after vehicle exit, none of which appeared to be a NerdTech vehicle. "Maybe he was driving his own private vehicle?"

"Perhaps, but a major part of these guys' branding is their bright green vans with the geek on top. There's a good chance though that this guy has nothing to do with NerdTech and was just using the ball cap as a disguise."

Prentice straightened up from the desk he had been leaning on and crossed his arms. "That's most likely it," he said, his tone indicating any more time spent on this issue would be a waste.

Eldridge wasn't sure. He wracked his brain, trying to remember what he had seen that night, and was almost positive the guy had a denim shirt with the NerdTech logo sewn on the pocket. "Wait, what's that?" Eldridge pointed to the screen.

"What?"

"Back it up slowly." Prentice leaned in again and paused the image, backing it up frame-by-frame. "There, pause it." Eldridge pointed at the bottom of the image. The roof of a vehicle filled the bottom of the screen, most of it out of the camera's view, but the smiling geek's profile was unmistakable. "NerdTech."

Prentice smiled. "Got him now."

Eldridge marveled at how quickly Prentice changed his view, but wasn't as quick to proclaim victory.

At least we have a lead that might actually lead somewhere.

"And when was the last time you heard from her?"

Trace sat at a dining room table, across from a very worried set of parents who had reported their daughter, Chelsie Birmingham, missing after waiting the requisite forty-eight hours. The initial investigation by uniformed officers had turned up nothing and had been bumped up to the detectives. She normally worked homicides or attempted homicides, but volunteered to take this case, what with every case she had been assigned this week having been handed over to Eldridge, and the detective squad already swamped. More often than not these turned out to be parental spats with the children, but she didn't think so in this case, since the daughter no longer lived with the parents, Shane and Melanie.

Chelsie's mother blew her chapped nose into yet another tissue, and looked at Trace, her red, swollen eyes betraying the hell she had been through the past several days. "Saturday evening on her way to the subway, just after her shift ended. She calls me every night, usually when she gets home but she said that she was feeling tired and was going to go straight to bed."

So far the mother had answered most of the questions. Trace turned her attention to Shane Birmingham. Though he didn't have the obvious signs of grief so clearly displayed on his wife's face, his vacant expression revealed a man who expected the worst, but was trying desperately to keep his fears from his wife. "Perhaps she was just making an excuse? Perhaps she was going to meet up with someone and she didn't want you to know?"

Shane shook his head. "No, I doubt it. She was very focused on her schoolwork. She was taking classes whenever she could, working toward becoming a nurse."

"And the address you gave me earlier, how long has she lived there?"

"About six months, she wanted some independence and we encouraged it. We were helping her with the rent, but we understood that for her to truly make a go of it on her own she needed her space." Shane's voice cracked as he spoke, finally letting go, days of emotions he had kept suppressed for his wife's sake, breaking through. "We should never have let her go," he sobbed. His wife burst into tears again, her head collapsing into her hands on the table as her husband leaned on her shoulder from behind, crying with her.

"It's a little premature to assume anything has happened," Trace said, trying to reassure the distraught parents. "The bar she was working at, how long had she been there?"

Shane lifted his head and took a deep breath, trying to compose himself. "About three months I think, she wanted to help pay the rent herself, said she felt obligated."

Trace nodded and stood, deciding there was nothing left to learn here, and that they had been through enough. "I'll look into this and keep you up to date with anything I find. In the meantime, try calling her friends, family, anyone you can think of. It could turn out to be something completely innocent, like a vacation she forgot to tell you about, road trip to Atlantic City with some friends. Any number of things." She left the Birmingham residence knowing full well they weren't convinced.

Aynslee sat in the back of a cab heading to her office, already on the phone with her producer, giving him the heads-up on the new video. "It's huge! Remember the explosion at the hospital the other night? Well, it was him!" She listened to her producer who at the moment sounded even more excited than her, then hung up the phone, looking impatiently at her new Boucheron watch, a gift to herself when she got her bonus yesterday.

I'm glad we have an agreement.

Eldridge's voice filled her head like a telltale heart. It had been driving her mad since the video arrived. *Fine!* She scrolled through her contact list, found the entry she had made for him earlier and called, relieved to get his voice mail. Her focus wavered as she listened to his voice, lost in a daydream about what she might say if they were dating. *Hi, hon, how are you?* The beep yanked her back to the real world. "Oh, ah, hi, this is Aynslee. How are you?" She cringed. "Sorry, Aynslee Kai, I, ah, just wanted to let you know that I got another video, sooo, if you want to come see me, see *it* I mean, then please feel free to come down to the station. Any time. I'll be there waiting for you. Well, not for you, but I'll be there. Or you can call me at home if you want. Well, I'm sure you'll get this before that. Can't wait to see you, bye!" She hung up. *Did I just say "Can't wait to see you"?* She smacked her forehead and let out a groan. *You might as well have said, "Hi, this is Aynslee and I just find you dreamy! If you asked me to the dance I'd say yes!"* She laughed out loud.

"You okay, miss?"

She looked at the cabby and nodded, stifling another laugh.

Eldridge's cell phone vibrated in his pocket as he merged into traffic, forcing him to let the call go to voice mail. It vibrated again a minute later indicating a message. Safely in the flow, he dialed into his voice mail and listened to Aynslee Kai's awkward message. *That woman is in waaay over her head.* He had been battling traffic for almost thirty minutes trying to reach the NerdTech offices in Manhattan, and was almost there. *She'll have to wait.* En route, the second photo from the subway had arrived on his phone. He didn't recognize the man but sent a message back to Frank to tell him to contact the case officer to see if any passengers had been identified during their initial investigation.

Lucking into a spot on a side street, Eldridge walked past several food vendors. The aroma of sausages and French fries that filled the air, along with the sizzle from the grills, triggered a Pavlovian response from his stomach. It growled. He beelined for a nearby vendor when he flashed on an image of his face with his partner's gut. He shuddered. *I can wait.* His stomach protested, indicating it couldn't. Eldridge marched toward the NerdTech building, popping a breath mint in his mouth to try and stem the hunger.

His stomach growled harder.

Entering the impressive marble lobby, he scanned the directory and found NerdTech had the entire twelfth floor. He boarded an elevator and by the eighth floor he and a young woman in a smart business suit remained. His stomach rumbled. Loudly.

She looked at him and smiled. "You should feed that thing," she said, a sly look on her face as she looked him up and down.

Eldridge wasn't sure what to say. "I will."

The bell chimed for the eleventh floor and the doors opened. She pulled a business card from her purse and stuffed it into the breast pocket of his suit jacket, running her finger slowly down his chest toward his stomach. "Does it like blondes?"

His stomach growled.

She smiled and exited the elevator.

The doors closed behind her and Eldridge laughed. *Vinny will hate me for this one.*

The elevators opened to a striking reception area, marble flooring and columns clashed with steel and glass, fusing the modern with the classic. In the room's center sat the reception desk and behind it, through glass with a large NerdTech logo smoked into it, Eldridge glimpsed what appeared to be hundreds of people answering phones. A striking young woman greeted him, her Hollywood white smile further enhanced by her deeply tanned skin, her nameplate proudly announcing Tracy Oswald was a Front Office Coordinator, *not* a receptionist.

"Welcome to NerdTech," she bubbled. "How can I help you today?"

Eldridge flashed his badge. "I'm Detective Eldridge, Homicide. I need to talk to somebody who can help me track one of your vans."

"Ummm, you probably want to talk to Mr. Gupta." She hit a button on her phone. "Mr. Gupta to reception please." She hung up and a moment later her voice echoed over the intercom system. She pointed toward a waiting area nearby. "Please have a seat. Can I get you anything while you wait?"

Eldridge shook his head as he walked to what appeared to be very expensive Italian leather couches. "No thanks." He sank into the plush couch, the gentle sigh it made echoed in his head as he remembered the uncomfortable chair at the office. Leaning back, he closed his eyes, enjoying the sensations as the soft leather enveloped his body, the rich aroma filling his nostrils. He let himself relax for a moment, then returned to the man from the stairwell. No matter how hard he tried to remember what the man looked like, he kept drawing a blank. After a few minutes Eldridge heard whispering at the desk. He opened his eyes and saw an Indian man talking to the receptionist. Eldridge rose as the man walked toward him, his somewhat portly frame disguised well by a very expensive suit.

"Detective? I'm Sanjiv Gupta. How may I help you?"

Eldridge shook the extended hand and immediately regretted it, his hand returned soaked. He successfully hid his disgust as he surreptitiously wiped it on a handkerchief he kept in his right pants pocket for just such occasions. "Detective Eldridge, Homicide. Mr. Gupta, I'm trying to track one of your employees. He was at the St. Luke's Hospital two nights ago."

"I'd be happy to check into that for you, Detective. Please follow me to my office."

Gupta's voice, and the wording of the response, reminded Eldridge of dealing with tech support for his laptop. *Your question is important to us, Detective.* Eldridge followed Gupta to a lavish office, a large mahogany desk filled a small portion of the back wall of floor to ceiling windows offering a breathtaking view of the city skyline. *I'm in the wrong business.* Comfortable chairs, along with what looked like a pullout couch against one wall, several glass and chrome tables and an impressive bookcase, completed the room. He eyed two other doors, one appearing to be an escape door to a back hallway in the event he didn't want to be found in his office, the other revealed a sliver of a granite countertop. *Private bathroom?* The art filling the walls impressed Eldridge until he noticed the little logo of an art bank in the corner of one. *Somebody at the art bank has good taste.*

Gupta sat behind his desk and punched up the appointment schedule on his computer. "I don't see any calls for St. Luke's here for over a month." He leaned back in his chair, pushing the tips of his fingers together, his elbows resting on the arms of his high-back leather chair. "Are you sure it was one of our guys?"

"He was seen wearing your uniform—"

Gupta chuckled. "Detective, we give away hundreds of those hats and shirts to our clients as promotional items," interrupted Gupta. "I think perhaps you're looking in the wrong place."

"—*and* one of your vans was seen leaving the scene," finished Eldridge, hiding the annoyance in his voice. This shut Gupta up for a moment.

But only a moment. "You saw one of our vans?" He looked back at the computer. "We have nothing here for that hospital." He hit a few more keys. "And we had nothing in the geographical area two nights ago either. Most of our calls in that area are during office hours. Evenings and weekends tend to push out to the residential areas. We have had several of our roof nerds stolen over the years. Perhaps it was one of those?"

Eldridge ignored the suggestion. "How many vans would you have had on duty that night?"

Gupta hit a few more keys. "Ninety-seven." Eldridge sighed. *It's never easy.* Gupta looked at him. "You said you were Homicide? What is this about?"

"I can't say. Do you have employee photos that I could look at?"

Gupta turned away from the computer and crossed his arms. "We do, but due to privacy laws I can't release them without a warrant, I'm afraid."

Eldridge nodded, the smug look on Gupta's face pissing him off. "Warrant it is. Have those files ready for me when I get back."

Gupta smiled. "I'm a very busy man, Detective. I'll wait to see if you're successful." He rose from his desk and offered his sweaty hand again for Eldridge to shake.

Prepared, Eldridge faked a sneeze into his right hand. "Better not," he smiled. "I think I'm coming down with something." As he rode down the elevator he began to have doubts. *Maybe it was just someone pretending to be from NerdTech with a stolen roof ornament?*

He looked at his watch and decided it was best to head to the television station to pick up the latest video, rather than wait for the lawyers to get it to him.

His stomach growled.

And then lunch.

His stomach growled again, as if in protest to coming second.

Aynslee paid the cabby and stepped out onto the sun baked concrete in front of her station's offices. She had barely closed the door when a large, disheveled man, stepped up to her, uncomfortably close, her personal space definitely violated. With the cab at her back, she had nowhere to go. He jabbed a finger at her.

"Are you Aynslee Kai?"

The tone of his voice set off alarm bells in her head. She knew she shouldn't answer him, just get away, but she also knew he was already fully aware of the answer. Before she could say anything, he reached out and grabbed her by both shoulders, then threw her to the side. It happened so quickly she had no time to react. She felt her entire body sail through the air, her feet no longer seeming to be in contact with the ground they were firmly planted on only moments before. Her waist then shoulders slammed against the hot, filthy sidewalk, followed by her head bouncing off the concrete. Stunned, she lay there for a moment as the world turned black before snapping back into focus.

"You heartless bitch!" he yelled. "How dare you broadcast that video of my baby being killed?" He spat on her and continued, "Her poor mother tried to commit suicide! Don't you people ever think of the consequences of your actions? Are ratings the only things you care about?" The man drew back his foot, the crazed expression on his face leaving no doubt as to his intentions. Aynslee raised her arms to protect her head from the impending blow and squeezed her eyes shut as she curled into a ball.

But the blow never came. Instead, she heard someone yell, "Hey!" She opened her eyes and saw the man turn toward the voice, a look of surprise spreading across his face. He was tackled full force by someone, their shoulder impacting her attacker's midriff, eliciting a gasp for air as they both tumbled to the ground next to her. She scrambled out of the way as the two men rolled around for a few seconds. Her savior flipped her attacker over on his stomach and shoved his arm behind his back and upward, causing him to howl in pain. The man retrieved a pair of handcuffs from his belt, expertly cuffed his prisoner and hauled him to his feet, prostrating him over the trunk of the cab. When he turned to face her, her heart leapt. *Hayden!*

"Are you okay, Miss Kai?" he asked, genuine, or at least she told herself it was genuine, concern in his voice as he reached out his hand to help her up. For a moment she stared at him in awe, feeling like the stereotypical maiden in distress, rescued by her knight in shining armor. Regaining her composure, she reached up and took his hand as she put on a brave face.

"I'll be fine." She stood and saw a large crowd surrounding her, in fact, slowly walking around her in a circle, as if she were the center post of a spinning merry-go-round. *But why are the buildings moving?* Confused, the scene turned into a blur as she collapsed.

At first all she heard was indistinguishable, a blend of voices and the sounds of a bustling city, no one thing standing out. As she pushed through the din, she thought she heard Hayden giving orders to somebody. She focused on his voice, the voice of her savior, and the sounds began to separate, but all she really heard was his voice. His calm, soothing voice. She felt a warm hand touch her face, the palm against her cheek, the fingers reaching under her neck and lifting. Something soft was placed under her head and the hand gently lowered her, but remained. She felt something cool touch her forehead and cheeks. *God, that feels good.* She concentrated on the sensation and slowly opened her eyes. At first everything remained an unfocused blur, but her vision slowly cleared, revealing the concerned face of Hayden looking down at her, his hand gently caressing her cheek. She smiled at him and leaned into his hand, enjoying the warmth of his skin on hers, trying to remember what had happened to get her into such a wonderful situation. She looked around at the crowd of onlookers and police, suddenly remembering where she was, and flushed. "What happened?"

"You fainted," he replied. She leaned forward to get up when he stopped her with a gentle hand on her chest. "There's an ambulance on the way. You took quite a blow to your head, you should rest until the paramedics get here." She nodded weakly and lay back down, abandoning all hope of trying to impress him with her iron will. She closed her eyes, trying to settle her spinning head, embarrassed by her display when she had first awoken, wondering if he had noticed. *I hope not!* In the distance the siren of an ambulance wailed as it battled its way through New York City traffic. The spinning continued, and she felt herself begin to black out again, her head falling to the side, held by Hayden's warm, steadying hand.

When she awoke she was disappointed to find Hayden's hand gone, replaced by the cold, impersonal, latex gloved hand of a paramedic checking her. At least this time she was lying on a soft stretcher. She looked around and quickly determined she was in the back of an ambulance.

"She's awake," said the paramedic shining a flashlight in her eyes. "Ma'am, you've had a nasty fall and hit your head. We're going to take you to the hospital for observation."

Aynslee at first didn't register what he said, then suddenly, as if hit by a defibrillator, it all came back. She raised her arm and looked at her watch. *Shit!* She sat up on her elbows. "No, I'll be fine," she said. "I have a broadcast to do."

"I really think you should listen to the paramedics, Miss Kai." *Hayden!* His voice sang out from behind her. She looked around and noticed the back of the ambulance was open, and they had not left her office building. He was standing at the bumper, looking at her. The sincerity in his voice almost made her agree. *Anything for you!* Gritting her teeth to hide the pain, she lifted herself off the stretcher.

"Ma'am, you really should let us take you to the hospital."

She shook her head and immediately regretted it. "No, I'm okay. Thank you for your help." Hayden helped her out of the ambulance, frowning, but saying nothing. She headed toward the studio entrance, Hayden following, the grimace on her face the sole outward indication of the discomfort she was in. On the elevator, she leaned into the corner and gripped both railings, her eyes focused on the floor. "Who attacked me?" she asked, not making eye contact.

"Don't know yet," he replied as he punched the button for her floor. "He had no ID on him. I had him taken to booking, hopefully we'll put a name to him shortly."

Aynslee gave a single nod, afraid to disturb the delicate equilibrium she had managed to establish. She knew she wasn't fooling him, but she wasn't willing to admit how horrible she felt. Her head throbbed, spun at the slightest movement, and she was still shaken from the terrifying experience of being assaulted by a complete stranger. She wanted to burst into tears and let the fear and frustration out. She wanted to be held.

"You're sure you're okay, Miss Kai?"

"Yes." *Hold me!*

He nodded. "Very well."

The elevator doors opened and they walked toward her office, coworkers popping their heads over their dividers asking if she was okay, most having already heard what had happened on the street below. She ignored them all, determined to reach her office without collapsing again, desperately hoping none of the drama queens came running from their desks to give her a motherly hug. Finally in the sanctuary of her office, she sank into her chair and rested her head against the back, using the swivel in its base to bring Hayden into her line of sight.

He stood at the side of her desk, looking at her. "Your message said you got another video?"

"Yes."

"I'm glad you decided to cooperate with the investigation."

"I promised to let you know, but I still get the exclusive," she replied as she logged into her computer. "This is airing tonight."

He stepped around the desk and leaned over her shoulder. "I would expect nothing less."

His mouth so close to her ear, his hot breath on her neck sent shivers down her spine, her pain forgotten. She caught a slight waft of his aftershave and inhaled through her nose, taking in every bit of his scent she could without making it too obvious. She had read about pheromones and his were working overtime on her. *Oh, God, I've got to ask him out!*

The video appeared on the screen, confusing at first, the image dark and the view shifting rapidly like a chase scene in Cloverfield. "He must be crawling in the air ducts. We're pretty sure that's where the shots came from," his gentle yet strong voice whispered in her ear. The image stabilized somewhat as it brightened and the killer stopped moving. The video showed an angle from above and ahead of the bed, the intended victim attached to various sensors below. He pointed toward the camera as the barrel of a pistol entered the view. There were five shots, the last two hitting their target in the chest. The image went dark again and bounced around as the shooter backed up. It ended with an intense flash of light. "That must have been the explosion at the end." He handed her his card with his email address. "Forward this to me. I'll also have the techs come down and try to trace the email again." He stepped back around the desk.

Aynslee dug deep for some courage. "Detective Eldridge?"

He turned to face her. "Yes?"

"Would you, ah, like to get some coffee some time?" Her cheeks flushed. She felt like a school girl.

"I don't think that would be appropriate, Miss Kai," he replied. "You're a witness in an active investigation."

"Of course." Aynslee, her mind reeling for a way out of the embarrassment, said, "Maybe when this is done?" *That wasn't it.*

"Perhaps," he said as he left the office.

Perhaps? Why not, "Yes! I'd love to!" Aynslee slumped in her chair, her head hitting the back. She winced. *Maybe I* should *have gone to the hospital.*

Detective Justin Shakespeare climbed into his car, keys in one hand, a dozen Krispy Kreme's in the other. He had over three decades on the force and only a few years left until he could retire with a full pension. Once a good cop, he himself would be the first to admit the last five years of his career were a joke. In his mid-forties he had inexplicably begun to gain weight, and as any self-respecting cop would tell you, you only go to a doctor if you've been shot. Twice. But he finally got concerned enough he at last went. Diabetes. He had tried everything to lose weight, to no avail, but he hadn't given up. Exercise, proper diet, medication, relaxation techniques, he had tried them all, but his blood sugar continued out of control, the weight continued its relentless march up.

And it was the diabetes that had sent his career into a spiral. Five years ago he had worked a crime scene for almost ten hours, going through the evidence collected with Vinny Fantino's crew and his former partner. With time of the essence, he rushed a weapon they found over to ballistics. On the way his blood sugar dropped, the now familiar yet still terrifying feeling of disorientation setting in. He knew if he didn't act quickly he could end up in a coma so he pulled over and grabbed a quick sandwich in a deli.

It had all taken less than fifteen minutes, but those precious few minutes were long enough to not only save his own life, but also for someone to steal the gun from his car. Disoriented from his hypoglycemic episode, he had left the evidence bag in plain sight, the car not only unlocked, but the windows down as well. Too ashamed of why he had pulled over, he told people he was hungry and had stopped to eat. He made no mention of his diabetes, and because of it, there was now no love lost between him and Vinny. Vinny had taken him to task in front of the entire precinct and the case was nearly lost. Fortunately Vinny's team came up with other evidence, but not before humiliating Shakespeare in public.

And that's when he stopped caring.

He knew people made fun of him behind his back, he knew his young partner had no respect for him, and he knew he was dying. After trying everything, he had given up and decided to enjoy his last few years by eating. He didn't have any family so he didn't feel guilty about leaving anyone behind, but deep down he was ashamed. He felt like a failure not only in his personal life but his professional life as well. But over the past few months he had begun to feel differently. He had met a girl. A great girl. A girl who loved him for who he was, warts and all, and it had made him want to live again. She had a great teenaged son who he had taken to, and they were talking about moving in together. He was even tossing around the idea of working out again. He eyed the donuts on the passenger seat of his car. *But not today.* With his personal life perhaps on the mend, he wondered if it wasn't time to try and salvage what was left of his self-respect in his professional life. He had heard the kid had caught an interesting case and decided perhaps it was time to give him a hand. *If he'll take it.*

While en route to the precinct, another photo arrived from the subway video, this one of a clearly terrified Ibrahim Jamar. On a hunch, Eldridge headed to the lab and found Frank alone, listening to Korn at full volume as he pecked away at a keyboard, his head nodding with the beat. "Hey, Frank!" he shouted, trying to be heard over the din of Twisted Transistor. The only response was a banging of the head. Eldridge stepped into Frank's field of vision, waving his arms, causing Frank to jump. He quickly hit the pause button on his keyboard.

"Sorry, Detective, just rockin' out. How can I help you?"

Eldridge plunked himself into a nearby chair. "Gotta a question for you."

"Shoot."

"Can you pull up the video from the subway and play it for me?"

"Sure thing." Frank used his right leg to propel the chair across the room to another computer. A few keystrokes later he had the image displayed on a large monitor mounted to the wall. Eldridge watched, keeping an eye out specifically for Ibrahim Jamar, but other than a couple of quick flashes of him in the background, there was nothing more.

Eldridge leaned back in the chair and crossed his arms. "What was the best still of Ibrahim Jamar you were able to get from this video?"

"You mean without running it through the NASA algorithms?"

Eldridge nodded.

Frank opened a folder on the computer showing several thumbnails of the passengers. He displayed three photos on the screen. "These are the best I could get."

Eldridge looked at them and shook his head. "There's no way you could recognize him from that."

"No, it doesn't look likely. Too much pixelization," agreed Frank.

"Then how the hell is our killer identifying the passengers?"

Frank shrugged his shoulders. "No idea, but it can't be from the video."

Eldridge headed from the lab and returned to his desk. *If he's not using the video, then he has to be identifying them in some other way.* Leaning back in his chair, he closed his eyes for a moment. He heard a groan from across his desk. Opening his eyes, he saw Shakespeare pour himself into his chair, his portly frame surging over and under the arms.

"Hey, kid, how's it goin'?" Eldridge watched as his partner opened a box of Krispy Kremes, his right hand poised over the warm, glazed donuts, three fingers twitching as if tapping out a tune on a piano, then like a hunter after its prey, his hand darted in and clutched one of the donuts, leaving Eldridge to wonder what made the decision so hard in the first place since they were all the same. Shakespeare polished off the donut in seconds and began the long process of sucking the glaze off his fingers.

Eldridge looked away in disgust. *Does he chew?* "Fine, just working on those video murders."

"Where're you at?"

"Just trying to figure out how he's identifying his victims." Eldridge leaned forward and set his elbows on his desk, crossing his arms. "They seem to all have been on the subway last year when the Arnette woman was beaten to death."

"Right." Shakespeare turned his attention to his index finger. "Wasn't there a video?"

"Yeah, but I looked at it and there's no way you can recognize one of the victims. He's sitting way in the back, he's almost a blur."

Shakespeare's index finger exited his mouth with a pop. "Maybe he's not using the video."

"Then what would he be using?"

"Well, if I were somebody looking at life in prison or worse, I'd—" He paused for a moment to lick his thumb. "—be looking to maybe get rid of some witnesses."

"Hmmm, maybe," said Eldridge. "But they've got these guys pretty much dead to rights."

"Yeah, but you know who has witness lists besides the DA?" asked Shakespeare as he decided upon which donut to inhale next. "Defense attorneys."

Eldridge wasn't sure. "It's a long shot."

"Want me to check it out?"

Eldridge nearly choked. "You want to check it out?"

"Sure, why not?" Shakespeare finished off another donut. "I haven't been to Rikers in a while. I'll go see the two perps and see if I can *persuade* them to come clean."

"They'll never see you without their attorney."

"Actually, I heard they just fired their attorney last week. Might be time they got a new one."

Eldridge raised his hands. "I don't wanna hear about it." He knew Shakespeare was going to pull something. "Just let me know if you find out anything. I'm heading to Interrogation One if anyone needs me." Shakespeare grunted an acknowledgement, his mouth full of his latest victim.

Eldridge headed down to holding and opened the interrogation room door, the tired, disheveled man sitting at the table looked up at him, a hint of defiance remaining, his two days growth of facial hair betraying the fact his problems went far beyond this afternoon's events. He had refused to cooperate on scene, but once taken downtown to be booked for assault, he had quickly changed his tune. *Fingerprints usually get the innocent to talk.* When Eldridge heard who the man was, he told them to wait before filing the charges, and had him placed in an interrogation room instead. It had been a few hours of waiting for the man, which Eldridge fully expected to have pissed him off, but it was better than Rikers, and possibly the State Penn.

116

"Mr. Coverdale, I'm Detective Eldridge, Homicide." Tammera Coverdale's father, Hugh Coverdale, glowered at him. "I'd like to ask you a few questions about your daughter."

Coverdale's anger, seething below the surface for hours without release, burst forth. "It's about goddamned time!" he yelled. "Do you realize that nobody has asked us any questions since the day you guys found her?"

Eldridge remained calm, letting the man vent, and sat in a chair across the table from him. "I'm sorry, sir. I've recently taken over the case as part of a larger investigation. Your daughter is one of at least four people that have been murdered recently by, we believe, the same perpetrator."

"Four?" This news trimmed Coverdale's sails. "You mean it wasn't some drunk who did this?"

Eldridge shook his head. "No, it definitely wasn't the man discovered with your daughter's body. We believe your daughter's death is in relation to the subway murder last year."

Eldridge watched Coverdale process this new information for a moment. Finally, the father sighed, the fight in him gone.

"She was supposed to testify in a few weeks." He leaned forward, placed his head in his hands and pulled at his hair. "I encouraged her to testify. Practically insisted." He looked up at Eldridge, tears welled in his eyes. "Do you think she was killed because of me?"

Eldridge lowered his voice and leaned toward the distraught man. "Sir, four people connected with the subway that night have been killed so far, with videos taken of all of the murders. One of them we didn't even know was on the subway until after his death. I don't think it would have mattered." He doubted this new information would help how the man felt now, but in time, he would come to realize it wasn't his fault. "Has your daughter said anything about any threats recently?"

Coverdale shook his head. "No, but I'm not the one to ask. She tells her mother everything."

Eldridge nodded. "I'll be by to question her later. But for now, as far as you know, your daughter hasn't had anything unusual happen to her, nobody following her, threatening her, hang-up phone calls, nothing out of the ordinary?"

"Nothing she's told me."

"Okay, thank you, Mr. Coverdale." Eldridge rose and opened the door.

"What happens to me now?" asked Coverdale.

Eldridge turned back to face him. "That depends if Miss Kai decides to press charges." Eldridge closed the door behind him, leaving Coverdale to dwell on what might happen to him next. Eldridge did feel sympathy for the man, his daughter killed and her murder played out for everyone to see as if a form of entertainment. He hoped Aynslee wouldn't press charges, but he'd have to wait and see what kind of woman she truly was.

Trace stood in front of Chelsie's apartment door and knocked again. She cocked an ear, trying to catch any telltale sound from inside. *Nothing.* She eyed the key to Chelsie's apartment the parents had given to her. If it weren't for this key, she wouldn't have been surprised to find the girl holed up in her apartment, eating a tub of cookie dough ice cream, mourning a breakup with the one true love of her life, a breakup that would leave her alone and miserable for eternity. She knew what young heartbreak was like. *Not much better than adult heartbreak, except you know it will happen again.*

But the key changed everything. The parents had already visited half a dozen times over the past days, so she knew what she was going to find. She slipped the key in the keyhole and turned. The tumblers clicked, and she turned the knob, pushing the door open. "NYPD, is anyone here!" she called, knowing full well there would be no answer. She stepped across the threshold and closed the door behind her. Her hand on the gun at her hip, she slowly entered, carefully examining every corner, every cavity, anywhere a person, or a body, might be hiding.

No smell, so if she's dead, the body isn't here.

She looked for a freezer, but found none.

She stepped into the apartment's lone bedroom and found it too empty, the usual mess of a young girl's life strewn about, toiletries and makeup cluttering the bathroom's vanity and countertop. No evidence whatsoever that she had packed anything for a trip. Her life was still here, untouched. She checked the laundry and found casual clothes near the top, but no evidence of the type of clothes her parents' had said Chelsie wore for her job. She checked out the floor, then the living area. Nothing. And there was no purse in sight, except a nice Gucci knockoff in the closet, empty. *Probably for her nights on the town.*

Trace stood in the center of the apartment, hands on her hips, her trained eye taking everything in. *She definitely didn't make it home from work.* She spotted a note on the kitchen counter and hurried toward it, momentarily excited it might be a clue, the emotion proving fleeting as it turned out to be from the parents. "Please call, we're worried sick! Mom & Dad."

She continued her search, but found nothing. No evidence of a boyfriend, no diary, no personal papers. A few bottles of beer in the well-stocked fridge told her she didn't have a drinking problem; there were no signs of drug paraphernalia. A few framed photos on the end tables and nightstands in her bedroom, all of her and her parents, did nothing to indicate anyone special in her life. The only thing setting it apart from any other single girl's apartment was the sheer volume of books. Chelsie appeared to be an avid reader of both fiction and non-fiction, mostly medical related.

This is a dead end.

Trace took a handful of photos with her phone, just in case someone might return to retrieve something, then left, deciding her time might be better spent interviewing people at the bar where Chelsie worked.

For the first time in years Shakespeare felt alive. Coming to Rikers was a crazy idea, especially with what he planned on doing. Hell, it was illegal, but he didn't care. He knew if he was caught he'd just be asked to resign; the department wouldn't want the scandal. But if he succeeded, he might bust open this case for the kid. He had no interest in furthering his own career. He didn't even care what the others thought of him. He just cared what he thought of himself. And right now, he was feeling pretty damned good as he entered the receiving area. Adjusting his large white Boss Hogg Stetson, he approached the front desk. "Howdy, I'm Justin Shapiro and I'm here to meet with my clients, Denzel Todd and Ian Temple." Shakespeare handed over fake ID matching the bogus name he had just given to the desk officer, relishing the guard's stunned expression as he took in the ridiculous spectacle in front of him. He had always found the more ridiculous the disguise, the more willing people were to believe it. And this was one of his favorite recurring characters to play.

"So those two bastards got another lawyer?"

"Hey, I won't have you talking about those two fine gentlemen like that!" said Shakespeare, enjoying the bombastic performance, a fake southern accent, curled mustache, bad hairpiece and loud white suit completing the disguise. "They're innocent until *proven* guilty."

"Whatever," said the disinterested Corrections Officer as he wrote down "Shapiro's" information in the visitors log. He called for the two prisoners to be brought to an interview room then pointed toward the waiting area. "Wait there until you're called."

Shakespeare didn't have long to wait. A CO led him into a small, depressing room, the drab, grey paint on the walls tired and chipped, the concrete scraped and pitted from decades of impacts with various items, most likely including the body parts of lawyers and convicts. A metal table, bolted to the floor, occupied the center of the room, four metal chairs, two of which were also bolted down, the other two, meant for the visitors, bore the scars of having been thrown around at one time or another, most likely contributing their fair share of the damage to their surroundings. The florescent lighting hummed overhead, augmented only slightly by the natural light coming in from a small window near the ceiling, too small to fit even the tiniest of adults, making the rusted bars crisscrossing it redundant. In the two bolted chairs sat his "clients", their feet and hands shackled together, the chains cuffed to a bolt in the floor.

"Thank you, Officer, I'd like to speak to my clients in private, if you don't mind," said Shakespeare, smiling as he held out his arm, ushering the guard toward the door. The guard nodded and closed the door, leaving Shakespeare alone with two of the most reviled young men in New York.

Shakespeare turned and faced the two prisoners, a broad smile stretched across his face. *They're only boys!*

"Who the fuck are you?" asked one.

Shakespeare sat down in the chair opposite them. "*You* must be Denzel," he said as he opened a brief case and pulled out two files. "Denzel Todd, twenty-two years old, mother died a crack whore, never knew who your daddy was. Says here you've been in and out of jail more times than you can count."

"Fuck you!" yelled Denzel, yanking at the chains.

"And *you* are Ian Temple," he said, turning to the other boy. "Nineteen years old, dad died in Iraq, mom is a legal secretary at a good firm." He leaned toward Ian. "What are you doing hanging around with a lowlife like this?" he asked, jerking his thumb toward Denzel. Ian lowered his eyes and looked at the floor.

"Hey, fuck you, man! Who the fuck are you anyway?" Denzel struggled against his chains, yanking at them with all his might, the rattling attracting the attention of the CO outside who knocked on the door and looked through the small Plexiglas window.

Shakespeare waved him off. "I'm your new lawyer, Justin Shapiro," replied Shakespeare, returning his attention to the boys. "I'm here to see if I can get you gentlemen off."

Denzel tossed his head back and laughed, no longer struggling with his chains. "Yeah, like that's gonna happen. What you been snortin' anyway? Got any left?" he asked, laughing and elbowing his partner, clearly impressed with what he perceived to be a clever sense of humor.

Shakespeare smiled and pulled another file from the brief case. "Well, I have some good news for you that might change your thinking on this." Shakespeare took four pictures from the file and spread them face down in front of him. He leaned forward and lowered his voice. "Whoever you hired has managed to eliminate four witnesses already."

Ian and Denzel looked at each other then back at Shakespeare. "What do you mean, eliminated?" asked Denzel.

Shakespeare flipped each picture over, revealing the faces of Tammera, Logan and Aaron, along with what remained of Ibrahim, to Denzel and Ian. "What do you think I mean?" asked Shakespeare, pretending to be exasperated. "Eliminated! Kaput, pushing up daisies, knockin' at the Pearly Gates, having dinner with Tupac, dead! What the hell else could I mean?"

Ian looked shocked. "Y-you mean f-four more p-people are dead?" he asked with a pronounced stutter, a look of wide-eyed horror on his face.

"Y-yes, I-I d-do," mocked Shakespeare.

"Hey, lay off him asshole or I'll mess you up!"

Shakespeare leaned back. *So, Denzel is Ian's protector.* "Okay, Denzel, you're in charge," said Shakespeare, playing to the boy's ego. "Your man has managed to eliminate four of the witnesses against you. There's still some more but he's got some time."

"W-we d-didn't hire any b-body," stammered Ian.

"Hey, of *course* you didn't." Shakespeare opened his hands in a dismissive manner and raised his shoulders. "Someone just *happens* to be out there *helping* you out. You never *asked* him to, he just *volunteered.*"

"Well, so what if someone is helpin' us out, that's a good thing, right?" Denzel didn't sound certain.

"Oh yeah, it's a great thing!" said Shakespeare with an exaggerated grin. "But here's the problem," he said, again lowering his voice and leaning toward them. "A new, *very* credible witness has come forward. I need to get their name to your guy so he can take care of them."

Denzel shook his head. "That's not possible, we can't get in touch with him."

"Sure you can. Listen, this is one hell of a witness. Friend of the DA. The jury's gonna buy his story, hook, line and sinker. There's nothing I can do to stop this guy from burying you. The only way is if he *can't* make it to the stand." Shakespeare gathered the pictures and placed them back in his briefcase. "Listen, I'll give you the name, you call your guy and give it to him, and everything is good, okay?"

"We can't get in touch with him," repeated a sullen Denzel.

"Fine." Shakespeare stood and headed toward the door. "It's your funeral."

"Wait!"

Shakespeare turned around to see Denzel looking at the floor. "What?"

"We didn't hire no hit man," mumbled Denzel.

"What was that?" Shakespeare rounded the table and leaned forward on his fists, cocking his ear in a larger-than-life manner. "I didn't hear you."

"I said, we didn't hire no hit man!" said Denzel, this time with a hint of desperation in his voice.

"What? Naaaw, I don't believe that for a second!" said Shakespeare, shaking his head as he sat back down. "You're telling me that you two had nothing to do with eliminating those witnesses?"

Denzel lowered his head and looked at the floor. "No."

"You're serious? Listen, now's not the time to grow a conscience. If we get rid of this one witness, you guys could end up walking."

Denzel raised his head and looked Shakespeare in the eyes. "If we had a guy on the outside, don't you think we'd give him to you?" yelled Denzel in frustration. "But we don't, there's nobody, nothing! Just a bunch of useless legal aide lawyers and that's it! We got nobody helpin' us 'cept you!"

Shakespeare stood and headed to the door. "And you don't even have me, ya pieces of shit." He rapped on the door and it opened. He walked out, leaving his two "clients" in confused silence. When he got into his car he called Eldridge's phone and was sent directly to voicemail. "Hey, kid, it's me. No way these two guys have anything to do with your murders." He snapped the phone shut and tossed it on the passenger seat. His stomach rumbled. *Well, that deserves a snack!* He put the car in gear and headed across the Francis Buono Bridge toward his favorite hotdog stand in Queens, ripping off his wig and fake mustache. He eyed the white suit. *Maybe I should change first?*

"What's got you so happy?"

Frank grinned at Eldridge as he entered the lab. "Watch this!" He hit a button on his keyboard and the subway beating video flashed on the plasma display, replaying the horror of that day. Eldridge opened his mouth to say something but Frank raised his index finger. "Wait!" said Frank, turning it into a two syllable word as he bent his finger and jabbed at the screen. The video paused on an image of Ibrahim Jamar sitting in his seat and sat frozen for almost a minute before continuing, the only difference between the original and the one found on the DVD player left at the hospital.

"Yeah, so it pauses on our victim. I already knew that."

"Yeah, but did you notice anything?"

"What?"

Frank backed up the video to where the image of Ibrahim had frozen and pressed pause. "Now do you notice anything?"

Eldridge raised his hands in exasperation. "What, what am I supposed to be noticing?"

"Do you recognize who that is?"

"Of course I do, it's Ibrahim Jamar, our cab driver who was abducted, shot and blown up!"

"Exactly." Frank had a satisfied look on his face. Eldridge stared at him. "Man, you cops aren't too bright are you?"

Eldridge recognized the Leo Getz reference for what it was, surprised someone as young as Frank knew Lethal Weapon. Then it hit him. His mouth opened and his eyebrows shot up, resulting in a look of relief from Frank.

"Got it? This image has been cleaned up! Whoever is doing this has access to the same technology I'm using here to clean up our video," gushed Frank. "This guy is good!"

Suddenly NerdTech didn't seem like such a stretch. "What kind of horsepower would he need?"

"I'm using some incredibly powerful multi-core processors here, very expensive stuff. There's no way some NerdTech employee owns this stuff."

"But he could have access to this kind of hardware? As part of his job, maybe?"

"Perhaps. But even so, the routines take a long time to run and I'd be surprised if anyone would leave hardware this powerful unattended for long enough."

"So then how's he doing it?"

"Well, there's nothing to say you can't do this at home, it would just take a *really* long time."

"How long?"

"Well, it could take weeks per image. If he's done this for everybody on the train, hell, it could have taken him months, maybe even longer!"

Eldridge nodded. "So, he's been working on this since the beginning."

"Holy shit, Detective," exclaimed Frank. "Do you realize how much work that is? He'd have to be obsessed to do something like this!"

Eldridge headed toward the door. "He's killed four of them already. I'd say that counts as obsessed."

Chelsie woke to find herself lying on something comfortable. Incredibly comfortable. She hadn't experienced anything so soft in days. She rolled onto her back, enjoying the sensation as she stretched her arms above her head and reached out with her legs, extending them as far as she could, working out the kinks. She opened her eyes and snapped them shut again, a bright light, the brightest she had seen in days, nearly blinding her. She opened her eyes a sliver, trying to adjust. The soft bed she lay in and the bright light caused her heart to pound in excitement. *Was I rescued?* It took a minute, but with each passing second her surroundings came into focus and her elation turned to despair, the dirt and concrete walls she had only touched until now, finally revealed by a light dangling from the ceiling, her soft, comfortable bed, nothing more than a thin mattress tossed on the floor of her prison. She lay her head down and closed her eyes, shutting out the horror surrounding her as her body heaved with sobs, a wave of self-pity taking over.

What did I do to deserve this?

She thought of her mom and dad, what they must be going through, what she would give to have her overprotective mother there with her right now, holding her, telling her it was going to be alright, to have her father there to protect her from her captor. *This isn't fair!* She hugged her knees to her chest, and tried to steady her crying. She pictured her parents. She could imagine her father's soothing voice. *Stay strong.*

She gasped, inhaling deeply, and held it for a moment, as if the air were steel, fortifying her against the horrors outside the fragile shell of her body. She slowly exhaled, letting the air audibly escape past her pursed lips.

I will, Daddy.

Eldridge exited the courthouse's underground parking, the warrant for the NerdTech employee files issued earlier that morning, sat on the passenger seat beside him. He steered his car toward the NerdTech offices, determined now more than ever he was on the right track. With both a NerdTech uniform and van seen in the vicinity, someone with advanced computer knowledge uploading videos on hijacked wireless networks, and extremely advanced photographic analysis software utilized to identify the victims, everything pointed to someone at NerdTech. The familiar feeling that came over him when he was about to break a case wide open, filled him with a natural high he would never get enough of. This was the turning point, he could feel it in his gut, and his gut was rarely wrong. This was why he became a cop, the excitement of knowing you were about to put a criminal in jail, especially a murderer, was something no drug could recreate. His spine tingled, anticipating the rush of seeing his suspect looking back at him from an employee file.

He also couldn't wait to shove the warrant in Gupta's smug face.

The traffic moved slower than usual, even for this time of morning. Creeping along for almost half an hour, the constant honking of horns slowly killing his joy, he finally came upon the cause of the chaos, a broken-down Jaguar in the middle of an intersection, hood up, its owner standing by the open driver's side door, the entire dash flashing with warning lights, as he screamed at the dealer on his cell phone about his six-figure lemon. Eldridge shook his head. *Everybody knows you don't buy Jags to actually get anywhere.* As he cleared the intersection, traffic finally returned to a normal pace and he soon arrived at NerdTech.

Gupta wasn't pleased to see him, the plastic smile failing to hide the knowledge he was about to taste his own shoes. He extended his hand regardless, and Eldridge, having planned ahead, passed him the warrant, struggling to keep his delight from being too obvious. "I need all of your personnel records for anyone who may have access to one of your vehicles."

Gupta read the warrant carefully, as if looking for some reason to not comply, then turned to the receptionist. "Get somebody from Legal in my office, ASAP." She nodded and turned to her computer to look up the extension. Gupta pointed to the couches. "You'll have to wait until our lawyers look at this."

Eldridge walked past Gupta and headed toward his office. Gupta, startled, ran after him, opening his mouth to protest. Eldridge cut him off. "Your lawyer can review it at his leisure. That warrant gives me immediate access, and you will provide me with the information detailed in that court order now, or I will have all of your computers seized and our techs will search for the information themselves. It should take a few weeks since they are very busy. Your choice." Arriving at the office, Eldridge held his arm out and beckoned Gupta in. "After you."

A subdued Gupta shuffled past him and sat behind his desk. "Do you want me to filter them somehow?"

"White males for now, we don't know anything else beyond that."

Gupta nodded and hit a few keys. The printer beside his desk powered up and began spitting out employee records.

Eldridge eyed the rapidly growing stack of paper. "How many does that leave?"

"One-hundred-forty-two."

"You're kidding me!"

"No, Detective." Gupta smiled, apparently garnering some satisfaction at the work ahead of Eldridge. "You are fortunate that you were able to specify a white male. Otherwise you would be looking at over three hundred."

Eldridge's earlier optimism waned as he leafed through the thick set of papers Gupta handed him, each with a photo and contact details for all NerdTech's white male employees. Determined not to give Gupta the satisfaction of knowing how discouraged he was, he shoved the stack of papers under his arm and dropped his card on Gupta's desk. "E-mail me that as well for our techs in case we want to cross reference it with anything."

Gupta nodded. "Of course, Detective."

Eldridge headed to his car with 142 sheets of paper under his arm, and his hopes of a turning point being reached, dashed. As he trotted across the street, a nearby Starbucks beckoned, his need for a pick-me-up greater than his need to return to the station. Sinking into a ridiculously comfortable chair, he sipped his Venti coffee with no sugar, no cream, no foam, no cinnamon and definitely no vanilla or caramel. *Just black, the way it was meant to be!* He flipped through the records, hoping to narrow down the list of possibilities. He knew some were not the man he had seen in the hospital simply by looking at them. Some too fat, others too old. When he finished, he had the list whittled down to a little under one hundred names. *Some progress.*

As he finished his coffee his phone buzzed with a message from the lab informing him a hijacked wireless network in SoHo was used to upload the latest video. He called Gupta and confirmed five employees from the list were in the area when the message was sent. Eldridge flipped through the pages and found all five, two of which he had already eliminated in his too fat/too old pile. *Real progress!* But maybe not. He looked at the photos, certain he hadn't seen the three remaining men before. One was a maybe, but he couldn't honestly say he was ringing a bell. He called Gupta back. "Were any of these five on duty three nights ago?" He heard Gupta hitting keys.

"One. Chris Messina."

Eldridge's heart thumped in his chest, his gut feeling returning. "Where is he now?"

A few more key taps echoed through the phone. "GPS has him here. Probably for a meeting."

"Keep him there."

"Are you serious? Greedo? There's no way he has anything to do with this."

"I'll be there in five minutes."

Eldridge snapped his phone shut, downed the rest of his coffee and rushed from the Starbucks, tossing his cup in the trash. A voice straight from the sixties yelled at him, "Hey, man, reduce, reuse, recycle, man!" Eldridge did a double-take at the Starbucks' resident-granola as the man reached into the trash to retrieve the cup he had tossed moments ago. With no time to get into an environmental debate, he continued on to the NerdTech offices and found Gupta waiting for him with his suspect.

"Detective Eldridge, this is Chris Messina," said Gupta. "Perhaps we should talk in my office?"

Eldridge nodded and followed several steps behind a clearly nervous Messina, his royal blue dress shirt stained with large, expanding sweat stains, beads of sweat trickling down his forehead and back of his neck, his pasty white face glistening and sickly pale. Someone opened the door to a photocopier room as they walked by and Messina jumped to the other side of the hall, grabbing his chest. *This has got to be him.* Eldridge reached under his sport coat and adjusted his holster. *But he doesn't look at all like the guy from the stairwell!*

"What's this all about?" asked Messina when the door closed. "Did I do something wrong?"

Eldridge looked at the man standing before him. He stood about five foot eleven, 190 pounds with salt and pepper hair, probably in his late-thirties. There was no way this man could be mistaken for the one from the hospital, that man standing at least a head shorter than Eldridge, and ten to fifteen years younger than Messina. *Then why is he so damned nervous?* He decided to play it out. "That depends, Mr. Messina. Were you at St. Luke's hospital this week?"

"St. Luke's? I've never been there in my life!"

"Where were you Tuesday night?"

"Tuesday?" Messina stammered. "Oh, thank God!" He breathed out a sigh of relief, a hint of color returning to his face. "I was with my wife and kid at a piano recital!"

"Can anyone confirm that?"

Messina bobbed his head, clearly relieved. "Of course, a couple hundred people!" Messina smiled and pulled a handkerchief from his pocket and wiped his forehead and neck.

"And between what times were you at this recital?"

"Between seven and ten."

Well, he couldn't have been at the hospital.

"But I have you taking a call around eleven," said Gupta, looking at his computer. "The notes say they couldn't reach you for almost three hours."

"Yeah, I was on call."

Eldridge detected a note of panic in his voice, the little color that had returned, quickly gone. *Why? He's already cleared himself.*

Messina wiped his forehead again, alternating his attention between Gupta and Eldridge, as if unsure of who he would get in more trouble with. He apparently decided on Gupta. "I'm sorry, sir, I hardly ever get called on Tuesday night and I needed the money, so I took the shift and went to the recital. I turned off my phone in the recital and then forgot to turn it back on when I got out. I'm sorry, Mr. Gupta, it won't happen again."

"See that it doesn't," warned Gupta. He turned to Eldridge. "Are we done here?"

"For now," replied Eldridge. *Another dead end.* He looked at Messina for a moment, then reached out to shake his hand. Messina took it, his hand shaking almost uncontrollably. *This guy is definitely hiding something.* Eldridge decided to sit on him for a while.

Aynslee looked in the mirror and smiled. *Definitely worth it.* Two torturous hours in the stylist's chair with a bruised skull had resulted in a new look that wouldn't launch a thousand ships, but just might launch her career those final few steps. When she had first sat down she said she wanted something bold, dramatic, different. Serge suggested leaving her hair long, straightening it, and going with an extreme change—from boring brunette to blonde bombshell. Aynslee hadn't been sure. Serge's "trust me, darling" were words she had heard numerous times before, and he had never disappointed. It was probably the throbbing headache rather than her innate trust in her stylist, that made her agree, but in the end, she loved the look. Her light brown complexion contrasted beautifully with the new color and heads were definitely turning in the studio. *I wonder if Hayden will like it?*

The attack by Tammera's father had shaken her up. When it happened, she had no idea who he was; he was nothing more than a man who screamed at her and shoved her to the ground. She remembered hitting her head and blacking out for a moment, coming to as he was about to deliver the finishing blow.

But Hayden had saved her.

She shuddered to think what would have happened if he hadn't shown up when he did, the ironic coincidence of him being there to view the video of a murder, resulting in the saving of a life. Her life. Since Hayden's rescue, her mind had created an extensive fantasy around the incident, a dream world she found herself escaping to whenever she had a moment to herself, something she hadn't done since her teenage crush days. She sighed and returned to reality as the director cued them for the supper hour newscast. Tonight, she was co-anchor. *One more step out of the way!*

Abby stepped from her Dojo and into the crisp evening air, chatting with a new student, Bruce, who had joined earlier that evening. There had been a time when she would never have considered talking to a strange man, especially on the street at night, but Karate had changed that. She signed up a year ago and was, in her opinion, doing quite well, considering she was testing for her green belt next week, was in the best shape of her life, and loved the feeling of confidence and security it gave her. Not to mention feeling sexy again after her bitter divorce. She looked at the young man and touched his arm. *You're incorrigible! He's barely half your age!*

"Oh, I'm sure you're going to love it," she said. "Shihan Jamie is excellent and very patient."

"I hope so," the young man said. "I've always wanted to get into it but I kept putting it off. I guess I just thought that you had to start as a kid."

Abby laughed. "I just started a year ago and I'm only thirty-five." *A little white lie never hurt anyone.* "I'm already testing for my green belt next week."

"Really? What made you start?"

She opened the trunk of her car with her key fob and tossed her gym bag inside. Pausing, she debated on whether or not she should tell him, but the eager expression on his innocent face made her trust him. "There was an incident a year ago on a subway where a girl was killed," she began.

"Really?" Bruce was wide-eyed. "What happened?"

"You never heard about it?" *Who hasn't heard of this?*

Bruce cast his eyes down, a hint of shame on his face. "To be perfectly honest, I get most of my news from the entertainment section of Digg."

Abby nodded. *What the hell is "dig"?* "Well, a year ago two guys beat a girl to death on the subway. I was there when it happened and I was too scared to do anything about it."

"It must have been terrifying."

"It was. I swore after that night I would learn how to defend myself and others. The next day I came to the Dojo and I've been going four times a week since."

Bruce nodded his head. "Yeah, it was a brutal thing that happened that day," he said, the tone of his voice dramatically different from moments ago.

Abby paused, suddenly apprehensive. "I thought you didn't know what I was talking about?"

Bruce looked directly at her, all expression drained from his face. His hand snapped out from his side and he clutched her wrist with an iron grip, pulling her toward the still open trunk. Abby, consumed with panic, couldn't understand what was happening, or what to do. She became light headed, exactly like a year ago, as her emotions took over.

"She was my—."

The reality of the situation rushed back with a roar. "No!" she yelled, anger and fear mixed in her voice. She broke his wrist lock with a move she had practiced for months, never dreaming she would have to use it in the real world, then followed it up with a front snap kick to his groin. Her attacker buckled forward in agony, trying to grab her again, as she yelled for help and ran toward the Dojo. Nearing the door, something hit her back then an agonizing pain shot through her entire body, every muscle contracting, her clenched fists and arms shaking uncontrollably. She collapsed to the ground, mere feet from the door, unable to reach out, every muscle and sinew taut and no longer under her control, her teeth, clenched together as if wired shut, not letting a sound escape. The pain stopped as suddenly as it had started, her muscles released, completely exhausted of energy, and she slumped to the ground.

She pushed herself on her back, her weakened muscles screaming from the effort, and saw Bruce stumble toward her, his outstretched hand aiming a Tazer at her. He squeezed the trigger and the electricity shot through her nerve endings from head to toe again, spasms wracked her body as she jerked around on the sidewalk, helpless. Releasing the trigger, he picked her up, threw her over his shoulder and dumped her unceremoniously into the trunk. He ripped the keys from her still clenched hand then slammed the lid closed, sealing her inside. As her strength slowly returned, she kicked at the trunk roof and yelled for help. The car screeched to a halt, sending her rolling. She heard the car door and a moment later the trunk lid was thrown open. Bruce leaned in, holding the Tazer in his left hand and a white cloth in the other. He pointed the Tazer at her head and pressed the damp cloth tight over her mouth, a pungent odor overwhelming her nostrils. Almost immediately the world swam around her, the chemical on the cloth causing her to breathe deeply, her sinuses tingling as if from the initial blast of a breath mint, then she went numb. She struggled but it was no use. Within seconds she was unconscious.

Aynslee sat in the makeup chair prepping to tape a segment for the evening newscast when her BlackBerry pulsed in her lap. She pressed the button on her Bluetooth headset. "Aynslee Kai."

"Is this Aynslee Kai, the reporter?"

"Yes." She motioned to the stylist working on her hair to get her a pen and paper. "How can I help you?"

"My name is Rafi Jamar, Ibrahim Jamar's cousin, the man who was killed in the hospital explosion."

Aynslee looked at the stylist with frustration as the woman searched for something to write with. Leaning forward, Aynslee snatched an eyeliner pencil and wrote on her hand. *Ibrahim Jamar.*

"I have information you may be interested in," the man continued, his thick accent and name making her think he was sub-Saharan African, not long in the country.

"Yes, what is it?"

"First, I want to know how much money you will pay me for this information."

"I'm sorry, Mr. Jamar, but we are a legitimate news organization, we don't pay for stories."

The man's voice became curt. "Fine, someone will pay for what I know."

You're going to lose him! "What is it you know, maybe we can work something out, perhaps get you on TV." Aynslee couldn't think of anything else to offer the man.

"TV doesn't put food on the table. Cash does."

She decided to try the oldest trick in the book. "Well, I'm sorry, sir, maybe if I knew what you were offering I could talk to my news director to see what we could do, but I'd need to know what it is you think is so valuable."

The man laughed. "Nice try, Miss Kai, I'm not going to tell you what I know without seeing some cash first."

Well, it was worth a shot. "I need some inkling, Mr. Jamar, just a hint. Work with me and I'll see what I can do." There was a pause for a moment. *Got you!*

"Fine, ask your news director if he knows about the DVD player that was found at the scene of the explosion. I'll call back in one hour then I go to another news organization."

Aynslee jumped from the chair, not to talk to Jeff, but to track down the lead just handed to her. She now knew the victim's identity and probably as much about the DVD player as this Rafi Jamar knew—the fact it existed. Rushing into her office, she came to a halt when she saw her chair. A CD sat on it, a handwritten label, "Love Songs for Aynslee" attached, along with a single, red rose. She shivered as she thought of Reggie in her office. *This is getting weird.*

Abby came to, tied to a chair in the living room of her house, a house hard won in the divorce settlement, a house she now lived in alone, a house where there was no one to save her. The tape across her mouth muffled the desperate screams that erupted when she saw Bruce sitting in another chair facing her, his impassive stare scarier than anything she could have imagined. He pointed a remote control at her DVD player and pressed play, the video from that night flashed on the screen, eventually pausing on an image of her terrified face as she fled the subway car. *What had he said? "She was my"? She was my what? What was she to him?* She screamed against the tape to no avail, the only response from the formerly talkative man to pull out a cell phone and video tape her. At that moment everything came together. *The killings on TV!* This time panic took complete hold. There were no self-defense moves she could use to get herself out of this situation, too tightly bound to the chair to move, her taped mouth unable to reason with her assailant, she knew she was going to die. Her eyes filled with tears as he pulled a gun from his belt. Struggling against the bindings, she watched him raise the weapon, his finger squeezing the trigger so slowly she wondered if it were her imagination, or the fact so few seconds remained in her life her brain was making each one of them count.

Throwing her weight to the left, she and the chair toppled to the floor, the crash rattling the china in a nearby hutch. Desperate, she rubbed her face against the carpeting, trying to remove the tape, it catching slightly on the pile, the sensation of the sticky backing pulling from her skin as he stepped toward her and knelt down so she could see his face. He continued to hold the cell phone out, recording everything, when the tape at last ripped away.

"No, please, wait!" she cried, gasping to catch her breath as the gun entered her field of vision. "I told you, I felt terrible about it, I felt so bad that I took Karate so that if it ever happened again I would be able to help!" The gun, now aimed directly at her forehead, its long, narrow barrel all she could see, the world around her an unfocused blur, the camera lens of her life now focused on only one thing, the final antagonist who would remove her from the second act of a life about to become nothing more than a supporting actor with no legacy, no children, an ex-husband who hated her, and a dead-end career where in a year no one would remember her name. "No, please don't, please!" She sobbed at the futility and closed her eyes, desperately searching for what she might say to make him stop. "Who was she to you?" she blurted out in one last attempt to appeal to his human side.

And it worked. He did stop. His finger relaxed on the trigger and confusion entered his eyes followed by what she thought might be the onset of tears. She decided to keep pressing. "You started to tell me, please, I would like to know who she was, why she was important to you." She fought to steady her voice, to try and reduce the adrenaline of the situation.

A single tear escaped his right eye, the sensation it made as it rolled down his face seemed to surprise him, ripping him back into the reality of the moment, his resolve taking hold again. "She was my—." He squeezed the trigger, forever silencing the answer.

SEVEN

Messina sat at one of the shared desks the techs were assigned when not out on calls, staring at his keyboard, a bundle of nerves that hadn't settled down since the meeting with the cop earlier in the day. He looked at the iced cappuccino he had switched to after a dropped stapler caused him to jump, spilling hot coffee all over his hand. It remained full, beads of condensation inched their way down the Styrofoam, mimicking the sweat trickling down his spine. His eyes glazed over, the single droplet he had focused on as it zigzagged its way toward the desk surface, lost in a blur as his head slowly dropped to his chest. His watch beeped, snapping the bead of condensation back into focus as it merged into the small puddle of water now encircling the cup. He glanced at his watch. Six o'clock. He raced to the elevators, his heart thudding in his chest as adrenaline rushed through his veins, once again bringing the events of today to the forefront. *What the hell has that bastard got me into?* From the safety of his van he placed a call to the person he had trusted to cover for him that night, and who had almost cost him his job, and possibly his freedom.

Eldridge sat in his car watching the parking garage exit at the NerdTech building. His ass ached, his bladder demanded attention, and doubt crept into his mind. Had he gambled wrong on whether Messina was driving a NerdTech vehicle or walking to the subway? He shifted in his seat, trying to provide at least one ass cheek with relief, when he saw a van with the NerdTech mascot on the roof pull up to the gate, this only the latest of dozens that had exited since he began his vigil. He leaned forward in anticipation, hoping this might at last be the one. The driver waved a pass in front of a sensor and pulled out onto the street. Eldridge had a clear view as the driver turned to do a shoulder check before merging into traffic.

Messina! He smiled, the discomforts plaguing him moments before forgotten, the thrill of the chase taking over. Pulling in behind him, he watched Messina yelling at someone on the phone through the van's side view mirror. *You don't talk to a client that way. That's either his wife or whoever he's covering for.* Eldridge noticed the van's window had been rolled down and decided to take a chance. As the van pulled up to a light, he rolled down his passenger side window and pulled alongside.

"—the hell did you get me into! The cops were here asking questions about Tuesday night! Were you at St. Luke's? You were supposed to cover for me! What the hell were you doing?" A truck pulled in behind Eldridge, drowning out the conversation. He leaned toward the window. "—when you get this message, you call me right away!" Messina tossed the cell phone and looked out the window, a desperate look on his face. Eldridge jerked his head back and settled in behind the van as the light changed.

As they drove, he watched Messina repeatedly look in his side-view mirror. *I've been made.* He turned at the next intersection, there being no point in following him anymore, and let Messina continue on his way. The gamble of listening in on the conversation had paid off. He now had no doubt he was on the right track, all he needed now was a subpoena for the cell phone records to see who Messina had called, but first, he had to keep a promise he had made earlier.

Messina's heart pounded in his chest, unsure of what he had seen. Was it the detective? Had he overheard the phone call? He replayed what he had said in his head, trying to remember how he said it and if it could incriminate him. *My God, what has he got me into?* He looked in his side mirrors and searched each car for the detective, soon finding him a couple of cars back. His heart leapt into his throat. *What am I going to do?* He knew trying to lose him would just make him look guilty. He had to keep his cool. He knew he had done nothing wrong from a legal standpoint, but he couldn't afford to lose his job either. The cell phone rang on the passenger seat and he jumped, grabbing it, the call display showing it was the son-of-a-bitch that had gotten him into this mess. Hitting the Ignore button, he looked in his mirror again and cursed, punching the steering wheel as he fought to keep himself from breaking down in tears, the desperation of his situation almost proving too much. *What did I do to deserve this?*

Elise Coverdale approached the door, expecting yet another neighbor, friend, or worse yet, reporter, expressing their condolences or asking questions. *Why don't they just leave us alone?* She didn't recognize the man through the window, and, after her daughter's murder, had become almost paranoid of strangers, especially strange men. "What do you want?" she called through the closed door.

"Mrs. Coverdale? My name is Detective Eldridge, I'm investigating your daughter's case," the man called out. She jerked back, grabbing her chest, as she heard something tap the window. It was his badge. "May I come in and ask you a few questions?"

She examined the badge. *How can I tell it's real?* She wasn't sure what to do. *But what if he is a cop?* She unbolted the door, opened it slowly, and peered out at the man. He presented his badge again so she could see it more clearly.

"I'm with the NYPD, ma'am, Detective Eldridge," he repeated.

His voice was gentle, almost calming, something she could use more of after the events of the past several days. "I'm sorry about that. I'm finding since my daughter's death I'm a little paranoid."

The man smiled at her as she opened the door. "No need to apologize ma'am, it's better to be overly cautious than careless."

His voice remained quiet, respectful, as if he truly understood the pain she was going through. She returned the smile, immediately taking a liking to him. "Can I get you anything, coffee, tea?"

"No, ma'am, I'm fine, thank you. I just have a few questions and then I'll be on my way."

"Of course." She directed him to a chair in the living room and sat across from him, folding her hands on her lap as she tried to regain her composure, her heart still racing a bit from the shock of seeing a strange man on her doorstep.

"I understand from your husband that you and your daughter were very close," he began.

"Oh yes, we're very close," she agreed. "We tell—." She stopped, her voice cracking. *"Told* each other everything." She looked at the fireplace mantle, her eyes filled with tears, a picture of her and her daughter at her college graduation flooded her with fond memories, and the realization those precious memories were all that remained. *No, no more tears!* She bit down on her cheek and blinked the tears away.

"Was there anything unusual happening in your daughter's life, any new friends, any unusual phone calls, anything that might help us?"

Elise shook her head. "No, nothing she told me. The only thing unusual is she was going to testify at the trial of those two cretins who killed that poor girl on the subway last year."

"Yes, I understand she was on the subway when it happened."

Elise nodded. "She felt terrible about it, about not doing anything, you know? But she told me she was terrified. Apparently someone had tried to help and one of the men had yelled he would shoot him if he got any closer."

"So one of them had a gun?"

Elise shrugged her shoulders. "Tammera said she never saw one, but it was enough to make people back off. Are you sure I can't get you anything?"

The detective rose and smiled. "No, ma'am, we're all done here." Retrieving a card from his pocket, he jotted a number on the back and handed it to her. "If you think of anything else, please call me right away," he said, and then, lowering his voice, he looked her straight in her eyes and said gently, "And ma'am, if you ever need to talk to someone, I've written the crisis hotline number on the back. There are people who can help you get through this."

Elise knew what he was talking about. Her suicide attempt had failed, her husband arriving as she poured the pills in her mouth. It had brought her back to reality, and realizing what she was doing, she had spat them out into the sink, but wasn't able to remove all the evidence before her husband walked in. When he saw what she had tried to do, he at last opened up, and they cried together on the bathroom floor, holding each other for hours. "Don't worry about me, Detective. There will be no more episodes like the other night. We'll get through this on our own, but I thank you." Elise led him to the door. "Detective, when can I expect my husband home?"

He frowned and spread his hands out in front of him. "I'm sorry, ma'am, but that is out of my control. It depends if Miss Kai presses charges. You have my word he won't spend a moment longer in jail than he has to."

Elise nodded, the response more or less what she expected. "Ok, thank you for your honesty, Detective." Elise locked the door behind him and leaned against it, her shoulders shaking as she tried to stifle her sobs.

Eldridge stood on the porch a moment, his mind racing. If there was a gun, or at least the threat of a gun, it explained why no one had helped. Why this piece of information wasn't generally known was curious, and perhaps why the DA hadn't pursued charges against the bystanders, despite the intense public pressure; if their lives were threatened as well, there was no requirement on their part to act. His faith in humanity restored, if only slightly, he stepped off the porch. His phone vibrated with a message. He flipped it open and found another photo. Tammera Coverdale. Now with three of four passengers identified dead, he needed to find the other passenger's identity soon, and place him into protective custody.

Before Trace had a chance to interview the coworkers of her missing persons case, she was called in on something far more interesting. A murder. She surveyed the scene in front of her, the upper-middle income home appeared quite well decorated, though she knew little of these things, knowing only what she liked. And she liked what she saw. Spoiling the near perfect setting, the victim, a woman identified as Abigail Teague, forty years old, recent divorcée. The woman lay on her side, tied to a dining room chair, hands bound together behind the chair-back, feet taped to the ornate legs, a piece of duct tape had at one point covered her mouth but was somehow loosened, either by her, or her assailant. It appeared a single bullet to her forehead had finished her off.

"So what do you think, Detective?"

Trace glanced at Vinny then resumed her survey. "No signs of forced entry, so she either knew her assailant or they had a key. According to the neighbors she's recently divorced, apparently quite the bitter one from what they said. She won this house in the settlement." Trace pursed her lips. "My money's on the ex-husband."

Vinny nodded thoughtfully. "Could be. But …"

Here it comes! She already knew what Vinny was going to say and was a little disappointed he had picked up on it so quickly. "What?"

"Well, this looks an awful lot like the Cell Phone Killer's M.O."

"Is that what they're calling him?"

"As of last night's newscast," confirmed Vinny. "Bound, gagged, single shot to the head. I'm willing to bet that newscaster is getting a video as we speak."

Trace knew he was right. *Dammit!* "I'll let Eldridge know." She walked toward the door then added, "*If* he sends a video." She was determined to get a little bit of investigating in on this before handing over her third straight case to Eldridge. She had over ten years logged in the detective squad, Eldridge was definitely her junior, and part of her resented giving up interesting cases to him, but she had to admit the kid had skills. *I'll probably be reporting to him someday.* Though she called him kid, he was only a few years younger than her. She had started on the force straight out of high school, but she had heard through the grapevine Eldridge hadn't joined until almost twenty-five, after a stint in the army. An image of him popped in her head, standing in front of her in combat boots. And nothing else. She chuckled.

"What's so funny?" asked Vinny.

"Oh, nothing."

Jesse and Martha Rochester were hard working parents that had failed. They admitted it to themselves privately, then they had to admit it to the nation publicly, after their son, Logan, had videotaped the murder on the subway. Jesse had kicked Logan out the same day he found out about the video. They had tried their best, but Logan had fallen in with the wrong crowd and was out of control. In a last desperate attempt to save their son they planned on moving from the city, hoping against hope removing him from this destructive environment might turn him around.

Then the subway incident happened. And Jesse had had enough. Martha at first protested but even she came around to supporting his decision after seeing the reaction to their son's heartless act. They had almost separated but eventually pulled through for the sake of their other child, thirteen year old Hope. Hit hard by the scandal as well, she now seemed to be coping. Jesse and Martha both prayed every night Hope wouldn't lose her way like Logan had.

The upcoming trial had brought the events of a year ago back into the forefront, but this time they weren't granting any interviews. As far as they were concerned, this was behind them. But then the news of their son's murder nearly tore them apart again. Having sworn off watching the news on television, they hadn't seen the murder of their son televised as if it were entertainment, instead, a police officer on their doorstep broke the news. Martha had collapsed in the doorway, screaming, Jesse, who had long ago thought he had buried his feelings for his son, fought hard to keep from breaking down, but it was of no use. He still loved his son, no matter how much he had disappointed him. And now he was dead because he had kicked him out.

But apparently that wasn't true. If this Detective Eldridge was right, Logan was targeted and there was nothing he could have done to prevent his son's death. It was of little comfort now, his son still gone, but perhaps someday, it may prove more.

"I'm sure your son received many threats after the incident," Eldridge said. "Did any in particular stick in your mind?"

"There were so many, it was overwhelming," remembered Martha. "There were phone calls, letters, things left at our doorstep." She shuddered at the memories. "It was terrifying."

"And it lasted for months," continued Jesse.

"Has there been anything recent?"

Jesse nodded and pointed to several file boxes stacked in the hallway. "A few. When you called I brought these up from the basement. They're all the threats we got. You can take them, we don't want them in the house anymore."

Eldridge rose and opened the top-most box, revealing letters, printouts of emails and more. He picked up a piece of paper from the top and unfolded it. In large capital letters was typed, "The day of judgment is coming!"

"That pretty much sets the tone," said Jesse, looking at the paper Eldridge was holding. "Take it and do what you want with it, we just want to be left alone."

Eldridge closed the box and reached into his pocket, pulling out a folded piece of paper. "I think there's something you need to see." He handed the paper to Jesse.

"What's this?" Jesse unfolded the page. Martha leaned over to read it with him, her hand immediately darting to her mouth to stifle a cry as they read the beginning of a letter from their son asking to come home.

Eldridge picked up the three boxes and left without saying anything, not wanting to interrupt the couple as they held each other, sobbing. As he loaded the boxes into the trunk of his car, another photo from the lab arrived, showing a woman he didn't recognize. *Yet.*

Chelsie explored her dungeon systematically, tapping every cinder block, kicking every square inch of the dirt walls, searching for a weakness. So far her efforts had yielded sore knuckles and toes, along with the taste of vomit in her mouth from when she found the scratches in the dirt walls. She turned her attention to the floor to make sure there was nothing she might use embedded in it, when she heard the chain rattle overhead, signaling the lowering of the platform she now stood directly under. She looked up and froze. *There's something written there!* It was hard to make out, the writing only slightly darker than the wood it was written on. She stretched as far as her toes would take her, straining her neck to read the words, but the light flickered out, frustrating her attempt. The platform inched lower, shafts of light from above cut through the black ink surrounding her, the bottom of the descending platform, bathed in total darkness, concealed its secret, its rectangular shape like the forbidden page of some great text, forever hidden, silhouetted against the intense light from above.

She returned to her corner and waited for the platform to reach the floor, her customary offering, a bottle of water and sandwich, sat in the center. She removed them from the tray and scurried back, careful to not look up, too terrified of what she might see. The chain rattled and the platform began its slow rise toward the ceiling, soon leaving her once again in her pitch black dungeon. The light remained off for several minutes and she decided to eat, her ravenous hunger demanding attention. The light blazed back on as she chewed the last of her sandwich. She took a swig of her water and returned to look at the platform, still unable to read the faint letters. Staring at it, she tried to take it a letter at a time, sounding it out, when what was written suddenly became terrifyingly clear. *Food Drugged!* She ran to the hole in the floor and vomited.

The retching in her stomach eventually subsided. She wiped her face and used some of the precious water from her bottle to rinse out her mouth. Collapsing onto her mattress, she curled into a ball, processing this new information. She hadn't been the first person here. How many had been here before? He was drugging her. What was he doing to her while she was drugged? How many times had he drugged her? How long was she out when he drugged her? And most importantly, what had happened to the other person?

She got to her feet and looked at the message again. The writing appeared almost dark brown. She was pretty sure it was written in blood, and if it were, it meant whoever had left the message was most likely dead.

And she was determined to survive.

Aynslee sat on her couch, holding an icepack to the back of her head as she watched a TiVo recording of her earlier debut as a co-anchor. *Damn I look good!* She had already watched it three times and was preparing to watch it a fourth when she found herself wondering if Hayden had seen it. *Why am I so obsessed with this guy?* Picking up her phone, she dialed his number at the precinct, having decided earlier to not press charges against Tammera Coverdale's father. Prepared to leave a voice mail, she was shocked when he picked up the line.

"Detective Eldridge, Homicide."

She was at a loss for words. *You're an anchorwoman now, you don't get tongue-tied!* "Oh, hello, Detective, this is Aynslee, Aynslee Kai."

"Good evening, Miss Kai, how can I help you?" His voice rumbled through the phone, affecting her at the very core of her being. She tingled.

"I just wanted to let you know that I don't plan on pressing charges against Mr. Coverdale," she said, impressed with how smoothly she was able to get that out.

"I'll have him released immediately then."

"Good, ah, very good," said Aynslee. *You're losing it!* "Umm …"

"Was there anything else, Miss Kai?"

Yes! I think I have a crush on you! "No, nothing else. Oh, there was one thing. Did you happen to see the newscast tonight?" *You idiot! Why did you ask him that?*

"No, I did not," he replied. "Was there anything I need to know?"

Yeah, that I'm fifteen again. "No, just, well, it was my first time co-anchoring the show."

Aynslee waited, the silence becoming awkward.

"Congratulations, Miss Kai. If there isn't anything else, I have a lot of work to do."

"No, I was just calling to let you know about Mr. Coverdale," she paused, desperately searching for something witty to say. Instead, she said, "Have a nice night, Detective."

"Good night, Miss Kai."

Then the conversation was over. *What a disaster!* Aynslee decided she better go to bed before she found another way to make an ass of herself.

Chelsie had to know if the message was written in blood, but with no way to reach the platform while raised, she waited. Her plan was to wet her hand and rub it on the bottom of the platform when it was lowered, to see if the color changed, but she wasn't sure how to accomplish this. It would mean waiting until the last second, something she had never done. And what if her touching the platform caused it to sway? If he caught her standing under the platform, he may get suspicious and investigate. Whoever had written the message couldn't have picked a more ingenious place. Each time he lowered the platform to enter the basement, he himself hid the message from view. Only his victims would ever see it, and she couldn't risk him finding it. If there were to be others after her, it was only fair they benefit from the knowledge someone, most likely now dead, was able to leave behind.

She wasn't sure why she wanted to know if it was blood. Did it make a difference? If it was blood, dirt or marker for that matter, did it change the content of the message, did it change how she would use that knowledge?

No, but her curiosity demanded she find out. She searched for alternatives that wouldn't risk the message being discovered, and, eying the hole, strode over and bent down, cupping her hands and filling them with water. Carefully walking back toward the platform, she positioned herself under it, and, looking up, tossed the water toward the faint letters above. The water splashed across the platform's bottom and immediately dripped down. She jumped back as she remembered she wore a white blouse with no means to clean it if stained. Removing the blouse and placing it safely in the opposite corner, she repeated the process, this time standing directly under the platform and letting the drops fall onto her hands and arms. What appeared to be dark brown overhead, turned a pale red on her skin. She rushed to the hole in the floor and scrubbed herself, now convinced it was blood.

Eldridge sat at his desk, sorting through the threats, when Shakespeare wandered in.

"Watcha doin'?" asked Shakespeare as he sat down, peering across the desk at the several piles of papers spread out in front of his partner.

Eldridge looked up, surprised to see him. *Where's the donuts?* "Going through the threats Logan Rochester received after posting that video of the subway attack on the Internet."

Shakespeare nodded and cracked his knuckles as if limbering up for some strenuous activity. "Want some help?"

"Sure." Eldridge pointed to a box on the floor, hoping his surprise hadn't been too obvious. "Help yourself."

"Anything in particular we're looking for?" Shakespeare wheeled his chair closer to the boxes and leaned over to pick one up, his shirt escaping the confines of his too tight pants, revealing the top of an impressive plumber's butt. He picked up the topmost box and wheeled back behind his desk, dropping it at his feet.

"If the killer sent a threat, I doubt he would have sent just one. These attacks show obsession."

Shakespeare tucked his shirt back in, snapped on a pair of latex gloves from his desk drawer, and removed the top from the box. "Makes sense. Found anything so far?"

"Look at these." Eldridge handed him three sheets of paper, all from a computer printer, typed in a large font, in all caps. Shakespeare whistled. "The Rochester's dated each one as they received them," explained Eldridge. "You can see the dates on the back."

Shakespeare flipped them over and read them in order. *"The day of judgment is coming.* Sounds biblical," commented Shakespeare as he flipped to the second one. *"Your blood is on your own head, for your own mouth has testified against you."* Shakespeare compared the first two pages. "Definitely look like they came from the same person."

Eldridge agreed. "Seems to be the same font used, anyway, and it seems to be unique amongst what I've seen so far, all very selective quotes from the bible."

Shakespeare held up the third one, dated three months ago. *"The Lord examines the righteous, but the wicked and those who love violence his soul hates!* Definitely seems like an escalation." He flipped through the box in front of him, looking for additional matches. The two detectives worked in silence for almost an hour before Shakespeare stopped. "Look at this." He held up another page and read, *"Your hands are stained with blood, your fingers with guilt."*

Eldridge took the page and compared the fonts. Turning it over, he looked at the date. "About a month ago." The two men dug through their boxes, looking for any more matches when Eldridge smiled in triumph. "Look! *Even now the ax of God's judgment is poised, ready to sever your roots."*

Shakespeare leaned back in his chair. "Definitely sounds like our guy."

Eldridge took the five sheets of paper and placed them in a large Ziploc bag from his desk. "I'm going to take these to Vinny and see if he can find out anything."

"Say hi to that whop bastard for me," said Shakespeare as he bent back down and continued searching the box.

Eldridge smiled. "Yeah, I'll be sure to." He found Vinny in the autopsy room with the coroner, Miles Jenkins, taking prints off a bloated corpse. "Hey, Vinny, another floater?"

Vinny grunted as he manipulated the corpse's left hand. "Be with you in a second, Detective," he said. "I just need to finish with our Jane Doe here."

"Where'd you find her?"

"The Hudson," replied Jenkins. "Some kids found her yesterday."

"How long had she been in there?"

"At least a couple of days. I'll know more when I'm done my examination."

Vinny stretched his back and winced.

"Back acting up again?" asked Eldridge.

Vinny nodded. "Yeah, damned thing'll never be the same."

"You got shot in the back," said Jenkins. "You're lucky to be alive so quit your bitchin' and get outta here. I've got work to do."

"Love you too, Miles," said Vinny as he blew him a kiss. Eldridge followed him back to the lab. "What can I do for you, Detective?"

"Shakespeare and I found some death threats sent to one of my vics that I need you to take a look at." Eldridge handed the envelope to Vinny. "Prints, trace, anything that might give me a clue as to where these came from."

"You *and* Shakespeare? You're telling me that waste of space did some real, honest to goodness police work today?"

Eldridge chuckled. "And he sends his love."

"The only love he'll feel is my fist up his—"

"Thanks, Vin," called Eldridge as he left the lab, "let me know as soon as you have something for me." Eldridge closed the door, cutting off Vinny's tirade.

Aynslee sat in the editing booth, her back to the door, spinning the control back and forth absentmindedly, the same footage racing forward, then back, with each flick of the dial. She heard a knock then the opening of the door.

Not Reggie again!

"Excuse me, I'm looking for Miss Kai?"

Aynslee smiled and spun around, immediately recognizing Hayden's voice. "Well hello, Detective." *Was that the start of a smile I saw?*

"Ah, sorry, Miss Kai, I didn't recognize you."

She flipped her hair with her hand. "You like?"

He nodded, any trace of a smile, if there had ever been one, nowhere to be seen. "It looks fine. You have a new video?"

I can't win. "Yup." She replayed the video and winced when the shot was fired. The fact she wasn't shocked at all by the latest video left Aynslee feeling ashamed. She had immediately called Hayden and her producer to let them know, then headed to the office to do a morning newscast followed by a couple of morning talk shows, the story now the talk of the nation, speculation running rampant as to what the connection between the victims might be, the fact two of them hadn't been identified publicly by the police only fueled the frenzy. "He was about to say something there at the end," said Aynslee. "And who is this *she* that she's talking about?"

"I have no idea," he replied. "Do you have a copy ready for me?"

Aynslee nodded and picked a CD up off the desk. Rather than handing it over however, she leaned closer to him, holding the CD between two fingers over her right shoulder. "So you like my hair?" she asked in a playful tone, not believing how bold she felt, but sure she had picked up a vibe from him when he first saw her.

He looked at her then reached out and took the CD. "Thank you, Miss Kai," he said, smiling from one side of his mouth.

Aynslee, a grin on her face, watched as he walked from the editing room. *Oh yeah, he liked it.*

Chelsie lay on her mattress, her eyes closed, her breathing steady, as steady as she could manage. She was wide awake, having decided not to eat any more food, a decision that terrified her. She had no idea what he did to her when she slept, though she was pretty sure he hadn't raped her. Yet. In fact, she was convinced he had only used the opportunity to clean the room, install the light and leave the mattress. But if he was going to rape her, did she want to know? The debate had raged in her head for some time, and eventually she decided her only opportunity for escape was to use this new knowledge to her advantage. And so she took the sandwich, stuffed it in the water hole, and lay down on the mattress, pretending to sleep.

It had been about an hour, or so she guessed, before she heard the familiar sounds overhead. Her heart insisted on pounding like a drum as the platform lowered toward her. She tried to control her breathing, to keep up her charade. If he discovered she was awake, what he might do to her terrified her. The rattling of the chains and creaking of the platform stopped. This time was different however. This time she heard something she hadn't heard yet. Something that had her clenching her teeth to hold back the scream threatening to erupt from within.

Footsteps.

Footsteps on the dirt floor, his shoes softly padding toward her. She could tell he was now standing over her, only inches away. Her heart thumped harder, the sound of terror rushed through her ears, the scream she knew might end her life only moments away from bursting forth. Desperate to take a deep breath, to calm her out of control nerves, she faked a yawn, drawing in a deep breath and letting it out slowly, doing her best to fake sleep, something she hadn't done since she was a child. It hadn't worked then, her mother always able to tell, but this time was different. He appeared fooled, most likely because he was fully expecting her to be drugged. She continued her deep breathing, regaining control enough to hopefully survive whatever was to come.

She felt him pick up her handcuffed wrist, then a clicking sound was followed by the feeling of the metal cuff being removed, her hand freed for the first time since she had been taken. It felt strange, almost light, as if he didn't continue to hold it, it might escape on its own. She felt his arms slide under her then pick her up. A few steps and he lay her back down on a hard surface that could only be the platform. The sound of the chain as it was pulled, followed by the feeling of the ground swaying, confirmed her suspicions. After almost a minute the platform stopped moving and he lifted her again, the ease with which he carried her suggesting whoever her captor was, he was strong. A sensation of bobbing up and down, along with heavy footsteps on a wood floor, convinced her they were climbing a set of stairs, followed by a hallway, the closed in sound of his footsteps changing as he made a turn, replaced with the sensation of a larger area, most likely a room, her belief confirmed when he placed her on what must be a bed.

A switch clicked to her left and her eyelids glowed pink from a light now turned on in the room. Creaking floorboards gave away the location of her captor as he walked about, then, to her horror, the bed shook as he climbed on it with her. *Oh no! Oh no!* He began by unbuttoning her pants then unzipping the fly. Pulling them off, he positioned himself behind her and lifted her back off the mattress. He reached around and pulled her top off over her head, removed her bra and gently laid her back down. He finished with her socks and panties.

She wanted to scream, her heart raced out of control. She knew what was coming. *Why didn't I eat the food? Oh please, God, please, don't let this happen.* The bed shook again as he climbed off, then his footsteps faded from earshot. Terrified, she didn't dare open her eyes to look. The creak of the stairs confirmed he was definitely gone, but still she couldn't bring herself to open her eyes. A few minutes later she heard him return. The thunderous beat of her heart filled her ears as he picked her up and carried her to another room. As he lowered her she was shocked by a strange sensation she at first couldn't place. *Water!* The warm liquid enveloped her body, helping calm her down slightly. *Surely he's not going to rape me in here?*

She heard him pick up something, then splashing, the water lapping against her breasts as whatever he did disturbed the surface. Struggling to maintain her unconscious façade, she almost yelped when he took her by the wrist and washed her with what felt like a sponge. Gently he scrubbed her arm, raising it over her head to reach her armpit, then down her side.

He started to hum.

And she tried not to gag.

She had had a sponge bath once before, her first boyfriend after high school had given her one, the experience of having a lover bathe her so erotic, he wasn't able to finish, her level of arousal demanding she pull him into the tub with her. The excitement of the unique situation, rather than the boy, still gave her goose bumps.

But this was nothing like that.

It was everything she could do not to throw up. She willed herself to take slow, steady breaths as he washed her breasts then moved to her other arm. When he washed her left leg she braced herself for what she knew was about to happen. Biting the inside of her cheek, she almost let out a yelp when he began to wash between her legs. She thanked God he didn't stay there long. He seemed intent on cleaning her; she sensed nothing sexual about this. When he moved onto her other leg she relaxed, realizing the worst was over.

Clanging noises were followed by the sound of running water from a shower attachment as it sprayed in the tub, then on her head and back as he rinsed her hair. After a minute the water turned off and she heard the sound of a shampoo bottle spurting, then his hands softly worked the shampoo into a lather in her hair. She had always enjoyed having her hair washed at the hairdresser's, and for a moment forgot where she was.

Then he started to hum again.

And the moment of pleasure was shoved aside as the stark reality of where she was and who was doing this to her returned. A moment of disgust with herself quickly turned. *He's pathetic!* Finished lathering her hair, he rinsed it thoroughly then removed her from the tub and carried her to the bed. He toweled her off, starting on her left arm. After finishing with her torso he raised one of her legs in the air and placed it on what she thought might be his shoulder, rubbing her skin dry, the towel inching toward her vagina.

She flinched.

And he stopped.

She held her breath for a second then thought that might tip him off. *Slow, steady breaths, slow steady breaths.*

But still he did nothing.

Oh, God, he knows! An idea sprung into her head. She flinched again, this time on purpose. She waited. Would he buy it? A fake flinch when he's doing nothing?

The humming resumed and so did the drying. She breathed a sigh of relief. In her head. He towel dried her hair then placed her in a sitting position, her legs dangling over the bedside, his hand firmly in the center of her back. He blow-dried her hair for several minutes and when done, positioned himself behind her, his legs wrapped around her waist, his groin pressed against her as he combed her hair. He hummed again, but this time gyrated his pelvis slowly into her back.

I'm going to be sick.

But that was all he did. After a few minutes, he lay her back down on the bed then left the room, the floor creaking as he made his way down the hallway. Emboldened by the knowledge he would be gone for a few minutes, she opened her eyes a sliver as she waited to hear the stairs creak. The glare from the lamps in the room blinded her for a moment, but she soon confirmed she was in a bedroom, lying on the left side of a four-poster bed, a door to her left, in the far corner, led to the hallway, and to her right, a window, thick with curtains blocking out any light or sounds from the outside. On the nightstand sat a pewter framed photo. She peered at it closer.

A creak from the doorway tore through the silence of the room. *He didn't go downstairs!* She snapped her eyes shut, thanking God her head faced away from the door. She listened as he approached then climbed on the bed with her. Something slid up her legs, and after a few seconds of uncertainty, she determined it was a pair of panties. He finished dressing her, the swiftness with which he was able to manipulate her limp body suggested he was well practiced. The ritual complete, he carried her downstairs and returned her to her basement prison. He placed her on the mattress and snapped the handcuff over her wrist. *It's almost over!*

Something warm, soft, and slightly moist pressed against her lips. *He's kissing me!* Panic set in as she realized she was about to get raped.

"Goodnight, my darling."

Then he left her.

"Listen you son-of-a-bitch, I don't know what you got me into, but I don't want any part of it!" Messina was in a panic. He hadn't slept all night and when he received another call back, he raced from the dinner table and into the garage. Lowering his voice, he continued, "I need to know, did you have anything to do with what happened at the hospital?"

"I think we should meet to discuss this."

The calm tone raised the hairs on the back of his neck. "What's there to discuss? Either you did or you didn't!"

"Let's meet for coffee and we can talk about it."

"The fact that you won't answer me tells me all I need to know," said Messina in a harsh whisper. "All I wanted was for you to cover a few calls for me while I dealt with my wife! I thought I was doing you a favor and now you've got me mixed up in some murder investigation!" Messina took a deep breath. "I'm calling the cops."

He hung up the phone and fished the detective's card from his wallet. He dialed and the call went to voicemail. He tried to calm himself, waiting for the tone. "Detective Eldridge, this is Chris Messina, from NerdTech, we spoke the other day." Messina trembled. "I need to talk to you about the hospital. I think I may know who did it. Please call me as soon as you get this message." He took a deep breath, then added, "I'm scared he might do something to me or my family."

Messina hung up the phone and sat on the step leading to the mudroom. *What am I going to do?* He took deep breaths, trying to calm himself before returning to the dinner table, not sure how he would explain the situation to his wife. A knock at the garage door startled him, setting his heart racing again. *Who could that be?* Again the knock, gentle but persistent. Messina rose and pressed the garage door opener on the wall. The door rose, revealing a pair of feet followed by the rest of the body. When he saw the face he nearly fainted.

"Greedo, we need to talk."

EIGHT

Aynslee knocked on the apartment door, glancing at her surroundings. The one light not stolen or broken, dimly lit the far end of the hallway, the rest swallowed in near darkness, thankfully hiding most of the filth the squalid building had an overabundance of. She nodded to her sound engineer Mike, and her cameraman, Steve, who flicked the light on his camera, bathing the entire area in a bright, white. "Ugh." Aynslee couldn't help it. She was pretty sure the dark mass near the door was feces. Garbage, needles and empty liquor bottles were strewn about the hall, the door she now faced, its chipped paint covered in grime and graffiti, sadly representing the home of a hardworking family man. A hardworking family man who would never cross its threshold again.

It had taken a fair amount of sleuthing to piece together Ibrahim Jamar's story. And a lot of charm tossed around the hospital. A little flirting with a file clerk and she had the wife's name and address, and a friend at the Transit Authority confirmed both Rafi and Ibrahim Jamar were cab drivers. She knocked on the door again, preparing herself for a rough experience. She never liked ambushing someone like this, but she had no other way to reach Fatima Jamar as they appeared to have no phone. They heard a scraping sound then something bump against the door. The sound of a chain being unhooked was followed again by the scraping sound. When the door opened, a little black girl, maybe eight years old, stood there, a chair she had used to reach the lock, beside her. Aynslee, caught off guard, didn't know what to say at first but quickly recovered. "Hello, what's your name?"

"Amina."

"Well hello, Amina. My name is Aynslee. Is your mother home?"

The little girl nodded but didn't move.

"Can I come in and speak to her?"

157

Again she nodded, but this time opened the door and stepped back into the apartment. "Amina, is someone at the door?" a voice called from the back of the apartment. Steve directed the camera toward the voice while Mike held out the boom. Aynslee stepped deeper into the apartment toward the room where the voice originated.

When Fatima Jamar entered the apartment hallway, she grabbed at her chest with one hand, the door frame with the other, steadying herself after the shock of discovering three strangers with a camera standing in her entranceway. Aynslee decided to press her advantage now that they were in the apartment. "Ma'am, my name is Aynslee Kai, WACX News. I'd like to ask you a few questions about your husband, Ibrahim Jamar."

It took only a moment for Fatima to recover. "Get out of my house!" She stormed toward them, shooing at them with her hands. "Get out!"

Steve and Mike backed away but Aynslee stood her ground, accustomed to irate celebrities facing her down. "Ma'am, I just want to know about the DVD player, what was on it?"

This stopped Fatima. "The DVD, how did you know about that?"

"Your cousin, Rafi, told me."

"Rafi, that dog, he is always trying to get my Ibrahim in trouble!"

"Why would Ibrahim get in trouble, ma'am? What was on the DVD?"

Fatima's jaw set, her glare, like daggers, signaled the end of the interview. "Out! I won't let you ruin his reputation! He couldn't have helped that girl, no one could have. Out!" This time she physically pushed Aynslee, sending her stumbling backward. Steve caught her by the arm before she fell, and the three backed out of the apartment, the door slamming behind them.

"What the hell was on that DVD?" asked Mike.

"I don't know, but definitely something she doesn't want anyone to know about." Aynslee removed the wireless mike from her collar and handed it to Steve. "But I know who would know." Pulling out her BlackBerry, she began to dial when Mike stopped her.

"Aynslee, we've got to get back to the studio, now. You go on in less than an hour." Aynslee looked at her watch and nodded.

"Fine, I'll call him later. We've got enough to go on for now."

Eldridge ran to his desk and grabbed the phone. Trace sat in Shakespeare's chair, looking frustrated. She opened her mouth to speak, but he raised a finger and cut her off.

"Eldridge."

"Detective, it's Vinny, I've got those results you wanted."

Eldridge hoped for a break, but Vinny's tone already told him everything he needed to know. "Go ahead."

"I'm afraid I've come up with nothing. No usable prints or fibers, it's a common font on common paper printed by a common printer."

Eldridge sighed. "Yeah, I was afraid of that. Thanks anyway, Vin."

"No problem. Oh, and tell that no good—"

Eldridge hung up and eyed the pulsing red light on his phone. He looked at Trace. She scowled. *Better not.* "What's up, Amber?"

Trace tossed a folder over to him. "Yet another one of my cases ends up being yours."

"You're kidding me!" He flipped through the file on the murder of Abigail Teague. When he reached the crime scene photos he nodded, immediately recognizing the woman as not only the latest victim, but also the latest witness emailed to his phone. "Yup, this is definitely the victim from the last video. Any leads?"

"One, but it's thin right now." Trace stood and leaned over the desk, flipping the file to a page near the back containing a witness statement. "Just before the shot was heard by a neighbor, she was at her Karate class. I interviewed some of her classmates and instructors and they said they saw her leaving with a new student."

"But?" Eldridge knew from her voice there was going to be a but. This case seemed to always have a but.

"*But*, he was a walk-in for a free introductory lesson. The name and address on the sign-up sheet were bogus. A Bruce Samson."

"Samson?"

"Yeah, mean anything?"

"And Samson said to them, 'Since you've acted like this, I won't stop until I get my revenge on you.'"

"Huh?"

"The bible, Book of Judges. Might mean nothing, might mean everything."

"A religious nut-bar?"

"Perhaps. There hasn't been any type of religious element to any of the killings that we've seen, but some threats we found against Logan Rochester were all quotes from the bible. Vengeance and judgment type stuff."

"Maybe he thinks they're all sinners?"

"Could be. Right now my best lead is this Messina character from NerdTech. I'm positive he's hiding something."

Trace stood and yawned. "I've got a missing persons case I'm working on so I'll see you later. Good luck!"

Eldridge nodded and dialed into the voicemail system, listening to the message from Messina. He snatched the NerdTech personnel record and ran to his car, determined not to give Messina a chance to change his mind.

Trace sat at her desk, the first file from a large stack opened in front of her, all missing persons over the past ten years, a photo at Chelsie's apartment having tweaked a vague memory. She was acting on a hunch, a hunch she hoped would be proven wrong. *Brunette.* She flipped the file closed and moved it aside, taking the next one off the stack. *Red head.* It wasn't until the sixth file she found what she was looking for. A young woman with long, blonde hair, missing for six months. *Merissa Gordon.* She set the file aside and continued through the stack, half an hour later finding another blonde with long hair, mid-twenties. *Kara McPhee.* Her sense of foreboding grew as she searched the files, finding more and more women matching many older photos of Chelsie, but not the most recent. According to her mother, Chelsie had changed her hair, but if she was a stalking victim, the initial attraction might be to the older style—long, straight blonde hair, teased up in the front.

She looked at the stack of files in front of her and shook her head. Almost a dozen young, blonde women, with the same hairstyle, all missing and never found, stretching back for years. *If this is a serial killer, then the L.T. will want to bring in the FBI and I'll lose another case.* She was damned if she was going to lose this one, and besides, no one had ever suggested a serial killer was targeting young blondes in the city. If she had looked through the pile for old brunettes she probably would have found just as many.

But her gut was telling her different.

And she always went with her gut.

Eldridge turned on to Messina's street on Staten Island, almost two hours after the message had been originally left. He knew he shouldn't have been surprised when he saw the flashing lights. *Dammit!* He slammed his fist into the steering wheel then parked behind one of several squad cars already on the scene. Two paramedics nearby packed their gear, their leaving empty handed speaking volumes. He headed toward the garage where most of the action appeared to be taking place when someone called his name. Looking over his shoulder, he saw Vinny pulling up in the crime scene van, waving to him out the window. Eldridge raised his hand in acknowledgement and entered the garage. Two uniforms watched over the scene, making sure nothing was disturbed. The Patrol Supervisor nodded, waving him through as he recorded his name in the scene log.

Messina lay in a pool of his own blood, a look of shock frozen on his face. Kneeling down, Eldridge examined the body. A small hole in the forehead indicated where the bullet had entered, the source of blood the larger exit wound at the back of his head. Eldridge had seen enough bullet wounds to know this was probably going to be a match to the other shootings. *Another life, and another lead, dead.*

"Detective, we've gotta stop meeting like this."

Eldridge didn't look up. "Then we'd be out of jobs, my friend."

"The day I can hang up my hat due to lack of business is the day I'd be happy to be unemployed."

"Amen to that." Eldridge leaned in over Messina's pants and pointed at his knees. "What do you make of that?"

Vinny looked. "Dirt?"

"Looks like it, maybe he was on his knees when he was shot?"

"Could be," agreed Vinny. "I'll be able to tell you for sure when I examine the angle of the wound, but judging from that spray pattern, I'd say he was definitely shot from a downward trajectory."

"Executed."

"Yup."

"Not like the others. The others were always tied up, made to suffer in some way. This guy was executed, not humiliated or tortured."

"Others? This linked to that case of yours?"

"Yeah, he was basically my only lead." Eldridge stood and examined the garage. The standard items most garages had, bikes, rakes, garbage cans and the other sundries required to maintain a home, were fairly well organized, most on hooks or racks. Careful not to disturb anything, he made his way around the garage. He reached the entrance and looked up, something catching his eye. *What the hell is that?* He stepped closer, and, realizing what it was, kept walking under it and past, as if to look at something else. Once past the object, he motioned to Vinny to join him. Vinny was about to say something when Eldridge raised a finger over his mouth then pointed up.

Nestled on top of a rafter in the garage sat a small round object, a red light blinking on it. "It's a fucking webcam!" hissed Vinny. "The son-of-a-bitch is watching us right now!" Eldridge nodded and motioned to Vinny to follow him into the yard and around to the side of the garage, out of the camera's sight.

"He must be transmitting the signal wirelessly," whispered Eldridge.

Vinny nodded. "That means he's probably close." They both looked around. Dozens of vehicles lined the street in each direction. "The range is probably a few hundred feet. He must be in one of the parked vehicles."

Eldridge whipped out his cell phone and called the tech lab. Frank answered. "Frank, it's Eldridge. Can you track somebody receiving a wireless webcam signal?"

"Huh? You mean a Wi-Fi cam?"

"I haven't a clue. I've got what looks like a wireless webcam broadcasting my crime scene."

"Holy shit, Detective! He must be close, the range on those is like nothing, maybe a thousand feet on a good day!"

"Exactly! I've got a multiple murderer probably within a few hundred feet of me but I've also got a dozen houses and even more cars. Now, can you track him?"

"I'm on my way!"

Eldridge flipped his phone closed and turned back to Vinny. "Okay, we need to let everybody know, we don't want somebody discovering it by accident."

"Okay, I'll go back in there and take my time, give him a real good show. You spread the word."

"Detective." Vinny's whisper barely registered. Eldridge looked at him without moving his head. Vinny pointed out the garage door with his eyes, all the while continuing to dust for prints. Eldridge followed his gaze and saw Frank walking up the driveway and past the garage, heading toward the front entrance.

"I think it's time to talk to the victim's wife," announced Eldridge, full volume.

"I'll come with you," said Vinny. "I need to get her prints for elimination purposes."

Vinny and Eldridge entered the house through the garage entrance and found Frank slowly turning in a circle, a handheld computer and a small device with two antennas connected to it held out in front of him. Vinny and Eldridge waited for him to complete his slow spin.

"Jesus Christ, kid, I coulda searched each car myself by now!" exclaimed Vinny, exasperated. Eldridge placed his hand on Vinny's arm and gave him a look. *Patience!* Vinny frowned but didn't say a word.

"Okay, I have sixteen distinct Wi-Fi signals in the area," Frank said.

"Can that thing tell where they're coming from?"

"Not really, but I can tell you when one gets stronger."

Eldridge jumped in before Vinny could say something. "Will you be able to tell if there's one in a car parked outside?"

Frank nodded. "If I walk down the street, one of the signals should spike near the car receiving the webcam feed."

"Well then let's go!" Vinny headed for the door with Eldridge and Frank following. "And try to not make it too obvious!" he said, looking at Frank as he held out the device, waving it about. Frank shot him a look but lowered the device and brought it closer to his chest. The three men exited the house, Eldridge and Vinny walking shoulder-to-shoulder in front of Frank as they strode down the walkway toward the street.

"I've got a strong signal to our right," whispered Frank.

"So, when is that bag of excess flesh retiring?" asked Vinny, turning right, onto the sidewalk.

Eldridge laughed with a little more drama than he intended. "Not too long from now I understand."

"Won't come soon enough. The less deadbeats like him on the force the better. My Granddaddy always said if you're good for nothin', you're nothin' good."

"It's getting stronger!" Frank's excited whisper wasn't acknowledged.

"Sounds like you had a wise Grandfather."

"Old stock, came across the ocean and landed right here in this city and never left his entire life."

"I think we're close, Detective. Maybe fifty feet." Frank's voice revealed his excitement.

Settle down, kid! "I'm sixth generation myself," said Eldridge as he casually looked about.

"Sixth?"

"Yup. Family came over from England, settled in Maine then my grandparents on my father's side moved here. I still live in the family house as a matter of fact."

"Really?"

Eldridge watched Frank gesture with his chin out of the corner of his eye. *Don't blow it!*

"It has to be one of these cars just ahead."

"Yeah, inherited from my folks after they died."

"How'd they—look!" Vinny yelled. A van three cars down pulled out into the street and sped off. Vinny gave chase on foot as Eldridge raced back toward his car, yelling at the officers, "Stop that van!" One, leaning on his squad car, immediately took off in pursuit. Another sprinted to his cruiser and jumped in at the same time Eldridge leapt into the passenger seat. The officer jammed the accelerator to the floor and the car surged out into the street after the other cruiser. As they sped by Frank, Eldridge noticed him still looking intently at his computer. It took only seconds to catch up to the other squad car that had cut in front of the van, blocking its path. The other officer, already out of his cruiser, pointed his weapon at the van. Eldridge's car squealed to a halt and both he and the officer jumped out, drawing their weapons.

Eldridge reached in and pulled the mike off the dash, flipping the knob to the public address system on the car's roof. "Occupant of the vehicle, turn off your engine and drop the keys out the window." The van idled for a few seconds then the engine stopped. The window inched down and a set of keys dropped onto the road. "Now let me see both your hands out the window!" A pair of hands dutifully appeared. *What the hell?* Eldridge looked at the hands. Then the arms. Arms covered in a pink blouse. He slowly circled around for a better angle on the driver. It was a terrified young woman.

Suddenly he heard two shots ring out from behind him.

Vinny heard the two shots and spun around to see Frank flying backward and an SUV peeling onto the street, pulling a u-turn. Sprinting toward Frank, he pulled his weapon and began firing at the fleeing vehicle, several shots hitting the back, shattering the rear window. It swerved from side to side a couple of times before turning left and out of sight. Vinny reached Frank and dropped to his knees at Frank's side. He couldn't see any blood but there were two clear holes in his shirt. "Jesus Christ, kid!" yelled Vinny. "Please tell me …" He ripped open Frank's jacket and breathed a sigh of relief at what he saw—two bullets embedded in a Kevlar vest. Ripping the Velcro clasps, he removed the vest to see if the bullets had penetrated. Suddenly Frank gasped and coughed. He winced in pain. "Take it easy, kid," said Vinny gently.

"Wh-what happened?"

"You were shot, kid." Vinny looked at the shirt under the vest and saw the bullets hadn't penetrated. "Your vest caught the bullets, you'll be okay." Vinny sat down on the ground beside Frank. "Your ribs'll be sore for a few weeks, though." They both looked up as Eldridge arrived, having sprinted all the way from the take-down.

"What the hell happened?"

"The kid's been shot twice in the vest. The bastard was in an SUV, literally two vehicles down from where that van pulled out. I got a few shots off, hit the rear window, but couldn't get a plate."

Another officer ran up to them. "Sir, they found the vehicle just a few blocks from here abandoned!"

"Any sign of the shooter?"

"No, sir, no sign of him but they're searching."

Eldridge nodded as he and Vinny helped Frank to his feet. "Tell us what happened," said Eldridge.

Frank took a few tentative steps on his own, slowly regaining his composure. "As soon as the van took off I knew it wasn't the right vehicle—the signal didn't get weaker, so I kept going, figured out it was the SUV and that's when I got shot."

"Did you see the shooter?"

"I saw the shots, that's it. I'm sorry, Detective, I should have been more careful."

Eldridge put his hand on Frank's back and gave his neck a gentle squeeze. "Don't worry, kid, you did good. You're alive and that's all that matters."

"I've got a question for you, kid," said Vinny. "Why the hell were you wearing a vest to a crime scene?"

Frank looked at him. "I'm a computer geek. I *never* get out of the lab. I'd have worn two if I could have found a second one."

Vinny laughed and slapped him on the back. Frank yelped in pain. "Sorry," said Vinny sheepishly. Turning to Eldridge, he said, "So, we've got nothing then."

"Not true," disagreed Eldridge. "We've got a vehicle to search and trace."

Vinny smiled. "Let me at it!"

As they neared the original crime scene an ambulance pulled up with several more squad cars. Eldridge handed Frank over to the paramedics then redirected the officers to help in the search and secure the now expanded crime scene. Vinny headed to the shooter's vehicle to process it, leaving the rest of his team to gather whatever evidence they could.

Eldridge entered the house to interview Messina's wife, who, in all the excitement over the webcam's discovery, he hadn't had time to speak with. He found her in the living room, hugging a child of about six. The wife's face appeared gaunt, almost anorexic, her cheek bones protruded through her skin, her head, devoid of all hair, seemed almost too large for her frail, emaciated frame, her skin, a pale grey, clung to her bones, her lips, thin and dry, were pursed, her right hand gripped the arm of the chair she sat in, determination holding her steadier than her weakened muscles could.

Eldridge was taken aback, not expecting this sight at all. "Mrs. Messina," said Eldridge softly, "I'm Detective Eldridge. May I ask you a few questions?" She nodded weakly. "Is there anything I can get you? Do you want me to get the paramedics?"

She shook her head. "No, there's nothing they can do."

Eldridge sat across from her, a concerned expression on his face. "Are you ill, Mrs. Messina?"

She nodded. "I'm terminal. My doctors say I won't see Christmas."

Eldridge's shoulders sagged. This was what he hated. The victim is always thought of as the person who died, but the real victims, the ones who have to now live with the death for the rest of their lives, were people like this. The poor little girl that probably wouldn't remember what her father looks like when she grows up. The dying wife who won't get to spend her last few days with her loving husband, left instead grieving his loss, knowing her daughter would soon be left all alone in the world. It broke Eldridge's heart. They were taught to not get involved personally, but sometimes he just couldn't help it, humanity had to enter the equation. "I'm sorry to hear that, ma'am. I truly am. I'll try to keep this brief." She managed a weak smile. "Did you see or hear anything that might help us?"

"No," she said, shaking her head. "I only heard the shot. I was too scared to go look, so I just called the police."

"I understand. Why was your husband in the garage?"

"He had a call on his cell and said he would take it outside so it wouldn't disturb me."

"Did he seem agitated in any way?"

She nodded. "As a matter of fact, he hasn't seemed himself for the past few days, something was bothering him. I asked him what it was but he just said it was work."

"Where were you last Tuesday?"

"Last Tuesday?" She scrunched her eyebrows. "I don't know, here probably."

"You weren't at a piano recital?"

"Oh, yes, that's right, I forgot." She hugged her daughter. "We went to see her class recital."

"I played Hot Cross Buns!" said the little girl, her voice filled with pride.

"That's one of my favorite songs!" said Eldridge, smiling at her. She buried her head into her mother's chest. Turning back to Mrs. Messina, he asked, "What time did it end?"

"Around ten, I think."

"And did you all return home?"

"Yes."

"Your husband didn't take a call from work?"

"No, he was off that night."

"So at no time on Tuesday evening did your husband leave you."

"No, he was with me all night," she said, her eyes drooping. "I'm sorry, Detective, but can we continue this tomorrow? I'm exhausted."

Eldridge rose. "Of course, ma'am. The crime scene unit will still be here and I'll be leaving an officer outside overnight. Is there anywhere you can stay? It could be busy in here for a while."

A determined expression crossed her face. "No, I only have a few months to live, and I'm spending every moment of it I can in my home."

"I completely understand," said Eldridge, admiring the strength she had. "If you need anything, don't hesitate to ask any of the officers. And here's my card, you can call me at any time as well." She took the card and thanked him.

Eldridge left the Messina residence and called Vinny. "Anything for me?"

"Nothing yet. The SUV was registered to Chris Messina so that's a dead end. I'm taking it to my lab to give it a thorough going over, see if we can get anything."

"Okay, keep me posted." Eldridge flipped his phone closed and walked over to Frank who had just finished with the paramedics. "How you feeling, kid?"

Frank grinned. "Pretty good, amazingly enough. Ribs are a little tender, but seeing how I should be dead, I'm feeling great!"

"You got damned lucky."

"Yeah, you're right," agreed Frank. "Listen, I'm heading back to the lab to see if any of those photos are finished, I just have three more."

Eldridge shook his head. "No, you go home, they'll be there tomorrow." He helped Frank into his car then turned back to his own when his phone rang. "Eldridge."

"Hello, Detective, this is Aynslee Kai. Just wondering if you had any comment on a story I'm running tonight, about a DVD player that was found at the hospital explosion?"

Eldridge was impressed with how she managed to keep finding out things that hadn't been released to the public. But then just as his job was investigating, so was hers. "I'm sorry, Miss Kai, but I can't comment on that."

"So there was a DVD player?"

Eldridge couldn't believe he had fallen in the trap of confirming a rumor. "Sorry, but I can't confirm or deny that there was a DVD player."

"Uh huh. Sounds like a 'yes' to me." He could almost hear her smiling over the phone. "Since we both know there was a DVD player there, can you tell me what was on it?"

"I'm sorry, Miss Kai, you'll have to ask your source that. Good night."

Hanging up the phone he chuckled to himself. *She might have this thing solved before I do.*

Chelsie remained lying on her mattress, too terrified to move, not knowing how long the drug should take to wear off. Eventually she drifted off to sleep, but not before noticing she wore different clothes than when she was originally taken. When she woke, it was to the sound of the platform lowering. She took the food and water and stood back as the platform rose to the ceiling. Sealed in once again, her light flickered on, and she shoved the sandwich into the hole and drank her water. Eventually she would have to eat, but in the meantime she would make every effort to gather whatever information she could about her prison in the hopes something might allow her to escape.

She guessed about an hour had gone by when once again she heard the platform lower. Her eyes shut, she pretended to be asleep, and, as he did the night before, he carried her to the platform and eventually to the bedroom. This time however she wasn't undressed. Instead, he held her right hand out and gently gripped her pinky finger. Her nail was squeezed and she heard a clicking sound. *He's cutting my nails!* Again he hummed the same tune from the night before, the tune vaguely familiar but something she couldn't place. It didn't take long for him to clip all of her fingernails short. The experience was vile. Not able to see what was happening as her nails were cut off one by one, she resisted the urge to squirm. But it was the incessant humming that threatened to drive her crazy. When he moved to her feet it proved almost too much. She didn't like anybody touching her feet, and having her abductor touch them was beyond uncomfortable.

She flinched.

She couldn't help it; her feet were just too sensitive. The humming stopped and she immediately flinched again, remembering how it had worked last time. He resumed his humming and she flinched as needed, her tension slightly relieved. By the time he finished, water boarding sounded good to her. He pushed her socks back on and carried her into what she knew was the bathroom. Placing her in a chair, he tilted her head back into a sink and then turned the tap on. Within minutes her long hair was wet. He towel-dried it then she heard him open a tube of something and begin to work it into her hair. At first she thought it was shampoo, but when the pungent, nostril searing odor of peroxide reached her nose, she realized what was happening. *He's dying my hair!*

NINE

Eldridge entered Vinny's lab and found him processing what looked like fiber evidence, hopefully from last night's fiasco. He had messages from both Vinny and Frank when he arrived, and now that his best lead was dead, he was desperate for fresh ones.

"Hey, Detective, have you seen our young hero from last night yet?"

"No, I just got in. Why?"

"He's everybody's sweetheart now," laughed Vinny as he looked up from the microscope. "Girls are fawning over him, guys are high-fivin' him. I gotta get me shot again."

Eldridge reached for his gun and Vinny waved him off. "No, please, no!" he yelled, laughing.

"You sure? I'd be happy to do it."

Vinny rounded the lab table, chuckling. "I processed your vehicle last night. Nothing much to identify the shooter, but I can tell you this. He's a he, and he's a blonde."

"DNA?"

"Yeah, we got lucky there, there were a few follicles on the hairs. No matches in the system yet, though."

"Okay, keep me posted."

"Always do, Detective," said Vinny as he headed back to his tests.

Eldridge ran up the stairwell and found Frank smiling at a volunteer police officer, a particularly attractive young woman with long blonde hair. She handed him her number as Eldridge walked into the tech lab.

"Detective!" yelped Frank as if caught with his hand in the cookie jar. *And what a cookie jar!*

"Call me," she said to Frank as she left, smiling at Eldridge.

Eldridge returned the smile and watched her sway out of the room. "I see you're feeling better," he said, turning back to Frank.

Frank laughed nervously. "Yeah, well, I guess word gets around."

Eldridge smiled. "What've you got for me?"

"A name and another photo," said Frank, returning to his computer. "I've got an ID on the second photo. His name is Nathan Small, I'm emailing you his details now. He's on the witness list for the prosecution next week. And here's your next photo," he said, hitting a few keys. The picture showed a young man, maybe mid-twenties, with sandy-blonde hair and his face partially covered by his hand. "Now what does that look like to you?"

"What do you mean?"

"Well, I've been staring at this for a while, and I get the impression he's trying not to vomit."

Eldridge looked at the photo again. "It does kind of look like that, doesn't it? Was there any found at the scene?"

Frank shrugged. "Hey, if it was programmable vomit, I could tell you about it. Plain ol' goop, that's Vinny's territory." Eldridge smiled, noticing a newfound sense of confidence in Frank not there the night before. *Maybe getting shot did him some good?* "I'll email you the photo right away."

Eldridge thanked Frank and returned to Vinny's lab. "Hey, Vin, question for you. The subway attack last year, you didn't happen to find any vomit on the train or the platform?"

Vinny looked up from his computer. "Don't know, I didn't process that scene. Let me pull up the file." He hit a few keys and within seconds the evidence list for the case appeared. "There were quite a few vomit samples taken, it is a subway you know."

"Were they processed?"

"No, we had the perps in custody before they were done so it wasn't necessary."

"Can you process them now for me?"

Vinny crinkled his nose. "Year old vomit? What for?"

"Just a hunch."

Vinny shook his head. "I should show *you* how to do it."

Eldridge smiled and ducked out the door before Vinny could throw the stapler at him he had just picked up. Back at his desk, he printed out the contact info for Nathan Small then arranged to meet him at his home in an hour.

Shaw had received the tip this time. An anonymous source (his favorite kind) in the police department had informed him the latest video was of an Abigail Teague. That little tidbit hadn't been released to the public yet, but *he* knew it. And he knew Aynslee Kai, the flavor of the month, didn't. And that was why he was stifling a grin in the story meeting as Aynslee told Merle she didn't know who the new victim was. *That's why I should be doing the story. I have years of contacts, contacts that you can only dream of having some day.*

"What's on your mind, Jonathan?"

It took a moment before Shaw noticed the entire room looking at him. "Pardon?"

"I know that look, Jonathan. Spill."

Shaw shook his head. "No, it's nothing."

Merle frowned. "We're a team. If you've got something, let's have it. Now."

Shaw turned slightly red then sighed. "Fine. I have a source at One Police Plaza that tells me the latest victim is named Abigail Teague." He watched with tremendous satisfaction the shocked expressions on the faces around the table.

"How good is your source?"

It was Aynslee that asked. *The nerve!* "Better than anything you've obviously got." *Zing! Take that, bitch!*

"And when did you find this out?"

This time it was Merle. "This morning." *This morning! I've known for hours and our wunderkind hasn't been able to find out anything!*

Merle's raised voiced caused him to jerk his head toward the head of the table. "You've known about this since this morning and you didn't tell anyone!" Shaw's jubilation quickly drained away. "We're going to air without a name, and now you tell me you've had one all along?" Merle slammed his fist on the table then stood. "Aynslee, find out everything you can on Abigail Teague." Shaw opened his mouth to protest when Merle spun toward him. "And you," he said, pointing, "My office, now!"

The room sat in stunned silence while Merle stormed out, a subdued Shaw in tow. Somebody giggled, breaking the tension, and everyone burst out in laughter. "What an asshole!" exclaimed the sports reporter, Mike Thomas.

"Yeah, it's about damned time that snob was taken down a peg."

Aynslee kept quiet but was grinning from ear to ear on the inside. Heading for her desk, she quickly tracked down Abigail Teague's ex-husband, grabbed her crew and headed to the parking garage.

Nathan Small sat on the couch in his tiny Greenwich Village apartment, remembering that day on the subway. There was only one way to describe it. Senseless. He had seen enough death in theatre, but that was war. You expected death in war. But in a subway? With a dozen people watching, doing nothing? That was senseless. That was an unnecessary death. He had been in the next car when he saw the commotion through the doors. He struggled to get there, his two prosthetic limbs slowing him down, the pain, still fresh from the IED that had shredded his legs less than a year before, almost overwhelming, but he pushed through. He reached the car as the subway screeched to a stop, too late to help the girl. He tried to chase her two attackers, but it was no use. The cowards on the train had disgusted him, most not sticking around for the police to arrive. He had. And he was going to testify and do whatever he could to help lock those two bastards in prison for the rest of their lives.

A knock on the door brought him out of his reverie. He looked at his watch, surprised. He strode over to the door, his ability to control his legs much improved since the year before, and opened it. "You're early, Detective." The blur of a hand, gripping something, greeted him. He ducked, but too late, the blow hitting the side of his head, knocking him out cold.

Small awoke, the searing pain in the side of his head reminded him of when he regained consciousness in the Blackhawk used to medevac him. He hadn't felt his legs, it was the impact his head had made with the side of his

Humvee that hurt. The real pain, followed by the phantom pain, came later. He opened his eyes and found himself tied to one of his kitchen chairs, his mouth taped. A young man stood in front of him, holding out a phone, a video of the subway attack playing on it. It froze on an image of his face. The man raised his gun and pointed it at Small's head. He watched the man's finger squeeze the trigger.

Never thought I'd go out like this.

A rapping sound at the door startled them both. His attacker whirled around, a look of panic in his eyes. *The detective!* He knew he had to warn him somehow, but couldn't move, he had no leverage with his artificial limbs. Trying to use his upper body to raise the chair, he managed to make a loud bang as the chair legs slammed back down on the hardwood floor. He was rewarded with a pistol whipping that sent him flying backward.

Eldridge, hearing some sort of commotion inside, drew his weapon and kicked open the door. Taking in the scene before him, he cautiously entered the small apartment, checking first to make sure no one was hiding behind the door. He heard a noise deeper inside, and as he entered the living room, saw movement coming from what looked to be the kitchen. His weapon leading the way, he rounded the corner and saw a man tied to a chair, lying on its side, then a flash of movement from outside the window. Running forward, he saw somebody on the fire escape, already two floors below. Looking back at the victim, their eyes met and he knew he was telling him, *Go!*

Eldridge jumped out the window and ran down the steps after his target, the rusted metal swaying dangerously under his feet. He heard the final steps slam to the ground, shaking the entire structure, and watched the suspect sprint from the alleyway, his blonde hair confirming what Vinny had discovered earlier. A few seconds later Eldridge launched himself off the final level and onto the ground, racing after the man. He exited the dark alleyway and ran headlong into a thick crowd of pedestrians. Desperately he looked around but found no sign of his suspect.

"Fuck!" he muttered, pulling out his cell. He ran back to the apartment as he called for backup and an ambulance. As he stepped back into the kitchen, he found Small where he had left him. Eldridge knelt down and removed the tape covering the man's mouth as gently as he could.

"Did you get him?" the defiant man asked.

"No, he was gone before I could get out of the alley." He pulled a small utility knife from his pocket and cut the tape binding Small's wrists and ankles. He noticed the prosthetics and was momentarily taken aback. "Are you a vet?"

Small gripped Eldridge's extended hand. "Afghanistan. Second tour, roadside bomb." He groaned as Eldridge helped him to his feet.

Eldridge nodded with respect. "My dad was in 'Nam." He looked up as two officers raced into the apartment, their weapons drawn. "Secure the scene, there should be a bus here any moment." Turning his attention back to his witness, he asked, "Can I get you anything?"

Small shook his head. "No, I'll be fine. Bastard pistol-whipped me a couple of times, though. I'll be feeling that for a while." He headed to his couch, the fiercely independent man waving off any assistance, and sat down.

Eldridge sat across from him. "Did you ever see your attacker before?"

"No, never."

"If we set you up with a sketch artist, do you think you'd remember enough to help us out?"

"Absolutely. You better hope I don't catch that punk before you do. I'll beat him to death with one of my legs if I have to."

Eldridge smiled, not doubting him for a moment. "Last year on the subway, did you see a gun?" asked Eldridge, deciding to go ahead with the questions he originally planned on asking, since his witness appeared determined to act as if nothing had happened.

"No, I didn't see anything. But I came on the scene late. I was in another car and came to help, but," he gestured at his legs, "these things held me up."

"Did you happen to see anybody vomit during or after the incident?"

"Huh?" Small looked surprised at the question. "As a matter of fact, yeah, some kid upchucked right in front of the door, on the platform. Why's that important?"

"Nothing, just clearing up some loose ends. Would you recognize him if you saw him again?"

Small shook his head. "No, I saw him from behind. I was more concerned with those two bastards."

Eldridge rose to his feet as the paramedics arrived. "Thank you, Mr. Small, I'll be assigning a protective detail just in case he tries to come back."

"Save your money, I don't need it."

"I'm sure you don't, Mr. Small, but I'll feel better knowing you're protected."

As Eldridge rode the elevator down, he called Vinny. "Have you started those DNA tests yet?"

"You mean you can't smell it from where you are?"

"I'll take that as a yes," laughed Eldridge, thankful he wasn't anywhere near the lab. "Test anything found on the platform, nearest the doors, first." Eldridge hung up and called Frank. "Hey, Romeo, any luck tracing the call Messina received?"

"Sorry, Detective, it was a disposable cell phone, no way to trace it."

"Okay, thanks." Eldridge was about to return his phone to his pocket when it rang. It was Shakespeare.

"Hiya, kid, it's me. I got someone down here you're gonna want to talk to, pronto."

"Who?"

"A priest, says he's got some info on your case."

"I'll be there in thirty minutes, keep him comfortable." Shakespeare grunted an acknowledgement and Eldridge heard him offer the priest a donut before hanging up. Walking quickly to his car, he mentally crossed his fingers, hoping he might be about to get a break in the case, every other clue so far leading to dead-ends, both literally and figuratively.

Aynslee was interviewing a clearly bitter man. If he wasn't careful, the police were going to start to suspect he was the killer. So she decided to ask him.

"Mr. Teague, did you kill your ex-wife?"

He laughed. "No, but I'd like to thank whoever did. That bloodsucking bitch took me for everything I had."

"You're glad she's dead?"

"Absolutely! She got my house. *My house!* I paid for the damned thing! Not her! Why the hell should she get to live there, and me, I have to live in this shithole of an apartment and send her four grand a month in goddamned alimony. There's barely anything left!"

Aynslee, content to let him ramble on, knew she already had quite a few great quotes from him that would make for a juicy segment, but she wanted to know something about the victim other than her ex-husband's thoughts on the subject.

"Hey, do you think I can get the house back?"

"No clue. Can you tell me anything about your ex-wife, like what she did for a living?"

"Nothing."

"Charities?"

"Nothing. Okay, that's not true, she did volunteer work for some hospice. I don't know, I didn't pay much attention to that. We mostly just fought."

"What did she do with all of her spare time then?"

"She took up Karate, I think."

"Karate?"

"Yeah, something happened about a year ago, I guess it scared the shit out of her."

"Any idea what that might have been?"

"No, I didn't give a shit."

Aynslee sensed no point in continuing. "Well, thank you very much for your time, Mr. Teague."

"Is that thing still on?"

Steve nodded.

"I'd just like to say thank you to the guy who did this. You've saved me a fortune in alimony and if they catch you, I'll help fund your defense!"

Aynslee signaled for Mike to turn the camera off and quickly headed from the apartment.

"Holy shit, I don't think I've ever met anybody that bitter!" exclaimed Steve.

"You've obviously never been divorced."

Steve turned to Mike. "You mean to tell me *you* hate your ex-wife that much?"

Mike paused for a moment. "No, definitely hated her for a while, but I guess I'd have to admit I was never at that level. That guy's really fucked up."

Aynslee nodded in agreement. "Let's get back to the station and see if there's any of this we can use, then we'll try to follow up this Karate angle, see what happened a year ago that scared her."

"You think it might be connected to the case?"

Aynslee shrugged her shoulders. "No idea, but it's worth a look." She typed an email to a lackey at the station to start tracking down what Karate studio their victim had gone to.

Chelsie sat on her mattress, satisfied enough time had gone by for any drugs she was supposed to have taken to have worn off. She looked at her nails, clipped short. *So I can't scratch him?* She grabbed a handful of her hair and examined it, the bright blonde almost unnatural. *Why would he dye my hair? Is he trying to make me into someone else?* She remembered reading about serial killers who kidnapped people who reminded them of someone from their past, but she had never heard of one kidnapping someone that *didn't* look like that person, then trying to change them. Then it dawned on her. She had been blonde until several weeks ago. *Could he have been watching me for that long?* She shuddered, realizing she may not be a random victim after all. She wracked her brain, trying to remember anything out of the ordinary. But she couldn't. Everything had been normal. Mundane. She went to school. She hung out with her friends occasionally. She studied. She worked.

Work!

Could it be the creepy guy who had given her the huge tip? She tried to picture him in her mind, but drew a blank. He was faceless, like so many other customers. Nameless, faceless, sources of frequent annoyance, and rare pleasantness. And occasional moments of creepiness. She was sure she hadn't seen him before however. She knew she would remember if she had recognized him.

Who else?

The bum sniffer? He was definitely weird. Assuming she hadn't imagined the whole thing. She couldn't be sure anymore. Her imagination was now in control, filling in the blanks with outlandish ideas, to the point she was no longer sure of what had happened.

Her stomach grumbled.

All she did know was she was starving. Which probably wasn't helping her memory. She hadn't eaten in three days and she felt weak. She knew she would have to eat the next time food was lowered. A thought dawned on her. Walking over to the hole in the floor, she reached in, fishing around for one of the sandwiches. She grasped something momentarily but it broke apart in her grip. Removing her hand she saw the leftover paste of the bun stuck to her fingers. *Yuck!* She shoved her hand back in the water and shook it to clean off the mess that was her hidden meal, no longer as hungry.

Eldridge was surprised to find Shakespeare and the priest laughing together and eating donuts. Correction. Shakespeare was eating donuts, although the priest did have evidence of an earlier dalliance, a little bit of powder on his otherwise perfectly black robe.

"Ahh, here he is, Father," said Shakespeare, rising to his feet. "Detective Hayden Eldridge, this is Father O'Neil." Eldridge shook the priest's hand. He was a tall, lean man in his seventies with brilliant silver hair and a thin, deeply lined face, weathered by decades of exposure to the elements. His simple, black robe, in immaculate condition, his collar as brilliant a white as the day he first slipped it on. The genuine smile on his face disarmed Eldridge, he at once felt like he could tell this man anything. Which if he was lucky, would be exactly what someone else had done. "Father O'Neil was my parish priest when I was a boy," explained Shakespeare.

"You went to church?" Eldridge hoped he didn't sound too incredulous.

"Mr. Shakespeare was an altar boy when he was younger." O'Neil looked back at Shakespeare. "But we don't see him that often anymore." Shakespeare looked briefly at the floor. "Something tells me you'd have quite the confession if you were to come in, son."

"Father, you don't have the time to hear my confession," smiled Shakespeare. "It would take *way* too long."

Eldridge had to agree. *If only the Father knew what had become of his altar boy.* "Perhaps we can take this into an interview room where we can have some privacy?" suggested Eldridge. "I understand you may have some information on a case?"

O'Neil nodded and followed Eldridge to a nearby room. "Yes, I think one of my parishioners might be involved."

"What makes you say that?" asked Shakespeare.

"Well, you understand, if I heard anything in my confessional, I couldn't say anything, but something I stumbled upon got me worried."

"We understand, Father," said Eldridge. "Please continue."

"There's a young man who has been coming to my church for probably four or five years," explained O'Neil. "He's shy and awkward, probably what you would call a 'loner'. He always came to church alone, several times a week and always sat as far back as he could in the pews. The first few weeks I respected his privacy, but after a while I decided maybe he was needing to talk to somebody. I approached him and we struck up a conversation. Over the following months we continued to speak and eventually I was able to discover that he was living on his own in a nearby apartment, his parents and older sister had been killed in a car accident and he had been on his own since he was seventeen."

"What was his name?" asked Shakespeare.

Father O'Neil raised his hand. "Patience, Justin, I see we still have the habit of jumping to the end of the book first." Shakespeare, suitably admonished, sat back and fidgeted with the arm of his chair. "Over the years we became closer but he never truly opened up until about three years ago."

"What happened three years ago?" asked Eldridge.

"He asked if he could help us on the computers. He was quite good at it and ended up helping me around the office. He became quite a whiz. He read about computers, networking, the Internet, everything, voraciously, at the library. Not a day went by where I wouldn't see him with a book under his arm." Eldridge and Shakespeare exchanged excited glances at this. "He networked my office, set up a web page, really brought us into the twenty-first century. Anyway, one day, about two years ago, he came to me very distraught, and said he had run into a man who said he was his uncle. He said he remembered the man vaguely from when he was a teenager, but hadn't heard from him since. He said the man had told him his mother had given up a child for adoption when she was a teenager and he had a sister out there somewhere."

Eldridge leaned back in his chair. "How did he take the news?"

"He was excited by the possibility and asked what he should do. I told him he should try to find her but to be prepared for her not wanting to have contact with him. From then on almost every free moment was spent looking for her, months of visiting adoption agencies, searching on the Internet, looking over birth notices, everything."

"Did he find her?" asked Shakespeare, the arm of his chair no longer of interest.

O'Neil nodded. "Yes, he did. He knew what hometown his mother had been born in, and somehow, I don't think this part was legal, got access to her hospital records, found out the date she gave birth and the name on the birth certificate. He used that to find his sister on a website that apparently caters to adoptees looking for their birth parents."

Eldridge leaned forward in his chair. "When did he find her?"

"About a year ago. They arranged to meet and as far as I know, he went to that meeting. I didn't see him for days afterward and I began to get worried it hadn't gone well. About a week later he showed up at the church and was a different man. He continued to help out, but never spoke of his sister again. I decided not to press it, figuring she had rejected him for some reason."

"But why do you think this relates to our case?"

"Two weeks ago he was doing something on the computer and turned it off as soon as I came in the room. He was acting a little strange and left quickly. I was concerned, so I decided to look at his computer. He hadn't shut it down properly, it was still stuck on a program and I saw one of the videos that's been on TV."

"Millions of people have been downloading those," said Shakespeare.

"Which is why I didn't think too much of it at the time. But then when he didn't show up for a couple of weeks, I decided to look at his computer and found these." He pulled a folder from a leather case he had brought with him. Eldridge flipped open the folder and whistled at the printouts of the same biblical threats the Rochester family had received. "I found these on the hard drive so I called Justin right away."

Eldridge examined the pages and nodded. "You were right to bring this to us. Do you have his name and address, we'll need to check him out."

O'Neil pulled another folder out and pushed it toward Eldridge. "His name is Jeremiah Lansing. This is everything I have on him." He turned to Shakespeare. "Please Justin, he's still just a boy inside who's been through an awful lot. Make sure nothing happens to him when you arrest him."

Shakespeare smiled and leaned toward O'Neil. "Don't worry, Father, we'll do everything we can to make sure he is brought in unharmed."

O'Neil smiled gratefully. "It may still be nothing, maybe he was upset over something, it might have been a joke."

Eldridge nodded but didn't believe that any more than Father O'Neil's voice suggested he did. "Perhaps. We'll check it out." He rose as did the others. "Thank you, Father, for bringing this to our attention." He shook O'Neil's hand. "We'll have his computer picked up as well, see if there's anything on it that can help."

"Of course." O'Neil turned to Shakespeare, taking his hand in both of his. "Justin, when are we going to see you in church?"

Shakespeare turned a tinge red and looked away. "Well, Father, I'm afraid I'd probably be struck down the moment I set foot in there."

O'Neil chuckled. "God loves everyone, even the sinner, Justin. You should come this weekend, you can let me know what happened with young Jeremiah."

Shakespeare nodded. "No promises, Father, but we'll see."

O'Neil tossed his head back and laughed. "I'm glad you didn't lie to me, Justin. But do somehow let me know what happens with Jeremiah."

"*That* I can do," promised Shakespeare.

After Father O'Neil left, they returned to their desks, excited at what they had just found out. "I think you might've finally got a break."

Eldridge nodded as he checked his messages. He hung up the phone and stood up. "Might have just got another. I have to go see Vinny, he's got something for me."

Shakespeare nodded. "I'll get to work on a warrant to search the kid's place."

Eldridge hadn't known Shakespeare to fill out any paperwork in ages, and not willing to look a gift-horse in the mouth, he headed down to the lab without commenting. "Yo, Vinny, what've you got for me?"

"Detective, your hunch paid off. I compared the DNA from our SUV shooter and from vomit collected on the platform and we got a match."

"I had a feeling. Our shooter, who we're assuming is also our killer, was on the train that day."

"Yeah, but if he was one of the passengers who did nothing, why is he killing the others? Shouldn't he just kill himself and get it over with?"

"Maybe it'll end that way. He could be his own final target."

Vinny nodded. "Serial killer-suicide? Maybe. But why?"

"Overcome with remorse at not helping, maybe? Decides he should kill himself, but if he has to die, then so should the others?"

"Could be. You can't always apply logic to a nut-bar's brain."

Eldridge agreed. "I assume there were no matches to anything else in the system?"

"No, Detective, you got lucky once today, don't push it."

Eldridge nodded and headed back to his desk. As he climbed the stairs, his phone vibrated with a message. Flipping it open, he saw another photo from Frank with a tag-line "No ID". It showed an elderly woman, clearly terrified, heading for the door.

Small sat on his couch, watching some mindless reality television drivel on mute, no longer able to stand the grade three dialogue. *I fought a war to protect this shit?* He brought up the guide, looking for something better to watch. He found an old Bogart war movie and flicked it on. *Navy? Bah!* He raised the remote to find something else when he heard what he thought was the officer's radio outside his door. A moment later there was a knock. He struggled to his feet and had to clutch the back of a chair as the room spun around him. Steadying himself, he cursed the bastard who had given him the concussion, and headed to the door. A glance through the peephole confirmed it was the officer. He opened the door.

"Sorry to disturb you, sir, but I just wanted to let you know that we've been called back to the precinct."

Curious. "Did they catch him?"

The young officer shrugged his shoulders. "Dunno. Must have. I can't see them calling off a protective detail if they hadn't."

"Ok, well thanks for sticking around as long as you did."

The officer nodded as Small closed the door. He turned slowly, then made his way back into the living room. Hovering over his couch, about to drop onto it, he heard another knock at the door. He swung his arms in circles to keep his balance, and chuckled.

"Forgot something, officer?" he yelled, as he shuffled to the door. Turning the knob, he yanked the door open. His jaw dropped as he saw the barrel of a gun pointed directly at his head, then the muzzle flash as it went off in his face.

Police Officer Daniels, only moments before called off his shit assignment, tapped his toe, eyeing the slowly descending floor indicator. He couldn't wait until he had a little more seniority, then he'd at least be the one sitting in the car. *You're a rookie, what do you expect?* He was almost at the ground floor when he heard the shot. *Shit!* He jabbed at the button for the fifth floor and grabbed his radio. "Shots fired! Shots fired!" The elevator continued its interminable descent, at last arriving at its destination. The doors inched open and Daniels waved off a man who tried to get on. "Police emergency!" The doors finally began to close, his repeated jabs at the *Door Close* button and string of curses failed to urge them on any faster. They had almost finished closing when a hand grasped the door and forced it open. It was his partner. "Did you hear that?" Daniels asked.

"Yeah, I called it in." The doors closed and they watched the indicator, their weapons drawn, as it inched toward the fifth floor. The elevator chimed its arrival, and the doors opened to silence. Daniels placed his foot against the door to prevent it from closing, while his partner took position opposite him. He peered out, toward the apartment, and saw nothing. His partner checked the other direction then motioned for Daniels to exit the elevator. He stepped out into the hallway, followed by his partner close behind. The hallway was clear, but the door to the apartment they were assigned to watch minutes before lay open. Daniels was first to see the body lying in the entranceway.

"How the hell did this happen?" demanded Eldridge. "You two were assigned to protect him! Where were you?"

"The detail had just been called off," explained Daniels' partner, Police Officer Davidson. "Maybe about two minutes before I heard the shot."

"Yeah, I was in the elevator on my way down when it happened," said Daniels.

"Called off? Who the hell called it off?"

"I don't know, it came over the squad car computer," said Davidson.

"The computer?" Eldridge knew immediately what had happened. They were dealing with a computer whiz, apparently good enough to hack the police system. Eldridge looked at the body of Nathan Small as it was wheeled out. *I've got to find that old lady before she gets it.* He stormed off, shaking his head.

Aynslee's new look had gone over big. For once *she* made the City page instead of those she used to cover. She was hot. Her image makeover had closely followed on the heels of her career makeover and she was now the co-anchor, having proved herself capable, and with ratings to back her up. Interview offers with national talk shows were still pouring in and she had at last received the phone call she was waiting for, CNN. She had just heard the message and didn't know what they wanted to talk to her about, but she knew the name was for someone she had heard was in their recruiting department. Cloud Nine had nothing on the way she was feeling right now.

She was heading home after the 11pm newscast when the CNN message arrived on her BlackBerry. Her immediate instinct was to return the call right away, but she decided against it, not wanting to appear too eager. When the second message arrived, she was almost home. It was another video. The exhilaration at receiving these messages had worn off, and she sometimes felt guilty she may achieve her lifelong dreams because some depraved person had picked her to be the recipient of videos depicting his vicious acts. Pushing the twinge of guilt away, she instructed the driver to head back to the station.

When she arrived at her office she pulled the video up on her monitor. The person recording it stood in front of a door, an outstretched arm held a gun, pointed directly at the peephole. The door opened, revealing a man who clearly had been expecting someone else, his jaw dropping at the sight of the weapon. There was a flash then the man collapsed backward. The video panned down to show him lying on the floor, then ended. Aynslee backed up the video to where the man answered the door and paused it. *He looks familiar.* She let the video play out then froze it on the body lying on the floor, two prosthetic limbs clearly visible. *I know him!* Her heart pounded in her chest as she realized she may actually have a connection to the victims. If she knew him, how many of the others might she have known, but just not recognized? She grabbed the phone and dialed Hayden's number.

TEN

Police Officer Stewart sipped his coffee, enjoying the last few minutes of his 10-63. He leaned back in his seat and closed his eyes, dreaming of the Dominican beach he and his girlfriend would be on next week. Sandy beaches, blue-green water, sunshine. No clouds, no rain. And beaches full of scantily clad women. *Life is good!* He'd have to watch himself; his girlfriend was the jealous type. He'd never dream of cheating on her, but a guy's allowed to look, just not touch. *That's what they invented sunglasses for.* A squeal of tires startled him and he opened his eyes in time to see a car careening toward him. He tossed his coffee and dropped the car into reverse, hammering on the gas. The car surged backward as the oncoming vehicle continued to gain. He spun the wheel to the right and the squad car jerked to the side, the other car narrowly missing him as it sped past and collided with a nearby light standard. He slammed his brakes on and breathed a sigh of relief, taking a moment to regain his composure. Turning his cherries on, he pulled in behind the car, blocking its escape, then radioed it in. He climbed out and drew his weapon. As he approached the car he saw the occupant asleep on the steering wheel. *Fucking drunks!* He holstered his weapon and pulled out his nightstick, tapping on the window. Nothing. He tapped again, this time harder. The man stirred and looked at him. "Howdy, Officer!" he waved.

"Please exit the vehicle, sir."

The man nodded, and, with difficulty, opened the door. He swung his legs out and tried to stand, only to be pulled back in by his still clasped seatbelt.

If this were a movie, it might be funny.

"Unbuckle your seatbelt, sir."

"Jusht a minute." After a few seconds of fumbling he freed himself and stumbled out, grasping the door for support.

"How much have you had to drink tonight, sir?"

"Nothing." He hiccupped.

"I'll need you to take a breathalyzer test, sir."

"I d-don't need that."

"Sir, if you refuse to take the test, you can be charged."

"Charged for not taking a test?" asked the man. "If I'm going to be charged, it should be for something—". He paused as if to vomit. "For something good," he finished. He swung at Stewart, catching him on the chin. Stewart staggered back and drew his weapon, calling for backup. The man stood laughing for a few seconds, then collapsed in a heap, passed out.

It was warm. Comfortable. Relaxing. Chelsie slowly woke, and it felt wonderful. She opened her eyes, preparing to moan in ecstasy, when the reality of the new world she lived in yanked her mercilessly back to the horror of her new life. She was in the bathtub, her captor stood not five feet away, his head in the medicine cabinet. And he was humming. That same, annoying, droning tune. He straightened as he removed something from the cabinet then flipped the mirrored door closed. Chelsie snapped her eyes shut, praying he hadn't seen her in the reflection. His humming continued.

She had been ravenously hungry, and had finally given in, eating half a sandwich. Not even half. But it had proven enough to knock her out within minutes. *How long was I out?* She knew he waited about an hour before collecting her, and her wet hair suggested he was finished cleaning her, which she thanked God she had been asleep for. *Half a sandwich means 90 minutes.* She'd know for next time to try a quarter.

The humming neared and she sensed he had sat on the edge of the tub. He picked up her leg and held it in the air, the water pouring then trickling off her leg, the warmth of it quickly replaced by the relative chill of the room. He rubbed something over the entire exposed surface of her leg. It felt soft, smooth. *Skin cream?* Something hard ran over her leg, accompanied by a scraping sound. *Oh my God, he's shaving my legs!* Her instinct demanded she kick out, try to stop him, but she resisted, knowing she had no hope of overpowering him from her current position. Or any position for that matter. She already knew he was too strong. She would need to outwit him somehow. Brains would win this, and that knowledge calmed her. She endured the grooming session, and after a few minutes, was carried into the bedroom, the ritual of toweling her dry and blow-drying her hair hopefully signaling the near end of tonight's activities.

She heard him walk into the hall again and then the definite creak of the stairs as he descended. Opening her eyes, she looked around. Deep red with gold gilded wallpaper adorned every wall, the plastered ceiling with deep cove moldings and gold trim, reminded her of her grandmother's place in Maine. Several expensive looking rugs accented the hardwood flooring, including a dated brown and burgundy afghan directly in front of a large dresser with mirror at the head of the bed. She raised herself up on her elbows and gasped. Her hair was a bright blonde, puffed into an almost eighties style hairdo. What shocked her more was she had worn it this way before, but only at her retro-eighties nights. *Could he have seen me at one of those?* She continued her search, finding no evidence of a phone or any other means of communication in the room. The window to her right, still covered by heavy drapery, disguised whether it was day or night. She looked again at the photo she had glimpsed last time. It was of a small boy, hugged by what he assumed were his parents, and next to that, a picture of two teenagers on a swing together, an awkward smile on the boy's face, a look of boredom on the girl's. Her stomach churned. The girl could have been her.

A creak on the stairs startled her and she lay back down, closing her eyes. He reentered the room and dressed her in clothes so warm they felt fresh from the dryer. He picked her up and carried her out of the room. Her head lay on his right, turned toward his back. She opened her left eye a sliver, revealing a tight stairwell, as if in an old house. When they reached the bottom, a doorway, clearly to the outside, shoes and several men's jackets in evidence, was tantalizingly close, but impossibly far. He turned and walked down a hallway stretching almost the length of the house, a living room with a phone sitting on a table, made her heart leap as they passed. They entered the kitchen, its modern appliances a drastic contradiction to the obvious age and style of the rest of the house. A cordless phone lay on the kitchen counter, almost within reach. She made note of this, thinking if her arm had been free, she might have been able to grab it, and perhaps hide it somehow from him. *Next time.* He placed her on the floor, near the kitchen's far end and she heard him pull the chain, triggering the lowering of the floor. *He obviously doesn't get any visitors.* A few more minutes and she lay on her mattress, waiting while he collected the water bottle and tray from earlier. Recalling what she had just seen, she built a mental map of the house in her head.

Clarice Viktora eyed her client, held between two bailiffs, his head lolled on his shoulder, reeking of God knows what. *Why do I always get the drunks?* She knew why. She was the low "man" on the totem pole, doomed to the shit assignments until a new crop of newbies came aboard, at which point shit would become crap, and with each new crop, she would work her way up, eventually, hopefully, switching to the prosecutor's office. But this was her first month in the Public Defender's Office, a stepping stone on the ambitious road she had laid out for herself. Her client belched then farted. *Oh, that's nice.* She took two steps sideways.

"How do you plead?"

Clarice smelt the vomit on her client's breath. He looked at the judge, the look of bewilderment almost comical. *He isn't answering.* He opened his mouth, then dropped his head to his chest and snored.

"Not guilty," she said.

"Bail?"

Thankfully the prosecutor replied before she had to think up some line of BS she didn't even believe. "Your honor, the plaintiff has refused to identify himself, has no identification, was driving while under the influence in a stolen car, and assaulted an officer. We recommend remand until such time as he can be identified."

"Defense?"

I just want to go to bed. "The defense has no objections to him being held overnight until his identity can be established."

"Very well, bail is denied until such time as identity can be established." The judge swung her gavel, ending the proceedings. Bailiffs led, or dragged, her client toward a holding cell, from which he would be transferred to

Rikers. Clarice stifled a yawn as she picked up the folder for the next case. *Oh goody, another DUI.*

Aynslee walked slowly toward her office, her now used "go" bag slung over her shoulder, a bag the life of a reporter had her in the habit of always keeping stocked with a change of clothes and toiletries to freshen up with in the station's gym facilities. She had slept at the station on a pull-out couch in her office, too afraid to go home. She couldn't believe Hayden hadn't come to protect her. Wasn't that his job? *Maybe if you hadn't scared him away!* She started to reassess their relationship. *Maybe I'm reading way too much into this?*

She stepped into her office and found Hayden sitting in a chair in front of her desk.

Thank God!

"Where were you?" she asked, the fear from the night before still in her voice. "I slept here all night, I was terrified!"

He stood up, his hands spread out in apology. "I'm sorry, Miss Kai." His calm, soothing voice, washed the fear that gripped her away. "I didn't get your message until this morning. What's changed that has you so scared?"

How could I ever have doubted him? She threw her bag behind the door, and sat down at her desk. She brought up the new video and pointed at the frozen image of the latest victim. "I knew him!"

His eyebrows shot up. "You knew him? How?"

"He took the subway with me," she explained. "I've seen him lots of times."

"Did you ever speak to him?"

"No, I usually just put my iPod on and tune out, but he's hard to miss with those legs. Could it be a coincidence?"

"I don't believe in coincidences," he said, shaking his head. "But you never spoke to him?"

"No."

He hit a few keys on his phone then showed her a series of photos. "Have you ever seen any of these people before?" He flipped through, Aynslee shaking her head to each one.

"No, sorry, he's the only one I recognize."

"Okay, I want you to stay in your office today. Don't leave the building until you hear from me."

She felt her chest tighten. "Do you think he'll come after me?"

"No, I know what the connection is between the other victims and I don't see any relation to you."

"You know the connection! What is it?" she asked, her reporter instincts kicking back in.

"Sorry, Miss Kai, I can't tell you that."

Worth a try!

His phone rang and he looked at the call display. "It's my partner, I have to take this. Stay here until you hear from me, okay?"

She nodded as he walked out of her office.

Ian tried to go about his business, but showering with twenty other men made that extremely difficult. He just wanted to survive. Prison was terrifying. And Rikers wasn't even real prison. He had no idea what he would do when he got to the real thing. Denzel would most likely protect him, until he got himself killed, and then what would he do? Every night he hugged his pillow, crying silently in terror and self pity, until eventually exhaustion would take him. Every waking moment was an exercise in avoidance, of people and situations, but some, like this, were mandatory, and he couldn't avoid them. He just prayed Denzel wouldn't start something. Where he avoided eye contact with everyone else, Denzel, showering beside him, defiantly looked about, trying to stare down anyone who would meet his glare.

"What you lookin' at crackah!" he yelled.

Ian looked out of the corner of his eye at the man Denzel had challenged, showering about five feet away. The rather slight, white man met Denzel's gaze then looked away slowly, apparently unconcerned with Denzel's outburst. *It's the small bitches you need to worry about. Ya never know if they're gonna try and prove they're tough.* Denzel's words rang through his head as he thumped his chest and looked about as if he had stared down a silverback gorilla.

The showers cut out and everyone toweled off then dressed. Ian finished buttoning his shirt and began to fold his towel when Denzel elbowed him in the ribs. Ian looked up and saw the man from earlier walking toward them. Denzel stepped forward. Ian noticed the man had his hand in the pocket of his jumper, and reached to warn Denzel. "W-w-wait—"

"What the hell do you want?"

"For you to die," the man said in a hoarse whisper. It happened so quickly, Ian never had a chance to finish his sentence. The man pulled his hand from his jumper and lunged toward Denzel, plunging a shiv made from a toothbrush into the side of Denzel's neck. Denzel clutched at the wound in shock, the punctured artery rhythmically spurting blood as he fell to the floor.

"No!" yelled Ian, jumping toward the man, grabbing at him. The man sidestepped Ian's awkward attack and flipped him around, grabbing him in a headlock. Ian saw the free hand reach over his head, the shiv, still dripping in his friend's blood, held high, plunged down and into his stomach then chest, as his attacker repeatedly pierced his body. He threw Ian to the ground next to his friend along with the shiv, then blended with the crowd of prisoners running away.

Everyone on the boards talked tough, bragged about hacking various company websites, the odd third-world government database, basically, the easy stuff. A few claimed to have hacked the big boys. The Fortune 500's, first-world government sites, DoD, or the holy grail, M$. Most of it was complete and utter bullshit. When the challenge had been put out there, to hack the police database to get someone out of jail, the usually busy chat room had quickly emptied, leaving him and the challenger, Lonewolf2048. The plan was simple, yet would take skills. Skills he had and was dying to test. Hacking the local stores and restaurants that offended him lacked the challenge he needed, so he had agreed to do his part in the craziest scheme he had ever heard of. The challenger, Lonewolf2048, would get himself arrested, and he, ElfLord666, hacker extraordinaire, would hack the police system and have him released.

He had waited all night for the call, and it never came. His head dropped into his chest for the umpteenth time this morning, when the phone rang at last.

"I'm in as a John Doe at Rikers, admitted at two-forty-five a.m. Let's see if you can do your part."

"No problem." His fingers flew over the keyboard as he broke through layer after layer of security. *These luddites haven't a clue!* Within fifteen minutes he had full access to their system and inserted a record indicating their John Doe should be released immediately, the charges dropped.

"ElfLord rules!" he yelled, raising his hands in the air.

"Winston, what's going on down there?" yelled a shrill voice from upstairs.

"Nothing, mom!" he called, turning back to his computer, erasing all traces of what he had just done. It took a couple of hours, but a message eventually popped on his screen. *Lonewolf2048 out of the den. Awesome work! You rule!* Winston leaned back, smiled and snagged a handful of Cheezies.

It turned out to be a wine bar Chelsie worked at. Upscale, snooty, all the staff wearing crisp white shirts and black pants or skirts. Trace made a note to not bother coming here, a beer and shooter girl herself, although perhaps getting sloshed in a classy place might be some fun. *With the right guy.* She found her thoughts drifting to Eldridge and quickly pushed them to the back of her mind. Relationships with fellow officers never worked out. *Who said anything about a relationship?*

A hostess led her to an office in the back where the owner, Yannick Leroux, was tasting several different wines. Fascinated, she watched as he swirled the glass, held it up and examined it, for what she did not know, then sucked it in, his tongue manipulating the wine as he held his mouth slightly open. The odd display wasn't what shocked her, it was when he leaned over and spat it out into a nearby bucket. *Why the hell's he wasting good booze?*

"How can I help you?" asked Yannick as he stepped around his desk to shake her hand.

She showed him her badge. "Detective Trace. I'm working on a missing persons case, a Chelsie Birmingham, I understand she works for you."

The man sat on the edge of his desk. "Chelsie's missing? I didn't know. She wasn't due to work here until tonight so I figured she was just late." He turned to the door and yelled, "Cynthia!" A moment later an impossibly skinny girl trotted in.

"Yes, Mr. Leroux?"

"When did Chelsie last work, was it Saturday night?"

"Yes, sir."

"Who was on security that night?"

"Denis was."

"Get him for me, will you?"

She nodded and disappeared.

"You need security here?"

"Occasionally we have problems, it is a wine bar so a lot of the young, rich snobs like to come here, spend a lot of money and get drunk, then they expect a little something in return for a big tip. Having a guy like this," Yannick motioned toward a hulking man in the doorway, "cures them of any of those thoughts pretty quickly." Just as Cynthia was impossibly tiny, Denis was impossibly large, probably six foot six, he had to be over three hundred pounds of muscle. "Denis, this is a detective, she says Chelsie is missing. Did you walk her to the subway on Saturday?"

Trace watched his reaction to the news closely, the look of surprise and concern on the massive head one of pure innocence.

"Of course, sir, just like I always do."

"Did you see her get on it?"

"Yes, sir, she was on the phone with her mother, I think, then she got on the subway, I watched until it pulled away."

"You're sure?"

"Yes, sir, I would never let one of the girls leave here unescorted."

"Of course you wouldn't." Yannick waved for Denis to leave, who nodded to Trace then lumbered away. Yannick lowered his voice. "Not the sharpest knife in the drawer, but a heart of gold. He treats every one of these girls like they were his sisters. I don't think he'd lie to me."

"Okay, I'll just need to find out what time she left here and I should be done."

"No problem, just see Cynthia, she can tell you what time she punched out."

Trace nodded and stepped into the hall and almost ran into Cynthia who was holding a piece of paper. "I thought you might need this," she said, her hand shaking as she handed the paper to Trace. "It's a copy of her timecard."

Trace took the paper from the terrified girl. "Thanks."

"Do-do you think we have anything to worry about?" stammered Cynthia. "I mean, whoever took her, could he—?" She stopped, unable to put the words together.

Trace looked at her short, dark hair. "No, I don't think you have anything to worry about." She looked at the timecard.

Time to look at some surveillance footage.

Eldridge parked in front of the rundown hole that was Jeremiah Lansing's apartment building. As he climbed out of his car, Shakespeare did the same, several cars down, and waved.

"Hiya, kid!"

"Hey, Justin. Any sign of him?"

Shakespeare shook his head as he mounted the front steps, pulling on the railing as he hauled himself up. "Not since I got here." At the top he stopped and took a deep breath. "I've got to get back into shape, this is ridiculous."

Eldridge didn't say anything, it being the first time he had ever heard Shakespeare even hint at exercise, he wasn't sure what to say. They picked their way through the filth littering the lobby and Eldridge headed for the stairs when Shakespeare gripped his arm.

"Whoa, where you goin'?"

"You want to take an elevator in this place?"

"Hey, if God had meant man to take stairs, he wouldn't have let man invent the elevator," replied Shakespeare as he pressed the button. The doors opened and he climbed on. "You comin'?"

Eldridge chuckled and stepped into the elevator with Shakespeare. "Fine. But if we die, I'm gonna kick your ass."

Shakespeare let out a bellowing laugh, pressing the button for the third floor. Then gasped. The stench of urine and things far worse consumed the air like a rancid soup. They rode in silence to the third floor, neither wanting to admit they were both holding their breath. At long last they arrived and both burst from the elevator, desperate for air.

Shakespeare looked back at the elevator as the doors closed. "What the fuck was that? I swear I've smelt that in the morgue."

Eldridge exhaled deeply, trying to rid himself of any of the remaining air. "I think you may be right. When we leave we should check the shaft for a body."

He was only half joking.

"Fuck that, phone in an anonymous tip, just in case you're right."

Shakespeare wasn't joking.

Partially recovered, the air in the hallway only slightly better, they approached apartment 308. Eldridge knocked and listened. Nothing. He knocked again, this time louder. "Police officers, we have a warrant to search the premises!" yelled Eldridge. Still no answer.

"Looks like we go in the old fashioned way," said Shakespeare, stepping back to take a run at the door.

Eldridge held out his hand. "I'll go find the super."

Shakespeare frowned. "Sure, take all the fun out of the job."

Eldridge took the stairs to the first floor and found the door labeled *Super*. He knocked and waited for a few minutes as sounds of movement and cursing from inside approached. The door flew open and an unkempt man in boxer shorts and a stained wife-beater t-shirt glared at Eldridge.

"Who the hell are you?"

"Detective Eldridge, Homicide." Eldridge flashed his badge. "I have a warrant to search apartment three-oh-eight."

"Yeah, yeah." The man snatched a large ring of keys off the wall and walked out into the hallway toward the elevator.

"Aren't you going to put some pants on?" asked Eldridge in disgust. The man looked at him as if his shoulder had grown a second head, then shuffled onto the elevator.

"You comin'?" Eldridge held his breath and rode to the third floor. Shakespeare did a double-take when he saw the Super exit the elevator, the flap in the front of his boxers failing miserably in hiding the man's shame. He unlocked the door and reached to open it when Eldridge stopped him.

"What's the layout?" he asked.

"Huh?"

"How many bedrooms?" asked an impatient Shakespeare.

"It's a bachelor."

Eldridge waved him back. "Ok, we've got it from here."

They both drew their weapons and took positions on either side of the door. Eldridge gripped the knob and looked at Shakespeare who held up three fingers and counted down, silently mouthing, "three, two, one," then pointing at the door.

Eldridge turned the knob and threw open the door, stepping into the apartment. "Police officers executing a search warrant!" he yelled as he steadily, but cautiously, cleared the entrance, with Shakespeare close behind. With only one room, a bathroom and a small kitchenette, they cleared it within seconds.

"Would you look at that!" Shakespeare whistled as he looked at one of the main room walls. Dozens of printouts, photos, handwritten notes and timelines were tacked to it, almost every square inch a testament to one man's obsession.

"What the hell is that?" asked the Super who had wandered in.

"Get the fu—"

Eldridge cut Shakespeare off. "Please wait outside, sir. This is a crime scene." He accompanied the man out to the hallway and closed the door. When he returned, Shakespeare was standing near the wall, reading some of the material.

"Know what this reminds me of?"

Eldridge nodded. "Yeah, working a case."

"Exactly. Look at this." Shakespeare pointed to the upper left and, moving his finger slowly toward the right, following the chain of documents. "This is his search for his sister. Internet searches, hospital records, birth records, it's all here."

Eldridge's eye was drawn to a series of photos half way down the wall and pointed. "See this? It looks like he met her." A series of photos taken of a young blonde man and a blonde woman, maybe ten years older, were neatly pinned in a row. She had her arm around him and the angle suggested the man had held out his arm to take their picture, as they both smiled broadly.

"This doesn't look like a meeting that went bad."

"No, these are two *very* happy people." Eldridge continued looking then stopped. "What the—" He pointed at several clippings of articles about the subway killing. He scanned ahead and found articles about the suspects' capture followed by a series of eight photos, the first seven he recognized as passengers on the subway, but from their everyday lives, not taken from the video. The eighth was of Aynslee.

"They look like surveillance photos," said Shakespeare. "This kid's been planning this a long time."

Eldridge stared at the photo of Aynslee. *Why is her photo here?*

Shakespeare reached out and pulled a photo of Jeremiah and his sister off the wall and held it up to a photo from a newspaper clipping showing the subway victim. "Look at this."

Eldridge gasped. "Patricia Arnette was Jeremiah Lansing's sister?"

"No wonder this kid's gone off the handle. You're alone, you find out you've got a long lost sister, and she gets killed right in front of you."

"Look at the date." Eldridge pointed to the timestamp in the corner showing the happy pair.

"Same day as the attack."

"They must have been travelling together after this meeting. My God, he's killing everyone that didn't help his sister!"

"And he's going to finish it off with himself, I'm willing to bet."

Eldridge pointed at Aynslee's photo. "I need to find out why she's on this wall." He took the photo of Jeremiah and Patricia then headed out the door.

Eldridge rushed into the infirmary at Rikers, having received a call from his LT about an attack on Denzel Todd, who had died immediately, and Ian Temple, who wasn't expected to last much longer. He knew he might only have minutes to get a deathbed confession from the boy, and of finding out who had attacked him. He had a hard time believing Jeremiah could kill someone from inside Rikers, but he had proven resourceful so far, and was certainly desperate enough to try anything. He looked around for someone who could direct him to Temple's room, when the doctor on duty approached him.

"You here to see Ian Temple?"

"Yes, is he still alive?"

"Barely. He's conscious, but you haven't got a lot of time."

"Okay, I'll need you as a witness." Eldridge entered the room where Ian lay on a bed, hooked to numerous machines, his bandaged stomach and chest showing where the shiv had penetrated. "Mr. Temple, I am Detective Eldridge. Has the doctor informed you of your situation?"

Ian nodded.

"Then you are aware you are dying?"

"Yes," he said, his voice extremely weak.

"Do you know what a death-bed confession is?"

"Yes."

"Okay, I'm going to ask you some questions. Did you and Denzel Todd kill Patricia Arnette on the subway?"

"Yes."

"Is this the man that attacked you?" Eldridge held up the photo of Jeremiah.

Ian nodded. "Y-yes."

"Had you ever seen him before today?"

"No."

"Did you or Mr. Todd have a gun that day?"

"No, b-but D-Denzel told everyb-body he d-did."

"Do you have anything else you want to say?"

"Just, just that I'm s-sorry I d-didn't stop him," said Ian as tears poured from his eyes. "I was sc-scared."

Eldridge looked up as a priest arrived to administer the last rites, surprised Ian was Catholic. Moving aside, Eldridge and the doctor watched, heads bowed, as the boy drifted off to sleep, unable to complete the sacrament. The priest continued with the blessing, Ian's heart monitor beeping erratically, and after a few moments, flat-lining. The doctor stepped forward and turned it off, allowing the priest to finish in silence as the entire ward looked on as a young man, with the wrong friend, paid for his mistake with his life.

Somber, Eldridge left Rikers Island jail and climbed into his car, sitting for a moment as he collected himself. In his job he had seen death, too much death, but usually he arrived after the fact, the corpse long cold, and almost always someone he had never spoken to. On rare occasions he was there when death took someone, sometimes by his own hand, and that moment, the moment of death, always disturbed him, and would remain something he would never grow accustomed to.

He sighed and started the car. As he drove to the television studio he left a message for Vinny to check the subway victim's DNA against the hairs found in the SUV, wanting to confirm what he already suspected, and what his killer was already convinced of, that Jeremiah Lansing and Patricia Arnette were half siblings. As he searched for a parking spot at the studio he received the final photo from the subway. It was Aynslee. He ran into the building and pushed his way through the end of day throngs and onto an empty elevator.

Aynslee looked up to see who had opened her door without knocking. *Hayden!* "Detective Eldridge!" She smiled and rose from her chair. "I'm so happy to see you." She looked at his face, jaw squared in anger, cheeks slightly flushed. *Uh oh, he looks pissed!*

"Care to explain this?" he asked as he held out his phone. She looked at the picture displayed on the tiny display. It was her, but she couldn't make out any details.

"What's that?"

"You were on the subway the night that Patricia Arnette was killed."

Aynslee fell back into her chair, the picture of her rushing from the subway, Blackberry to her ear, snapped into focus as a flood of emotions overwhelmed her. Like a movie, those few minutes replayed themselves in her mind, each face becoming clear as if it had happened yesterday.

"Oh my God," she exclaimed, gripping the arms of her chair, her knuckles turning white, as the realization dawned on her. "We were all on the subway that night!"

"Yes." He seemed to calm down slightly as he showed her a photo of a young man and slightly older woman. "And so was he," he said, pointing to the man. "Jeremiah Lansing and Patricia Arnette were brother and sister. She was killed the day they met for the first time."

"What do you mean first time?"

"She was given up for adoption before he was born. He searched for years and finally found her. They met *that day* for the first time. On their way back from *that* meeting, she was murdered in front of him. He has been killing everyone he can identify from the YouTube video. As of a few minutes ago, he's killed everyone on that tape except for an unidentified senior citizen and yourself. Earlier today he managed to somehow infiltrate Rikers Island and kill Denzel Todd and Ian Temple, the two men who killed his sister."

"How—how did he do that?" asked Aynslee, terror gripping her. *If he can kill in there, nowhere is safe!*

"We're still working that out, but he's a computer genius and we think he may have used that to somehow get himself in and out."

Aynslee's throat went dry and the room closed in around her, Hayden's voice becoming distant as she became dizzy. She clenched the arms of her chair tighter. *Get a grip!* She steadied herself and focused on the bottle of water sitting on her desk. She reached forward and took a drink. "He's going to come after me, isn't he?" She couldn't hide the fear in her voice. And she didn't care. This was no time to put on an act of false bravado.

"I think we can be sure of that."

"Will you protect me?" she asked, almost embarrassed by how meek it sounded.

"We will do everything we can. But first I want you to tell me what happened on the subway."

Aynslee took a deep breath and closed her eyes, remembering that night on the train. "I was heading home after doing the evening entertainment report. There were maybe a dozen people in the subway car with me. I was sending some emails with my BlackBerry, sitting near the back. Two guys got on and they definitely seemed to be on something, or at least that's what it seemed like. Anyway, these two got on and one of them was really loud. He knocked one guy's newspaper, flipped somebody's hat off and then one of them, the loud one, sat down beside the girl—Patricia was it?" Hayden nodded. "—sat down beside Patricia and put his arm around her. She said something like 'Get your hands off me, creep' and then he jumped to his feet and started yelling at her, things like 'what, you think you're too good for me, you're better than me?', that type of thing. So she gets up and tries to go to another car with this other guy that was sitting across from her, but the loud one—"

"That would be Denzel."

"Yes, Denzel, yells 'don't you walk away from me, bitch' and shoves her from behind. She flew forward and hit her head on one of the seatbacks. She fell to the ground and this Denzel guy started to laugh. The guy she was with—"

"The one in the photo I showed you?"

"Yes, he yelled at them and that's when this Denzel guy shoves his hand in his pocket and starts making like he's got a gun and yells that he'll shoot anyone who gets in their way. Well, the guy in the photo, I think he fainted because he just collapsed to the floor. Then this Denzel guy said something like 'she's my bitch now and I'll do to her what I want'. Then he kicked her, hard. She screamed and then he started kicking her over and over. I was in shock, I couldn't believe what was going on, I was so terrified. I didn't know if he had a gun or not. So he keeps kicking her and then tells his friend to kick her as well. His friend," she paused. "What was his name?"

"Ian."

"Yeah, well it didn't look like he liked what was going on, kind of reluctant, you know? Anyway, he did a few half-hearted kicks and then when the train was coming to the next stop he pulled his friend away, but his friend went back and stomped his boot down as hard as he could on that poor girl's head. I swear I could hear her skull crack. I just knew she was dead. Anyway, I'm embarrassed to say this, but I just ran with everyone else."

"You didn't stay to talk to the police?"

Aynslee dropped her head in shame. "No. I was going to call the next day but then that video hit the Internet and the terrible things people were saying about us, the ones on the subway who didn't help, well, it just made me think that I didn't want to get involved, to be one of those people that everyone was vilifying. Do you understand?"

She could tell he was no longer angry, his soft, caring features had returned, the face she so yearned to hold in her hands looked at her for a moment before speaking.

"I understand a little better, now that I've been looking into this further. Due to the lack of witnesses, nobody knew about the threat of a gun. This is an important factor. People have a duty to assist another person in distress, but not if it means putting their own lives at risk. It makes me wonder if Jeremiah even remembers the gun?"

"This Jeremiah, he's the brother?"

"Yes, I'm assuming half-brother, but we believe he's our killer."

"And that was the first time they had ever met?" Tears filled her eyes. "How sad, no wonder he's gone mad."

"And if he fainted, then he's probably ashamed and embarrassed by what happened and blames himself for her death."

Aynslee looked at her watch. "Oh my, God, I'm on in half an hour. I need to get ready."

"Miss Kai, I need to place you in protective custody immediately."

"You'll do no such thing, I have to go to air."

"Your life is in danger."

"Listen, he's sent a video of every killing to me so far, right?"

"Yes."

"Well, the old lady is still alive, right?"

"We don't know," he replied. "Perhaps we just haven't found the body yet."

"No, we know she's still alive because he hasn't sent me a video yet."

He frowned. "Are you willing to bet your life on that?"

"Yes. I need to go to air."

"Not a word about what we've spoken about. He can't know that we know who he is."

Aynslee blew a breath out between her lips hard in frustration. "Fine! Now get out of here, I need to get ready."

"I'm going to have a squad car out front and an officer shadowing you. They'll be here in about half an hour."

"Fine, whatever you feel is necessary, but I need to get ready. And, Detective," she paused and looked him in the eyes. "Thank you for helping me. I mean, I'm sure you don't have to come down here every time I get one of those videos, you could send someone else or just have me email it to you. I appreciate that you take the time to come and see me."

"I'm just doing my job, Miss Kai."

She stepped a little closer to him. "Why don't you call me Aynslee, it's my name too."

A smile flashed across his face for a moment, but it quickly returned to his usual formal expression. "That wouldn't be appropriate, Miss Kai."

Aynslee waved her finger at him. "I'll break through that cold exterior one of these days, Detective." She detected the corner of his lip curl slightly, revealing a hint of a smile.

"I'll have those uniforms here shortly, Miss Kai." And with that he left her standing there, more determined than ever to have him, and even more impressed at the level of confidence she now felt. *It must be the new job! Or the look?*

"Oh, Eunice, what to do, what to do!"

Eunice Henry muttered to herself as she rocked in her chair, knitting yet another scarf for yet another niece or nephew. "There's nothing to worry about, you've got food, you've got water, you've got all the basic necessities of life. You can hold out until Friday." Her knitting needles clicked together as her skilled hands never dropped a stitch. Frustrated, she tossed her project aside and reached over to check the phone again. And again no dial tone. "Sugarollie double-plum fairy! Darned phone company."

She hadn't left her apartment in twelve months. After witnessing the attack on the subway, she had gone straight home, locked the door and hadn't set foot outside since. Anything she needed could be delivered, it was New York after all, and she had family to do the rest. She never answered the door unless she expected someone or recognized them through the peephole. There were times, even just yesterday, when strangers would knock on the door, sometimes insistently, but she would ignore them. Her distrust of people in general overwhelmed her, an all-consuming problem she knew she would never overcome. Not after seeing that poor girl beaten to death on the subway that day.

But her lifestyle had one flaw. She needed a phone. And today her phone wasn't working. She couldn't call anyone to get it fixed nor go out to tell anyone it needed to be fixed. And worst of all, she wasn't expecting anybody for several days.

She started at a knock on the door. As usual, she ignored it but became very quiet. *They'll go away, they always do.* Again the knock.

"Mrs. Henry, this is Verizon, I'm here to fix your phone!"

She looked at the door. "Oh my, what to do, what to do?" she whispered to herself. "Well, you have to answer it, you need your phone. But you don't know who he is. How do you know he's actually from the phone company? You could ask to see his ID? Yes, but those could be faked. Well, your phone is out and how would some criminal know that?" She nodded to herself and rocked to her feet. "You're right, how could he know? Coming!" she called.

Shuffling to the door, she looked through the peephole and saw a young man smiling. *Oh, he looks sweet, just like Jamie.* She began the long process of unlocking, unbolting and unchaining her myriad of devices aimed at keeping intruders out, and herself in. With one chain remaining, she turned the knob and opened the door. "Can I see some ID, please?" she asked, peering through the narrow opening. The young man stepped back and suddenly kicked the door hard, ripping through the chain and hitting her square in the shoulder. She tumbled backward and landed hard, a searing pain shot through her entire body as the man stormed in and slammed the door behind him. She tried to speak but the pain was so intense, she couldn't. Having broken her hip once before, she knew she had done it again.

The man gripped her wrists and hauled her to her feet, sending excruciating jolts of pain up and down her body. She yelped in agony as he carried her and dropped her unceremoniously on her couch. The soft cushions provided little relief, but she managed to see through the pain and focus on her attacker.

"What do you want?" she cried.

He held a cell phone in front of her and pressed a button. A video played, a video of that horrible day a year ago, and when it finished, it froze on an image of her, climbing out of her seat. She looked at the cold expression on his face, and she knew why he was here. As he drew a gun and pointed it at her, a strange calm washed over her, a sense of peace, acceptance of her fate. She knew she was going to die, and it was okay.

"You knew her, didn't you?" He didn't respond but she could see it in his eyes. "My boy, you must do what you must do. I am truly sorry for what happened to that young girl. I can offer only my age as an excuse, albeit a poor one. I can see you are in pain and if my death brings you some sort of peace, then I am willing to give my life for it. Was she your girlfriend?" Still, no response. "Your sister?" This time she saw a reaction, a slight increase of moisture in his eyes. "That's it, isn't it? She was your sister. I am very sorry, my dear, for your loss. You must have been very close." Leaning forward, she tried not to wince from the pain. "Tell me, son, is there anything you would like me to tell her?"

This got a reaction. Her attacker hesitated, a look of uncertainty on his face. "I—" he began then stopped.

"Yes? It's okay, dear, you can tell me."

His eyes filled with tears. "Tell her that I wish I had gotten the chance to know her. That I'm sorry for not helping her."

Eunice was a little puzzled by his statement. *Gotten the chance? Did he not know his own sister?* She smiled gently. "I will tell her, dear, I will tell her." He raised his gun again, his hand shaking. Eunice closed her eyes, waiting for him to pull the trigger, silently praying. When the shot didn't come, she opened her eyes to see what was wrong.

He was gone.

Eldridge arrived at Jeremiah's apartment building and was more than a little stunned to see Shakespeare walking toward his car, having put in what amounted to a full day's work, but something told him they were both taking this case personally. He honked his horn and Shakespeare waved at him, walking toward the car as Eldridge parked.

"So, why was your lady friend on the wall?" asked Shakespeare as Eldridge rounded the vehicle.

"She was there that day. Just like the others, she just watched it happen."

Shakespeare grunted. "Chances are she's on the list then."

"Agreed. There's only her and the old lady left."

"Is she in protective custody yet?"

"She refused. I've got a couple of uniforms on her, though. She should be safe for now since there's been no video of the old lady yet. If he follows the pattern, he should send that first."

"*If* he follows the pattern. Big chance."

"Have you ever tried to convince a reporter not to go to air?"

"Yeah, like trying to convince Vinny to forget what happened."

Eldridge decided not to bite. "Are the lab guys still in there?"

Shakespeare nodded. "They're still processing, probably going to be awhile. What are you looking for?"

"Well, this guy's been working on this for a year now so he might have a lead on who the old lady is. If we can get to her first, she might stand a chance."

"Didn't help the last guy."

"Yeah, but hopefully no screw-ups this time."

Shakespeare nodded and walked toward his car. "Okay, I'm off, there's a Philly melt with my name on it somewhere."

Eldridge waved as Shakespeare pulled away. Across the street a small throng of onlookers watched the couple of squad cars plus the CSU vehicle, most likely hoping to catch a glimpse of a dead body. Ever since CSI started airing, the CSU guys had been getting a lot of attention. Eldridge thought half the city expected Garry Sinise to come strolling out and solve the case in forty minutes plus commercials.

A shock of blonde hair caught Eldridge's eye. He looked closer but didn't see it again. He walked toward the apartment building entrance, all the while keeping his eye on the crowd across from him. Then he saw it again. Just a flash of blonde behind several people. Normally he wouldn't have paid it any mind, there being several blondes in the crowd, but this one stood out. Where everyone was jockeying for position, trying to get a better view, this one was in behind. Eldridge turned and walked toward the crowd when he saw the blonde hair again followed by the face of Jeremiah, looking directly at him. Eldridge, stunned to see his suspect standing maybe fifty feet from him, stopped in his tracks. Jeremiah smiled at him then bolted.

Eldridge ran as hard as he could, slowly gaining on his suspect, when Jeremiah ducked into an alleyway. He heard the sound of an engine turn over as he rounded the corner, almost running headlong into a small motorcycle as it tore from the alley, Jeremiah perched atop it. Eldridge lunged at him, but Jeremiah ducked over to the other side of the bike and roared onto the street. Spinning around, Eldridge sprinted after him, but it was no use, Jeremiah bobbed and weaved amongst the traffic and quickly left Eldridge gasping for breath in the middle of the road.

Walking back toward the apartment he phoned in the bike's description and the direction it was heading, but he knew nothing would come of it; he was long gone. He phoned Shakespeare to let him know what had happened, then met Vinny in the apartment as he catalogued the papers tacked to the wall.

"Detective! Looks like you've ID'd your killer!"

"I'd rather have him in a holding cell, but at least we've got a name and face to go with the handiwork. Anything on the location of the old lady amongst all this stuff?"

Vinny shook his head. "No, haven't really had a chance to go through this stuff in detail. I'm just cataloguing it so we can process it all at the lab."

"Okay, have your team keep an eye out for any names or addresses. I need to ID that old woman. And make sure you get a copy of the photo of her sent to me because it looks like he's got a better one than I do, maybe we can air it, get some help from the public."

"Will do, detective. By the way, why'd you want me to compare the subway vic's DNA to the SUV driver? Another hunch?"

"No, just want to confirm something. Assuming the SUV driver was Jeremiah Lansing, they were apparently half brother and sister."

"You're kidding me!"

"Wish I were. Looks like this all started a year ago. I want you to compare the SUV DNA to some samples from this apartment. It should remove all doubt that Lansing is the killer. I'll bring you up to speed later, right now I've got to check in on a stubborn witness."

"Our cute little reporter?" Vinny smiled slyly.

"Yes."

"I wouldn't mind checkin' in on her if you know what I mean," laughed Vinny. "She could read the news to me any day, if you know what I mean. I'd like her to speak into my microph—"

"I think I've heard enough," said Eldridge, cutting him off. "I'll see you tomorrow."

"Hey, did I say something wrong?" asked Vinny, feigning hurt feelings. "You got something going on with this girl?"

"Good night, Vinny!"

"Wouldn't blame ya, she's a hottie!"

Eldridge smiled as he headed down the stairs.

As Shakespeare headed off to Brooklyn to get his favorite sandwich, he drove by his old boyhood church. Much to his surprise he found himself going around the block and parking outside. *You're here, might as well make it worthwhile.* As he climbed from the car he saw Father O'Neil waving to him from the church steps.

"Justin! So good to see you!"

Shakespeare waved half-heartedly. "Hiya, Father, don't get your hopes up, I'm just here on official business."

"One can always hope, Justin." O'Neil entered the church, forcing a reluctant Shakespeare to follow him if he wanted to continue the conversation. As they headed to the rectory O'Neil pointed to the confessionals and looked back at Shakespeare. "You sure?"

"Nice try, Father, but neither of us have that kind of time."

O'Neil laughed and held the door to his office open for the detective. "Now what brings New York's Finest here this evening?"

'Bout the nicest thing anyone's called me lately. "We searched Jeremiah Lansing's apartment today and have confirmed he's the man we're looking for. We think his sister was beaten to death on the subway about a year ago. That's what started this whole thing off."

"My God, that poor boy!" O'Neil sat down in a nearby chair and said a quick, silent prayer. "Were you able to catch Jeremiah without hurting him?"

"No, my partner spotted him just a little while ago outside of the apartment but he managed to get away on a motorcycle."

"Is Detective Eldridge okay?"

"Oh yeah, that kid can take care of himself. But now that we've confirmed Jeremiah is the killer, I need you to be careful, Father."

"Why should I have anything to worry about?"

"He knows he can't go home now, so he'll be looking for other safe havens. He feels safe here so he may come back."

"And I'll welcome him with open arms. If he comes here, I'm sure I can convince him to turn himself in."

"He might not even be looking for you," replied Shakespeare. "Listen Father, he's been coming here and helping out for years. That means he knows the place. He could hole up somewhere here and not even tell you. You or one of your staff could just stumble upon him and he's dangerous."

"I can't believe he would hurt me."

"Would you have believed yesterday that he could kill ten people?"

"I put my fate in God's hands, Justin. It is my duty to help Jeremiah, and I will."

Shakespeare rose from his seat. "Just call me, Father, if he comes here, don't try and be a hero."

O'Neil laughed. "Not a hero, son, just a man of the cloth."

"Yeah, well just be careful, Father, that cloth isn't bulletproof and I'd hate to see anything happen to you."

O'Neil draped his arm across Shakespeare's shoulder and led him back toward the church entrance. "I'm an old man, Justin. If God decides I can serve him better by his side, then he will take me. If not, then I will be fine. Either way, it is out of our hands."

Shakespeare didn't put much stock in religion, but he did respect Father O'Neil and had many fond memories of him from his younger days, before his job had jaded him to the point where he had lost his faith. Decades of seeing the worst in people had made him question how any God could let people the likes of what he dealt with on a daily basis be born. Over time, he just stopped believing. He figured as long as he kept his head down and out of trouble, Saint Peter would let him past those pearly gates even if he had a deathbed conversion back to the side of the believers. "Just watch your back, Father."

"I will, I will, don't you worry about me. Now off with you, I've got to close up." Shakespeare headed to his car and looked back to see O'Neil shut the heavy church doors.

That bastard better not touch him.

His stomach grumbled and his mouth watered as he pictured a toasted Philly melt sandwich, smothered in sautéed onions with a side of au jus gravy. He pressed a little harder on the accelerator.

Eldridge sat in the viewing booth he had been shown to when he arrived at the television studios, watching the live newscast taping. He had to admit to himself it was kind of exhilarating to be behind the scenes, seeing how it was all done. And despite himself he couldn't take his eyes off Aynslee. She *was* quite attractive, and seeing her in her element, very good at her job. Delivering an update on the murders, he was pleased to see she didn't reveal any of their conversation, simply rehashed already known details. The broadcast closed with the typical casual banter between the various on-air personalities, followed by Aynslee saying goodnight to her audience.

"And we're clear!" he heard someone yell. He watched as Aynslee stretched in her chair then got up and tossed good-natured jabs back and forth with her co-workers. She spotted him in the booth and waved, a huge smile on her face. He was surprised at how good it made him feel. *You got something going on with this girl?* He could hear Vinny's voice in his head. *Can't get involved with a witness.* He smiled back.

Aynslee rushed into the booth and before Eldridge could stop her, she had given him a quick hug. Catching a waft of the scent from her hair, he found himself almost reaching around to return the hug but he recovered in time and instead coughed. She let go and stepped back. "So, what did you think?"

Eldridge looked about him at the rapidly emptying control room. "Very impressive."

"Sooo, how was I?" she asked, fishing for a compliment in none too subtle a manner.

Eldridge had to smile. "You were fine, Miss Kai, very professional."

She playfully slapped his arm. "Oh, do stop, you'll embarrass me. Now, how can I help you?"

"I'm here to escort you home."

"But, Detective, we haven't even been on a date yet!" she said as she took his arm and led him toward her office. "First, we should have dinner, *then* we can see where the evening leads."

"Aaah," was all Eldridge managed. Aynslee let go of his arm and laughed.

"You need to work on your sense of humor a little bit, Detective, if you're going to take me home, even if it is to just be my bodyguard. Remember, Kevin did fall for Whitney in the end."

"Huh?"

"The Bodyguard, Kevin Costner, Whitney Houston?"

"Oh, yeah," said Eldridge. He had no clue what she was talking about.

"It's a love story with guns," explained Aynslee as she gathered her things. "You'd love it."

"I'm sure I would," replied Eldridge as they headed to the elevators where Aynslee was accosted by several of her coworkers trying to convince her to join them for drinks, but a quick look at Eldridge's expression put the kibosh on that idea. As they approached the entrance, Eldridge waved over the two uniforms still parked out front. Leaving Aynslee with them, he looked around, inspected his car, and, satisfied, motioned for the officers to bring her out. In less than a minute, the two-car motorcade was underway, the squad car trailing behind them, making sure they weren't followed.

"Do you really think I'm in danger?"

"Absolutely, however you haven't received what we assume is the final video, so I believe we have time before he acts."

"And the old lady, any idea who she is?"

"Not yet, but we're going through all of the stuff that was found in his apartment. Hopefully we'll find a name or address."

Aynslee tossed her head back against the seat in frustration. "Ooh, I hate this!"

Eldridge looked in his rearview mirror then over at her. "Don't worry, you're in good hands."

Looking back at him she smiled. "I know." Eldridge looked back at the road ahead and said nothing. "Detective, can I ask you something? And you have to answer truthfully, I am a marked woman after all." Eldridge nodded, knowing where this was going. "You're not gay, are you?"

Ok, wasn't expecting that. "Ah, no."

"Do you find me attractive?"

Eldridge paused before answering, then, without making eye contact, he said, "Yes."

The smile on Aynslee's face made it clear to him that was the answer she was hoping to hear. "Okay then, it must be my personality. There's something about me you don't like."

"Why would you say that?"

"Because I've been practically throwing myself at you these past few days and you've been, like, completely ignoring me."

Eldridge didn't say anything.

"Like now."

He was on duty. Doing his job. He wasn't required to respond, but he felt he had to. "I can't get involved with a witness, especially one under my protection."

"Yeah, yeah, I know, but when this is all over, promise me one thing?"

"What?"

"Coffee. At least one coffee together, just you and me, no talk about this case, and let's just see if there's something there. If there isn't, we drink our coffees quickly, if there is, we order refills. And if we're lucky, we both order refills."

Despite himself Eldridge was finding it hard to keep the wall up. He found something about her voice intoxicating, as if he could listen to her talk all night and never get tired of hearing it. *Perhaps that's why she's a news anchor?* He hadn't realized it, but he had already said, "Fine." This appeared to satisfy her and she drew quiet for a minute, humming a tune he didn't recognize.

"Here's my apartment just up on the right." Eldridge parked behind a squad car already waiting and exited the vehicle, carefully scanning his surroundings.

"Can I have your keys, Miss Kai," he asked, leaning in the passenger side window.

She handed them over. "Nine-C."

The trailing squad car pulled in directly behind and its occupants joined him as the two officers already waiting trotted from the building's lobby and approached the group. Eldridge eyed the traffic, watching for any cars parking unexpectedly. "Status?" he asked, still watching the traffic.

One of the officers from the lobby replied. "We've done a thorough search, all exits seem secure, the security systems are working and the security company has been told to send any alarms to us immediately."

"Good work. I'll want one of you in the car, and one at the entrance inside," said Eldridge, pointing to the two officers already on scene. "I want you two in eye contact at all times." He handed them a photo of Jeremiah. "This is our suspect. He's proven very resourceful and has been known to wear disguises. He is armed and has already killed over ten people." He handed the keys to an officer from the trailing car. "Nine-C, check it out, make sure it's clear. If everything is okay, one of you come back down and we'll proceed." They nodded and ran inside. A few minutes later one returned and waved from the lobby the all clear. Eldridge opened the door and helped Aynslee out, ushering her into the building and directly into an elevator the officer had blocked open with his nightstick. Silence ruled as they ascended to the ninth floor, everyone tense. The doors opened and Eldridge cautiously poked his head out, looking both ways. The other officer, halfway down the hallway, holding open the door to Aynslee's apartment, waved. Eldridge, one hand on Aynslee's back, the other holding her elbow, marched her toward the apartment then inside. Eldridge heard Aynslee breathe a sigh of relief as the apartment door closed behind them.

"My God, that was intense. I don't think I realized how scared I was." She kicked off her shoes and sat down on her couch as Eldridge searched the apartment, including closets and under furniture, satisfying himself it was empty. He returned to the living room to find Aynslee waiting.

"I'll be leaving one officer outside your door. If you need anything, they're just outside." Aynslee nodded and walked with him to the door as he spoke to his two officers. "I want one of you at the door, the other a rover. Check out the hallways, stairwells, everything. Alternate between the four of you as necessary, I'll have you relieved at the end of your shift. Make sure you don't leave this door for anything, even a piss break." The men nodded and left to take their posts. He turned to Aynslee. "Again, if you need anything, please call one of the officers. They will accompany you to your office in the morning when you're ready. I will see you tomorrow."

She gripped his arm as he was about to head out the door. Leaning in, she gave him a soft peck on the cheek. "Thank you, Hayden."

Not trusting himself to make eye contact, he paused then stepped out into the hallway. "Good night, Miss Kai. Lock the door behind me." She nodded and did a small wave to him as she closed the door.

Chelsie was ravenous when the food and water arrived. She sat back on her mattress and eyed the sandwich. Picking it apart, she surveyed the ingredients, a generous helping of smoked meat, Swiss cheese, lettuce, tomato, and mustard, set between two halves of what looked like a homemade sourdough roll. She had to admit the sandwich looked delicious. *But which ingredient is drugged?* It had to be the mustard. It was the easiest. She scraped as much off as she could with her finger and rinsed it in the water hole. Tearing the sandwich in two, she disposed of the second half. *Just in case it isn't the mustard.* Starving, she practically inhaled the sandwich, afterward leaning her back against the wall. Within minutes her eyes drooped. *It's not the mustard.*

She awoke, lying in the now familiar bed, but this time with something pressing her into the soft mattress. It took only moments for her to realize what was happening. Her captor's hot, sweaty flesh was pressed against her naked body, his breath heavy in her ear as he thrust at her, his hands gripping her buttocks as he tried to penetrate her with a non-existent erection. She smiled inwardly, both satisfied and relieved at this turn of events. His feeble attempts continued for several more minutes, his groans of pleasure, sounding more and more forced, eventually turning into growls of frustration.

Then he stopped and lay perfectly still on top of her, the only movement that of his heaving chest as he caught his breath. After a few moments, she felt him shake, the sounds of sobs filled her ear, a hot splash of a tear on her shoulder, as he broke down and cried. "This still isn't right," he whispered in her ear. *Is he talking to me?* He sniffed and pushed himself up, removing the now uncomfortable weight. The bed rocked as he climbed off and she heard the sounds of clothes being put on nearby. "This *still* isn't right!" he said, this time louder. "She not right, she's not the same." *What is he talking about? I'm not the same as what? The girl in the picture?* "No, she won't do."

Now fear set in. If she wouldn't do, did that mean he no longer had any use for her? He continued to mutter as he left the room. *You have to get out of here. Now!* She heard the creak of the stairs, and as quietly as she could, she crawled from the bed and tip-toed to the window. Opening the drapes, her heart sank as she found it boarded over. She tiptoed to the doorway, fearful with each step the old floors would give her away. Gingerly, she crept down the stairs, leaning heavily on the railing, trying to prevent the stairs from creaking. As she neared the bottom she saw the doorway and freedom. She stole a glance down the hall and saw a bright light shining from the kitchen doorway, cutting into the darkness. She heard him moving around, continuing to mutter, as he did something in the kitchen, a kitchen thankfully out of her line of sight, and therefore, she out of his. She stepped to the door, flipped the deadbolt and removed the chain. Turning the knob, she felt the door start to open in her hand. Her heart raced. A final glance back to make sure she was still alone and she slowly pulled the door open.

A chime beeped three times from behind her. She spun around and saw a security panel on the wall, a red light indicating the door she had just opened. The noise in the kitchen stopped, but only for a moment. She heard footsteps then her captor charge from the kitchen. She threw the door open and ran headlong into a screen door. Screaming, she pushed at it and then, seeing the clasp, fumbled with it. "Help! Help me!" she cried repeatedly, hoping someone would hear her, the darkened street mere feet away, houses on the other side, some with lights on, urging her forward. She threw her weight against the door and the clasp gave way. She shoved the door aside, the pounding of footsteps right behind her now. Hurtling herself from the house she ran onto a porch then down several steps to a stone path. She heard him hit the screen door as it bounced back at him. Running as fast as her bare feet could take her, she raced to an opening in a thick hedge surrounding the property, then was hit hard from behind. She smacked the ground, her attacker on top of her, her naked body scraping against the walkway, the rough stones tearing at her flesh. She rolled over as he lost his grip and looked up to see the face of the man from the subway glaring down at her, his fist cocked over his shoulder.

Chelsie awoke to a curious sensation. Darkness surrounded her, and she felt cold. Very cold. She lay naked on something soft and moist. It wasn't a mattress, it wasn't the basement floor, she wasn't sure what it was. She tried to reach out but found her hands bound in front of her. She heard what sounded like a sob from somewhere above her. She looked up and saw what appeared to be the night sky, then something blocked the shaft of light, falling toward her, spreading out as it neared. The bulk of it hit her stomach, taking the wind out of her, the rest sprayed over her flesh, cool and damp. Looking up she heard the sound of a shovel hitting dirt followed by another pile sailing into the hole she lay in. *Oh my God! He's burying me alive!* "Help!" she screamed, but it was no use, her mouth taped shut, her hands and wrists bound, she struggled to free herself from her bindings. Shovelful after shovelful hit her, each one slowly immobilizing her further, soon leaving her unable to move her legs, then her upper body.

A pile hit her face and she snorted hard, trying to clear the dirt from her nose, exhausting the air in her lungs. She sucked against the tape, trying to force precious oxygen through, to no avail. She shook her head, attempting to rid herself of the dirt. She opened her eyes and again another pile fell on her face. She shook it off but was hit by another, then another. She tried to hold her breath, but it was no use. Her heart beat harder and harder and she felt the pressure as her body demanded she take a breath. Finally giving in, she took a deep breath through her nose, sucking the dirt into her nasal passages, immediately clogging her airways. The musty scent crept into her throat as she sucked more and more in, desperate for air. Her heart thumped in her chest and she began to feel lightheaded. Bright lights streaked all around her like a Fourth of July fireworks display, despite her eyes being firmly shut. As she slowly passed out, her gasps became less and less frequent, until, at long last, they stopped.

ELEVEN

Eunice lay against her door, her ear pressed to the cold wood, hoping to hear someone, anyone, pass by. She had remained sitting on her couch for the longest time after her attacker abruptly left. In excruciating pain from her broken hip, she eventually managed to reach the nearby phone, only to find it remained dead, the endeavor expending all the energy she had. She yelled for help until hoarse from the effort. Hours later she decided she had to at least get near the door; she would worry about working up the courage to open it to strangers later. It took almost two hours to drag herself by her hands, across the floor to the doorway. She nearly passed out several times, but was determined not to be found by her son dead in two days when he was due to visit her. She managed to get within reach of the door, but the knob proved too high.

It was hours more before she heard two people talking. She recognized the voices as a neighbor couple, Paul and Joanne Russell, who lived across the hall. She banged on the door with the last of her strength. The talking stopped then she heard a knock on the door. "Mrs. Henry, are you okay?"

"No, please call an ambulance and the police," she cried at the door. "I've been attacked!" She heard them try the door and push against it. Dragging herself out of the way, they managed to open it and enter the apartment.

"Oh my God!" Joanne exclaimed. "Call nine-one-one!" Paul was already on his cell phone and within minutes police arrived, followed shortly by paramedics.

Eldridge sprinted toward the hospital lobby. It wasn't until the next morning the connection was made with his case. An elderly lady, one Eunice Henry, had been attacked, and the officer who had taken her statement had mentioned in the locker room about the attacker showing a video on a cell phone. Someone familiar with his case had made the connection and contacted him. Arriving in the lobby, he found the protective detail of four officers he had ordered milling about. He flashed his shield, bringing the group not quite to attention, but at least to a respectable at ease. He flipped open a file folder and handed them the suspect's photo.

"This is him. The last time he was in a hospital, the damned thing blew up, so let's keep an eye out." He pointed to an officer. "You are?"

"Haynes, sir."

"Haynes, I want you in the security booth. Get copies of this photo made and have them handed out to every employee in the building." Haynes rushed off to fulfill his assignment as Eldridge motioned the others to follow him to the elevators. The crowded elevator prevented him from continuing the briefing until they exited. He pointed at two officers as he strode toward Eunice's room. "I want you two to do a room by room search, every room, including bathrooms, janitor's closets, everything, and make sure this floor is clear, then I want you at opposite ends of this corridor, go!" The men rushed off as the remaining officer struggled to keep up with Eldridge's rapid pace. When they arrived he stationed her outside the door.

Entering the private room, he saw Eunice Henry comforted by a middle-aged, balding man. He looked up and protectively placed himself between Eldridge and the frail looking woman. "Who are you?"

Eldridge flashed his badge. "I'm Detective Eldridge, Homicide. You are?"

"Jonathan Henry, I'm her son. What's going on?"

"Sir, ma'am, here's the situation. Your attacker is involved in over ten murders in the past week. He's killing everyone he's been able to identify off of a video of a subway attack last year that resulted in the death of one Patricia Arnette. You were there, Mrs. Henry."

"You saw that happen?" asked Jonathan. "No wonder you've been terrified to go out!"

She nodded and smiled at her son. "Yes, I was there and I did nothing. I'm ashamed to admit it, but I was too terrified to do anything."

"Mother, you're over eighty years old, what could you have done?"

She shrugged her shoulders. "I still have my voice, and I didn't use it."

Jonathan turned to Eldridge. "You said he's killing people from a video, do you mean the one that was all over the news last year that those two morons made?"

"Yes, he used advanced computer software to pull faces from the video. We believe him to be quite adept at computers and this is how he managed to track everyone down who was on that train. We're still piecing it together, it's early on. I can tell you there are only three people still alive who were on that tape. One is the killer himself, the other a reporter that he has been sending videos of the killings to, and you, Mrs. Henry."

"Aynslee Kai on channel nine?" asked Jonathan, the slight rise in his voice betraying a piqued curiosity. His mother slapped his wrist. Jonathan blushed.

"Yes, I believe that your mother will be his next target as he always sends a video of the murder to Miss Kai before moving on to the next person. Since he didn't succeed the first time with you, ma'am, we expect him to try again."

"Oh, I don't think he'll be coming for me, dear," said Eunice shaking her head.

"Why is that?"

"There's a flaw in your logic, young man. It wasn't that he didn't succeed in killing me. It was that he changed his mind."

"What?" Eldridge wasn't sure he understood her correctly. "Please explain."

"I spoke to him. I knew I was going to die so I asked him if there was anything he wanted me to tell the girl."

"You did what?" Jonathan stared at his mother, searching for words. "What were you—why did—how could—wait a minute!" He turned back to Eldridge. "He knew the girl on the subway?"

"Yes, we believe he was her half-brother."

"Aaah, I figured either sister or girlfriend," said Eunice. "He said that he wanted me to tell her that he wished he had gotten a chance to know her better and that he wished he had helped her."

"And what did you say?" asked Eldridge.

"I said I would tell her."

"And then what happened."

"He walked out of the apartment."

Eldridge processed this new information. *If he changed his mind, then he won't be killing her, which means there will be no video.* "There's not going to be a video!" he muttered as he turned on his heel and raced from the room, reaching for his cell phone.

Father O'Neil rose from his knees, made the sign of the cross, bowed, and turned to see he wasn't alone, a man in a pulled-up hoodie sat in the back row. He looked at O'Neil, rose, and walked toward the confessional. O'Neil hadn't expected to be taking confession at this moment, he had other duties to attend, but none more important. When he reached the booth, the man had already entered. Sitting down, O'Neil prepared himself then slid the panel open.

"Bless me, Father, for I have sinned. It has been two weeks since my last confession and these are my sins." The man paused. But this was no man. O'Neil recognized his voice from the first word. *Jeremiah!* His heart pounded, his mouth went dry.

"Please continue, my son."

He heard a deep breath on the other side of the thin booth. "I have broken the fifth commandment." *Oh no, he did do what they said!* "I have murdered my fellow man."

"And what made you break God's commandment?"

"They did nothing to help my sister, they were sinners for not helping *their* fellow man."

"And they are to be judged by God for their sins, not by us mere mortals."

"But as instruments of God, shouldn't we do what we know He would want? They let her die and they should burn in hell for it!" Jeremiah's voice was getting louder, in the end almost hysterical. Fear gripped O'Neil. Choosing his words with care, he tried to calm him.

"And if God judges that they were indeed sinners that cannot be forgiven, then they will, my son, they will. You can rest easy that if God wills it, they will get a punishment far more harsh than anything you or I could ever mete out."

He heard a sob from the other side. "They let her die, Father. They just stood there and watched as they killed her. I never had a chance to even get to know her."

O'Neil desperately wanted to go to the other side of the booth and comfort the poor boy, but he knew he couldn't, it would be a violation of the confessional. "I know, my son, it was a terrible tragedy. She was taken from us far too soon. And the men who did this will pay for their sins."

"I was bringing her to meet *you*, Father. That day on the subway, I was bringing her to meet *you*!" His voice was almost maniacal. O'Neil's heart leapt in his throat. He had to figure out a way to defuse the tension.

"And it would have been an honor to meet her, my son." His voice shook. "And one day I will, I will meet her in heaven amongst the angels."

"Yes, you will meet her." The sudden calm in the voice terrified O'Neil. "But first, I want you to forgive me for my sins."

"I-I can't do that, my son, I don't think that you are truly sorry for what you have done. I cannot forgive you your sins unless you are truly sorry and won't commit them again." He heard something knock against the wood of the confessional wall. "I can however counsel you. Please let me take you to the police, Jeremiah. Please let me help you end this so that no one else gets hurt, including yourself."

"I don't care if anything happens to me. If I die, then I'll be with her, but only if you absolve me of my sins!"

O'Neil, shaking all over, gripped his rosary. "You know that I can't do that, Jeremiah. Only God can."

A sigh came from the other side. "Very well." He heard a loud popping sound followed by splintering wood, then a curious sensation from his stomach. He looked down and saw his black robe rapidly becoming wet. Reaching with his hand, he touched the liquid spreading from his stomach and was shocked to see it was red. As the adrenaline of the situation subsided, the pain took over. He felt himself getting weaker as the confessional door ripped open. Jeremiah stood looking down at him, his tear stained face betraying the horror of what he had done.

"I-I'm sorry, Father, I'm so sorry." He knelt down beside O'Neil and put his hand over the wound.

O'Neil reached up with his hand and held it against Jeremiah's cheek. "I forgive you," he whispered before blacking out.

Eldridge's phone rang as he raced toward the television studios. He snapped it off his belt and flipped it open, putting it on speaker. "Eldridge."

"Hello, Detective, Vinny here. I've confirmed the DNA from the subway vic, Patricia Arnette and our John Doe, presumably this Jeremiah Lansing, are related maternally."

"Figured. I think there's little doubt John Doe and Jeremiah Lansing are one and the same."

"Should have DNA results from the apartment any time now, that will confirm it for sure. We've also been going through the papers and computer found at the apartment, as well as the church computer. We've found extensive Internet searches and video surveillance of the subway system. It looks like he was able to hack the surveillance footage and track the people on the subway that day. As well, he had a copy of the witness list we think was stolen from the defense attorney's computer. Detective, this guy has been working on this for a year. He has surveillance, schedules, everything. This is well planned. It looks like he was just waiting for the final piece."

"And what was that?"

"It looks like he needed a partner to get himself out of Rikers. We found several postings on known hacker boards putting out a challenge to get a prisoner out and someone took him up on it. Shakespeare is picking him up as we speak."

"Shakespeare?"

"Yeah, didn't believe it myself. Hopefully he doesn't fu—"

"So this hacker got him out of Rikers?"

"Yes, from the timestamps on everything it looks like he just needed that final piece and then he began eliminating everyone in the order they were most likely to be able to flee. He killed Tammera Coverdale because she was leaving on a business trip, then Logan and Aaron as well as William "Lance" Hanson because their lifestyles were more transient. The cab driver, Mr. Jamar and Abby were pretty stable but moved around the city in their day-to-day activities. He knew Nathan Small and Eunice Henry hardly ever left their apartments, so he eliminated Denzel and Todd first."

"And all that leaves is Miss Kai."

"Yes, he seems to have singled her out, probably because he's using her to get publicity for what he's doing. We never see him on anything though and he never has a message attached, so what kind of publicity he's hoping for, I don't know."

"He doesn't seem to have any fear, hell, he killed Small while under our protection. He may have expected we'd figure it out and then release the information, scaring the shit out of his next victims. I'm almost at the studio, I've gotta go."

Eldridge flipped his phone closed and pulled up to the entrance behind a squad car already there, the officer leaning on the hood. Eldridge motioned to him and he walked over, leaning down to face him. "Make sure no one blocks the parking garage exit, we're going to be coming out of there fast." The officer nodded and stepped back as Eldridge pulled the car into the building's underground parking.

I see you, Detective! Jeremiah sat across the street in a car he had borrowed from the church, watching Eldridge speak to the cop. He had left the webcam in Greedo's garage to find out who was investigating him, and he had to admit, was quite impressed by how the detective had almost caught him that night. His foresight had paid off however, and he had determined Eldridge's name and then a quick hack of the police computers had given him the rest of what he needed. He had been shocked when they had found his apartment, but it didn't take him long to realize it was Father O'Neil who had most likely told them.

He felt terrible about killing the Father, he was the first person he had killed he had personally known, the rest all strangers. He had gone there intending to kill the Father, though. Not only had he figured out it must be him that told the police about where to find him, if the Father hadn't encouraged him to seek out his sister, she would still be alive today. And if he hadn't been bringing her to meet him, then she never would have been on that train. No matter how he looked at it, it was always Father O'Neil's fault. But he had doubts. In the confessional, hearing the Father's voice, a voice that had helped him for all these years, was hard. He was happy he didn't have to see the Father's face before killing him, but when he had opened the door to make sure he had hit him, his resolve had wavered. His momentary weakness disappeared as soon as Father O'Neil had said he had forgiven him. *For all my sins.* The actual words were unimportant. Jeremiah knew the intent of Father O'Neil's last words. They were in the confessional, and the priest had said he had forgiven him. He was dying so he just didn't have time to finish the ceremony. He would do that himself after this was all over. He would do his penance.

But first, he had to kill Aynslee Kai.

Eldridge ran up to Aynslee who was just stepping back into her office.

"Hayden, what's going on? Why all the excitement?"

"We found the old lady," said Eldridge as he looked around, eyeing everyone with suspicion, especially the pimply geek looking through the plastic window of a nearby divider.

"But I never got a video," said Aynslee as she leaned over her desk and checked her email to confirm.

"And you won't. He didn't kill her."

"What?"

"He attacked her but it appears he had a moment of doubt and left her alive."

"But that means—"

"There won't be another video. You are in immediate danger."

Aynslee raised her hand to her mouth to stifle a gasp. "What do I do?"

"First we have to get you out of here. This place is too public, too exposed."

"The police station?"

"No, we already know he can hack any of our systems. We'll go back to your apartment. It's a secure location, easily protected with limited access." Aynslee nodded and threw her jacket on. Eldridge shook his head. "No, give me that," he said. "And your sunglasses." Aynslee handed them over, puzzled. Eldridge leaned out the office door. "She here yet?"

"She's coming up now," said the officer standing outside. A few minutes later a woman walked into the office. She smiled at Eldridge and extended her hand.

"Officer Kordas, reporting as ordered, sir."

Eldridge looked her up and down. She was about the same height and build as Aynslee with blonde hair tied up in a bun. "Let your hair down, please." Kordas removed the clips holding her hair and shook out her long, blonde tresses. Eldridge looked at Aynslee who walked over and faced the officer.

"She's supposed to be me." It wasn't a question, but a statement. Aynslee took the coat and glasses from Eldridge and handed them to Kordas. "Here, put these on." Kordas donned the jacket and sunglasses. Eldridge and Aynslee stood back and looked at her, then at each other, smiling. "Perfect!"

"Almost," said Eldridge. "Give her your purse." Aynslee handed it over. "Now, she's perfect," agreed Eldridge. "Okay, let's go." The three were joined by two officers already in the hall. Eldridge trailed behind Aynslee, looking all around him for anyone acting suspicious. The problem was everyone was standing, gawking at them.

Perfection. Absolute perfection. Her hair was gorgeous, the way it swayed back and forth as she walked, the golden blonde she now wore the exact shade he remembered. The posture was perfect, her shoulders thrust back, made her breasts appear even bigger than they already were. Her long, perfect neckline gave no indication of any excess weight. *She will have a perfect body, I just know it! She's just like her!* His heart pounded in his chest as he thought of the life they would spend together. He felt a stirring in his loins he hadn't had in years. *She will definitely do!* He admired the sway of her hips, his eyes drifting to her perfectly shaped buttocks. He imagined grabbing on to her as they made love, screaming each other's names in ecstasy, as they climaxed together, forever sealing their bond. *I have to possess her. I just need to get her alone!* He smiled to himself as his plan unfolded in his mind.

It won't be long now.

Eldridge, Aynslee, Kordas and the other two officers climbed on an elevator one officer had run ahead and held. They descended toward the parking garage, and after a few stops where the officers blocked anyone else from getting on, they reached their destination. The two officers led the way, making sure it was clear. Eldridge held the back door of his car open for Aynslee and Kordas. "Okay, Miss Kai, I want you to lie down on the floor as best you can. You will need to keep out of sight until I tell you, it's going to be awhile, though."

"Anything, let's just get the hell out of here, something doesn't feel right."

Eldridge knew how she felt. Something definitely didn't feel right. Looking around the busy garage he couldn't help but think any one of the vehicles might hold their killer. Getting in the driver's seat, he started the car and headed toward the exit.

There you are! Jeremiah watched as the detective's car pulled from the parking garage. The squad car at the entrance led the way, its lights flashing and siren wailing, a second squad car, also in the garage, pulled in behind the procession. And so did he. It didn't take long for him to lose them in traffic but he wasn't worried. He eyed his laptop, a map displayed on it showed a red blip. He had already low-jacked the detective's car days ago at Greedo's house. *She's not getting away from me, Detective!*

Eldridge pulled the car in front of Aynslee's apartment building and shut off the engine. He turned back to face Kordas, careful to not look down at Aynslee. "Get the keys out of her purse." Kordas complied and Eldridge exited the car after the four officers in the accompanying vehicles had taken their positions outside the entrance. He tossed the keys to one. "You two secure the apartment." The two officers ran into the building as Eldridge warily eyed each passing vehicle.

"All clear," came the call over the radio. He opened the rear door and helped Kordas from the vehicle, unable to avoid looking at Aynslee who lay grimacing on the floor, in obvious discomfort. She gave a weak smile. He didn't acknowledge her, instead slammed the door shut and swiftly escorted Kordas toward the building entrance. His eyes continually scanned their surroundings as his hand, placed firmly on the small of her back, urged her toward the elevator. Once in the safety of the apartment, Eldridge breathed a little easier and turned to Kordas and the other two officers. "Okay, I want you two in the hall, keep your eyes open for anything suspicious. This guy has no fear so don't get cocky." He turned to Kordas. "And *you* might as well get comfortable. Make sure you don't answer the phone."

"Yes, sir."

"Frank from the lab should be here any minute to wire up some surveillance gear so we can get some eyes and ears on the place. This is all last minute, we were expecting more time."

"It's all good," she said, shrugging her shoulders. "Hopefully he'll take the bait and we can get him."

Eldridge placed his hand on her shoulder and looked directly in her eyes. "Don't take this lightly. He's killed over ten people already. He *will* find a way to get to you and you need to be ready."

He watched her pale slightly and gulp. Her feeble, "Yes, sir," confirmation the message had made it through.

Eldridge left the apartment, made sure both officers were in position, then waited for the elevator. When the doors opened he ran almost headlong into Frank. "Oh, hey, Detective. Sorry it took me so long to get here, I needed to get approval and then get everything together and—"

Eldridge raised his hand. "Fine. Just wire the place, I don't want anything happening to another uniform."

"Will do, I'll be in and out in a few minutes, everything's wireless and we're not really trying to hide anything so it should be quick."

Eldridge looked at Frank. "Something bothering you, you seem kinda jumpy tonight?"

Frank blushed. "Well, it's my first time out of the lab since, well, you know, since I was shot, so I'm kinda shittin' my pants right now."

Eldridge laughed and slapped him on his back. "Get your work done, then get out of here, you'll be okay. Where are you guys going to be set up?"

"We've got a delivery truck across the street."

Eldridge nodded. "Okay, scram, get it done," he said, motioning Frank toward the door as he climbed aboard the elevator and pulled out his cell phone. *Now for the final part of the plan.*

Jeremiah watched from outside, his car tucked in amongst a long row of parked cars. He had seen a police tech arrive a few minutes ago and the van that dropped him off park only three spots ahead. As he listened to the police dispatch frequency in the background, something caught his attention. He turned up the volume and listened.

"—required immediately at the station, repeat, Detective Eldridge is required immediately at the station. Over." He watched as the officer at the door acknowledged the call on his radio then triggered it again to call his partner upstairs. A couple of minutes later he watched Eldridge exit the building, talk to the officer briefly, then climb in his car and pull away.

Big mistake, Detective. Jeremiah's fingers flew over the keyboard as he put his plan into motion.

When Shakespeare knocked on the door he wasn't sure what to expect. What he got wasn't it, but did seem to fit with the yard's unkempt look in an otherwise pristine middle-class neighborhood. A short, morbidly obese woman with a surly expression, stained shirt and spandex pants answered the door. "Whatdaya want?" she yelled. "Ya better not be one of them Jehovah's Witnesses!"

Pulling out his badge, Shakespeare held it up with the warrant. "Detective Shakespeare, Homicide. I have a warrant to search the premises." He stepped across the threshold, handed her the warrant and motioned the other officers with him to proceed.

"What the hell is this?" she asked as she looked at the piece of paper he had handed her.

"I'm looking for someone who identifies himself as Elf Lord Six-Six-Six on the Internet." Shakespeare looked around at the mess inside. *Disgusting.*

"The Internet? I don't have no time for that crap!" She tossed the warrant back at Shakespeare. "You've got the wrong house, fatso!"

Shakespeare bit his tongue. *I'm fat? Look in a mirror, lady. If you can find one big enough.* "Does anyone else live here?"

"Yeah, my good for nothin' son lives in the basement. Maybe he's this Shelf Lord or whatever the hell you called him." She turned her head and raised both hands to her mouth. "Winston! Get your lazy ass up here, now!"

Shakespeare cringed at the shrill voice. *Poor Winston!* He heard an, "Awww, Mom!" come from down a set of stairs to his right. He motioned to two officers and they rushed down.

"Move away from the computer!" he heard one yell as he followed them down at a much slower pace.

"Hey, what's goin' on here?" he heard someone cry as he reached the bottom. He turned the corner and couldn't believe what he was looking at. Stacks of pizza boxes, Diet Pepsi cans, crumpled candy bar wrappers and chip bags were strewn everywhere, and tucked in amongst the garbage, a very impressive computer setup with eight flat panels and at least half a dozen computers within sight, and God knows how many hidden behind the mess. He smiled as he saw the fat, bearded geek with long hair, barely tucked back in a ponytail, the hair-tie about to fall out. *Talk about stereotypes.*

"Are you Elf Lord?"

"Who wants to know?" said the kid with false bravado, the desk he gripped with one hand the only thing keeping him standing.

"I'm Detective Shakespeare, Homicide."

"H-Homicide?" The look of fear on Winston's face let Shakespeare know interrogation wasn't going to be a problem. "Hey, I didn't do anything!"

"Someone at this location, and I'm guessing it wasn't your mother, hacked into the Rikers Island computer system and freed a prisoner earlier this week."

Winston's sun starved complexion turned greyer, his eyes darted to the floor. "That wasn't me."

"Really." Shakespeare moved closer to the boy and glared at him. "Talk now and we may go easy on you," he growled.

And growling was all it took to open the floodgates. "Okay, it was me but I didn't do it for me I did it for Lonewolf. He contacted me over the net on one of the boards, it was just a bet, it was just a bet, no one was supposed to get hurt, he said he was just going to get himself arrested for fun and then I would get him released." Winston had spilled his guts so hastily he was out of breath by the time he finished.

"And what did you get out of this?"

"Nothing, there was no money, I swear, it was just a bet."

"Just a bet. So you're telling me that two people died just so you could have bragging rights?"

"Two people died?" This sent Winston to the floor. Shakespeare leaned over and slapped him on the face a few times. Winston came to and looked around confused before remembering where he was. "Oh shit, I had nothing to do with it, no one was supposed to get hurt!"

"Have you ever met this, what did you call him, Lone Wolf?"

"Lonewolf-Two-Zero-Four-Eight. No, I never met him, only online in a chat-room." Winston's adrenaline fueled rapid-fire response reminded Shakespeare of a meth addict.

"So you don't know who he is, never met him before?"

"No," said Winston. Shakespeare turned and looked at all the equipment. "But I can find him."

"What?" Shakespeare spun around. "What do you mean you can find him?"

"Well, if he's jacked in I mean. Let me show you." He darted toward one of several keyboards. An officer snared him by the collar, halting the large bulk from reaching the keys.

Shakespeare waved him off. "Okay, *Elf Lord*, let's see if you can find our killer."

Winston paled further and typed feverishly, desperate to save his neck. In under three minutes he stood in triumph, pointing at a screen. "There!" Shakespeare looked. It showed a map with a red circle covering about a block.

"What's this?"

"That's where he's jacked in, dude."

"How do you know?"

"I know, dude. This is him. He's tapped some yokel's unsecured Wi-Fi and is using it for access." Shakespeare's puzzled expression elicited a smirk. "You cops aren't too bright, are you?"

"Downtown!" said Shakespeare, pointing over his shoulder with his thumb. He pulled out his phone and called Eldridge but it went to voicemail. He looked again at the screen, the red circle covering the same block where Aynslee Kai's apartment was. As he pulled himself up the stairs he called dispatch.

Trace rubbed her eyes, yawned, then looked back at the screen. An overly cautious ADA, concerned about privacy laws, had delayed her from gaining access to the security footage from the subway. She had eventually prevailed, but had still lost over a day, a day she prayed wouldn't cost this poor girl her life. The great thing about technology was that digital footage was much easier to go through, so she was making quick progress. She was already watching footage of Chelsie walking onto the subway platform and waving goodbye to the walking wall that was Denis.

"Ok, switch to the subway."

Mario, the lackey assigned to her by the Transit Authority, hit a few keys on the keyboard, and the view switched to the subway car. "Just give me a moment to synch up the time codes."

Trace didn't have a clue what he was talking about, but didn't let on. "Ok."

A few seconds later the view leapt ahead, and she saw Chelsie stepping through the doors and onto the car, sitting in an empty seat near the front. She appeared to be listening to music, her head leaning against the window. At the next stop people shuffled on and off, but she remained, joined by a man reading a newspaper.

"That's odd," muttered Trace.

"What?"

Trace pointed at the screen. "There's a couple of completely empty seats. Why'd he sit with her?"

"Umm, hot chick?" suggested Mario.

Trace glanced at him then back at the footage.

Possible.

A few more stops went by when they watched as Chelsie rose, and exited the subway. Trace looked at the stop. "That's one stop before her normal stop!" Trace leaned back in her chair. "Why would she get off one stop early?"

Mario shrugged his shoulders. "Running an errand? Meeting someone?"

Trace snapped her fingers. "Show me the platform footage."

Mario tapped a few keys and within moments they were watching her exit the subway, rushing toward the stairs, looking over her shoulder frequently.

"Looks like she thinks she's being followed."

Thanks, but I'll be the detective here.

"Perhaps." But he was right. She was definitely looking behind her. *But for what?*

"Let's roll it back to the train, see if she spoke to anyone."

"I didn't see anything," said Mario as he tapped away at the keyboard.

"Can you zoom in on her while she's seated?" A few more taps and the footage, now very grainy, showed her sitting against the window, soon joined by the man. As she got up, Trace pointed. "Slow that down!"

Mario complied. "Why? What do you see?"

"Watch."

Chelsie slowly rose. The man swung his legs into the aisle, and Chelsie squeezed by. The man's upper body distinctly lifted off the back of his seat, and leaned toward her. As she cleared the seat, he leaned back into a proper position, but Chelsie's head had rapidly turned toward the man, then back again, and her pace quickened. *Had he said something, or touched her somehow?*

"Let's follow him."

Mario let the tape play forward, and at the next stop they watched as he rose from the seat, and walked directly under the camera as he disembarked, giving them a clear shot of his face.

"What the hell is he doing there?"

"Who?"

Trace ignored him. *It can't be!* "Zoom in on his face and enhance it as best you can."

Mario did as told, and the face became even clearer. There was no doubt who it was.

And it scared the hell out of her.

She flipped open her phone and made a call her wildest nightmares couldn't conjure. "Dispatch, I need the current location of Vincent Fantino, Crime Scene Unit."

Police Officer Kordas, Janet to her friends, eyed the apartment, disappointed. *Not what I expected.* One bedroom, a cramped kitchen, but a decent sized living area. Either this reporter wasn't that successful, or liked to live frugally. *Recent success?* There was evidence of a lot of new purchases including a large Panasonic plasma, sitting on its stand but not yet hooked up. She wasn't much into TV, especially the news, which may explain why she had never heard of this reporter they were protecting, but this night was going to be awfully boring without a television to distract her. She wandered into the bedroom and began to poke through the drawers before the cameras arrived. *At least you're in here, and not out in the hall.* With only two years on the force, she knew she was chosen for this assignment for one reason. *Blonde with big tits. Oh well, maybe the girls will get me noticed for the right reason if I help catch this guy.* She opened a dresser drawer. *Ooh, these are nice!* She reached in to feel what appeared to be the reporter's lingerie store when there was a knock at the door.

She slammed the dresser door shut, as if caught with her hand in the silk cookie jar, and quickly made her way to the entrance, her guilty heart pounding in her chest. She knew it had to be the lab tech, Frank "something", what with two of her buddies in the hallway. She opened the door, expecting dweeb central and was pleasantly surprised at how cute he was.

"Hi, you must be Frank," she said, extending her hand.

He was carrying several cases and stuck his hand out, the case it was already carrying almost falling to the floor as his eyes dropped from her face to her chest and back up. "Uh, sorry, I, ah, well, ah."

Dweeb it is. Oh well. "Let me give you a hand with that," she said, taking the case instead.

"Thanks," he said, smiling awkwardly. "I'll just need a few minutes and I'll be out of your hair."

She followed him into the living area and placed the case on the floor. "Anything I can do to help?"

He flipped open one of the cases then looked at her, shaking his head. "No, thanks, I'm faster when I work alone."

She sat down, one foot on the floor, the other up on the couch, her knee in the air, her pose a little provocative. *Why not have a little fun?* Frank looked at her for a moment, and dropped one of the cameras. He looked back at the case, and went about placing cameras and other equipment throughout the apartment, careful to never look in her direction. He came out of the bedroom and closed the cases.

"All done, I guess I'll be outta here," he said, continuing to avoid looking at her.

Now to close the deal. She got up off the couch and stepped closer, smiling. "Would you mind hooking up the TV for me? It's gonna be incredibly boring if I have to sit here all night with no entertainment."

His Adam's apple bobbed as he gulped. "Aahh, I don't know, I'm not supposed to touch any of her stuff."

She could tell he just needed a little more convincing. "What did you say your name was again?"

"Brata, Frank Brata."

"Oooh!" she gushed. "Aren't you the guy who got shot in the chest the other night!"

He smiled shyly and looked at the floor. "Yeah, that was me."

She stepped forward and placed her hand gently on his chest, a slight pout pursed her lips. "Do your ribs still hurt?"

"Yeah, they're still pretty tender." Taking a step back, he looked over at the TV. "You know, I guess there's no harm in hooking this up, it'll just take me a few minutes."

Schoolgirl act works every time! She watched as he busied himself hooking up cables and within minutes he was true to his word.

"You're all set!" he said, grabbing his cases.

She leaned over and gave him a peck on the cheek. "Thanks, Frankie!" He blushed as he scurried for the door. She chuckled to herself as she sat down and flicked on the TV.

Once he's been on a few dates, he could be a heartbreaker,

Jeremiah pulled up to the parking garage entrance to Aynslee Kai's apartment building and swiped the parking pass he had cloned weeks before. The garage door rose, and he drove in, parking as close to the elevators as he could. He had planned this for some time. It was relatively easy to hack the condo's computer system and find an apartment above Aynslee's undergoing renovation and therefore empty. He climbed out of the car and looked about for any of the protective detail he had seen earlier. Finding the garage empty, he removed a large duffel bag from the trunk, entered the elevator and hit the button for the twelfth floor. *This is too easy!* He rocked back and forth on his heels as he watched the numbers count up, bypassing all of the police there to stop him. The light flashed on the ninth floor, the floor that he knew his target lived on, and his heart skipped a beat as his imagination had him thinking it was about to stop. The tenth floor lit and he exhaled.

On the twelfth floor, the doors opened and he poked his head out, looking in both directions. Again he was alone. He quickly headed toward the vacant apartment, and opened it with the key he had made a copy of by breaking into the super's apartment two weeks before.

Secure in the apartment three floors directly above his target, he threw the duffel bag in front of the balcony doors and opened it, removing a climbing harness and a length of rope. Donning the harness, he fastened the ropes to the balcony's steel frame, then attached them to his harness. His heart pounded. He had only done this in an indoor rock-climbing park previously, never twelve stories in the air. He stepped over the balcony railing and placed his feet on the edge. Pushing off, he let some rope slip through his carabineer and he dropped like a stone, his poor technique leaving his legs swinging under the balcony of the floor below him. He let some more rope out and dropped to the tenth floor balcony railing. Seeing someone watching TV inside, he immediately let himself drop some more and purposefully overshot the ninth floor. Dangling precariously in between the eighth and ninth floor balconies, he reached up and steadied himself on the underside of Aynslee's balcony. He took a moment to catch his breath, then slowly pulled himself back up to where he had a view of the apartment from the bottom of the balcony railing.

Holy shit!

Janet checked the TiVo to see what a television celebrity taped when she thought she spotted something out of the corner of her eye. She threw the remote down and grabbed her gun, adrenaline pumping through her veins. *Something moved!* She was sure of it. Something had definitely moved out there. Walking to the windows occupying the entire outside wall, she peered out to see what had drawn her attention, but all she saw was the city skyline. *Must have been a reflection on one of the buildings across the street.* Turning, she sat back down on the couch and placed her weapon on the table in front of her, cursing herself for her paranoia. She kept eyeing the balcony. *But I'm sure I saw something.* She stood up, deciding to check the bedroom.

Jeremiah was pissed. Staring down the barrel of a gun had at first scared the shit out of him, but when he focused on who was holding the gun, it had turned to anger. This was not Aynslee Kai. The woman did bear a striking resemblance to her, but it definitely wasn't her. *Well done, Detective!* He had to admit a begrudging respect for this man who had managed to find him sooner than he had expected, and had now delayed him achieving his final goal. He gripped the edge of the balcony, frozen in place, until she finally left the window and put her gun down. He let out the breath he was holding, and took stock of his situation. He couldn't stay, he had to move. Up wasn't an option with her staring out the window, and he didn't have enough rope for down.

Then came his break. She suddenly stood up, and left the room. He furiously pulled on the Jumar ascender, reaching the next floor before she returned. He continued his ascent, and soon grasped the bottom of the twelfth floor balcony and pulled himself to safety, tumbling over the railing and onto his back, his muscles screaming in agony. He lay for a moment, gasping, then slammed his fists on the concrete, willing himself to his feet. He scrambled out of the harness and raced from the apartment. He ran to the elevator, hit the down button, then sprinted toward the stairwell at the other end of the hall.

Janet checked the windows again, and, satisfied they were still secure, headed back into the living area. But something still bothered her. She was sure she had seen something. Her weapon still drawn, she approached the door to the balcony. Looking carefully, all she saw were the city lights spread out across the entire view. Then she saw it. Some lights twinkled. She turned the lock for the balcony door and slid it open. Peering up and around to make sure the balcony was clear, she inched toward the railing and looked over at the ground below. Something hit her arm. She jumped back and spun her weapon around but saw nothing. Suddenly it jumped out at her as clear as if it were daytime. *Ropes!* She rushed to the railing and leaned over backward, pointing her weapon up. The ropes dangled above her but she couldn't tell what floor they came from. Rushing back into the apartment, she snatched the radio from the table.

"He's here!"

Janet's call sent everyone in the surveillance van into a panic. Immediately a call went out for backup as they scrambled to find out what she was talking about, none of them having seen anything. "Get in that apartment!" yelled Frank over the radio. He watched Kordas run to the door and open it for the officers stationed in the hallway. A moment later her voice came over the radio.

"There's ropes hanging outside the balcony! It looks like he rappelled from above!"

This new information had them rolling back the living room footage that included a view of the balcony. "There!" said Frank, pointing at the screen. For a brief instance they saw somebody drop from above then a few minutes later climb back up. Frank looked at the time index and got on the radio. "He began climbing up less than five minutes ago, he's gotta still be in the building!" They pored over the footage, desperately trying to find any sign of their suspect.

"This is Calvin in the lobby, there's an elevator coming down from the twelfth floor, it could be him, over."

Jeremiah flew down the stairwell, taking the steps two and three at a time. He knew if they were on to him, the elevators would be suicide. He suspected his little diversion would keep the officer in the lobby occupied, but would it be long enough? Leaping over the stairs he rapidly made his way down, and in less than a minute, passed the ninth floor where he was sure most of the officers were stationed. He knew if he were chased it would most likely be from above, but with one cop in the lobby, and one outside, he could still be intercepted.

Police Officer Calvin pressed the buttons to call elevators both up and down. The second elevator door opened, its up indicator lit. He reached in and sent it to the top floor, then pressed the up button again and waited, his weapon drawn and pointing at the door. The elevator stopped on the third floor then resumed its descent. "Elevator stopped on the third floor, he may have got off there, over," radioed Calvin. His partner raced in from outside and drew his weapon as well. Calvin's heart pounded as the chime sounded and the doors opened. They were met with a scream and barking as a young woman holding a lapdog in her arms covered her face. Calvin reached in and pulled her from the elevator as his partner entered, confirming it was empty. "Was anyone else on this elevator with you, ma'am?"

"N-no," she stammered. "What the hell were you thinking?"

"What floor did you get on at?"

"What?"

"What floor!"

"The third, the third floor!"

"Did anyone get off at that floor?"

"No, it was empty when I got on."

Calvin frowned and got on his radio. "Suspect was not in the elevator, repeat, suspect was *not* in the elevator. We're going to check the stairwells, you two stay where you are, he may make another attempt, over."

"Where's the stairwell?" he asked the still frightened woman. She pointed a shaking finger to the other side of the lobby. Turning to his partner, he said, "Okay, you cover the entrance, I'll check the stairwell." Running toward the lobby's far end he tore open the door and listened for footsteps. Nothing.

Jeremiah heard the door above him open as he entered the parking garage. Wasting no time, he ran to his strategically parked car, jumped in and turned the key he had left in the ignition. The engine roared to life and he floored it, heading to the exit.

Calvin listened intently for any sound but heard nothing at first, then a door clicked shut below him, the pneumatic hinge having finished its job. With weapon drawn, he rushed down the two flights of steps and cautiously opened the door. Peering out, he saw no one, and triggered his radio. "He might be in the parking garage, over." He stepped into the garage and spun around with his weapon and flashlight held out in front of him. A squealing of tires to his right sent him running toward the garage exit. Grabbing his radio, he yelled, "Stop anything coming out of the parking garage!"

Officer Parker heard the call come in but it was too late. He had already gone inside to join his partner in the parking garage when the call came in about the car. Sprinting outside he saw nothing, the perpetual traffic of the busy New York streets providing ample cover for any car that may have just exited the parking garage. His radio crackled. "Be advised, Homicide has reason to believe your suspect is in the vicinity, over."

Gee, ya think? "Roger that dispatch, suspect has *already* fled the vicinity, over." He watched as his partner rushed from the entrance to the parking garage and looked over at him. He shrugged his shoulders, raising both hands, palms upward.

Aynslee waited for the automatic garage door opener to finish its job. It had been over an hour, and she was in more pain than she ever remembered being in, making the garage door's interminable descent seem even longer than it was. She heard the motor stop and Hayden turned around, looking over the seat at her. "Okay, it's safe now." He got out of the car and opened the back door.

"It's about time, I thought we'd never get here!" Aynslee had lost all feeling in her legs and her side ached. She took Hayden's hand and he helped pull her out. She took a tentative step but collapsed, her legs numb. He caught her and helped her toward the door. "Thanks." She winced as her feet began to tingle. "Oh my God, that hurts."

"What?"

"I'm just starting to get some feeling back in my feet," she said as she tried to walk, leaning heavily on Hayden. "God, I hate that feeling!" He helped her into the house and placed her on a couch in his living room. "Thanks," she said gratefully as she gingerly placed her feet on the floor. Grimacing through the pain, she wiggled her toes and tried moving her feet around. Slowly the tingling spread upward and eventually subsided as her circulation was restored. Now only the pain in her side remained. She began stretching to try and work it out as she looked at her surroundings. It wasn't at all what she expected. It was clearly a carefully restored older home, the furnishings and accessories matching the period. "This is a beautiful house you have, Detective." Her stomach grumbled. Hayden smiled. "You heard that?"

"I think the neighbors did too."

"Yeah, I guess I'm pretty hungry."

"Okay, I'll go fix us something, you wait here. The remote's on the table." He headed toward the kitchen as she turned on the TV. She feigned interest for a couple of minutes then decided to take the opportunity to pursue her latest hobby, detectives named Hayden. Walking down the hallway she found him busy in the kitchen arranging various cold meats and cheeses on a tray. "Feeling better?" he asked.

"Yeah, still pretty stiff but I can walk again." Looking around she saw a quite modern kitchen that ran contrary to the remainder of the house. An antique kitchen table and chairs sitting atop an ornate oval rug at the opposite end from the cupboards was illuminated by an elaborate antique lamp hanging above. She watched as Hayden deftly sliced a tomato. "You're pretty handy in the kitchen."

"Well, I'm not a fan of processed foods. I guess as a kid I just learned to like the taste of fresh ingredients, so it was either learn to cook for myself or accept the blandness of boxed food."

"Oh, you wouldn't like my fridge then. The freezer is just a stack of microwaveable food and the fridge is leftover takeout and condiments."

He finished quickly and carried the tray to the kitchen table. "Grab the buns, please?" Aynslee flashed to another pair of buns she'd like to grab, but picked up the basket on the counter instead. "Can I get you something to drink?"

"Red wine if you've got it. I could really use a glass." *Or three.*

"Of course," said Hayden as he walked back to the counter. Removing a cork from an already opened bottle, he poured a glass. Returning with her wine and a glass of water for himself, he sat down and motioned to the tray. "Bon appétit!"

Aynslee smiled and assembled a sandwich, ravenous with hunger. When the flurry of activity ended, Hayden began preparing his own as she waited politely for him to finish.

"Please, go ahead, I know how hungry you must be."

"Thanks." She took a huge bite, and had eaten half of her sandwich before he finished making his. She took a sip of wine and wiped her mouth with a napkin from the tray. "I'm sorry, I must disgust you, but I haven't eaten since lunch and that was only soup and a salad."

"No need to apologize, it's always a pleasure to see someone enjoy a meal you've prepared." He took a large bite of the ham and Swiss sandwich he had prepared for himself.

After devouring the rest of her sandwich, Aynslee sat back and sipped the wine. She looked over at Hayden and realized it was the first time in a week she felt truly safe. She smiled at him.

He finished chewing his food and swallowed. "What?"

"Oh, nothing," she said. "Do you think your little ruse worked?"

He nodded. "Yes, it came in over the scanner that he was at your apartment just as we got here."

Aynslee shivered. "Is everybody okay, that cop who's pretending to be me? Is she okay?"

"Yes, no one got hurt but unfortunately he got away."

Her anxiety returned. "There's no way he could know we're here, is there?"

"I don't see how. We were twenty minutes away when he was sighted at your building. Nobody knows you're here so we should be fine." He watched as she took a long drink of her wine, draining the glass. "Another?"

"Please." He retrieved the bottle, poured another glass and sat down. They continued in silence for a few minutes as he finished his sandwich and she enjoyed the relaxing feeling of the wine as it spread through her system.

"Can I get you anything else?"

Aynslee yawned. "No, I'm stuffed, thanks."

"Well, would you like to go to bed now, or relax in the living room? Your choice."

She did feel sleepy and knew she could fall asleep right now, but she wanted to have as much awake time with Hayden as possible. "Let's go in the living room for a while, I'd like to unwind a little before going to bed."

He nodded and cleared the table. She got up to help him but he waved her off. "No, I'll take care of it. You go see if there's something interesting to watch on TV."

She smiled appreciatively and headed from the kitchen, enjoying the sounds of Hayden cleaning up, humming as he did so. She walked toward the living room then felt strange, as if the wine had hit her harder than she expected. She stumbled into the wall as the world spun around her. *What's going on?* Holding herself up with the wall, she knew something was definitely wrong. *This isn't the wine, I've been drugged!* Panic overwhelmed her as she slid to the floor, losing control of her legs, wondering how she would warn Hayden. She looked down the hall toward the kitchen and saw Hayden step into the hallway. "He's here," she slurred, looking up at him as he knelt down in front of her.

TWELVE

Jeremiah sat in his car, staring at the home of his nemesis, Detective Hayden Eldridge. After escaping the trap set for him, it had only taken ten minutes to track Eldridge's car to his home on Staten Island, then thirty minutes to arrive at the location. His anger over being tricked hadn't lasted long. In fact, for the first time since he began his work, he finally felt challenged, exhilarated by the thrill of the chase. Where most of the others had been easy, this was the first time he was in real danger. And he felt alive. Something he hadn't felt in almost a year. When his sister had been murdered, he had withdrawn from the few around him he had previously let in, including Father O'Neil. Once the news had revealed the identity of Logan and Aaron, a few minutes on the computer had netted him their home addresses. At first he had contented himself with the knowledge their lives as they knew them were over due to the media attention, but when he finally let himself go back to the church, a sermon about judgment day tweaked something inside him. When the DA had refused to press charges against the bystanders, he knew judgment day for the guilty wouldn't come from the court of man, but from the court of God. And he wasn't willing to let them live the rest of their lives before facing His judgment.

He set his plan into action after doing some research into enhancing security camera footage with computer software. It didn't take long to track down the software, and after befriending Messina on a bereavement chat room, he had access to the necessary hardware to do it. Messina needed someone to cover some shifts for him while he took care of his dying wife, otherwise he might lose his job. Jeremiah offered to cover for him and split the pay. Messina had jumped at the offer, and Jeremiah used the NerdTech credentials to gain access to computers far more powerful than he had access to.

It took months before he finally had all their faces. As each bystander became recognizable, he began tracking them down. Hacking into the Public Defender's computer had netted him Tammera Coverdale, William Hanson and Nathan Small. Logan and Aaron he already had, and Aynslee Kai he recognized from television. The other three had proven a challenge. He spent months going through hacked footage from the subway security cameras, and spent every spare moment on the subway looking for them. But in the end he had found them all. Abigail he found by tracking back what stop she boarded on, then by seeing she had used a transit pass. He hacked the database, got the records for everyone who had gone through during the same time window, and found her. Ibrahim he stumbled upon six months into the process, on the same route as that night, returning home from his work as a cab driver.

It was Eunice Henry that had proven to be the most trouble. She had disappeared. He tracked her from the subway, but then couldn't find her. This was where NerdTech had helped. By using his credentials and the van, he was able to visit businesses near the subway exit and pretend to be on a service call. He would access their security footage and after painstaking work, found bank footage of her hailing a cab. Video enhancement revealed the cab number, and a quick hack of their database revealed the destination. Posing again as a NerdTech employee, he knocked on each individual apartment door, until he had it narrowed down to one unit, a unit where an old lady lived, an old lady who hadn't stepped from her apartment in months. That was when he knew he had the last one, and his plan could begin.

And tonight it would finally end. *Today is your judgment day, Aynslee Kai.*

He took a deep breath and exhaled slowly. *This is it!* He took the gun off the seat beside him and stuffed it in his belt. Popping the trunk, he climbed out of the car and removed a crowbar. Gently closing the lid, he looked around the quiet neighborhood to see if any nosy neighbors were about. Seeing no one, he walked purposefully toward the opening in the hedge, and once through, darted to the side of the house. Peering into a darkened window he saw nothing except the faint glow from a light elsewhere in the house. Moving to the next window, a bright sliver of light shone between two heavy curtains blocking most of his view, the little he could see appeared to be a kitchen. He leaned in closer, pressing his face to the glass. His heart leapt as he saw the detective walk directly in front of him.

Aynslee's vision was blurred, but she could still make out Hayden as he reached out and caressed her cheek. *What's going on?* Her emotions were a bundle of confusion. She had to warn him, but shouldn't he be wondering why she had collapsed? And why was he touching her face? He was finally showing her the attention she had craved, and it was freaking her out. *Something is wrong!*

"You'll do perfectly, my love." He leaned in and kissed her on the lips.

Her heart pounded in excitement and fear. *This isn't right!* Why was he kissing her? Why wasn't he concerned she was lying on the floor? As he continued to kiss her, his lips moving against her frozen mouth, it became terrifyingly clear. He *drugged me! Not Jeremiah!* Any trace of excitement was wiped away, leaving only a terror that pulsed adrenaline through her veins, giving her a moment of control. She opened her mouth to scream, but instead found him shoving his tongue in her mouth, moaning in pleasure, as if she had willingly parted her lips to participate in his twisted assault. *Oh my God, he's crazy!* She tried to pull away, but her muscles were no longer hers to control, whatever drug he had given her now having taken over. She felt the last threads of consciousness leaving as she slid down the wall, mercifully breaking the kiss she had so longed for.

Eldridge looked down at her and smiled. *She is beautiful.* The kiss had been perfect; his raging erection proving to him that she was the one. She would be his forever. Together they would become one, fulfilling each other's desires, the end of a quest almost two decades in the making, finally at an end. He scooped her tenderly off the floor and lifted her head higher toward his face. He inhaled deeply, her delicate perfume, mixed with her natural scent, intoxicating. He kissed her neck and she gave a slight whimper but remained asleep. Careful to not hit her against any walls, he carried her into the kitchen, and laid her gently on the floor. He bent over and grabbed the edge of a large mat and tugged, pulling the kitchen table and its four chairs, toward the center of the room. He moved his precious cargo to the floor previously occupied by the table, and reached up, unhooking several chains disguised to look like part of the lamp hanging overhead. He hooked four of them to bolts in the floor, then unwound a long, looped chain, letting the slack fall to the floor with a clatter. Gazing down at the sleeping figure, he smiled. *Absolute perfection. She's the one.* Pulling on the chain, the floor slowly lowered.

And he began to hum.

Shakespeare slammed his phone against the roof of his car. *Where the hell is he?* He stood in front of Aynslee Kai's apartment building with four uniforms, one officer in disguise, and two surveillance techs. And nobody knew where Eldridge or Aynslee had gone. When Shakespeare questioned them, everyone knew about the decoy, but none the end game. Eldridge had told him nothing, which wasn't surprising with the way their relationship had been over the past several years, but for him to not tell anybody made no sense. He had placed almost a dozen calls to Eldridge's cell phone but it kept going to voice mail. And it wasn't like him to turn off his phone. Shakespeare was officially nervous. Eldridge was alone with the killer's target, at an unknown location, and the killer had escaped the trap, apparently so well hooked into every facet of the case, he just might know what they didn't.

Where the hell did they go?

"Where would I go?"

"Huh?"

Shakespeare looked through Frank as an idea formed in his head. "Somewhere safe. Somewhere I knew."

"Home?"

Shakespeare nodded. "Can you pull up his home address on one of your computers?"

"Who needs a computer?" Frank whipped out his phone, and a flurry of thumbs later, he handed it to Shakespeare. "Here you go."

Shakespeare took the phone and saw Eldridge's home address displayed on the screen, along with a map. He jumped in the car and squealed away from the curb, leaving the others wondering whether or not they should be sticking around.

What the hell is he doing?

Jeremiah watched the detective through the window as he pulled on a chain and slowly lowered out of site with his target. *This is fucked up.* He wasn't sure what was going on, but with Eldridge apparently in the basement, this was his opportunity to get inside. He crept further down the house and stopped at a window he was certain was far enough from where Eldridge last was to not be heard. He shoved the crowbar between the window and the sill, working it around until it at last slid under. He yanked down and the wood splintered as the window ripped from the lock inside, rising about an inch. He shoved the window up with the crowbar then tossed it aside. Hoisting himself onto the ledge, he peered inside, the ambient light from the street lamps casting a pale glow, revealing a small powder room. He struggled the rest of the way onto the ledge, then swung his legs inside, careful to not bump anything that might alert Eldridge to his presence. His feet planted firmly on the floor, he pulled his gun from his belt and stepped toward the open door.

Eldridge gazed at his latest, and last, candidate as she slept soundly, a peaceful smile on her face, her hair, a perfect gold, splayed across the platform. Crouching down, he picked her up and walked over to the mattress on the cellar floor he had dug out years before in his quest to replace the only woman he had ever loved. New candidates didn't normally merit a mattress, they had to earn it. Good behavior was important. If they ate their food and drank their water, they would be rewarded with a mattress and a light. After all, he did want them to feel at home. If they passed all of the tests, the successful candidate would become his wife. He wasn't a fool, he knew they hated him, but they would learn to love him eventually. And when that day came, they would live forever happy in each other's arms. And this candidate, this perfect specimen, had fallen right into his arms. He hadn't even been looking and she had turned herself into the perfect vision. And she already liked him, he knew. Her constant flirtations hadn't gone unnoticed. She would be much easier than the others, she would love him. *She's the one.* Looking down at her, the stirrings of an erection sent his heart racing with excitement. *It's been so long since I've felt this!* He was on fire, elated he had found her, had found the one. Caressing her face, he straightened her hair and leaned in to place a kiss on her full, sensuous lips. *She wants me to kiss her, just look at her. She wants me to!*

A floorboard overhead creaked.

Jeremiah froze, his heart in his throat. He lifted his foot slowly and the floorboard creaked back up. He cringed. *There's no way he didn't hear that!* Walking as near the floor edges as possible, his gun extended in front of him, he crept toward the light at the end of the hallway. He rounded the corner and entered the kitchen. *What kind of twisted shit is this?* He found the table and chairs that he had witnessed the detective move earlier, all sitting on a large mat, out of place in front of the cupboards, and, where the table should be, lay a hole in the floor, maybe six-foot square, with chains hanging from overhead, extending down and out of sight, into what he imagined must be a basement. *What the hell kind of basement doesn't have stairs?* He listened but heard nothing. Certain they were in the basement, he inched forward and peered over the edge and down. About ten feet below, the dark brown dirt of the floor contrasted starkly with the bright white of a mattress off to one side. And his target, Aynslee Kai, lay atop it, a chain with a pair of unfastened handcuffs, rested in front of her. *What is he doing with her? This isn't right!* He stepped around the hole to see another angle when the long, floor to ceiling curtain to his right fluttered.

Jeremiah spun as a figure surged from behind the curtains, raising his hands to try and fend off the impending blow. His attacker's outstretched hands made contact, shoving him backward toward the opening. He twisted around and flung himself at the other side of the gaping hole, but fell short. One foot fell into the void and the fingers of his left hand barely gripped the other side of the floor as he desperately tried to hold on to the gun with his right. He reached forward but slipped further, both legs now dangling into the emptiness below. The hand holding his gun slipped down to his side and he let go of the weapon, reaching now with both hands as he tried to pull himself up, the gun clattering on the platform beneath. As he swung from the edge, he eyed the basement below and knew if he fell inside he would never get out. He raised his head and saw Eldridge staring down at him as he slowly stepped around the hole. Eldridge lifted his foot and stomped on the fingers of Jeremiah's right hand. He cried out in pain as he yanked them back. Now dangling from just four fingers, he watched Eldridge raise his foot again but before he could lower it, Jeremiah let go, tumbling backward into the basement below. Hitting hard on his tailbone, he continued backward and smacked his head against the wood of the platform. His vision blurred as he began to black out, but within moments it cleared, revealing Eldridge dangling from the edge, then dropping to the floor from above, Jeremiah scrambled back, trying to get to his feet, but Eldridge rushed forward and grabbed hold of Jeremiah's shirt, dragging him toward Aynslee and the handcuffs.

Eldridge snapped the handcuffs on Jeremiah's wrist and stepped back to assess this new situation. He had reacted instantly upon hearing the floorboard creak, his height proving an invaluable advantage as he leapt and grabbed the edge of the floor above, swinging himself up into the kitchen, and secreting himself behind the curtain just before his intruder entered. *What the hell am I going to do now?* He looked at Jeremiah as the young man gingerly touched the back of his head, glowering at him. "Jeremiah Lansing, it's a pleasure to finally meet you."

"Likewise, I'm sure." Jeremiah's voice dripped with sarcasm as he looked around him. "What the hell is this place?"

Eldridge looked around, his eyes finally resting on Aynslee's sleeping form. "It's a place you were never invited to, a place you were never meant to see. A private place, a place for remembrance, for rediscovery." He paused, took a deep breath, and whispered, "A place to find something I lost." His eyes focused on her breathing, her chest slowly rising and falling, as she lay there, innocent, like the day he had first laid eyes on her. He smiled and turned his gaze to his prisoner, raising his voice. "And it's where *you* will be shot, trying to kill your final victim, by me, the heroic police officer, just doing his duty."

"You're one sick fuck!" spat Jeremiah. "What were you going to do with her?"

Eldridge's gaze returned to Aynslee and he stepped toward her, kneeling down. "I'm going to make her mine," he said as he stroked her long, blonde hair. He heard her sigh and his heart leapt in joy. He caressed her cheek with the back of his hand, feeling the warmth of her skin on his, the gentle touch of her breath as he traced his fingers over her lips. He sighed.

Jeremiah's stomach churned as Eldridge pawed at Aynslee's face. He looked around for a way out. He had intended to die, but a death-by-cop situation was more what he had in mind, not death-by-psycho-cop. "You're one of those sick freaks you read about, aren't you?" Eldridge stopped and looked back at Jeremiah. Jeremiah gulped. He had to buy time. "What are you going to do to her?"

Eldridge rose and looked down at him. "I don't see what concern it is of yours."

Jeremiah tried to act casual, shrugging his shoulders. "Hey, I don't care what you do with her, I'm just curious. You know what I was going to do."

Eldridge frowned. "Yes, I know, Mr. Lansing. You've left quite the trail behind you, and as a police officer, I would normally arrest you. It's unfortunate I'm going to have to kill you, but if I don't, Sarah and I may not get a chance at a life together."

"Sarah?" *Who the hell is he talking about?*

Eldridge looked momentarily confused and glanced at Aynslee. "Miss Kai."

Jeremiah needed to get Eldridge to lower his guard, and his clear obsession with Aynslee was his best chance at doing it. Looking over at her, he smiled. "You know, I don't blame you, she is gorgeous."

"Yes, she is," said Eldridge, returning his attention to Aynslee.

"Do you love her?" asked Jeremiah, in as caring a voice as he could muster.

"I've loved her most of my life."

Most of his life? But I know he just met her? "How did you meet?"

"It was on Coney Island. We were both teenagers. Our parents had brought us there and we met in the lineup to get cotton candy." Eldridge knelt back down beside Aynslee and turned her face toward him. "She didn't have enough money with her so I gave her the extra quarter she needed. She thanked me and kissed me on the cheek." His voice cracked as he ran his fingers through her hair, lifting his hand and gently letting the strands stream through and back down to the mattress. "When she sat on a nearby swing, I asked if I could join her. I had never asked a girl anything like that before, but there was something intoxicating about her that gave me the courage to ask. She said yes and we sat on those swings for hours, eating our cotton candy and just talking. It was the last time I can remember being truly happy." He smiled at her then turned his head toward Jeremiah. "Have you ever known love?"

Jeremiah shook his head. "No, never." He was surprised at how much it hurt to say.

Eldridge nodded and looked back at Aynslee. "Neither had I until that day. I knew at that moment I wanted to spend the rest of my life with her."

"What happened?"

"We made arrangements to meet, but on the way home, there was an accident." His voice cracked. "My mother was killed." Tears rolled freely down his cheeks and Jeremiah couldn't help but feel sorry for him, knowing how he had felt when his sister had died. "I wasn't able to meet her. My father ripped up her number when I said I wanted to call her." He wiped the tears from his face and continued, his voice barely a whisper. "I've been looking for her ever since. A lot of times I thought I had found her, but they turned out to not be her." He wiped away a tear that had fallen on her cheek. "When I saw her I knew she was the one I had lost so many years ago. It was fate that brought us together."

Jeremiah hesitated to ask, but his own curiosity won out. "How many women have there been?"

"Dozens over the years."

"Dozens?" Bile began to rise in Jeremiah's throat.

"Oh, don't get me wrong, most I found out quickly weren't her, there's only been a handful I've invited home."

"Invited? Is that what you call it?" Jeremiah immediately regretted his question.

Eldridge's head snapped toward him, his eyes glaring. "You're just trying to delay the inevitable." Eldridge pulled Jeremiah's weapon from his belt and motioned toward the far wall. "Against the wall!" Jeremiah stood and backed toward the wall as Eldridge stepped onto the platform and pulled on the chain, slowly raising the platform until he disappeared.

Jeremiah immediately reached in his pocket and fished out a handcuff key he always carried, just in case he might need it some day. He unlocked the cuffs, then looked around but saw nothing he could use as a weapon. Aynslee moaned and rolled onto her back. Jeremiah walked over, knelt down beside her and slapped her face lightly, trying to revive her.

"Come on lady, wakeup!" He slapped her again, this time a little harder. "Wake up!"

The sting of something hitting Aynslee's face sliced through the fog filling her head. The earnestness with which the voice urged her on forced her to focus as she willed her way to consciousness. Another slap, this time harder, stung enough for her to gasp and open her eyes, revealing a blurred image of someone looking down at her. She blinked several times and the face came into focus, sending her heart racing as her chest tightened in terror. *Jeremiah!* She scrambled back, hitting a wall behind her. "Stay away from me!"

Jeremiah raised a hand to calm her down. "Listen lady, I'm not going to hurt you. We've got bigger problems, you hear?"

Unconvinced, Aynslee quickly glanced around then scrambled into a far corner. "Wh-what do you mean?"

Jeremiah threw up his hands. "Jesus Christ, lady, look around you, you're in a fucking dungeon!"

As his words echoed in her head, her memories flooded back. The meal. Her feeling like she had been drugged. Eldridge looking down at her then kissing her. She looked around. *Where the hell am I?* "What is this place?"

"We're in the basement, under his kitchen." Pointing at the kitchen floor over their heads, he traced the platform's outline above them. "He's got some kind of pulley system that raises and lowers a platform in here."

"But why?"

"He seems to think you're some long lost love of his named Sarah."

"Sarah?"

"Yeah, and looking at this setup, I don't think you're the first one he's had down here."

The fog in Aynslee's head cleared, she took stock of her situation. Looking at the young man in front of her, the irony of *her* serial killer being the victim of her *other* serial killer struck her as oddly humorous. But not enough to make her laugh. *God, what did I do to deserve this?* "He's going to kill us, isn't he?"

Jeremiah shook his head. "No, he's going to kill *me*. *You*, I think he's going to marry."

"Marry? That'll be the day." She felt a twinge in her heart. If Eldridge had simply asked her out, she would have said yes, and may have never known the true psychopath he was. *There but for the grace of God ...*

"Something tells me he won't take no for an answer. This guy's in love. You should've seen him. Creepy."

A harrumph escaped Aynslee's throat. "You're one to talk."

Jeremiah looked at her and chuckled. "Yeah, I guess, eh? You're a reporter. Did you figure out why I did what I did?"

"You mean kill all those people?"

Jeremiah nodded.

"Patricia Arnette was your sister. You killed the people from the train who didn't help her."

"Right. And you were one of them."

"Maybe you should know some things. You remember Tammera Coverdale?"

"Of course."

"I did a piece on her after you sent your first video, after the police identified her. She was engaged to be married."

"Yes, I knew that. I watched them all for months. I probably know them better than they know themselves."

"Did you know that her father was so distraught he attacked me and was arrested, that her mother tried to kill herself? He was put on suicide watch while he was in custody, *that's* how distraught he is over his daughter's death."

Jeremiah remained silent.

"Ibrahim Jamar, the cab driver, was married with a young daughter."

"I know."

"Did you know he was forced to watch while his wife and daughter were brutally raped by the Janjaweed in the Sudan?"

Jeremiah paused. "No. No, I didn't know that."

"Yes, and now because of you, that poor woman has experienced tragedy for the second time in her life, and has to live with not only the memory of the rape, but the murder of her husband before her very eyes." She looked into Jeremiah's eyes, searching for some sign of remorse. "Nathan Small, the amputee? He fought in Afghanistan and saved his entire platoon in an ambush. He was rushing onto *your* subway car to try and save *your* sister, and even tried to chase the men who attacked her but was too slow because of his legs. Did you know that?" demanded Aynslee.

"No," Jeremiah mumbled.

Aynslee continued. "And you may have had a problem with William 'Lance' Hanson being gay, but he was a loving brother to a young sister who adored him, and now she's lost her brother just like you lost your sister." She watched for a moment as tears welled in Jeremiah's eyes. "Those people you killed, they were real people, with real people who loved them, and now, thanks to you, those people feel just as alone as you do without your sister."

A single tear rolled down Jeremiah's cheek as his heart thumped in his tightening chest, the rush of blood filled his ears as the growing pit in his stomach threatened to heave with guilt. *What have I done?* He pictured his sister and her beautiful smile that had lit his heart for the last time. He remembered the excitement of discovering he wasn't alone, the excitement they had both felt. Her eyes had reminded him so much of his mother's it had brought tears to his eyes when he first looked in them. The moment he spotted her sitting in the booth at the Brooklyn Diner he had an immediate connection. She was family. A family he was certain he had lost forever. He had felt happy. Truly happy. Truly happy for the first time since his parents had died. And he had wanted to share this by bringing her to meet the closest thing to family he had had until he met her, Father O'Neil, for it was Father O'Neil who had encouraged him to find her and he couldn't wait for them to meet. He collapsed to the floor and looked up at the ceiling above, piercing it with his eyes as he tried to reach out to his beloved victim.

"Forgive me, Father!"

The night's events rushed back, fresh for the first time in a year, the waiting on the platform for the subway to arrive, the two black teenagers racing down the stairs, the doors opening and he and Patricia stepping aboard as the two teens jumped through the doors, laughing loudly. He remembered Patricia squeezing past them and taking a seat, and when he tried to join her, the one loud kid yelled at him when he made eye contact, thrusting his chest out at him, hammering it with his fist and yelling something about respect. He had immediately dropped his gaze, but it was too late. His challenger shoved past him, sending him into a nearby seat occupied by a woman busy on her BlackBerry. *Aynslee!* He watched in horror as the teenager sat down beside his sister and placed his arm around her. She yelled at him to get his hands off of her and he immediately started cursing, jumping from the seat, flailing his arms about. Patricia pushed her way toward where he was and they headed for the doors when he was yanked from behind and thrown to the floor. He remembered looking up to see the horrified expression on the face of a woman as she stared at him, her eyes wide open. *Abby!* He felt hands on him as someone tried to help him up but he had struggled against them and pushed them away. *Lance!*

He had watched, paralyzed in fear, as the boy shoved Patricia from behind, causing her to stumble forward and fall to the floor. He winced at the memory of his sister being kicked, over and over, all the while her attacker cursing at her, spitting on her, mocking her cries for help. He had struggled to his feet and rushed to help her, but as soon as he saw the outline of a gun pointing through the pocket of the attacker's jacket, the menacing look as he threatened to shoot him, he collapsed. The memory of fainting brought an overwhelming sense of shame as intense now as it was then. When he woke a few moments later they were still kicking his sister, but, too terrified to move, he played possum. He remembered seeing a black man gripping his chair, staring at him, an elderly woman crying, and those two damned bastards taping the whole thing. And then he remembered it. Something he hadn't remembered until this very moment. It was a man, yelling as he struggled through the adjoining car's door. It was Nathan Small, his artificial limbs slowing him down in his effort to reach the attackers.

Someone had *tried to save her.*

He looked back at Aynslee, tears freely flowing down his cheeks. "Detective Eldridge asked me if I had ever known love." He paused and

259

took a deep breath, stifling a sob. "I said no, but I lied. I did know love once. It was for my sister. From the moment I laid eyes on her I loved her, with all my heart. And I only got to love her for three hours and forty-two minutes." He looked at Aynslee. "That's all I got to spend with her. Three hours and forty-two minutes! And then those two animals killed her and I was too terrified to stop them." He lowered his chin and sobbed, his shoulders shaking out of control.

Aynslee reached out and laid her hand on top of his. "We all were, Jeremiah. We were all terrified." He looked up at her but couldn't speak, his body racked with sobs. "Your sister didn't deserve to die, but neither did those other people. You know that now, don't you?"

Jeremiah nodded as he continued to cry. "I'm sorry," he wailed. "Oh, God, what have I done?" *Father, I'm so sorry!* He covered his face with his hands as Aynslee put her arms around him. He buried his head in her shoulder as she rubbed his back. The overwhelming grief and shame he had felt for over a year, the grief and shame he had kept bottled inside, finally released, and it felt good, it felt good to be held, to remember what had happened not only to his sister, but to him. It felt good to feel like a victim should feel, sad, angry, the roller coaster of emotions that came with grief, a roller coaster kept in its gate for a year, finally rushing down the track in a torrent of emotion so cathartic, his sobs soon stopped, a tremendous weight lifted off his shoulders, and another, heavier weight, a weight of realization of what he had done, beginning to set in.

He pulled away and looked at Aynslee. "I'm sorry, Miss Kai, I'm sorry for everything I put you through."

She smiled at him, a smile that made him feel some day, some day he might be forgiven for what he had done. "I know you are, Jeremiah."

The distinct rattle of the chain overhead startled them both. The platform creaked and dropped several inches, sending Aynslee scrambling for the corner. Jeremiah grabbed her arm and pulled her close, cupping his hand over her ear. "When the platform's half way down I'm going to jump him. You go for help." She nodded, lay back down and closed her eyes, feigning sleep. Jeremiah turned his attention to the platform as it inched lower, revealing more of their captor with each pull of the chain. He hugged the wall and edged his way around their prison, positioning himself at

Eldridge's back, waiting for the platform to be low enough for Aynslee to jump onto, but not too low for Eldridge to be able to see he was hiding from him. His heart pounded in his chest, his fingers dug into the dirt wall as he took a step forward and leaned over, ready to charge, surprise essential to saving their lives. He wiped a bead of sweat off his forehead as Eldridge's torso came into view.

The descent stopped.

Eldridge leaned forward and reached behind him, pulling out the gun tucked in his belt. Jeremiah sprang forward and shoved the platform hard, swinging it violently away from him. Eldridge stumbled backward and grasped at the chain, trying to steady himself. Jeremiah jumped up, his chest now on the platform, and grabbed Eldridge by the ankles, pulling with all his might as he let his body drop off the platform. Eldridge fell forward hard, the upper half of his body tumbling over the unstable platform's edge then onto the hard floor below. Jeremiah dove on top of him, struggling for the gun still firmly in Eldridge's grasp.

"Go, Aynslee, go!" he screamed as he wrestled with Eldridge. He watched Aynslee jump up and struggle onto the still swinging platform then lost sight of her as Eldridge flipped them both onto their fronts. The rattling of the chain as Aynslee pulled on it, all the while screaming for help, urged him on in his struggle with the bigger and more powerful man. He knew he would ultimately lose this battle, but he just had to hold on for a few more minutes.

He had to fight dirty.

He sunk his teeth into Eldridge's shoulder, the yelp of pain renewing his confidence momentarily. Eldridge threw his elbow back and shook Jeremiah free. Jeremiah fell onto his back and caught a glimpse of Aynslee scrambling into the kitchen above. He kicked at Eldridge's legs and made contact, shin to shin, leaving him hoping Eldridge was feeling the same stinging pain now racing through his leg. Eldridge fell forward, his hands stretched in front of him to break his fall. As he slammed into the floor, the gun, still gripped tightly in his right hand, fired, spraying dirt from the wall in their faces. Jeremiah jumped on his back but Eldridge was ready, this time swinging back with his elbow and catching Jeremiah squarely in the nose. The blinding pain caused Jeremiah to grab his face, rather than

Eldridge, who immediately took advantage of his opponent's momentary disorientation. He threw Jeremiah off his back and rolled away, jumping to his feet.

Aynslee had watched the fight through slightly opened eyes, and as soon as Jeremiah yelled, she sprang to her feet and rolled onto the swaying platform. Steadying herself with the chain, she pulled on it as fast as her shaking hands would allow, the platform slowly, painfully, inching toward the floor above as the death struggle below continued. She screamed for help at the top of her lungs, hoping someone outside the house might hear her. In less than a minute she was high enough to pull herself over the edge and onto the kitchen floor. She stole one last glance at the two men below and raced for the front door.

A loud crack from behind shocked her motionless. She had never heard a real gunshot before, and despite the fact it didn't sound like what she expected, terror gripped her as she realized Jeremiah was probably dead, and Eldridge would soon be after her. She resumed her dash, reaching the door at the end of the hallway, and fumbled with the locks. A second shot rang out and she heard the platform creak as she turned the final lock, yanking the door open. A blast of crisp, cool night air greeted her, but a latched screen door blocked her path. She pushed against it, the frame rattling but not budging. She reached for the clasp, the heavy sound of footsteps gaining speed on the floor behind her caused her hands to shake. She screamed as she tried to slide the latch with her trembling thumb.

Shakespeare parked in front of his partner's house, worried. He still hadn't reached Eldridge, and knew this was a gamble, but could think of no other place the kid might be. *This is where I'd go.* He looked around at the almost impossibly quiet neighborhood. Tall hedges circled many of the properties, casting long shadows from the streetlamps above, the neighboring houses mostly in darkness, their occupants long retired, only the occasional porch light suggesting anyone might be home, or expected home later. He looked at the neatly trimmed hedge, over twelve feet high, surrounding his partner's house, and shook his head. *I really don't know anything about the kid.* He found the narrow entrance in the center of the hedge, and squeezed through, cursing at Eldridge for not making it wider. Finally free, he walked up the path toward the front door as he fished his cell phone out to try calling him once more. His thumb hovered over the Send button when he heard the front door open. He smiled, pleased his hunch had paid off, as he recognized Aynslee Kai. He reached for his badge to identify himself when he heard a scream erupt from her unlike anything he had ever heard, evoking every feeling of terror and desperation he could imagine.

He raced toward the entrance as the screen door flung open. Aynslee burst through, her head turned back into the darkness, and ran straight into him. Shakespeare caught her in his arms and steadied her. Her head whipped around and she made eye contact with him, the look of fear, of pleading desperation, of pure terror, scared even him.

She wrenched herself from his grasp and pointed toward the entrance. "Help me! He's crazy! He's trying to kill me!" She tripped over an edging strip lining the walkway, and fell onto the grass. Shakespeare stepped forward to help her but she scrambled backward on her hands and feet. "He's coming!" He heard the pounding of feet from inside the house. Spinning, he drew his weapon and pointed it into the darkness of the entrance, a barely discernible shadow inside rushing toward him, burst from the entranceway.

Shakespeare breathed a sigh of relief as he saw Eldridge come to a halt on the porch, his own weapon drawn. "Jesus Christ, kid, you scared the shit outta me!" Shakespeare lowered his weapon and Eldridge did the same. "Did you see him?"

Eldridge shook his head but before he could say anything, Aynslee yelled, "No! *He's* the one trying to kill me!"

Shakespeare turned toward her, confused. "What the hell are you talking about?"

She pointed at Eldridge. "Look out!"

Shakespeare spun around and saw Eldridge's weapon pointing directly at him. Shakespeare immediately raised his own weapon, and, stepping sideways, positioned himself between his partner and Aynslee.

"Get behind me!" he yelled to Aynslee. Raising his left hand, he tried to calm Eldridge. "Listen, kid, lower your weapon, please."

"Don't get in my way, Justin." Eldridge slowly walked toward Aynslee as Shakespeare stepped backward, keeping himself between them. With his left hand, he motioned behind his back for Aynslee to move.

"Listen, kid, we can work this out, nobody has to get hurt." Beads of sweat formed on his forehead, his heart raced as he tried to grasp what was going on. *The kid is the killer?* None of it made sense. He knew Jeremiah was the killer, there was no doubting that. *What the fuck is going on?* He didn't want to shoot his partner, but at this exact moment, he couldn't see any other way out of this. "Just calm down and give me the gun."

"I won't let you take her away from me."

Eldridge's eyes shifted their focus from Aynslee to Shakespeare. Shakespeare paled as the muscles in Eldridge's face relaxed, a look of calm sweeping across his features, as if an important decision had been made. Shakespeare had seen the look enough in the past to know what was about to happen.

He squeezed the trigger.

Aynslee screamed as Eldridge stumbled backward, the bullet shattering his right shoulder. He grabbed the wound with his left hand and stared at Shakespeare, wide-eyed with surprise. "Why? Why are you trying to stop me from being happy?" He grimaced and took another step toward Aynslee. "Please, Sarah, you know I could never hurt you." Shakespeare reached back and pulled Aynslee to her feet, careful to keep himself between her and Eldridge.

"Please, Hayden, drop the gun, please," she pleaded.

"Don't I deserve to be happy?"

"Of course you do," said Aynslee. "We all do."

Shakespeare nodded. "We all do, kid, we all deserve to be happy." *This isn't going to work.*

"We were happy once, you and I, don't you remember."

"Yes, of course I remember."

Eldridge dropped his chin onto his chest and whispered, "It was the last time I was ever happy." He raised his head and looked at Shakespeare. "Until I finally found her again." He leaned back, trying to raise his weapon in his now nearly useless arm, then, with his good hand, grasped his arm and lifted it. "And now you want to take her away from me again."

"Please, Hayden, don't make me do this!" pleaded Shakespeare as Eldridge slowly slid his good hand toward the gun to squeeze the trigger. *God forgive me.* Shakespeare fired again, this time striking Eldridge square in the chest, the force of the impact knocking him off his feet, his shoulders, arms and neck rolling forward as his torso flew backward toward the porch. His body slammed onto the steps, his arms flailing to his sides, the hand holding the gun releasing its grip as it smacked the concrete edge of the top step, sending it skidding to the far side of the porch, and out of reach.

Aynslee gasped, covering her mouth in horror as she saw the man who, only hours before, she had been falling for, gasping for breath as blood spread across his crisp white shirt. Hidden behind Shakespeare, who was now calling for an ambulance, she looked Hayden in the eyes, the eyes that had never stopped looking at her. He raised his left hand and motioned to her.

"Please," he whispered, his eyes begged her forward, and she was shocked to find herself stepping around the man who had just saved her, and toward the man who had tried to kill her. The expression on Hayden's face, so pitiful she couldn't help but feel sorry for him, urged her on. She felt a hand on her shoulder.

"Miss Kai."

She turned slightly toward her savior, but didn't take her eyes off Hayden. "Yes?"

"I'm Detective Shakespeare. I need you to stay here. I'll be back in a few seconds, I just need to get the street number for the ambulance."

She nodded as he headed down the path toward the hedge, her feet continuing to carry her slowly toward Hayden who smiled as she neared. Kneeling down, she took his outstretched hand in both of hers and held it gently to her chest. She felt a slight squeeze as he used the last of his strength to hold on, his eyes, never leaving hers, gradually closing as he bled out. "I love you, Sarah," he sighed, his hand releasing its slight grip as the last of his life drained from his body.

Aynslee gripped his hand tighter, sobbing, the conflicting emotions overwhelming. A man who she thought she could love turned out to be a kidnapper, and the serial killer who only hours before had tried to kill her, had died trying to save her. Her mind didn't know who to feel sorry for. She didn't even know if she should feel sorry for anyone. She just knew, at this very moment, she was tired of death. She gently placed Hayden's hand on his chest, and rose.

Shakespeare finished his call and returned to find Aynslee standing over Eldridge's body.

"He's gone," she whispered.

He leaned down and checked his partner's pulse. *Nothing.* He sighed, lowering his head and making the sign of the cross. In all his years he had never killed anyone, and he had never imagined it would be a fellow officer, let alone his partner.

Jeremiah!

He jumped to his feet and looked around, drawing his weapon. "Jeremiah escaped the trap Eldridge set for him at your apartment. We should get you out of here immediately."

Aynslee, still staring at the smile on Eldridge's face, shook her head. "No, he's inside. He died trying to save me."

"What?" Shakespeare was sure everyone was off their rocker tonight. *Her would be killer died trying to save her from her would be killer?* "Are you sure?"

"Follow me." Aynslee led Shakespeare into the house and down a hallway. They rounded a corner and entered a kitchen. What Shakespeare saw brought him to a halt, his mouth agape.

"What the hell is this?" Slowly he approached the hole in the floor and peered over the side. About four feet below, there was a platform suspended by chains, and another half dozen feet below that, the dirt floor of a basement. Aynslee reached out and grabbed the chain, pulling on it. Shakespeare watched in amazement as the platform began to rise.

A groan from below the platform caused Shakespeare to step back, pointing his still drawn weapon at the hole.

"He's alive!"

Before Shakespeare could stop her, Aynslee jumped on the platform and swung herself to the floor below.

"Jesus Christ!" Rushing to the hole's edge, he eyed the swaying platform. *No way I'm jumping on that.* Clutching the chain, he raised it a couple of feet, stepped down, and lowered the platform with both hands until he could duck down enough to see what was going on. He found Aynslee cradling Jeremiah's head in her lap, her hand pressed against a large bloodstain on his shoulder. *What the hell happened here?* Bewildered, Shakespeare tried to fathom what could make a killer's intended victim care for him so quickly. Pulling on the chain, he lowered the platform until about two feet off the floor, and jumped down with a grunt, immediately regretting it as he felt a twinge in his ankle. "Is he okay?"

"Call an ambulance, quick!" cried Aynslee.

Jeremiah looked up at her and smiled. "Let me die. I don't deserve to live."

Tears filled Aynslee's eyes. "There's been enough dying," she whispered.

Above them shouts followed by the pounding of feet echoed through the house as backup arrived. "Down here!" yelled Shakespeare. The floor creaked overhead then two faces he wasn't expecting peered over the edge, weapons drawn. "What the hell are you two doing here?"

Trace and Vinny holstered their weapons, their expressions revealing they were just as shocked at seeing him as he was of seeing them. Vinny spoke first. "Amber figured out Hayden might have been involved in a missing persons case she was working on, so she called me rather than get the department involved, just in case she was wrong."

"Looks like I wasn't."

"Fine, fine, we'll talk about that later."

More people running the length of the house sent Vinny and Trace spinning, reaching for their weapons. Shakespeare, pretty sure everyone he had to worry about was either shot or dead, turned his attention to Jeremiah.

"How is he?"

"He's lost a lot of blood," replied Aynslee. "At least I think he has. I just don't know."

Yelling upstairs had settled down after badges were shown to the newly arriving uniforms, who now joined Trace and Vinny at the edge. Shakespeare looked up at them. "I've got a wounded man down here, is that bus here yet?"

"It's outside, just waiting for us to give the all clear," replied one officer.

"Well give it, dammit!"

The officer turned red as he grabbed his radio and stepped out of sight. Within seconds two paramedics were staring over the edge.

"What the fuck is this?" asked one of them.

"Never mind, just get your asses down here!"

The first one threw his bag down to Shakespeare, leaned forward and gripped the chain, shimmying down far enough until he could safely jump to the platform below. His partner followed suit and they were quickly attending to Jeremiah.

"Is he going to be okay?" asked Aynslee, now standing against the wall, her clenched fist gently tapping her grimacing teeth.

"He's lost a lot of blood, but he's stable. He should make it."

Aynslee breathed a sigh of relief as the paramedics carefully moved Jeremiah to the platform. "I'll go first," said the lead paramedic. "Not sure how much weight this thing can handle." He looked up at the officers above. "Ok, bring us up, slow and steady. I don't want him falling off this thing." The officers above pulled on the chain, raising the platform inch by inch until if finally reached the top, sealing Shakespeare, Aynslee and the other paramedic inside.

Shakespeare looked around. "What the hell kind of place is this?"

The paramedic pointed toward several scratches in the walls. "Looks like he kept somebody down here."

Aynslee shivered, unable to look. "I need to get out of here."

The chain above rattled again and the platform began to lower, ending the speculation. As soon as it was low enough, the second paramedic jumped up and swung himself onto the platform then the kitchen floor. The officers finished lowering the platform to the floor and waited for Shakespeare and Aynslee to step on, then pulled them up. As they neared floor level, they saw the two paramedics pushing Jeremiah out the door on a stretcher. A few more pulls and they were able to step safely into the kitchen. Aynslee sat hunched over in a kitchen chair, elbows on her knees as she tried to pull the stress out through her hair.

"What the hell happened here?" asked Trace.

"Yeah, who shot Hayden?" asked Vinny. "Was it that Jeremiah kid?"

Shakespeare shook his head. "No, it was me."

Both their jaws dropped. "Are you shittin' me?" asked Vinny.

"No." Shakespeare looked at Aynslee. "Listen, place the kid under arrest, I'll fill you in later." Trace opened her mouth to speak when Shakespeare cut her off, motioning with his eyes at Aynslee. "Let's have some breathing room for a few minutes, okay?" They both nodded and left the kitchen. Shakespeare sat across from Aynslee. "Do you feel up to telling me what happened here tonight?"

Aynslee nodded. "Hayden, I mean Detective Eldridge, had me hide in the back of his car to trick Jeremiah into thinking I was at my apartment, then brought me here. He drugged me and when I woke up I was in the basement and Jeremiah was there with me. We talked and in the end he said he was sorry for what he had done and then he helped me escape by attacking Hayden so I could climb out. I heard two shots then that's when you arrived."

Shakespeare shook his head through her entire story. "I can't believe Hayden would do such a thing. He kept calling you Sarah. Any idea who that is?"

"Jeremiah said it was some long lost love, or something like that. I don't really know."

"Ok, I'll let you rest for now, we can do this later." He stood as Vinny entered the room. Shakespeare eyed him warily.

"Oh, hi, Detective," said Vinny awkwardly, looking around the room and finally, after looking everywhere else, making eye contact. "Listen, Justin. I know we've had our differences, but I'm really sorry about your partner. He was a great guy."

Shakespeare nodded. "Yeah, he was. No matter what happened here tonight, he was a great cop."

"The best," agreed Vinny, joining Shakespeare at the platform edge. "What have we got here?"

"Not sure, but I saw a mattress down there, so I'm guessing he intended for Miss Kai to stay awhile."

"I'll check it out." Vinny lowered the platform as Aynslee stood.

"I need some fresh air."

Shakespeare nodded. "Me too." He unlocked the patio door and held it open. "I'd recommend the back yard, the front is probably a madhouse."

Aynslee stepped out onto a stone patio with Shakespeare joining her. Looking around them, Shakespeare whistled. "He was one hell of a gardener, apparently." Before them lay a beautifully manicured lawn surrounded by a lower, eight-foot hedge, with half a dozen rectangular flower beds laid out across the back of the yard, each with an assortment of flowers, carefully arranged and weeded, except for the flowerbed farthest to the right, which, though freshly tilled, had no flowers.

"He was."

"Detective!" Shakespeare turned at the sound of Vinny's voice. "You gotta see this!" They both walked back into the kitchen as Vinny pulled himself from the basement. "Look at this!" He held out a plastic bag containing dirt.

"What's this?" Shakespeare took the bag and held it up to the light.

Aynslee gasped and pointed. "Look at that!"

Shakespeare gulped. "It's a fingernail." Aynslee ran to the sink and heaved.

"Yeah, there's a lot of evidence someone stayed down there long-term. I found that embedded in the wall, as if they were scratching at it." Shakespeare was about to comment on the revelation when he suddenly turned on his heel and rushed out to the backyard. Vinny and Aynslee followed him and watched as he grabbed a shovel and began to dig furiously at the flowerless flowerbed.

"Oh shit," whispered Vinny. Picking up a nearby hoe, he ran over and together they dug as fast as they could.

"Wait!" yelled Shakespeare as his shovel hit something. They both got on their knees and, reaching in, began digging with their hands. It was Vinny who found her first, a pair of hands, taped together, that appeared to be held up, fingers splayed as if trying to stop the dirt piling on top of her. Shakespeare uncovered her face, the resemblance to Aynslee immediately evident. Sitting back on the grass sweating, he looked at Aynslee. "It appears you were damned lucky, Miss Kai."

"She hasn't been in here long, maybe a day or two." Vinny continued to scoop out the dirt surrounding her as Shakespeare caught his breath.

Trace rounded the house and immediately gasped at what she saw. "That's Chelsie Birmingham, my missing person!"

Shakespeare ignored her. "You don't think—" Vinny stopped digging and followed Shakespeare's gaze. In a neat row, five manicured flowerbeds, each about six feet by three feet, lay in front of them.

"Oh my god!" whispered Vinny. "Hayden, what have you done?"

Aynslee fainted.

When she awoke she saw Shakespeare leaning over her as two paramedics ran around the side of the house. Shakespeare stepped back to give them room to work. "She was drugged earlier, don't know with what."

One paramedic nodded. "We should take her in just to be safe. They can run some tests there and see if they need to flush her system." He helped Aynslee to her feet. "Do you think you can walk to the ambulance or do you want us to get a stretcher?"

Aynslee shook her head. "No, I think I'll be okay, just a little dizzy that's all." The two paramedics supported her as they walked slowly toward the ambulance.

Shakespeare turned to Vinny. "I know you were close to Hayden, but we've got to do this by the book, no matter how we feel. Process this scene like you would any other."

"Don't tell me my job, Detective," snapped Vinny. Shakespeare turned to walk away when he heard Vinny clear his throat. "Listen, I'm sorry, Justin. I'm just upset, I considered Hayden my friend and tonight I discovered he was a completely different person than I ever thought imaginable."

"Don't worry about it. We're all upset." Turning to Trace, he said, "I want you to take over the investigation, I'm too close to it." He headed to the ambulance to check on Aynslee and found her already loaded in the back, sitting on a stretcher. "Want some company?"

She nodded. "Please." She had never met this man who had saved her life before tonight, but she felt an immediate connection with him. Not only did they share in the grief of losing someone they thought they had known, they both were trying to deal with the horror they knew was about to be uncovered.

Aynslee stepped into the hallway, having been given the all clear, the Rohypnol now out of her system. She found Shakespeare sitting in the hall waiting. He rose as soon as he saw her. "How are you feeling?"

Aynslee shrugged her shoulders. "Physically? Fine. Everything else? I don't know what to feel."

Shakespeare nodded, a grimace creasing his face, betraying his own confusion. "We're going to have to take a witness statement from you at some point. It can wait until tomorrow if you don't feel up to it."

"Tomorrow, please." Aynslee didn't feel like going over what had happened to her again, not now. "Any word on the backyard?"

Shakespeare nodded. "Six bodies. The crime scene guys think it goes back almost a decade."

"My God!" Aynslee shook as she realized what had almost happened to her. "Are they going to be able to identify them? Give those poor families some closure?"

"They'll do their best."

Aynslee pressed a hand against the wall to steady herself. "Is Jeremiah here?"

"End of the hall, under guard."

"What will happen to him?"

"He'll be charged, arraigned probably here in the hospital. I doubt he'll be granted bail so they'll transfer him to Rikers as soon as he's well enough to be moved to their infirmary, then stand trial. He'll be going away for the rest of his life, I'm sure."

Aynslee felt a twinge of sympathy for the poor boy who had tried to kill her, but had ultimately saved her life. "Can I see him?" Shakespeare nodded and led her down the hallway.

Leaving Shakespeare out in the hall, Aynslee entered the room where Jeremiah lay hooked to various monitors, handcuffed to the bed. His eyes were closed, his breathing shallow but steady. Walking over to the bed she took his hand in hers and watched as his eyes slowly opened. "We made it."

"Yes," she said, smiling. "Thanks to you."

Jeremiah smiled weakly. "Any time." Aynslee squeezed his hand as Jeremiah's eyes filled with tears. "I'm so sorry for what I've done."

"Make sure you tell the judge that."

"I don't care about that. I deserve to rot in a prison cell for what I've done. I have no excuse."

Aynslee sat on the edge of his bed, and dabbed his eyes dry with a tissue. "Why don't you tell me about your sister."

Jeremiah took a deep breath and smiled.

Shakespeare listened to the voices murmuring in the room then eyed a snack machine at the end of the corridor. His stomach rumbled. Walking toward it he heard a voice call out as he passed one of the rooms. "Justin, is that you?" Puzzled, he walked back and looked into the room.

"Father O'Neil!" Shakespeare's jaw dropped at the shock of seeing his spiritual guide from so many years ago lying in a hospital bed, hooked to machines monitoring his weak vital signs. "What are you doing here?"

O'Neil smiled and beckoned him over. "I'm afraid I wasn't careful enough, my son. Jeremiah shot me."

"What? When? Why didn't you call me?"

O'Neil waved his hand to cut him off. "Yesterday, in the confessional. Luckily someone heard the shot and called for help. I just woke up a few hours ago here. Did you find Jeremiah?"

"Yes we did."

"And is he okay?"

"He was shot, but he'll survive. He's down the hall."

"Shot, how?"

Shakespeare pulled a chair up to the side of the bed and sat down.

"Father, have I got a story to tell you."

AFTERWORD

Selling books is marketing, and as part of that, I have held several contests on my website and Facebook page. I would like to take the time to thank several people who helped spread the word through entering the contests and inviting their friends to join. Having read *Depraved Difference*, you may recognize their names as characters in the books: Brent Richards, Tracy Oswald and Steve Scaramell. As well, a special thanks to an old high-school buddy Justin Shakespeare, who is similar to my character in name only, and to Regis Giasson, who, as is his nature, played a *very* small but important role in reminding me to put together these acknowledgements.

I'd like to thank my parents for reading endless drafts, my wife Esperanza (another name in the book), and my daughter, Niskha (next book!), for tolerating the hours of my delightful company lost to the keyboard, and my friends for listening to me drone on about plots and the publishing business, including, but definitely not limited to, Paul Conway, the best friend anyone could ask for.

And finally, a very special thanks to you, the reader. You have this author's humble gratitude.

The Protocol
A James Acton Thriller

Book #1

For two thousand years the Triarii have protected us, influencing history from the crusades to the discovery of America. Descendent from the Roman Empire, they pervade every level of society, and are now in a race with our own government to retrieve an ancient artifact thought to have been lost forever.

Caught in the middle is archaeology professor James Acton, relentlessly hunted by the elite Delta Force, under orders to stop at nothing to possess what he has found, and the Triarii, equally determined to prevent the discovery from falling into the wrong hands.

With his students and friends dying around him, Acton flees to find the one person who might be able to help him, but little does he know he may actually be racing directly into the hands of an organization he knows nothing about...

Brass Monkey

A James Acton Thriller

Book #2

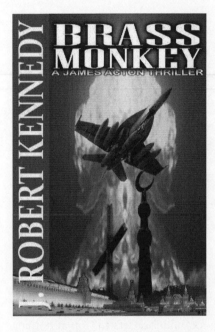

A nuclear missile, lost during the Cold War, is now in play--the most public spy swap in history, with a gorgeous agent the center of international attention, triggers the end-game of a corrupt Soviet Colonel's twenty five year plan. Pursued across the globe by the Russian authorities, including a brutal Spetsnaz unit, those involved will stop at nothing to deliver their weapon, and ensure their pay day, regardless of the terrifying consequences.

When Laura Palmer confronts a UNICEF group for trespassing on her Egyptian archaeological dig site, she unwittingly stumbles upon the ultimate weapons deal, and becomes entangled in an international conspiracy that sends her lover, archeology Professor James Acton, racing to Egypt with the most unlikely of allies, not only to rescue her, but to prevent the start of a holy war that could result in Islam and Christianity wiping each other out.

From the bestselling author of Depraved Difference and The Protocol comes Brass Monkey, a thriller international in scope, certain to offend some, and stimulate debate in others. Brass Monkey pulls no punches in confronting the conflict between two of the world's most powerful, and divergent, religions, and the terrifying possibilities the future may hold if left unchecked.

Broken Dove

A James Acton Thriller

Book #3

With the Triarii in control of the Roman Catholic Church, an organization founded by Saint Peter himself takes action, murdering one of the new Pope's operatives. Detective Chaney, called in by the Pope to investigate, disappears, and, to the horror of the Papal staff sent to inform His Holiness, they find him missing too, the only clue a secret chest, presented to each new pope on the eve of their election, since the beginning of the Church.

Interpol Agent Reading, determined to find his friend, calls Professors James Acton and Laura Palmer to Rome to examine the chest and its forbidden contents, but before they can arrive, they are intercepted by an organization older than the Church, demanding the professors retrieve an item stolen in ancient Judea in exchange for the lives of their friends.

All of your favorite characters from The Protocol return to solve the most infamous kidnapping in history, against the backdrop of a two thousand year old battle pitting ancient foes with diametrically opposed agendas.

DEPRAVED DIFFERENCE

From the internationally bestselling author of Depraved Difference and The Protocol comes Broken Dove, the third entry in the smash hit James Acton Thrillers series, where J. Robert Kennedy reveals a secret concealed by the Church for almost 1200 years, and a fascinating interpretation of what the real reason behind the denials might be.

The Templar's Relic
A James Acton Thriller
Book #4

The Church Helped Destroy the Templars. Will a twist of fate let them get their revenge 700 years later?

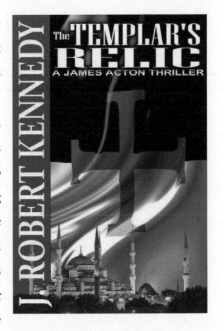

The Vault must be sealed, but a construction accident leads to a miraculous discovery--an ancient tomb containing four Templar Knights, long forgotten, on the grounds of the Vatican. Not knowing who they can trust, the Vatican requests Professors James Acton and Laura Palmer examine the find, but what they discover, a precious Islamic relic, lost during the Crusades, triggers a set of events that shake the entire world, pitting the two greatest religions against each other.

Join Professors James Acton and Laura Palmer, INTERPOL Agent Hugh Reading, Scotland Yard DI Martin Chaney, and the Delta Force Bravo Team as they race against time to defuse a worldwide crisis that could quickly devolve into all-out war.

At risk is nothing less than the Vatican itself, and the rock upon which it was built.

DEPRAVED DIFFERENCE

From J. Robert Kennedy, the author of six international bestsellers including Depraved Difference and The Protocol, comes The Templar's Relic, the fourth entry in the smash hit James Acton Thrillers series, where once again Kennedy takes history and twists it to his own ends, resulting in a heart pounding thrill ride filled with action, suspense, humor and heartbreak.

The Turned

Zander Varga, Vampire Detective

Book #1

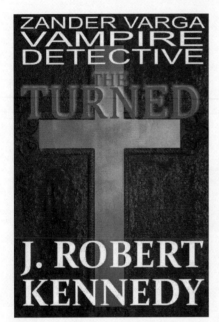

Zander has relived his wife's death at the hands of vampires every day for almost three hundred years, his perfect memory a curse of becoming one of The Turned—infecting him their final heinous act after her murder.

Nineteen year-old Sydney Winter knows Zander's secret, a secret preserved by the women in her family for four generations. But with her mother in a coma, she's thrust into the front lines, ahead of her time, to fight side-by-side with Zander.

And she wouldn't change a thing.

She loves the excitement, she loves the danger.

And she loves Zander.

But it's a love that will have to go unrequited, because Zander has only one thing on his mind. And it's been the same thing for over two hundred years.

Revenge.

But today, revenge will have to wait, because Zander Varga, Private Detective, has a new case. A woman's husband is missing. The police aren't interested. But Zander is. Something doesn't smell right, and he's determined to find out why.

From J. Robert Kennedy, the internationally bestselling author of The Protocol and Depraved Difference, comes his sixth novel, The Turned, a terrifying story that in true Kennedy fashion takes a completely new twist on the origin of vampires, tying it directly to a well-known moment in history. Told from the perspective of Zander Varga and his assistant, Sydney Winter, The Turned is loaded with action, humor, terror and a centuries long love that must eventually be let go.

Depraved Difference
A Detective Shakespeare Mystery
Book #1

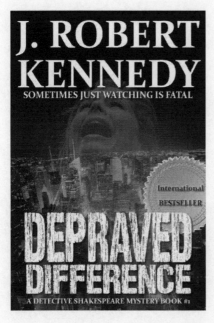

Would you help, would you run, or would you just watch?

When a young woman is brutally assaulted by two men on the subway, her cries for help fall on the deaf ears of onlookers too terrified to get involved, her misery ended with the crushing stomp of a steel-toed boot. A cellphone video of her vicious murder, callously released on the Internet, its popularity a testament to today's depraved society, serves as a trigger, pulled a year later, for a killer.

Emailed a video documenting the final moments of a woman's life, entertainment reporter Aynslee Kai, rather than ask why the killer chose her to tell the story, decides to capitalize on the opportunity to further her career. Assigned to the case is Hayden Eldridge, a detective left to learn the ropes by a disgraced partner, and as videos continue to follow victims, he discovers they were all witnesses to the vicious subway murder a year earlier, proving sometimes just watching is fatal.

From the author of The Protocol and Brass Monkey, Depraved Difference is a fast-paced murder suspense novel with enough laughs, heartbreak, terror and twists to keep you on the edge of your seat, then knock you flat on the floor with an ending so shocking, you'll read it again just to pick up the clues.

Tick Tock

A Detective Shakespeare Mystery

Book #2

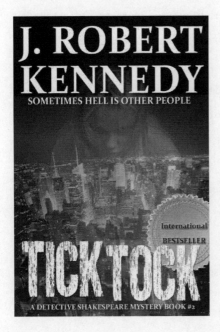

Crime Scene tech Frank Brata digs deep and finds the courage to ask his colleague, Sarah, out for coffee after work. Their good time turns into a nightmare when Frank wakes up the next morning covered in blood, with no recollection of what happened, and Sarah's body floating in the tub. Determined not to go to prison for a crime he's horrified he may have committed, he scrubs the crime scene clean, and, tormented by text messages from the real killer, begins a race against the clock to solve the murder before his own co-workers, his own friends, solve it first, and find him guilty.

Billionaire Richard Tate is the toast of the town, loved by everyone but his wife. His plans for a romantic weekend with his mistress ends in disaster, waking the next morning to find her murdered, floating in the tub. After fleeing in a panic, he returns to find the hotel room spotless, and no sign of the body. An envelope found at the scene contains not the expected blackmail note, but something far more sinister.

Two murders, with the same MO, targeting both the average working man, and the richest of society, sets a rejuvenated Detective Shakespeare, and his new reluctant partner, Amber Trace, after a murderer whose motivations are a mystery, and who appears to be aided by the very people they would least expect—their own.

Tick Tock, Book #2 in the internationally bestselling Detective Shakespeare Mysteries series, picks up right where Depraved Difference left off, and asks a simple question: What would you do? What would you do if you couldn't prove your innocence, but knew you weren't capable of murder? Would you hide the very evidence that might clear you, or would you turn yourself in and trust the system to work?

From the internationally bestselling author of The Protocol and Brass Monkey comes the highly anticipated sequel to the smash hit Depraved Difference, Tick Tock. Filled with heart pounding terror and suspense, along with a healthy dose of humor, Tick Tock's twists will keep you guessing right up to the terrifying end.

The Redeemer
A Detective Shakespeare Mystery
Book #3

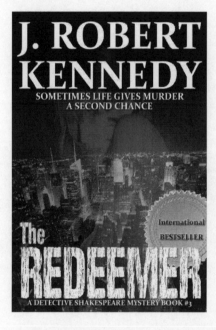

Sometimes Life Gives Murder a Second Chance

It was the case that destroyed Detective Justin Shakespeare's career, beginning a downward spiral of self-loathing and self-destruction lasting half a decade. And today things are only going to get worse. The Widow Rapist is free on a technicality, and it is up to Detective Shakespeare and his partner Amber Trace to find the evidence, five years cold, to put him back in prison before he strikes again.

But Shakespeare and Trace aren't alone in their desire for justice. The Seven are the survivors, avowed to not let the memories of their loved ones be forgotten. And with the release of the Widow Rapist, they are determined to take justice into their own hands, restoring balance to a flawed system.

At stake is a second chance, a chance at redemption, a chance to salvage a career destroyed, a reputation tarnished, and a life diminished.

A chance brought to Detective Shakespeare whether he wants it or not.

A chance brought to him by The Redeemer.

From J. Robert Kennedy, the author of seven international bestsellers including Depraved Difference and The Protocol, comes the third entry in the acclaimed Detective Shakespeare Mysteries series, The Redeemer, a dark tale exploring the psyches of the serial killer, the victim, and the police, as they all try to achieve the same goals.

Balance. And redemption.

3148646R00150

Printed in Great Britain
by Amazon.co.uk, Ltd.,
Marston Gate.